To my husband, Tom, who supports my
writing endeavors, and to our
granddaughter, Sydney, who is the perfect
granddaughter and the delightful model for
Meghan.

# Her Highland Rogue

## Leanne Burroughs

Vintage Romance Publishing

Goose Creek, South Carolina

www.vrpublishing.com

*Leanne Burroughs*

# Her Highland Rogue

ISBN: 0-9770107-9-1
PUBLISHED BY VINTAGE ROMANCE PUBLISHING, LLC
www.vrpublishing.com

# Praise for Highland Wishes (prequel to Her Highland Rogue)

Well written, *Highland Wishes* had me turning each page anticipating what would happen next.

I do have to say the dialogue was the best I have ever seen in regards to the Scottish words and pronunciation. It was refreshing to actually read words as they are truly spoken in Scotland, and in my own family's homes.

For a really good Scottish story with secrets, love, insecurities, evil, battles, and laughter, *Highland Wishes* fills the bill. I look forward to [the author's] sequel, *Her Highland Rogue.*

--*Catherine McHenry, Romance Reviews Today*

I truly enjoyed reading this book. It is one book that cannot be put down once you begin. From cover to cover, you are drawn into the story. I would recommend this book to anyone who loves to read Historical romance.

--*Tangela William, The Romance Readers Connection,*

*Highland Wishes* is a meaty, Scottish historical romance. Topping 650 pages, it is obvious that Leanne Burroughs has painstakingly researched her setting. The author transports you to a new place, a new time, and holds your attention from beginning to end.

--*Tracy Farnsworth, Roundtable Reviews,*

***

This reviewer was easily captivated by the story and was enthralled by it until the end. The reader will laugh

and cry as you read this wonderful story. The reader feels all the pain, torment and disillusionment felt by both main characters, but also the joy and love they felt.
--*Dawn Roberto, Love Romances, www.loveromances.com*

\*\*\*

*Highland Wishes* is a great Scottish historical romance with memorable characters. We look forward to Ms. Burroughs' next book, the sequel to *Highland Wishes*.
--*Susan, Fallen Angel Reviews*

*Highland Wishes* is every reader's dream of the perfect story! Author Leanne Burroughs has penned a majestic tale filled with romance, history and adventure.
Wonderfully written, with vibrant characters, this story is a masterpiece of historical fiction.
-- *Joyce Handzo, www.inthelibraryreview.com*

'Wonderful Medieval Debut Novel'

*Highland Wishes* is a first time Historical Romance by a new writer Leanne Burroughs. What hits the reader immediately is her true love for the romance of the period. Burroughs has written a wonderful Scottish Medieval full of heart and adventure.
Her next book, *Her Highland Rogue,* is in the works, so I am sure everyone will be looking forward to another heartfelt saga from this wonderful writer.

*DeborahAnne MacGillivray, The Best Reviews*

## Acknowledgements

*To the best critique partners in the world – my online critique partner, DeborahAnne MacGillivray, and my local critique partners, Cheryl Alldredge and Rebecca Andrews. You're the best, and I couldn't have done this without your help and support! Thanks for making me push to be better.*

*Scotland, 1304*

# Chapter One

Duncan MacThomas braced for the worst. He'd not seen that look on his father's face since the day he'd been fostered. The day that changed his life forever.

His father confronted the issue directly, knowing he crossed the sword's edge of Duncan's temper. "Recently, I had correspondence with an Englishman, Lord Nigel Gillingham. The two of us, at King Edward's bidding, drafted a wedding contract."

Duncan walked closer to his father, each step measured. "You intend to wed? Are you not a bit long in the tooth?"

"Dinnae be daft, Duncan." MacThomaidh locked eyes with his son. "It little suits you. You shall wed Gillingham's daughter within a fortnight."

"*What*?" Duncan slammed down his ale tankard. Missing the table, his knuckles hit the edge, the drink spilling on the floor. He rubbed his other hand over the skinned knuckles.

"'Tis done, the match is made." Determination crossed MacThomaidh's weathered features. "We leave on the morrow to arrive in London within a fortnight."

"You are daft. I willnae marry to please you." Duncan's voice rose. "You gave up the right to tell me what to do the day you left me to the *care* of strangers."

"Fostering is the Highland way, son."

"Never seeing your child again is not!"

Duncan crossed the large room to the double doors in three long strides. He flung the garden doors open, sending dust motes swirling in the sun's muted rays. As a child, the garden's beauty often calmed him. His mind roiling in black fury, this time he saw nothing. How dare his father—the man who'd sent him to foster with a clan that abused him—now presume to rule his life?

"You shall do as I say. You defied me afore and wed a woman no better than a harlot."

"Why cannae you leave me alone? You did whilst I grew up."

"You are my son! Regardless of past mistakes—mine or yours—you shall one day be Chief of Clan MacThomaidh."

Turning back to face his father, Duncan's face twisted in a mixture of pain and anger. He opened his mouth to reply, but his father forestalled him. "'Tis time you produce an heir. You have obligations to your clan and need acknowledge them."

"I willnae leave for London—or anywhere else—in the morn," came Duncan's angry growl.

Nothing had changed. His father always brought out the worst in him. His words bitter, Duncan gave his father no quarter. "You actually believe I would agree to the machinations of an *English king*? The Hammer of the

Scots? That *you* support him disgusts me."

Duncan braced his feet. The MacThomaidh's grim expression sent a foreshadowing of doom stealing up his spine.

"Sometimes we must make decisions we would rather not. You have been away these past years."

"Fighting the English king," Duncan retorted, "for Scotland—for freedom. Now you expect me to accept a royal edict from Longshanks? Faugh!"

"The contract has been signed and according to their religious beliefs Lord Gillingham posted banns."

Duncan scoffed. "The Bishop waits to hear if anyone objects? I object!"

"I swore our clan's fealty to the king. This war against England dips into our coffers. Whether you believe it or not, I am nae traitor to Scotland." His father's angry voice cut into Duncan like a broadsword. "You thought the war won with Stirling's battle, but 'twas only the beginning. Since Scotland refuses to bow its knee to Longshanks, we battle still. As Chief I must protect our clansman. The woman's dowry shall keep us fed many a year." He swept his arm around the high ceilinged Great Hall. "Look around you. The castle needs work. I might regret the necessity of this, but she shall be an asset to our clan and shall be a good lady wife for you, breed you fine sons. I dinnae choose lightly."

Duncan grunted, unable to find words to express his disgust.

"You do remember your kinsmen, dunnae you? Holding our *honours* cost dearly, with the Kirk with hands out for their tithe and Edward wanting his twelve percent. You defied me afore. See where that got you. You shall do it my way nonce. We leave on the morrow."

MacThomaidh turned and stormed from the room.

"I bloody well will not!" Duncan yelled to his father's retreating back. In three strides he reached the Great Hall's massive oaken door, flung it open and crossed the yard. He snatched his horse's reins from the groom, leapt onto the stallion's back and galloped toward his home as though wolves nipped at his horse's heels.

\* \* \*

MacThomaidh opened his bedchamber door. He shook his head, dismayed at the sight that greeted him. His wee granddaughter pushed a stool to the wall, stood on tiptoes and stared out the window slits, watching her father ride away. He walked behind her and wrapped his arms around the three-year-old's waist. She tilted her head and gazed up at him. Tears pooled in her bright blue eyes and glistened on her lashes before one trickled down her right cheek. Her lower lip quivering, she turned in his embrace and threw her arms around his neck. "Grandda."

"Och, dunnae cry lassie. Grandda will make everything aright." Why hadn't he thought this through? Knowing full well Duncan would balk, he should have addressed the issue at Cray Hall. It was his fault as much as his son's that his granddaughter, Meghan, was unhappy.

"Da dinnae visit me." She hiccupped from her sobs. Her tear-filled eyes looked into his.

He drew her to his chest, gently rubbing her back,

the bones of her small body so frail under his large calloused hands. He hoped loving Duncan's child in some way made up for the love he'd been unable to show his son.

Bending, he kissed the top of her head. "Sweetling, your da loves you." Often he left Castle Glenshee to allow Duncan time to visit Meghan, though his stubborn son never realized it. Neither did Duncan witness how he hungered for a visit himself.

"Den why…?"

"He is upset with Grandda. We must travel on the morrow, but he wanted to stay with you." He bent to kiss her soft cheek.

"I want Da. I wuv him." Her mouth scrunched up and tears flowed down her delicate cheeks.

The light of his life, his granddaughter's pain lanced through his heart. Unfortunately, the one person who had the power to make her smile just galloped away. He lifted her and carried her to her bedchamber, cradling her tenderly. "Grandda and Da must go away, Sweetling."

"Can I go wif ye?"

Hope sprang to her eyes. When he shook his head, her shoulders slumped.

"Not this time, my heart, but I shall return anon."

Meghan appeared crestfallen. "Will Da come back?"

MacThomaidh assured her with a hug, "Naught could keep him away." He smiled and leaned forward, touching her forehead with his. He gazed into her face, hoping for a smile. None came.

He found her rag doll and placed it beside her, knowing she never slept without it. Her aunt gave it to her and Meghan adored it. She fell asleep as he rocked her, her arms wrapped around her doll. He laid her on her small bed and covered her with soft white lamb's fur.

He walked slowly to the narrow window slits and stared out. *Och, why dinnae I share such moments with Duncan? So many years wasted. Faugh! I let pride get in the way of showing my love. Whyever was I daft enough to consider his illness a poor reflection on my manhood? Foolish pride. Can we yet establish a bond?* His hands tightened into fists. *Time runs out.* Regardless, having a stubborn streak as long as Loch Ness, he wouldn't reveal his heart to his son. Again, foolish pride.

Certain of one thing, his granddaughter was a blessing from God, he'd let nothing — or nobody — hurt her the way he'd hurt his son.

\* \* \*

Duncan galloped away from his family castle, but soon slowed his horse to a trot. He reined in near a copse of trees, thoughts swirling through his mind. *By the saints, what did I do? I stormed away without seeing Meghan. Never have I been there and not visited her.*

He ran his hand behind his neck to massage away tension. *How could I do that? Am I a horrible father like MacThomaidh was to me?* He turned his face to Heaven. *Lord, I vow I shall make this up to Meghan.*

He stared out over MacThomas land, blessed with rich soil for crops and cattle to keep everyone fed. The only problem was their neighbors, the Farquharsons, reiving cattle and trying to claim MacThomaidh land. Scotland's struggle against Longshanks caused hardships not just in coin, but in number of warriors lost in battle —

and the fight wasn't over. Every summer saw Longshanks once more above the Tweed River vowing to suppress the Scottish rebellion once and for all.

Castle Glenshee's pristine beauty dimmed, needing coin to restore its splendor. He'd seen signs of change, but hadn't wanted to face them. Now he must.

*Why did MacThomaidh drag our clansmen into the discussion?* Duncan forced himself to admit his father was right. At what cost to himself?

Alex, Angus, and Dohmnall rode out to meet him, bringing a smile to his face. "Too impatient to wait until my return? I shallnae keep you in suspense." He related the details as they rode slowly home.

"I cannae walk away from my duty. For Father to mention the clan's well being means he worries about its future. If only my future to consider, I'd fetch Meghan and keep riding, nae qualms about stopping. But I owe it to everyone to support you—even in a manner I abhor."

Clan loyalties ran deep in a Scot, he was no exception. The invisible bond shackled him to the welfare and future of MacThomas clansman, from the lowest servant to his sister Tamara.

\* \* \*

In a crowded London pub, a burly man sat alone. He leaned back in his chair and barked to the serving wench, "Ale."

His ears picked up the conversation at a nearby table about news worthy of celebration. The men laid bets on banns called in kirk that morn.

"Believe you King Edward ordered Gillingham's daughter to wed a heathen Scot?" someone commented.

Already drunk, he knocked his goblet over, spilling ale onto his brown chausses. He jumped up and swore, the others laughing at his clumsiness.

Wiping the ale with a cloth, he sat. "'Tis passing strange with the king holding Gillingham in such high regard. We all paid court the wench, only to be turned away. Personally, I thought her father set his sights on the Duke's son." Men grunted their agreement.

"Who did the priest say she had to marry?"

"Mac something."

The group laughed.

"They're all mac something," joked another. "The priest said MacThoms or MacThomas. Aye, that's it—Duncan MacThomas."

"I bet a groat it does not take place," an elderly man said, approaching the young men's table.

"You shall lose, old man, but we will be happy to take your money. The chit has no choice about the wedding. The king ordered it."

Erwin couldn't believe his luck. Duncan MacThomas would soon arrive in London. His lips twisted in an evil smile. The wedding saved him the long trip to Scotland. He could sit back and wait to kill his nemesis.

# Chapter Two

Shadows dappled the earth as the MacThomaidh entourage arrived at London's Brentwood Estate. Duncan found it difficult to believe a fortnight had passed, though his backside assured him otherwise. "It seems I just began this journey from hell and we are here already." Riding abreast of his men, his eyes took in his betrothed's home. "Bloody hell. Those *perfect* trees probably took a servant a sennight to trim." He shot a look at his father. "Pretentious—as I imagine *her* to be. The last attribute I want in a wife."

Escorted to his room by way of a well-scrubbed staircase and long corridor, Duncan was no more impressed with the home's inside. Portions of stone floor were covered with thick tapestries, clearly imported from the Continent. "They walk on these? I would hang them on my walls and be proud of it." Fancy iron works graced the ceiling and sunlight poured through stained glass windows. He groused, "Look at this house. A waste of good coin."

His sister Tamara shot him a frown. "Duncan, hush."

After arriving at her home in Melrose, her presence had been the only pleasant aspect to the journey.

He groaned. "I must relinquish my freedom to obtain this Englishwoman's hefty dowry. Yet her family throws coin around as if they possess an endless supply. And you want me to hush?"

"Aye, you are being rude." Tamara's eyes shifted to their escort.

Duncan ignored Tamara's glare. All he'd ever wanted was a woman to love much like his friend's wife, Tory. She was charming, a healer, and a born storyteller. Everything a man would want. Well, she was a hellcat— but a man could overlook a few flaws for perfection in everything else.

He certainly never planned to wed a woman he never met. He knew nothing about his betrothed except her name—Catherine Gillingham. Even that sounded pretentious. Did she dread the marriage as much as he? Or was she so meek she did all bidding without question? Considering the English's hatred of Scots, he couldn't imagine her being pleased at the prospect. After living in luxury, she'd find things different in the Highlands. She'd see no excess in his home.

Duncan stripped off his clothes and climbed into bed. He stretched his large frame and laced his hands behind his head, certain he'd have the last laugh. Now he could sleep.

\* \* \*

Catherine Gillingham stared out her chamber window at white clouds floating in the clear blue sky. Birds chirped happily. Such a beautiful day and yet it would be the worst day of her life. Her brother, Trevor, sat on her unmade bed. She knew he tried to cheer her, but his silence told her he could think of no comforting words.

Struggling to regain her poise, she turned to face him and wiped away tears.

"Trevor, what shall I do?"

He rose and came to her side, holding her securely in his embrace.

"Shh, Cat." He carefully ran his hands over her long, dark brown hair, cascading down her back. Her lady's maid, Rowena, had scattered seed pearls throughout and they shimmered with every movement. Trevor gently brushed back soft wisps of hair at the sides of her face, one stray lock coming loose on her forehead.

Fear of the unknown welled within her. "Oh Trev, I assumed Father would secure a good husband for me. Not be bartered off by Edward to some heathen in payment for Scotland's loyalty." She sobbed, "Why can I not marry Marquess Pemberly? Have I aimed my sights too high? Jason cares for me."

Trevor said nothing, but stroked his hand over her back. She took his silence as agreement. "What about Lightsey? I overheard Jeremy ask Father for my hand."

"Overheard?" Trevor teased.

"Aye, I was—"

"Eavesdropping, as usual?"

"I do not eavesdrop, Trevor Gillingham. I glean facts," she huffed. "And the few I learned of this marriage make me wish to escape to a convent."

She buried her face in his shoulder.

"We have no choice, Cat. Edward decreed it."

"Blast the king!"

Trevor whipped his head around to search the doorway, his face drained of color. "Hush, Cat. The king has ears everywhere. You must watch what you say—for all our sakes."

Seeking comfort, Catherine flung her arms around her older brother's neck and sobbed. "How shall I manage without you? You were the one constant in my life." She raised tear-filled eyes.

He held her, giving her no doubt he relinquished his role as protector reluctantly.

"You shall be fine," he said, his voice soothing, although she steeled herself against the words. "You can handle anything you set your mind to."

"What if…?" Words failed her. She tightened her grip around his neck. As a child, he'd protected her. Though he no longer lived at home, their bond remained strong. She'd thought nothing would separate them. Until now.

Catherine's eyes brimmed with tears while he studied her face, caressing her cheek with his knuckles. As if reading her mind, his voice soothed, "Call for me, Cat. Send a missive and I promise I shall come."

His eyes held only sadness.

"You must dress now, sweet sister." He cast an eye at her rumpled robe. "I shall leave so Rowena may return."

She watched him leave, too distraught to utter anything but a sob.

\* \* \*

When the priest asked for Catherine's voice of consent, her eyes slipped sideways to appraise the angry man beside her. His stony silence seemed as eloquent as any bard's tale. He wanted nothing to do with her.

He'd not joined them at supper the prior eve, so she'd still seen only his back and profile. His dark brown hair fell to his shoulders. When her father escorted her to the chapel's outer steps, she'd noticed her betrothed's height and the breadth of his shoulders. He wore a white linen shirt with a blue and green *plaide* revealing long, strong legs. His profile looked chiseled in rock, clearly revealing his anger.

She feared her knees might buckle. How could she bear the burden of her father's expectations to wed as the king decreed? He'd been in Edward's favor for years. Couldn't he change the king's mind? Was being granted a new title and another estate more important than her happiness? His sharp admonition 'to make me proud' echoed in her mind.

Her eyes sought her father's, pleading for a final reprieve. After leaving her to stand beside a stranger, he'd gone to her mother. She saw no love in his hazel eyes, only steely determination. Having always treated her kindly, Catherine wondered why he suddenly cared naught about her feelings. How much wealth had the king promised?

Her mother stood beside him, wringing her hands. She'd been in tears for sennights, upset over Catherine's fate. Her dark brown eyes were rimmed with red. Her hair, always lustrous black, now grayed. Never one to challenge her husband's decisions, Lady Gillingham wouldn't intervene.

Shoulders stooped in defeat, Catherine turned back to face Brentwood's priest. It felt like forever, yet mere moments had passed. Her voice cracking, she barely whispered the words that would forever alter the course of her life. "I will."

The man beside her stood rigid as she gave her response. He exhaled loudly and said through clenched teeth, "Aye, I will."

Despite the palpable tension, the priest completed the holy message, then moved inside the chapel to offer communion and bless the marriage.

Catherine couldn't believe the priest's audacity when at ceremony's end he smiled at Duncan. "You may give your bride the kiss of peace."

# Chapter Three

Duncan eyed the priest coolly, then turned for the first time to face his lady wife.

Trying to keep his expression unreadable, his gaze traversed the length of her body, stopped at her breasts, her hips. Seal this unwanted union with a kiss to show the families joined together with no ill feelings? He'd *not* do it. All he'd needed do was tell the priest he protested. The ceremony would have gone no further. He couldn't do it. His clan needed him. Before he left home he'd decided not to stay with her after the wedding, wanting nothing to do with a woman his father selected. He planned to leave as soon as he took her home. He wouldn't change his mind now.

He stood resolute—and unable to breathe—for he stared at one of the loveliest women he'd ever seen.

He moistened his lips and watched her proudly stare up at him.

He reached out to touch her face, but drew back at the last moment.

Rimmed with long black lashes, her large brown eyes had golden flecks shimmering throughout. Her lips pressed together to hide her nervousness. Failing, the corner of her mouth trembled. Duncan had the ridiculous urge to take her in his arms and kiss her. An image flashed through his mind—of her body trembling with desire as he sheathed himself inside her woman's heat.

He had to slow his breathing as his gaze drank in her every nuance. A sheer wimple flowed down her back and covered her shimmering auburn hair. Seed pearls and ivy formed a circlet atop her head. Her ivory-colored kirtle was form-fitted over ample breasts and draped over well-rounded hips. Hips perfect for carrying a bairn—his bairn. The sleeves were long and loose flowing, befitting her family's extreme wealth. The côtehardie, cut to show the gown beneath, was trimmed with martin fur.

Give her the kiss of peace? He intended no such thing, although he couldn't take his eyes from her lips, wondering if they'd feel as soft as velvet. Overwhelmed by her beauty, it took every ounce of willpower to tear his eyes from her face. He turned and left her standing at the altar, a collective gasp from onlookers echoing throughout the chapel as he walked out alone.

He cared not what anyone thought of his actions, but knew he'd hear about it from his sister. Tamara wouldn't hesitate to tell him he'd just been a cold-hearted, insensitive boor.

He saw her from the corner of his eye, her green eyes wide with dismay when he moved past her. She said naught, but he clearly heard her thoughts. 'Duncan, how could you leave that lovely woman standing alone?'

Determined not to stay in this Godforsaken house a moment longer than necessary, Duncan returned to his chamber and rang for the chambermaid. Upon her arrival, he ordered, "Inform my lady *wife* we leave within the hour. I expect her packed and ready."

Observing her shocked expression, he coolly added, "Inform her any *luxuries* not down the stairs shall remain behind." He turned his back in dismissal.

\* \* \*

Catherine felt a rush of annoyance and glared upstairs at her unseen husband. When he'd first turned in her direction, she'd lost herself in the fathomless depths of his blue eyes. She thought him one of the handsomest men she'd seen. She had the urge to reach up and brush the shock of dark hair from his forehead — until the rude man turned and left her standing alone.

"How dare he insult me and issue such an order? Does he not plan to partake of our wedding celebration?"

She stormed upstairs, her mother, sister, and lady's maid closely at her heels. "That arrogant man may think he won," she grumbled, "but he doesn't know whom he deals with yet. He probably believes I shall turn into a hysterical female. Well, I shan't."

She turned to the women she held dearest. "With your help, I intend to put my husband in his place." Her eyes softened as she looked to her sobbing mother, her shoulders shaking with the force of tears. "Mother, please do not cry. I need your help."

Determined to show *that man* he'd wed a force to be reckoned with, Catherine packed with haste. With time to spare and wearing her brown traveling mantle, she stood in the parlor, trying to project a calm façade. Inside, she seethed.

Her husband approached the staircase landing, probably expecting to see a group of wailing women ready to plead for additional time. Instead, a smile spread over her face when he stopped mid-step. She delighted he saw the woman he'd just issued a ridiculous order to waiting calmly, her traveling retinue around her.

Their gazes met and locked.

She gave a mocking smile. "I thought mayhap you were going to be late, my lord husband."

A twitch of his lips and a quirked brow seemed to say, *And so the battle begins.*

\* \* \*

With a haughty turn of her head, Catherine reached up and drew her mantle's hood over her hair.

Walking out the door, she fought the urge to glance back.

She stopped outside and turned to Rowena. "I shall miss you." She touched the tears freely flowing down the woman's cheeks. "I would love to have you accompany me, but would not subject you to that horrible ma...my lord husband." She smirked, her gaze sweeping to Duncan. He stared right through her, his face impassive, as if her derogatory words meant nothing.

Kissing her family farewell, she headed across the courtyard and stood beside the waiting conveyance.

Elizabeth ran to her, throwing her arms around her neck. "I shall miss you. Who shall I spend my days with? Who shall—?"

"Rowena shall care for you, Beth." Catherine lifted her chin and glowered over Elizabeth's head at her new husband. Lowering her head to her sister once again, Catherine whispered, "I love you."

Catherine nudged her toward Trevor.

26

He gathered Elizabeth in his arms and endeavored to console her. Failing, he raked his fingers through his hair, unleashing it from the leather strap. Trevor attempted a smile. The best he mustered was a crooked grin.

Angered to be placed in this predicament due to the king's whim and her father's greed, Catherine impatiently tapped her foot. She wondered how MacThomaidh planned to return home since this was his litter. It mattered not.

* * *

Duncan watched from the courtyard, readying his horse for the long journey. He rolled his eyes as he watched his new lady's every movement. The unyielding vixen stood beside the litter and didn't move. He walked toward her, opened the conveyance's curtains and extended his hand, waiting for her to accept it.

She shot him a withering glare. Surprisingly, he found her tenacity oddly pleasing.

Sense prevailed and although she glared back, her chin stubborn, she placed her hand in his. After settling her inside the cushioned litter, Duncan jumped atop his stallion.

*I misdoubt I shall be happy again. Not after being leg shackled to this English female.* At least she was pleasing to the eye, though it would be easier to hate her if she was a crone.

He rode ahead of the litter. *What to do with a wife I dunnae want – other than tumble with her atween the sheets?* Merciful saints, she was beautiful. When those big brown eyes looked at him he'd felt an overwhelming urge to pull her into his arms and crush her to him. He'd never felt such an immediate surge of lust as when he turned to face her. Nay, he couldn't keep her. He'd continue with his original plan. He might have to wed her to keep his clan safe, regretted he'd have to take her virginity to seal the bargain, but not once had he agreed to stay with her. He'd leave as soon as he took her to his home.

He'd laughed at the smug expression on her face when she awaited him in her parlor. Aye, the lass had bested him at his own game. He credited her with not falling apart.

* * *

After a hard ride, an uninvited guest arrived at Brentwood, the celebration feast still going on. People were well on their way to becoming drunk. He'd waited for this opportunity over seven years. Ever since his bloody laird deprived him of the woman he wanted. Tory should have been his—as should all of Clan MacThomas.

This night Duncan MacThomas would die.

Joining the milling throng, Erwin overheard men talking.

"Gillingham is not pleased the heathen departed after the ceremony. He's grumbled all night about the fête's expense, but I misdoubt he will complain to the king."

"Damnation," Erwin swore, slinking into the shadows. "I missed MacThomas again." He surveyed the gathered crowd, reached down to adjust his dark brown over-tunic. "For this I wore leggings? I feel like a bloody court jester. How can men wear these loathsome things?" Tomorrow he'd be back in chausses. He'd been embarrassed the last time.

The next time he searched out MacThomas, he'd plan better. The man would pay.

Erwin headed out the door to return to town. "Mayhap I shouldnae be so quick to kill him, should make him suffer before I end his life. He deprived me of the woman I wanted—twice. Now that he is wed, mayhap I should strike where it will hurt the most." He laughed mirthlessly. He needn't rush, would take his time and plan MacThomas' downfall carefully.

* * *

Catherine glanced around the inn, her eyes growing accustomed to the dim light. The large room, cluttered with wooden tables and chairs, appeared clean, free of vermin. Exhausted, every bone aching, she reached up to remove her mantle.

Beside her, Duncan informed the innkeeper, "We have traveled long this day. I require your best room and rooms for my men as well. Also, have a tub sent to mine." Turning, he gave Catherine a smile.

The first smile she'd seen upon his face, Catherine blinked surprise. She'd thought him handsome before. Without the perpetual grim lines bracketing his mouth, he was beautiful. Her heart pounded in her chest and she found it hard to see anything but Duncan.

His eyes roamed over her blue côtehardie, the long garment's skirt girdled at her hips. "I am certain after the dusty day's ride my lady wife would relish a warm bath."

Catherine's hand shook as she situated the mantle around her body, her spirit almost breaking. *He pretended to care.* She closed her eyes against a wave of pain.

As if the brute had regard for her feelings. She'd thought he never planned to stop. Having been tossed from side to side in the litter, she'd be surprised if her entire body wasn't bruised. At the very least, she should kick him a time or two to make him hurt.

She reached down to brush dust from her mantle, giving her time to regain her composure. Two could play whatever farce he engaged in. Catherine plastered on a come-hither smile and faced her knave of a husband. "I appreciate your kindness, my lord."

Before anyone uttered another word, she headed upstairs to the only room with an open door. She went inside and firmly closed it.

\* \* \*

Leisurely soaking in the tub filled with buckets of warm water, Catherine peered around the room. It had a bed and a small table that looked like it would collapse if anything was placed on it. Elsewise, the room appeared as stark as the common room downstairs. She stretched out an arm to lather it when the door opened and Duncan entered.

She squealed in shock realizing she'd not placed the wooden bar through the latch! What had she been thinking? Did this man make her forget all sense?

Outraged, she sank lower. The bubbles did little to hide her nudity and her breasts kept rising above them. She quickly crossed her arms over her chest.

"What are you doing here? Get out!"

"We were wed this day. I have every right to be here."

"But...but I bathe," she said as if he were an idiot.

His eyes lowered to take in everything the water didn't hide.

She wanted to wipe away the smile tugging at the corner of his mouth when he announced, "Och, aye, I see that."

Seeing the gleam in the depths of his blue eyes, she tried to slip lower in the tub. "Get out!"

Ignoring her, Duncan closed the door. "To grant you a measure of privacy, I cleaned up with my men, but this is *our* room." He unbelted his sporran and placed it atop the small wooden table beside the bed. Unfastening the brooch from his blue and green tunic, he folded it and set it on the floor. All he now wore were his white linen undershirt, leggings, and shoes.

Her eyes widened at the sight of him removing his clothes. "What are you doing?"

"Do your eyes not work? They didnae tell me you were blind. No wonder they were quick to wed you to a Scot." He chuckled and relished teasing her. "Since you are sorely afflicted, shall I describe my actions?"

Catherine gulped. "You are ta...taking off your clothes."

His eyes danced with mischievousness. "Och, the lass isnae blind after all, but is perceptive. A fine quality in a lady *wife*. Have you other afflictions or deformities I havenae been told about? You have been so silent, I feared you were addled."

Flustered at the sight of his disrobing, Catherine ignored his jibe. "Why?"

"Why did I think you addled?"

"Why do you remove your clothes?" Her breathing quickened at the sight of him.

"I told you, lady *wife*, I intend to spend the night." Duncan walked to the bed and sat, pushing on it to test its comfort. His eyes never leaving her, a hint of a smile lifted the corner of his mouth.

Catherine's trepidation grew at the implied threat of his actions. The very spot where he meant to take her virginity.

"Have the decency to turn your back while I don my n…nightrail."

She wanted to scratch his handsome face when laughter appeared in his eyes. Rising from the bed, he placed his shoes and leggings beside his folded *plaide*. He looked around the room, then headed to the small bench. Muscles in his strong legs rippled when he bent to retrieve the green chemise. All he wore now was his linen shirt. Her mouth went dry.

He held the garment out to the light of the fire, appraising the thin material.

"This?" he asked with arched brows.

Catherine nodded.

"Fine material, almost transparent," he said, appearing satisfied. "Though it willnae afford much protection." He wiggled his brows, mocking her.

She gulped.

"Turn my back? Why? You are my lady *wife*, are you not? Your family bought me as one might a blooded stallion."

Ashamed and furious that he should make such a comment, Catherine's cheeks flushed.

"Aye they did, and considering your rudeness it appears I received the worst of the bargain."

Duncan shrugged, but she heard the edge to his voice. "I shall be more than happy to hand you the chemise."

He extended his arm, held the garment out. She reached over the tub and tried to snag it without rising. "How dare you treat me thusly?"

Duncan's lips curved upward at the fury on her face. He stepped back.

"Give me my nightrail," came her shout of frustration.

"Why, I am," he said with a hint of a smile. Crooking a finger, he beckoned her over.

Catherine's eyes widened.

He tried to hold back his laughter when she grabbed for the garment once more. Failing, she didn't need to voice the unladylike thoughts swirling through her mind. Her smoldering eyes told him all.

His face impassive, he watched her every reaction. *Och, she's a spitfire. Not the least cowed by my actions.* For reasons he couldn't explain, that pleased him. Nothing like he'd expected, she was beautiful and spirited.

His body tensed when she rose, rivulets running down her long, shapely legs. He took in every curve of her body—the full breasts, narrow waist, and rounded hips made for breeding bairns, ending at…the dark hair on her woman's mound. He caught his breath and forced himself to look at her face. He didn't know what he'd expected, but it wasn't this.

She was beautiful—she was his. Knowing the king

would order it, he'd planned only an obligatory mating, but now he intended to have her moaning beneath him. Shouting his name with her release.

Duncan closed his eyes to stop his lustful thoughts. She'd drive him daft if he continued, yet his body had a mind of its own and his eyes opened. He'd look his fill. Drink in every delicious part of her body.

His manhood throbbed to life, shocking him with its intensity. He wanted to claim her, all of her. Not just her body. Wanted to mark her as his. Feelings he hadn't had in a long time.

# Chapter Four

Catherine stepped gingerly from the tub.

As she reached for the chemise, Duncan yanked it away, causing her to lose balance. Dropping the garment, his arm caught her and drew her toward him to brace her fall.

She froze the instant his hands touched her bare skin, her body firmly planted against his, separated only by his thin linen shirt. Her nightrail forgotten at their feet.

He brushed his lips over her bare shoulder. Goosebumps instantly arose. He felt them as he skimmed her skin with his lips. Ordered to wed, there'd been no question about consummating the marriage. He hadn't planned on wanting to do so, yet her quiet strength intrigued him, drew him.

"Do not touch me," she ordered, her body quaking.

Placing his thumb beneath her chin, he tilted her face up.

He lost himself in her whisky colored eyes. She had the longest, darkest lashes he'd ever seen. She tried not to meet his gaze and her lips trembled. From fear? She'd done that at their wedding, too. He couldn't think of anything he wanted more than to taste those lips and stop that quiver. He wanted to claim her, plunder her mouth with his tongue, make her totally his.

Why did this woman so affect him?

He flexed his arm so she pressed fully against him. Her skin, wet from her bath, felt soft and smooth. He lightly ran his fingers down her spine, causing her to shiver. The fragrance from her lavender soap clung to her like a breeze caressing a flower's silky petals. Soft, yet tantalizing. The heady scent aroused his senses.

Her body tensed at his touch. His hardened even more.

Catherine spoke. "You may release me now. I should like to dry my hair and don my n...nightrail." Her voice quavered.

When she moistened her lips with her tongue, the lips he couldn't keep his eyes from, Duncan thought he'd perish from need. Right now he could think of nothing besides bedding her.

Sliding his hand up her back, he stared into her beautiful eyes. He bent to brush a kiss over her lips. A feather of a touch, but all he needed to tell him they were soft as he imagined. The sensation was enough to make him want to touch her all over—her mouth, her neck, her breasts, her... Blessed Saint Ninian, he had to stop these thoughts!

Obviously, she didn't return his feelings. She'd frozen at his touch.

"Och, more's the pity," he sighed in frustration, "but aye, you may have your nightrail." Bending to retrieve it, he handed it to her and walked away. He sat on the bed to place distance between them and forced himself to gather his wits.

What spell did this woman cast that so affected him? She wasn't some lush courtesan trained in ways of pleasuring a man like those he'd encountered on his travels. She was naught but a rich, spoiled *Sasunnach*. The woman he wanted nothing to do with.

His body had other ideas and screamed for release. He desired her, no denying that. He shifted position to hide his erection, unwilling to let her think he had no control or she had any effect on him.

Upset that he craved her when he didn't want to be wed to her, he lashed out, "We could save time if you got into bed naked. I want this wedding nae more than you, but to make this sham of a marriage valid, we must consummate it." His words sounded crude even to himself.

Slipping the chemise over her head, Catherine swung around to face him, eyes wide with shock. "B...but..."

"'Tis our wedding night, lass." He softened his tone, hoping his voice didn't betray his mixed emotions. Having seen her wet and naked, his body responded immediately.

"B...but I thought..."

She appeared terrified. Having never bedded a virgin, Duncan wondered if all women were frightened their first time.

"I wouldnae demand my marital rights?"

"Aye." She pressed her lips together to stay the quiver.

"'Twas a legal ceremony afore God," he clarified, watching her mouth tremble. "I regret I must take your

37

virginity for a marriage neither of us desire, but I intend we do what our fathers and the king demand of me." He couldn't tear his eyes from her face, reached his hand up to move a stray lock from her forehead. "You might thank me lady wife."

"For what?"

"By whisking you away from your home, I saved you the humiliation of having the priest and half of London witness the bedding ceremony."

Catherine's brows furrowed. "Bedding ceremony?"

Duncan closed his eyes and sighed. Was she really that innocent? "Surely you knew we would be watched."

"W...watched?" she squeaked.

Duncan groaned. He should have kept his mouth shut.

"Mother said I would be taken upstairs and undressed. She meant to help me into the new nightrail she had made for my wedding night."

"Nay, she meant undressed...naked," Duncan clarified.

Catherine's eyes widened. "But—"

"Let me explain. I would have been expected to circle you, inspect your nakedness." He watched her eyes. She looked appalled. "Your priest would ask if I found you free of defects and accepted you as my lady wife. You would have done the same with me."

Her eyes widened in disbelief.

"If Edward hadn't had previous obligations, he'd have been there. He would have been one of the observers, would have insisted the priest, your father and mine stay in the room." His voice held an edge of

38

disgust. "Whilst they would allow us to draw the bed curtains, they wouldnae leave until I bedded you and presented them with the bloodied cloth from beneath you."

When she said nothing, but clutched her chemise like a cloak of armour, Duncan soothed, "'Twillnae be bad. I shall make it as painless as possible." A thought occurred and his eyes narrowed. "Or are you not a maiden?"

Furious at his insulting words, Catherine rushed toward him and raised her hand to slap him. He grabbed it and jerked her down atop him.

Catherine struggled to sit, only to wind up straddling his hips. She inhaled deeply in an apparent effort to calm herself.

Before she could scramble off, he tumbled her to the bed and kissed her. His kisses grew hungry, demanding. Shifting position, he had her beneath him, cupped her breast through her nightrail and moved his thumb over her nipple. When it grew taut, he grabbed his shirt and yanked it over his head, throwing it heedlessly to the floor. Breathing heavily, he moved her arms above her head. He tugged the chemise over her head and arms.

Catherine's eyes widened at the sight of his naked chest. Duncan laughed when she frantically tried to stay his hands. "Stop it. You cannot touch me…like this."

He caught her hands again and lifted them above her head, imprisoning both within one of his. "Och, but I can. As your lord husband, I can touch you anyway I want— anywhere I want." And he intended to do just that. He'd never felt such overwhelming desire, couldn't wait to sample every delectable part of her body. Leaning down, he kissed her forehead and slowly trailed his lips down the side of her jaw. His mouth slanted over hers. He teased her with his tongue to coax her mouth open, at the same time shifting his body closer to hers.

Catherine gasped when his manhood touched her belly, and Duncan seized the opportunity. His tongue explored her mouth. As her breathing grew ragged, he pulled back and gazed into confused brown eyes. Had she never been properly kissed? He smiled at the possibilities. "I mean no offense this time," he said truthfully, knowing no other way to ask the indelicate question. "I must know if you are indeed a maiden. Your answer shall determine the pace I set."

Eyes wide, Catherine nodded. She'd stopped fighting him.

He gazed at her long and hard. Long black lashes swept down over fathomless brown eyes. When the corner of her mouth quivered, Duncan was lost. He'd not only claim her lips, molding them to his own, he'd claim her body. He'd not wanted her, but now she was his— and that pleased him. He lowered his mouth to hers.

His breathing quickened as his lips wandered over her cheek and down the curve of her neck. Wherever he placed kisses, he released her soap's fragrance, found it intoxicating. When he flicked his tongue over her earlobe, Catherine shivered. Glancing down, he noticed bruises on her shoulder. Caused by the journey? A shard of guilt blasted through him. Hellsfire, he'd not meant to hurt her.

His mouth returned to hers. He wandered lower.

Down her collarbone, over her chest, to his next goal—her breast. By the saints, she was soft. The total opposite of himself. He couldn't get any harder. Pulsing with need, he ran his fingertips lightly down the insides of her silky thighs. Her skin felt soft and smooth as a butterfly's wings.

Duncan heard her sharp inhalation as he laved his tongue over the sensitive bud of her breast. A perfect breast, he thought. Full and firm. When he turned his attention to her lips, Catherine arched against him.

Duncan took his time and kissed her until her body strained against his, her tongue tentatively mimicking his actions. In the grip of passion, he positioned himself above her. She tensed, clearly surmising his intent. Sighing heavily, he closed his eyes and reined in his passion, reminding himself she was a virgin. He stilled, let her peruse his body. Her cheeks flushed when her eyes lowered and saw his solid manhood. She scrunched her eyes together and moaned. He leaned down, recapturing her breast with his mouth in an effort to rekindle her passion. He murmured, "'Tis all right, lass. There is nae rush. We have all night."

Catherine's face revealed her uncertainty. Clearly her body wanted something, but didn't know what.

When she instinctively arched against him, he shifted and eased himself inside her tight sheath until he reached the expected barrier. He withdrew, paused only the briefest instant before pressing forward, breaching her maidenhead and making her completely his. An unexpected surge of contentment washed over him.

At her cry of pain, he stilled.

She shifted under his weight, her movements causing him to slip farther inside. Her eyes widened at the unexpected feelings the motion provoked.

"Are you all right?" he questioned with concern, his eyes watching pensively. He found her enchanting. Certainly a far cry from the detested woman he envisioned when told of the marriage.

Stretched to his limit on staying his movements, he exercised more restraint than he thought imaginable. He had no desire to hurt her. To his immense relief, she nodded.

"The pain is gone?"

"'Tis not bad."

He needed no further answer and began the slow seductive moves to bring them to the peak of ecstasy. Catherine soon cried out and he covered her mouth with his to muffle the sound. His men knew what would occur this night, but he saw no need to announce it to the inn's occupants. His release followed and he collapsed atop her. His heart thumped hard and fast, but he finally roused himself enough to move, rolled over and brought her to his side.

He felt amazed. He'd vowed to hate her, yet he'd just experienced feelings he'd never had before. Not just the sex. He'd had more than his share of willing women.

Duncan found himself unable to explain his emotions.

"Are you all right?"

"Aye," came her surprised answer. "I never thought..." She blushed, her eyes lowering and voice trailing off. Pressed closely against his chest, her lashes fluttered, caressed his skin. They felt as light as a butterfly. A whimsical thought crossed his mind — a butterfly kiss.

"Joining our bodies could be so nice?" he finished and laughed. He delighted in completing this enchanting woman's statements.

"Well..." came her embarrassed stammer, "aye, but...but I never imagined I would feel so — "

"Wonderful? Complete? Sated?" he playfully offered. He enjoyed seeing her blushes. In truth, he enjoyed everything about her. A stray tendril swept across her face. He reached up to push it behind her ear. "Stop me when I find the correct word," he boasted good-humoredly.

Catherine wiggled free. "Lord MacThomas, please. I — "

"Wish to couple again?" he teased and kissed the tip of her very blushing nose. "Aye, m'lady, if you insist."

Before Catherine voiced her shock, he drew her closer and nuzzled her neck. He raised his head to look into her eyes. The way her lashes fluttered was one of the most arousing things he'd ever seen. It reminded him of a butterfly he'd seen in his sister's garden. His butterfly. His passion once again unleashed, he lowered his head to her soft lips. Words were forgotten as he brought them both to fulfillment.

# Chapter Five

Duncan awoke with a smile, no longer in a hurry to return home. Once over her initial shyness, Catherine surprised him with her passionate lovemaking. He stretched his arm across the bed to pull her close.

She wasn't there.

Springing from the bed, he reached to the floor to grab his plaide. He wrapped the yards of cloth around himself with practiced hands.

"I knew I couldnae trust her. Did the bloody woman already leave?" He stormed out the door only to meet Catherine halfway down the stairs. She carried a tray piled with food. A smile crossed her face, but faded at his scowl.

His eyes took in her tousled appearance. What had the daft woman been thinking to leave the room looking so desirable? Had she no qualms about his men seeing her thusly? Well, he bloody well did! Look at her! She didn't even have on shoes.

He had no intention of his men—any man—seeing such intimate parts of her body. She was his.

The primal reaction perplexed him. Why respond so strongly to her disappearance? If he didn't want her, why did it matter?

She moved past him, placing the tray on the wobbly table. "Good morrow, m'lord."

He slammed the door closed. "What were you doing

below stairs?"

Catherine looked perplexed and hurt. She glanced from him to the heaping tray. "As you asked me yestereve, do your eyes not work? I fetched food to break our fast."

The moment the words left his mouth Duncan realized how daft he sounded.

He closed the space between them and wrapped her in his arms. "I dinnae mean to yell. I just..." How could he tell her his fear of being abandoned? That both his father and first wife left? He'd appear weak.

Unable to find the right words, he propelled her toward the table. "Let us eat afore the food turns cold."

\* \* \*

Later that morn he led Catherine to the stables and lifted her atop his stallion. Mounting behind her, he drew her close. Their pace was slow, his men behind them, enjoying the solitude and peacefulness of the quiet meadow. He nuzzled her hair, inhaled her scent. Today she smelled of roses.

Choosing a secluded location with a brilliantine loch, he dismounted and lifted her from his horse. He moved her slowly down the length of his body before bending to kiss her. Ah, those beautiful lips. Soft, pliant. He released her reluctantly, removed his plaide and spread it on the ground. Catherine knelt, but he surprised her by continuing to discard clothes.

She stared, mouth agape. "What are you doing?"

"Going for a swim. Join me?"

"Here?"

He nodded, eyes glinting with merriment as hers

rounded in surprise.

"Now?" She gulped, able to say only one syllable words.

"Aye."

"Go into the lake? I could not possibly…" She finally found voice, but her words stopped when he removed his last article of clothing. At her shocked expression, he laughed.

Catherine blinked, a blush rising to her cheeks.

Duncan couldn't contain himself. He wanted to love her and protect her at the same time, but didn't comprehend such conflicting feelings. Make love he understood. If he didn't put space between them, she'd be on her back on his plaide. He wanted to kiss her eyes, her nose, her graceful neck, her breasts, every inch of that lush body. But where had the feelings to protect her come from? Running to the water's edge, he dove in.

Catherine followed and stood on the bank, watching his steady strokes. His legs were long. His strong arms sliced through the water. He looked like he could maintain that pace endlessly. She could watch him all day.

"Join me."

She smiled, but shyly shook her head.

Finally tired of swimming, Duncan exited the water and grabbed her hand, leading her toward his plaide. He sat and drew her beside him, shaking his hair like a puppy, releasing water droplets. Catherine squealed as cold water sprayed her.

"Come, Sweetling, the water feels good."

Catherine's refusal to join him in the water piqued Duncan's curiosity. "Cannae you swim?" He grinned playfully.

She tried to laugh off his question, but he wouldn't be deterred. "Then I must teach you."

He undid her kirtle and tugged it over her head, leaving only her chemise. He drew in a ragged breath at the sight, grabbed her hand and yanked her toward the water.

She resisted. "Nay, I do not wish to…"

Ignoring protests, he lifted her effortlessly and walked into the water.

She screeched, "'Tis cold."

Standing waist deep, he set her down, letting her feet touch the loch's bottom, and wrapped his arms around her. She trembled. He coaxed her to relax, teaching her to float. He slipped his hand under her lacy chemise. Wet, it concealed nothing.

A flick of his thumb over her nipple revealed she was either cold — or aroused. Believing both, but focusing on the latter, he moved her closer, placed her arms around his neck and captured her mouth with his. He shifted his hand from her breast to cup her woman's mound, pressed his fingers forward. She moaned, those beautiful lashes trying to veil her thoughts.

Duncan couldn't stop himself. He preened like a peacock. Blessed Saint Andrew, she wanted him. He'd overcome her inhibitions yet. And he'd never tell her those lovely brown eyes gave away her innermost feelings. A man had to have some secrets.

Reaching down, he wrapped her legs around his hips, kissed her neck, her ear, and finally her mouth. Places he'd fantasized about only moments before.

"So much for a cold swim helping," he groused, heading back toward the shore.

"What?"

"Never mind."

Kneeling, he reached forward, intent on unlacing her bodice, his eyes locked on hers with a predatory gleam.

"Duncan, we cannot possibly…"

Laughing, he eased her down. "Why not?" He spread the bodice laces apart and exposed a full, creamy breast to his view. "Nae one is about," he murmured, his head descending, capturing her breast. He didn't mention his men were never far away, protecting them from harm.

"Duncan," Catherine gasped, "we are outside!"

He mumbled agreement, but didn't release her breast. By the time he moved to the other side, she didn't seem to care they were outside.

* * *

"I am starving," he laughed, after heading arm in arm with her to the shore. They'd taken another dip in the loch after their lovemaking. Glad he'd had foresight to bring food, he watched her eat with relish.

Throwing a chicken bone over his shoulder, he laughed when she licked her fingertips. "Is that something a proper lady would do?"

She blushed. "Mother would die of embarrassment. She insisted I comport myself properly."

"That must have been tiring…*comporting*."

A grin crossed her face. "It was, but that is how we were raised. She had great hopes of my wedding a wealthy husband." She gasped, her hand flying to her mouth. Her eyes shot to his. "Forgive me. I did not mean—"

He cut her off. "You need not apologize for the truth. I dunnae misdoubt I wouldnae be your mam's choice had Edward not decreed it." Turning away, he repacked the food.

* * *

Married a sennight and rarely separated, Duncan and Catherine spent days learning about the other. At night they wrapped themselves in each other's arms.

Walking in the countryside, Catherine removed her hand from his and hurried toward a multi-colored field. She bent to pick a handful of flowers.

"Look! Think you that sour goodwoman would like these in her common room?"

Duncan heard her talking, but couldn't focus on the words. Desire wrecking havoc with his senses, he could only stare at her very rounded bottom.

She threw a petal at him and teased, "I am glad to discover you are not a barbarian, my lord husband."

He reached out to tuck a flower behind her ear, replying just as lightly, "And I am pleased to discover you are not completely spoiled."

She lowered her eyes and looked away, biting her bottom lip. He'd bruised her feelings. *Hellsfire, I but meant to tease her.* Disgusted with his choice of words, he looked down at his hands and closed them into fists. *Och, these hands are fashioned to hold and fight with a sword, but I am bloody ill equipped to woo a wife with simple things like words.*

He wanted their journey pleasurable. If within his power, he'd extend it indefinitely, but reality had a horrible way of interfering.

He held her close. "*Mo Chride*, I meant no harm. I may have thought that when first I heard of you, but quickly learned elsewise." He bent to kiss her.

Catherine gulped, managed a weak smile. "*Mo Chridhe*. What does it mean?"

My heart, he'd called her in Gaelic. Was he falling for this Sasunnach wife? Dread rolled up his spine. He'd once said those words to a woman—a wife—only to have them tossed into the mud with his pride. He couldn't give this fae wife such power to use against him.

Not wanting to tell her the meaning, he grasped for any diversion. Focusing on a distant sound, he grabbed her hand and pulled her after him.

Her soft brown eyes widened in delight when she saw the waterfall.

"'Tis breathtaking. Have you ever seen anything so magnificent?"

"Mmhmm." He meant her, but said, "We have one on MacThomas land."

Her eyes glistened with excitement. "You must take me to see it."

The memory of those wispy lashes fluttering on his chest made his manhood stir. Blessed Saint Michael, but she enticed him. Innocent, yet seductive. Pulling her into his arms, he nuzzled her silken hair, inhaled the heavenly scent of her.

Knowing he took the coward's way out—again—he never answered. Instead, he said, "I never made love near a waterfall, lass. Come." He held her close, his bold, insistent tongue mating with hers. *Aye, making love by a waterfall is the perfect way to end the day.*

* * *

Giving the newlyweds space, Duncan's friends trailed behind for security, but didn't join their outings. They ate together in the common room, eyeing Catherine critically. Duncan realized his friends' opinion changed when they drew her into conversation. Catherine laughed at their stories.

"Dohmnall, that cannot possibly be true."

The redhead faked offense. "You dunnae believe me? Every word is true."

Men around him guffawed and Catherine joined their laughter. Heads turned at the musical lilt of her voice. Duncan frowned at the strangers' attention, but thought his men's acceptance important. They'd serve and protect her once they arrived home. He nodded, pleased they drew her into their circle. Her face lit up as she smiled and a spurt of jealousy shot through him. Batherskite! It mattered not that she smiled at his men. No doubt her intentions were innocent.

But what if…? Thoughts of Helen swirled through his mind. Of knowing she bedded other men thinking to punish him. Would Catherine do the same? Would she be dissatisfied with his home—with him—and turn to other men? One of many questions Duncan had no answer to was what he'd do after they returned home. Would he—could he—still leave as originally planned? He didn't want to anymore.

Several days later, reaching a friend's castle in the Borders, Duncan finally relaxed.

Catherine sat on a stool, brushing her long hair. She

turned to the door when Duncan entered. "Have you seen the garden outside? Can we walk there later?"

"I will if you wish me to, Sweetling, but I had far more interesting things in mind for us."

Giving an exasperated sigh, she threw her brush at him.

What a delight she was to tease, Duncan thought as he changed for the fête that eve.

Extending his arm, he escorted her down the long winding staircase. Her auburn tresses flowed down the back of her emerald green côtehardie, its low cut bodice form fitted. Duncan thought her ravishing. Before they entered the Great Hall, he stopped and brushed wisps of hair from her face, his fingers tarrying moments longer than necessary. How had this delightful woman come to be his? Och, his father had chosen her, a fact that rankled still, but mayhap God had intervened. If so, did he have the right to leave? Torn, Duncan had no idea what he'd do.

They dined on roasted duck, bread, neeps with cream sauce, and sweet bread with nuts. Soon tables were dismantled and cleared away.

A bard sang, "The beautiful visiting lady and her laird husband..."

Catherine blushed when she realized he'd woven her and Duncan into his tale, especially when verses grew bawdy.

Soon her host and his wife were dancing. "Come, Catherine." Duncan helped her to her feet and whirled her into his arms.

"You dance well, my lord husband," she said,

amazed.

Duncan feigned a hurt look. "I danced often during years I spent in the king's court in Spain and France."

Changing the subject, Duncan flirted shamelessly. He reached up, letting his fingertips linger lightly on her cheek and gently wander down her neck. His hand brushed her breast when he placed his arm around her to bring her to his side.

Her cheeks blushing hot, she shuddered in anticipation.

They stood near the wall catching their breaths. Duncan stood behind her, his arms wrapped loosely around her waist. A young man enquired, "Might I have this dance, Lady MacThomas?"

Duncan's grip tightened. Shifting her position, he anchored her protectively to his side. "My wife and I share this next dance." He swept her onto the floor before the man could say more. He repeated his actions throughout the night, with the exception of their host.

Ian's eyes searched her face as she danced with him. "You have captivated my friend. I dunnae remember seeing Duncan act so possessive. After his first wi...I am sorry, what I meant to say was, rarely has he cared for women other than for the usual sport. You he watches like a hawk." His eyes shifted to Duncan. "Even now, dancing with my lady wife, he knows where you are at all times."

* * *

Their trip home had taken a moon and a half's passing, yet when they started on the journey's last leg, Catherine voiced, "The trip passed too quickly."

Duncan was quiet. On previous days' journeys he'd moved close and held her while they talked inside the litter. Now he sat stiffly on the opposite side and stared out through the curtains.

Reaching Duncan's home, Catherine's eyes took in everything. The litter crossed the outer bailey. She sighed in relief when he placed strong hands around her waist to help her down. She couldn't deny nervousness.

The area teemed with activity. Duncan grabbed her hand and led her toward the hall. "Well-come to my home. Come, Catherine."

Men shouted, "Well-come home, Duncan" and "Good to see you."

He stepped inside the door and tugged her hand, but Catherine balked. He turned to face her.

"Catherine, come."

She held her ground.

"Woman, what in the name of all the saints is wrong?"

Catherine whispered for his ears alone, "Are you not going to carry me inside?"

Duncan grinned, bent low in a gallant bow and swept her into his arms, carrying her into his house. "Aye, I wouldnae want you to trip and fall, bringing us ill fortune."

Setting her down, he wrapped his arm around her shoulders, drawing her close. "Everyone, well-come my lady wife, Catherine." He waved his arm to encompass everyone. "Catherine, these are members of Clan MacThomas. My family and friends."

Catherine swallowed deep and tried to greet

everyone with a smile. "How do you do?"

Her gaze darted everywhere, took in everything. Duncan's home was much smaller than she'd expected and had a masculine feel. Banners and swords were displayed on walls, unlike elegant tapestries gracing walls back home. Primitive weapons the likes of which she'd never seen covered grey stone walls.

Duncan took her hand. "Let me show you my home." He took her to the kitchen. "Cook, this is my lady wife."

The sullen woman glared.

Catherine smiled and looked around the room. Though small, everything seemed neat and in place.

Her new home had none of the amenities she'd been accustomed to. The first room they entered was large, had a raised dais with a long trestle table. Two massive chairs sat in the middle, benches flanked each side. Around the hall, long tables had been dismantled and leaned against whitewashed walls. Back in London, their tables and chairs were solid and gleamed with a high sheen, her father importing furniture from Europe's finest establishments.

Just as Duncan drew her toward another room, the house grew quiet. Duncan stiffened. Catherine turned to glance at him. He stared at the front door where a large man stood, his face encased in a spiteful smile. Catherine remembered seeing him, but couldn't remember where.

The man announced, "I see the lass I ordered you to wed dinnae turn out as bad as you thought. It took you long enough to return home. Clearly you enjoyed yourself with her."

# Chapter Six

MacThomaidh didn't hide the smirk on his face. "I didnae think you'd dally this long. Next time I order you to do something, mayhap you willnae argue." Not waiting for Duncan to answer, he turned and strode out into the bailey, the light of triumph glittering in his eyes.

Stunned by the belittling words, Catherine turned to Duncan. His face mottled with fury, he followed his father.

"Halt, auld man," Duncan shouted as his father mounted a chestnut brown mare. His father turned the horse, but Duncan reached out and grabbed the reins.

"Dunnae come here again and fash me or my people. As to that woman," he said, pointing back toward the hall, "you selected her, but you erred. You picked one with heart. 'Tis something you would know naught about, not having one yourself."

"And you learned this from the journey home?" MacThomaidh taunted. "Tangling with someone betwixt the sheets dunnae recommend them for sainthood."

"If you think so little of women, why choose this one?"

"I told you afore. We need her family's money. You need a wife. She is trained to run a large household, so she will do well at Castle Glenshee. Now that you wed, you must fetch her there rather than staying in this hovel."

"My home isnae a hovel."

"You saw where living in a wee home got you with Helen," MacThomaidh interrupted. "Dinnae drive another wife away. You need an heir. This woman comes from fine family. Her bloodlines are impeccable."

"I have an heir—Meghan."

"You need a son, and considering how often you probably bedded the lass, she may already be breeding. Dinnae do anything to make her leave. You dinnae want a repeat of Helen."

His father jerked the reins from his hands and twisted the horse around, causing its huge body to knock Duncan backward.

\* \* \*

Catherine stood alone in the center of the Hall while Duncan spoke with clansmen, particularly Angus MacCombe, his Captain of the Guard. The man's weathered, craggy features were creased with disapproval. Duncan hadn't looked pleased when he'd returned from the bailey. Pleased? Nay, he'd been furious. Had his father's words outside been as crude as what he'd said in the Hall? She'd recognized him the instant he spoke. His tone had been as condescending as it had been the night before her wedding.

She glanced around the Hall. Though small, it looked clean and neat, lovely in its simplicity—except for the floor. Catherine grimaced. Rather than the stone floors she'd been raised with, this had a covering of rushes. She'd seen them in some homes in London, but hadn't expected to find them where she'd live. She'd thought to live in a home like the Duke's castle, with intricately woven fabrics on the floor.

Duncan stormed toward her. She raised her chin to meet his frown. *This doesn't bode well.* She wanted to shake him out of his anger, wanted their homecoming pleasant. It was awkward enough without him being in a foul mood.

He grabbed her arm and wound his way up the narrow stone staircase, flinging a door open, causing it to crash against the wall. Seeing the sturdy four-poster bed, Catherine assumed this his bedchamber. Her belongings were already there.

"You must be tired after our journey," Duncan stated matter-of-factly. "I shall leave you to lie down."

Catherine frowned at his clipped voice.

How could she get him out of his dark mood? Looking around the room, her eyes landed on the bed. She knew one way to get his attention. Would he be shocked if she initiated their lovemaking? Might be just what the big oaf needed to dash away his dark mood.

Not stopping to deliberate, she reached to untie her brown mantle, laying it across the back of a chair.

"Nice bed," she teased, climbing up the three wooden steps and leaning over to push on it. She wiggled her bottom temptingly and turned her head to maintain eye contact just as he'd done the night they'd wed.

Sitting on the bed's edge, Catherine beckoned with her finger. He'd done that, too. She blushed, remembering the night vividly.

Duncan hardened in an instant, his father forgotten. His blood aflame, he approached her in two long strides. "You tempt me, wife?"

Her fingers shook, but she reached up to unfasten the brooch. Unwrapping the plaide, she dropped it to the floor. She slowly edged his shirt up over his chest, her soft fingers trailing along his warm skin, teasing the soft whorls of hair.

"Does this feel good?" Catherine teased, shifting her fingers to his back to run them lightly down his spine.

Duncan moaned, not expecting such behavior. He pushed her onto the bed, claimed her mouth with his own. He could stand it no longer. Rather than showering her with tenderness, he urged her mouth open with his tongue, mimicking what he intended to do with his manhood. His kiss was forceful, demanding. Catherine lifted her mouth to his, meeting his kiss with equal heat.

He reached to untie the laces at her shoulders, but had no patience. When laces refused to open, he yanked, tearing them from the fabric.

"Duncan!"

He groaned, his eyes searching hers for understanding. "Your come-hither eyes pushed me too far. I want you, wife — now."

Catherine removed his hands from her bottom and sat up. She drew him to the middle of the bed. Moving closer, she straddled his hips and stayed his arms with her hands. "Let me pleasure you this night." She wanted to take the pain from his eyes.

Leaning close, she nibbled his lower lip, feathered them with her own. A smile crossed her face when she stood and stepped back to look at him. "You look stunned, husband." She felt heady with power. If he hadn't already been lying on his back, she'd have brought her man to his knees. Oh my, when had she started to think of him as hers? Was she falling for her Highland rogue?

Taking a deep breath, she moved her hands lightly across his ribs, over his flat stomach, down to his...She stopped. Could she do this? Aye. Somehow she understood he needed her to erase some deep seated pain.

Duncan could stand it no longer. Didn't she know how she affected him? When her hand brazenly wrapped around him, he bucked uncontrollably. With a swift move he shifted position and had her beneath him, his mouth slanted on hers. All he cared about was bringing his young wife to a shattering release. His mouth devoured hers, his fingers roamed, touched every intimate place.

He heard her gasp of surprise when his tongue followed the trail of his fingers. He wanted her to need him as much as he needed her.

He said nothing, but caressed her. He wanted to memorize everything about her. Moving back up her body, he reclaimed her mouth, nipped her lips with his teeth.

Wild with abandon, Catherine offered herself completely. Duncan groaned in pleasure at her response. With her he'd found contentment. Why did happiness have to be so fleeting? Why did life have a way of twisting happy times into bad?

"Duncan…"

Calming himself, Duncan measured his pace, moving in and out slowly, bringing her to a pitch as fevered as his own. He wanted her to remember everything—as he would for the rest of his life.

He raised his lips to hers, claiming her mouth, his hands caressing her breasts. They were perfection. He lowered his head to lave first one, then the other.

Catherine screamed out her pleasure. With a few final thrusts, Duncan found his own. Sated, he cradled her in his arms.

He'd not thought about his father on the journey home and actually enjoyed this woman's company. He'd made the mistake of caring. How had he allowed that to happen? As his father so callously reminded him, she was chosen for him. And, Duncan acknowledged, the woman seemed perfect. Too perfect. Her flaws would reveal themselves soon enough.

The time he'd chosen a wife on his own blew up in his face. She left him for another man—men actually—turning quite the whore. She abandoned him just like his father had. Everyone left him. Would this woman leave, too? The little minx had just taken him to the heights of passion. Would she do that if she didn't have feelings? Men used sex to solve everything. Women didn't. They had to *care*. At least that's what he'd been told.

*Does she care for me as I have her?* His new wife scared him, having never loved a woman before. Lust and sex, aye. Love, never. And after Helen, he'd distanced himself emotionally. His father taught him never to trust anyone. Helen reinforced those feelings.

*But what if...I could make this work. We could bring Meghan home, ignore my father, and live happily.* Duncan smiled, his arms wrapped around Catherine's waist. All was right with his world.

* * *

Catherine stirred and stretched like a satisfied cat. Her body snuggled against his back. She trailed her fingers lightly over it, felt the muscles bunch beneath her fingertips, wondered at the scars. She'd noticed them on their wedding night, but had been too afraid to ask about them. She'd decided to wait, let him mention them. That hadn't happened.

Duncan turned his head to smile at her. He turned so he held her in his arms.

"I see my plan worked," she teased.

"Plan?"

"Aye, to make you forget your anger."

"MacThomaidh brings out the worst in me."

"He matters not. We shall ignore him." Catherine thought that would be easy. During their journey home, she'd learned there were secrets from Duncan's past that haunted him.

Determined she'd not let anything interfere with her newfound happiness, Catherine trailed her fingers down his chest—and lower. She felt immediate proof of renewed interest.

"You didn't know you released the wanton in me, did you, husband?" She teased, "Did you enjoy the temptress you turned me into?" Catherine felt him tense, but continued to tease, "Am I as good as any courtesan you had in the king's court?"

Duncan moved away and rose from the bed, began pacing restlessly. *Did you enjoy the temptress you turned me into?* Helen had said those very words.

*Damnation, have I done it again? Turned my wife into a temptress? Mayhap it was my fault Helen became a harlot. Mayhap I'm not meant to be happy.*

It mattered not, he thought as he bent to pick up his plaide. He'd been right from the beginning. He'd not stay with someone his father *forced* on him. His father and Helen left, betrayed him — and no one would ever hurt him like that again. He'd intended to leave right away, just as he planned before wedding her. Then she'd seduced him with her tantalizing body and made him forget leaving.

Was Catherine no better than Helen? Than his father? He'd been such a fool to think she would be different.

Catherine rose and stood in front of him, her long brown hair cascading gracefully over her breasts. The breasts he'd just worshipped with his hands and mouth. As he'd worshipped all of her.

She'd used her body to bend him to her ways, just as Helen tried to do. When it hadn't worked, she'd left. Just as this woman would.

Duncan vowed he'd leave first. No one would ever leave him again.

Foolish enough to think she cared, he'd been cruelly reminded that would never happen.

If wishes could come true, he'd wish to stay forever. But she'd come from a large, beautiful home. Did he actually believe she'd be happy here? Helen turned against him within a fortnight of arriving at Cray Hall. He'd seen the way Catherine looked around his home—the surprise on her face when she'd seen rushes on the floor. If he stayed, how long would it take before she returned to her fancy home? He wished... Nay, it mattered not. No sense dreaming about what he could never have.

Right now he needed to leave. Aye, he'd do that. After he held her one last time.

If things had been different, he would have... *I cannae think of what I cannae have*. Ah, but he'd remember her. He'd remember what they just shared for the rest of his life.

# Chapter Seven

Catherine ran her hand through the mass of dark brown hair on Duncan's chest. She thought him the most wonderful of husbands.

Duncan covered her hand with his, pressing it lightly to his chest. Feeling his heart beating, she felt a frisson of fear when he said, "I cannae stay, Catherine. Had we met under different conditions, something might have grown between us. However…"

"What mean you, 'however'?" She laughed, thinking it a jest.

"My clanspeople shall treat you well. If you need aught, let Angus MacCombe know. He shall provide whatever you desire."

Catherine stared in disbelief.

"You'll not be here?" she finally found the presence to ask.

"Nay."

"You are leaving?"

"Aye."

"We just arrived. Could you not stay a few days before departing?"

Duncan didn't answer.

"Have you pressing business?"

Still, Duncan didn't answer.

Catherine shivered when he dressed and walked toward the door. "How long will you be gone?"

"Forever," came his shocking reply.

"Forever?" Catherine's voice sounded a mere squeak before she lapsed into stunned silence.

Her question stopped his footsteps and he nodded.

She finally found her voice. "You do not plan to return?" Her eyes held her disbelief.

Duncan slowly shook his head.

"Is this some cruel jest? You plan to leave me with people I know not?" Her voice rose.

"'Tis nae jest."

Catherine narrowed her eyes at the lines of strain etched on his face. "You truly believe you need not explain your actions? You merely think to leave?"

He didn't answer.

"Why?"

Duncan sighed heavily. "I decided on this ere I left to wed you. 'Tis why I have things ready to take with me." He pointed to a small bundle beside the wardrobe. "I hadnae counted on…enjoying your presence and for awhile thought things might work. However…"

"'However' again. Suddenly I hate that word." Catherine's lips quivered as he shrugged. "You are leaving." This time she said it as fact rather than question. She finally believed him, just didn't understand why.

After an accusing silence, she cast him a glare. "I was a fool to believe—"

"You shall lack for naught."

"Are you so thick headed you think that my greatest

fear? I am not worried about *things*. I wish you to take me into your arms—never to let me go." She stopped. "But that shall not happen—shall it?"

"Nay."

Tears built in her eyes. "If you really…did not wish to wed with me, why did you go through with the ceremony?"

"I wasnae given a choice," Duncan grumbled. His body looked taut with anger after the reminder of their wedding day.

"Feel you no remorse about leaving? What about everything we shared?"

Duncan groaned as if in pain. "Och, woman, stop turning my emotions upside down."

"*Your* emotions? What about mine? Care you not what I feel?"

"I care too much," Duncan shouted, "but it matters not. I made it clear I dinnae wish to wed you."

Shocked into silence, Catherine felt like he'd slapped her.

She stared at him, trying to fight threatening tears, her voice husky with emotion. "How *silly* of me to forget."

"I dunnae wish to discuss this." Being upset, Duncan's brogue thickened.

Before he changed his mind, he headed to the door. "I must leave." Tilting his head, he glanced out the room's window slits. He still had hours before the sun set. This time of year it stayed light most of the night. Could he wait and leave on the morrow? Nay. If he didn't depart now, he'd never do so. He'd lose himself in her, in the illusion of her love.

At the door, Duncan turned back, surprised to see her large brown eyes clouded with tears of disappointment. He didn't want to think about the time they'd spent together. How could he leave if he remembered her in his arms, yielding her body to his touch? Shouting her ecstasy as he brought her to her woman's passion? Moaning his as his seed spurted into her body?

He shook his head, closed his mind against such thoughts. "The servants shall let you know when 'tis time to sup. I suggest you rest until then." After one last look, he took a fortifying breath. "I wish you well, Catherine."

"And I wish you well, too, my lord husband," she said proudly, her back straight and chin tilted. She stood before him naked, with no hint of shame. *So unlike our first night together.*

"I hope you have a safe journey until you return."

Duncan's mouth dropped. He tried to focus on her words rather than the lush curves of her body. "Dinnae you hear a word I said? I shallnae return."

"Aye, you will," Catherine asserted. "You may have planned to leave and for some silly reason still think you must, but we shared too much on our journey. We didn't just have sex together. You made love to me, Duncan MacThomas. *We* made love. There is a difference."

At that Duncan smiled. He couldn't help himself. "You are an expert on the subject?"

"Aye, I am. I had a good teacher." Duncan raised a brow in challenge. "All right, so I didn't know much when I first came to your bed."

Again, he cocked a brow.

"Very well. I knew naught." She strode to him and poked her finger against his chest. "But it changed."

Duncan couldn't stop himself. He knew he should walk out the door, but he couldn't. Blessed Saint Michael, but this woman delighted him. Why did she...? Why couldn't he...? It mattered not. He asked simply, "What changed?"

"You taught me the ways of love." Duncan watched her intently, evoking a blush. "Oh, I know you enjoyed it that first time, but our joinings were different near the end of our travels. You feel something for me. Deny it as you wish, but I know 'tis true. You shall never convince me otherwise."

Duncan shrugged in sangfroid.

"What about what we just shared? Are you telling me our lovemaking meant naught?"

This woman was too perceptive. Unable to stop himself, Duncan tugged her close and kissed her hard. He had to do something to prove her wrong. Had to prove it to himself. He backed her to the wall, pushed her against the door. His firm manhood pressed into her belly. Her eyes grew wide.

"A man is always ready to rut. It means naught." Pushing away from her, he moved her from the door. She looked hurt. He'd meant to be crude and clearly succeeded.

"I shallnae be back, Catherine."

Before he did more than devour her mouth again, he picked up his bundle and walked out the door, closing it firmly behind him.

Knowing she'd hate him, he slid the wooden bar and locked her inside. He heard her trying to open the door.

"Duncan MacThomas, don't you dare lock me in here." The door rattled. "Open this door."

Descending the stairs two at a time, he heard her shout, "You will be back. You hear me? You *will* be back."

\* \* \*

Duncan resisted the urge to race back to his chamber, to Catherine. *Dear God in Heaven, am I doing the right thing?* He hadn't known her when he planned to leave. Now he did — very well.

Mounting his black stallion in the courtyard, Duncan informed Angus, "I shall be in Crieff with Grant and Tory should you need me."

"Lad, you do shame leaving the lass here with strangers," Angus chided. "Give it time. Things will work out if you just —"

"I made up my mind, Angus. While at Drummond Castle I shall decide where I go next."

Catherine pulled at him. Made him want to stay, but pride raised its ugly head. He couldn't do so without his father thinking he'd bested him. Never would he allow his father to control his life again. His father abandoned him, sent him to foster with another clan and Duncan hadn't seen him again until he was grown and returned to Glen Shee. Did the man know he'd been abused? Would he care? Duncan vowed he'd never let The MacThomaidh know the mistreatment he'd experienced or have a say in his life again.

His first wife hadn't stayed. What made him hope

Catherine would be different? Just because he enjoyed bedding her more than any woman before didn't mean she'd stay. Once she realized how small his house was compared with the castle, this Sasunnach might leave faster than Helen had.

He'd not let her cuckold him. He'd leave before he fell further under her spell. Before he *loved* her more.

Mayhap he'd set her aside. Nay, he couldn't do that. He'd never do that.

He looked back at the door. Although he'd locked her in his room, he almost expected to see the stubborn woman in the doorway glaring at him. She wasn't there. Duncan clenched his teeth and a muscle in his cheek twitched. He turned to Angus and surprised himself by saying, "Meet me in Dunkeld a fortnight from now to report on how the lass fares."

Forcing himself to do the hardest thing of his life, Duncan spurred his horse away from his home—from the woman he wanted to spend the rest of his life with. Before riding through the front gate of his stronghold, he twisted on his steed and called out, "On second thought, meet me in a sennight."

He rode away before Angus could comment.

# Chapter Eight

Catherine knelt on the floor, tried to breathe deeply to stave off the horrible feeling. It didn't work. She threw up in the chamber pot.

*I haven't eaten much. Whatever upsets my stomach?*

The chamber door flung open and a maid entered.

"Lady Catherine!" Siobhán rushed forward and knelt. "Angus sent me to see to you. He worried when you dinnae break your fast. Is there aught I can do?"

Raising her head, Catherine shook it and moaned.

Siobhán rose and hurried to the basin to moisten a cloth. She knelt and wiped Catherine's sweat-drenched face.

Catherine clutched her belly, everything coming up again. She moaned, thinking, *there cannot be any food left in me.* Finally she sat back on her heels. "Something I ate must not have quite agreed with me."

"Wish you I should help you down the stairs to break your fast?" Siobhán queried.

Catherine groaned at the thought of food. "Nay, I could eat naught."

"Then return to bed," Siobhán insisted. "Rest. Get your strength back." She helped Catherine rise.

Feeling miserable, Catherine clutched her belly. Could things get any worse? After bringing her here,

Duncan left. No explanation, no excuses, just left. Bloody man! And now this. She'd been retching her insides all morning.

She tried to sleep, but couldn't. Thoughts swirled through her mind. She hadn't felt well since Duncan went away. After he'd left, she'd tried to run Duncan's abode, make him proud when he returned. He *would* be back. She allowed no doubts. Well, mayhap a *few*. Bloody hell, she had no idea what her *lord husband* planned!

Before the nooning she felt fine. Catherine stood before the wardrobe and selected a simple kirtle. Having no lady's maid, she'd paid close attention to her clothes, had worn none that fastened up the back.

She brushed and tied her hair with a ribbon to match her dark blue gown.

She headed downstairs and took her place at the table. The women were making tallow and ash candles and she hated missing that. She wanted to watch the entire process this time, although she wouldn't touch them like she had a sennight earlier and burned her hand. *I certainly do not remember Mother burning her hand after picking up freshly formed cakes of soap or newly made candles.* Catherine chuckled. *Mother may not have had such mishaps, but I've used enough violet leaf salve to heal my burns since arriving here. Thank goodness Rowena packed some for me before I left home.*

Cook brought out food for the head table. Eyes narrowed, she stared at Catherine. "Fare you better? Angus said you took ill."

"Much better. Thank you for asking." Catherine watched the woman walk away. What a difference in attitude. She remembered the first altercation she had with Cook when she approached her to plan meals.

"What might you be qualified to do? Cut vegetables?" Cook queried snidely.

"Nay," Catherine admitted, standing straighter. "I have never cut vegetables, but I am qualified to run this abode." She'd made an effort to keep her voice level. "I wish to start no argument, Cook, but you will not drive me away. Whether you like it or not, I am Cray Hall's mistress."

Cook stomped about the room, bumping into and clanking metal pots. She'd stormed to a table and angrily kneaded bread dough. She slapped it down onto the table then slammed her hand into it.

Catherine tried to hide her smile from the angry woman. She imagined Cook delighted in thinking the dough was Catherine's head.

Later that day servants changed rushes in the large Hall. Catherine suggested, "Mayhap we could sprinkle the new rushes with flower petals. Think you it might make them smell better when stepped on? Let me fetch some petals."

Angus had grown used to her saying *we* whenever anyone did a task, but this morn Catherine thought he seemed upset about it. He'd argued, "Lady, I willnae have you running up and down the stairs helping with chores. You were ill this morn and should rest."

"I feel fine now," she insisted, "and I believe Lord MacThomas would enjoy fresh worts in the rushes." In truth, she had no idea what he'd like.

Angus frowned. "Duncan will be angered when he

discovers how you work yourself."

"If you will not let me see to the rushes, then I have a boon to ask."

"What have you need of?"

"I know 'tis early in the year, but I would like to fetch flowers."

"Indeed," he said, quirking a brow, "I shall have someone look for some."

A brilliant smile transformed her face. "I wish to gather them myself. 'Tis such a lovely day."

"You need not ask permission to go outside."

Catherine smiled engagingly and headed toward the door.

She experienced the same illness the next morn. Laughing and crying at her misfortune, she clutched her belly, its contents emptied into the chamber pot. She turned to Siobhán for help rising. "I hope this is not a forecasting of things to come, to spend the rest of my days on my knees before a chamber pot."

Siobhán eyed her with compassion.

After sending her away, Catherine lay abed, alone and dejected. Duncan hadn't returned. Her husband abandoned her. Had she done aught to make him leave? Nay! Oh, she was English and some hated her for that, but such things no longer mattered. She wasn't the pampered *wench* these people thought her and the sooner everyone discovered that, the better.

As the wave of nausea hit, Catherine cared little about proving anything. She jumped out of bed and lurched to the chamber pot, thinking surely she was dying.

By the nooning she felt fine, though panicky. Something seriously afflicted her. Why else would she sicken each morn? She couldn't speak to Angus about this. He was but a man. Instead, she asked Siobhán, "Have you a healer?"

"Not one specific healer, m'lady. We have several women we see for different ailments." She gave instructions on how to find one in the nearby village. "Maddie is the one we use most. If she cannae help, she shall direct you to another."

Catherine walked to the village, taking advantage of the beautiful weather. She hated Duncan's men accompanied her through the lush countryside, but they refused to let her walk out the gates unattended.

She'd complained, "My absent husband cares naught what I do." He'd made that painfully clear. Her lower lip trembled. She'd grown used to Duncan comforting her when she was upset. He'd been tender and patient. A gentle caress with his fingertips, the tender brush of his lips…

Where had that thought come from? Aghast at her thoughts, it mattered not what he'd done before. Indeed, he was the cause of her upset.

Catherine easily found the small brown hut Siobhán described. She ducked her head to enter the darkened room, the smell of herbs overpowering. Seeing a woman in the far corner, she introduced herself. "Good day. I am Catherine Gillingham."

The old woman grunted. "I know you, Lady MacThomas." She emphasized MacThomas. "I am Maddie. How may I help our Lady?"

Suddenly afraid, Catherine couldn't stop her tears. "I fear I am dying." Her hand covered her mouth.

"Dying?" A look of surprise crossed the crone's face. She narrowed her eyes. "You are as healthy as one of Laird MacThomas' steeds."

Catherine inhaled sharply. Could this wizened old woman actually believe those words a compliment? Striving for composure, she sniffled and explained, "I sicken each morn. At first I thought I'd eaten something spoiled, but 'tis obviously more."

Maddie steadied her lady and offered a chair when she swayed. The healer asked several questions, but listened inattentively as if she already twigged the answers. Eventually Maddie rose from her wobbly wooden chair. She crossed to Catherine, helped her rise and escorted her to the door. She squeezed Catherine's hand and smiled encouragingly.

"Go home, Lady MacThomas. I can do naught to help you."

Catherine's eyes widened. "'Tis as I feared. I am dying then?" She felt hurt when Maddie's mouth twitched in a smile, clearly trying to keep from laughing.

"Nay, lady, as I sayeth, you are as healthy as a horse."

"But you said you could not help."

"I cannae help you *now*." The crone's wrinkled hands patted Catherine's. "In about seven moons I will be delighted to deliver a braw laddie or a bonnie lassie."

Catherine's mouth dropped. "I am...?" She could say no more.

The auld woman chortled, her eyes crinkling as she

smiled. "You breed with Laird Duncan's child."

"But how…?"

Maddie cackled. "Only one way for that to happen."

Catherine walked slowly back to the Hall, her emotions in a dither. One moment her heart swelled with the news and the next it plummeted to her belly as she considered the implications.

*A baby.*

Visions of a handsome face flashed through her mind. Why did Duncan leave? Couldn't he have stayed to work out whatever problem he thought they had? Surely between them they could have come up with a solution.

Angus met her coming in the Hall. She forced a smile. "I shall be upstairs. I had a pleasant walk, but wish to rest." She needed time to think.

\* \* \*

The next morn again found Catherine kneeling on the floor, leaning over the chamber pot. Siobhán went to the basin and returned with a wet cloth and pressed it to Catherine's forehead.

Catherine stared into her maid's green eyes. "I am with child, Siobhán. What am I to do?"

The maid reached out to embrace her hand. "What mean you, Lady Catherine? You shall birth a beautiful bairn. Laird Duncan shall be pleased."

Catherine rose. Pulling her garment tighter around her still flat belly, she walked to the small arrow slit and looked toward the majestic mountains. Upset at the turn of events, she saw naught.

"Lord Duncan has no intention of returning."

Catherine turned to face the young maid. "Please tell no one. I must decide what I shall do first." She paced the room.

Siobhán hesitated, bit the inside of her cheek, then mumbled, "Everyone already knows."

Catherine's head snapped around. "They know I carry Lord Duncan's child?"

Siobhán nodded.

"How? I said naught."

"We knew afore you went. 'Tis why you sicken each morn," Siobhán answered truthfully.

"Am I the only one—aside from my lord husband—who knew naught?" Catherine sank onto the large bed and absently traced the intricate ancient Celtic designs on the bedpost. Feeling self-conscious, she moved her hand into her lap. "How can I face everyone? I have no husband."

Catherine spoke as if the verity didn't bother her. Nothing could be farther from the truth. She wanted Duncan to return. She thought they'd formed a bond on the journey home. Showed how little she knew about men—or love.

"How can I face people with them knowing that? I want no one's pity."

Catherine's eyes brimmed with tears as they rose to meet Siobhán's.

"In spite of what others say, I believe Laird Duncan shall return. If he doesnae, shame on him and the loss is his—not yours."

Catherine realized a bond had been forged between her and the young woman offering encouragement.

With a weak smile and determination driven by desperation, Catherine walked out the bedchamber door and downstairs to formally announce Lord Duncan would soon be a father.

# Chapter Nine

Angus rubbed the back of his neck as Catherine gathered her blue mantle. A whirlwind of energy, this woman befuddled him. Though no one expected to like her, she'd not acted the spoiled Sasunnach, and wormed her way into their hearts.

He informed her, "I must leave Cray Hall. Torchil shall be in charge. Inform him if you need aught."

"I can care for myself, Angus, but I thank you for your concern." Her eyes lit with mischief. "Will you be gone long?"

"I am away to Dunkeld. Hardly long enough for you to miss my handsome face."

Catherine laughed, a beautiful, lilting sound. "Travel safe. I shall miss you. Carry tides to my lord husband. I look forward to his return."

She disappeared before he answered. However had she known?

\* \* \*

Duncan sat inside Dunkeld's inn and wondered why Angus hadn't arrived. After all, he needed to check on Cray Hall, be sure everyone had enough food. He needed to know they had enough peat to get them through the winter.

Peat? Winter? Och, why couldn't he just admit the

only thing he craved to know—how fared the wife he ridiculously stayed away from? Vexing, in the time they'd been together, she'd somehow become part of him, as important as his next breath. Could he live without such a vital part of himself?

Alone at the rear of the crowded inn, Duncan spotted Angus when he walked in, looking tired, worried. Watching his friend's painful movements, Duncan berated himself for suggesting meeting here.

Unwilling to share his thoughts, Duncan stood to greet him. "Angus, how fare all at Cray Hall?"

"We lost cattle to the neighboring Farquharson's, but it dinnae take long to recover them."

"Plus a few more?" Duncan chuckled.

"Och, aye." Angus nodded, merriment in his eye. "How fare Laird Grant and his Lady?"

"Still sparring."

He'd hoped to have such a home. A place where love and happiness abounded. He doubted that would happen. Would contentment forever elude him?

Angus sat, drinking ale. Frustrated, Duncan growled, "Enough! I wish to know about the woman."

"The woman?" Angus chuckled, his mouth full of food. "You mean the lass you brought home and abandoned."

"I didnae abandon her." Duncan sat up straighter, masking his response before Angus surely saw regret in his eyes.

"Aye, you did."

"I left her safe." Duncan's eyes flashed his annoyance.

"Aye, and she seems grateful." His tone forced Duncan to meet his eyes. "So grateful, she cried every day after you left."

"Cried?"

"Aye."

Weary, Duncan swiped a hand across his face. "I thought she might be pleased to be rid of me."

"Dinnae be daft. She is stubborn. Almost as unyielding as you."

"What mean you?"

"She insists on caring for herself. The only thing she allows is men to fetch water." Angus laughed. "She does like bathing."

Duncan said nothing. Memories of Catherine naked flooded his mind. He could still feel the softness of her wet skin, smell the gentle scent of her hair.

"She can do whatever she wishes. She is my wife."

"Och, you remember? How would you feel if someone dumped you amidst strangers?" Before Duncan responded, Angus pounded his point home. "Och, you *do* know how that feels. MacThomaidh did the same when he fostered you with Clan Kerr."

Embarrassment flooded Duncan's face. For a fleeting instant he couldn't breathe. Memories those words brought back were too painful.

"What I did is naught like that," Duncan said through gritted teeth. "MacThomaidh abandoned me because he wanted naught to do with me."

"What you did is different?"

"I left her with people I trust. MacThomaidh dinnae care where he took me. His only desire to be rid of me, he never checked to see if Laird Kerr hurt me. I probably wouldnae have lived out the year had Laird Drummond not arrived one day and taken me to Drummond Castle. They became my family." Duncan ran his hand over the back of his left shoulder to ease building tension, the phantom pain of scars lingering in his mind. Had Angus' cruel charge meant to evoke the dark memories? What he'd done in no way compared to his father's actions. Yet a frisson of doubt niggled at his mind.

"Your mam was proud of the man you turned into. On her deathbed she forgave your lord father for sending you away. Said his actions forged you into the finest man in all of Scotland."

Duncan silently cursed Angus' insight. It twisted his insides to hear his mam had been proud. He'd never known. "Mam may have forgiven MacThomaidh. I never shall."

"'Tis the only reason why you are not with your young wife. Because MacThomaidh chose her. You lie to yourself if you think to deny your feelings for the lass."

Duncan forced his fisted hands to relax. "After what happened with Helen, I swore never to wed again. She was no better than Father. She left, just like he did."

"Not all women are like Helen."

"Are they not?" Duncan grumbled.

"Och, you are stubborn. You are more like your da than you know."

"I am naught like MacThomaidh!"

"Mayhap if you returned and got to know the lass better."

"I did get to know her," Duncan said, shaking his

84

head as memories of their journey home burned into his memory and his heart.

Angus drove his point home like a pike into stone. "Aye and you liked what you saw."

There was nothing Duncan could say. Angus was right.

"You must admit naught," Angus said softly. "Your feelings were plain as heather on the hills."

Duncan rubbed his hand across his chest. It hadn't ached before Angus started yattering about the lass.

"It dunnae matter." He handed Angus a bag of coins and pushed his hands against the table to rise. "For whatever she desires. I had no other choice than to leave, Angus."

Angus stared long and hard while Duncan's emotions roiled with a disturbing combination of pain and loneliness.

"You always have a choice. Just as your da did," Angus said sadly. "He chose wrong. You chose wrong. 'Tis what you do that makes the difference."

"I am tired, old friend. Come share my room. We can break our fast afore we depart."

Angus yawned widely. "I am tired." He stood and stretched, threw coin on the table for the food.

Just as Duncan blew out the candle on the bedside table, Angus murmured, "Goodeve, lad. Sleep well. Och, afore I forget, you are going to be a da."

Duncan stared in amazement as Angus rolled onto his side and faced the far wall. He was going to be a father? His Catherine carried his child?

He shook Angus and thrust his face close to the

elderly man. "What mean you I am going to be a father? Dunnae be spouting such words and think to ignore me."

Angus rolled over and looked up at Duncan, a smile on his cagy face.

\* \* \*

There was no point denying it—he wanted to go home. Duncan paced the Great Hall in Crieff, but turned when he heard footsteps. He smiled at the interruption. "Tory."

Another pair of brown eyes flashed through his mind. Shaking his head, he realized Tory spoke to him. "I am sorry. I dinnae hear what you said."

Tory sat in the chair her husband made for her. "You woolgathered. About your wife? Plan you to go home to her where you belong?"

"Aye, but I worry about returning to the woman MacThomaidh shoved down my throat. What if she wants naught to do with me?" Turmoil roiled in him. Fear.

Grant entered the room. His childhood friend. Now a tall, imposing man with black hair and hazy grey eyes. He bent and kissed Tory.

Heartsick for what his friend had when he wanted the same, Duncan knew the only reason he didn't have it was stubborn pride. He sighed and crossed to fill a pewter cup with whisky.

"'Tis a wee early for that," Tory scolded.

Duncan breathed out frustration. "Your woman has nae pity for me, Grant."

"If you wish not to be chided as a bairn, cease acting like one." Tory smiled her taunt.

Grant stood beside his wife, one hand resting on her shoulder. "Leave the man be, Tory. He is returning to Cray Hall. He just needs a wee dram of courage."

"'Tis more than that." Duncan sat with a thud on a bench. "Angus said I am to be a father. I dunnae know what will happen when I return, but I must be there. I shall return to my wife and fetch my daughter home as well. Angus waits outside." His eyes met theirs, his own unsure. "What if Catherine dunnae want me?"

Grant and Tory clasped hands and smiled at each other. Duncan reminisced about Grant holding her prisoner and Tory trying to escape. Foolish. They'd learned their mistakes the hard way.

He'd made mistakes, too. Leaving Catherine had been the worst mistake of his life.

\* \* \*

Catherine fretted about the birth of her child. These clansmen were nice, but they weren't family. This wasn't her home. She missed Trevor. She needed his support, his shoulder to cry on. Needed someone strong to hold her and assure her everything would be fine.

She put a hand to her stomach. She had her babe and must be strong for its sake.

Downstairs, she saw Torchil. "I have decided to return to London."

He looked incredulous. "You cannae, My Lady."

"I did not ask, Torchil. Merely gave an order," Catherine said sadly. "Make preparations.

She crossed the Hall, rushes catching on the toe of the soft leather shoes she'd begun wearing shortly after her arrival. Her mother would be appalled at her lack of fashion. She'd adjusted well to simplicity of Highland life. Surprisingly, it suited her. Could she go back to a life that now seemed inconsequential?

Pacing nervously, Catherine walked to the garden doors, opened one and gazed outside, fighting for composure. "When I am gone, Lord Duncan can return. He should not have to stay away for something our fathers did. He—"

"Is a damnable fool for not returning," Torchil ranted.

Catherine smiled at the vehemence behind the man's words and the dark expression crossing his face. She gently touched his arm. "Thank you for being so kind."

"You dunnae like it here?"

"Please believe...I have come to love you all, love this Hall..." Tears clogged her throat.

"Stay and fight for what you want. 'Tis the Highland way. You are a Highlander's wife now," Torchil said.

Catherine closed her eyes. He made it sound so simple. "Fight for Duncan to love me?" Not meaning to reveal her innermost thoughts, her hand flew to her mouth.

Torchil locked eyes with her and nodded. "Only a fool couldnae love someone as bonnie as you."

"Thank you. I was raised to run a castle, see to my lord husband's happiness. Not to be a warrior." She sighed. "Were I not with child, I might consider staying forever—and Duncan could live elsewhere. 'Twould serve him right for leaving me." She laughed guiltily. "But I must make a life for myself and my babe, one where we are wanted."

"You are wanted here. The MacThomas child should be born here."

"Please do not make this harder for me." She raised a hand to stay his retort. "I am homesick, Torchil. Until I wed Lord MacThomas, I'd never been away from home more than a sennight."

Peering outside, she took in the surrounding area. "I always thought I would live in town, near my family. Although...I have never seen such majestic mountains." She glanced over her shoulder, discovered Torchil behind her. Lost in concentration, she hadn't heard his approach. She gazed back outside. "We have naught like them in London, you know."

"Because you dunnae have mountains," Alex grumbled from the doorway. "You have naught but wee hills." Catherine heard unwanted emotion in his voice.

"I did not realize you were here, too, Alex. I should like to leave on the morrow." Defeated, she battled tears. "Afore I change my mind."

"You cannae take Duncan's bairn. It must be raised here."

Exasperated, she told them, "I need my family, especial my brother." She looked at the land around Cray Hall. "I love it here, but my mind is made up."

Torchil shook his head, turned, and walked away, muttering with each step. "Angus left me in charge. Faugh! Laird Duncan may have my head." He swore as he strode out the door.

* * *

Men loaded Catherine's belongings onto a cart. Tears pooled in her eyes as she bade farewell. She didn't care if anyone considered hugging servants proper or not. Instantly her mother's voice sounded in her head. *Catherine Gillingham, what are you thinking? These are villeins.*

Villeins? *Nay, they are friends, family.* Her shoulders sagged as she bade Siobhán farewell. Following a strong urge, Catherine brushed a tendril of hair from the woman's cheek as Duncan had always done for her. She fought for composure at that memory. And lost.

*Why is this so difficult? Everyone has only been kind because Duncan insisted they must.* The moment she thought it, Catherine knew it for a lie. They'd befriended her of their own accord, had showered her with love. How could she leave? How could she stay? In London her brother could help. She twisted her hands in her skirt.

She wanted to leave—but wanted to stay. God help her, she didn't know what she wanted.

*I cannot wallow in self-pity.* She straightened her shoulders. *I must do what is best, shall never tell my child its father abandoned us.* Remembering how patient he'd been teaching her to swim, she imagined Duncan would have been a good father. Before she changed her mind, Catherine climbed into the litter and left for London.

# Chapter Ten

Early morning mist dissipated as Duncan rode his garron through the gate. He couldn't wait to see Catherine. Och, why had it taken him so long to come to his senses? This is where he belonged. How had he been fool enough to leave?

*She bears my babe.* The thought echoed through his mind for the hundredth time. Was her belly flat or could he tell his bairn grew in her body?

After Helen's betrayal, he'd never planned to wed again, never thought to have another child. *Now I can bring Meghan home as well.* Life was good.

Torchil rushed to meet him as he and Angus slipped from their horses.

"Praise the saints. You heard."

"Aye, 'tis the best news I've had in years." Duncan's grin split from ear to ear.

Around the busy courtyard, clansmen stood staring.

"Have I suddenly grown two heads—like a Viking troll?" He chuckled as he walked toward the house. "Is my lady wife inside?"

Torchil placed his hand on Duncan's arm.

Duncan stilled. He stepped away from Torchil and rushed toward the house. Something was amiss.

As his hand touched the door, Angus called,

"Duncan, lad. The lass isnae there. She's gone."

His face ashen, Duncan didn't move. His heart, that had only moments before been full of hope and love, now beat in pain.

Torchil reported, "Lady Catherine returned to London."

Duncan turned, placing his hand on the doorframe to steady himself. He swallowed before he spoke. "What... did...you...just...say?"

Torchil bit his lip, repeated his words, clearly one of the hardest things he'd ever done.

Duncan cursed and slammed his fist against the stone wall, scraping skin off his knuckles.

Torchil explained, "When you dinnae return, she said she needed to be with her family."

Duncan's voice filled with regret. "*We* are her family. *This* is her home."

"We know that, son," Angus consoled. "Clearly the lass was confused, scared. She—"

"Left me," Duncan completed for him. "Like everyone else."

"Not because she wanted to," Angus explained. "She liked it here."

"Not enough to stay," Duncan retorted.

Torchil tried to calm Duncan. "Lad, she was afeared."

"Of what?" Duncan pushed the door open with such force it slammed against the wall. "No one would dare hurt her."

"Of course not," Torchil sighed impatiently, "but you werenae here. She felt she needed a da for her child."

Duncan froze on his way inside the hall. "She thinks to find some other man? Did she say she meant to—?"

"Nay," Angus stormed, following Duncan. "She isnae like Helen."

"What plans she?"

"Live with her parents or near her brother," Torchil answered. "She claimed he would find her someplace near his home."

Duncan glared at that logic. "She took my child with her."

"We tried to convince her to stay, but she wouldnae listen. She is as stubborn as you," Torchil said.

Angus shot him an 'I told you so' look.

Duncan crossed the hall and grabbed a tankard of ale. Draining it, he slammed it on the table. "She is my wife and belongs here." He stormed out the front door.

"Where go you?" Angus queried.

"To fetch a mount," Duncan called over his shoulder, "and fetch my lady wife home." He saddled a fresh horse, not pausing to see if his clansmen followed. Jerking the cinch tight, he muttered, "Fire and damnation! I finally come to my senses and the daft woman loses hers."

\* \* \*

Upset over Catherine's leaving, the lines around his eyes revealed Duncan's volatility.

Pain flowed through him as he rode south. He'd pushed his men to ride to Crieff without stopping, hoping Grant would accompany them. Thinking with his heart rather than common sense, he'd wanted to shout his anger when he first heard Angus' words. Once again, someone left him. Was he right to follow her? Or should he let her go? He'd said he wanted naught to do with her, yet freely admitted she fascinated him. That was all he felt. Fascination. Certainly he didn't love her. He'd never let his guard down enough to love anyone, never trust anyone enough to gift them with that power.

Pouring rain increased his gloom. Why couldn't he forget her? Why did the taste and smell of her haunt his every breath?

"Curse her," he shouted to the wind. How dare she leave his home, the protection he offered? She was his wife. Pain lanced through him when realization struck. He'd done the same to her. Left her. Without a worthy reason. Choking back his emotions, he tried to understand why it mattered if she left. In a moment of honesty, Duncan realized he'd lost her the instant he walked out on her. "I was a fool—a damnable fool!" he muttered to himself, the rain drowning out his words.

* * *

They continued to the last place Duncan wanted to go—London. Where his marriage to Catherine had taken place. A marriage he wished he hadn't discounted so quickly. Aye, the wee lassie was his wife—and he wanted her back.

After arriving at Tamara's house in Melrose, his sister insisted, "Spend the night, Duncan. Your men grow weary and the animals need rest. You can set out at dayspring."

"Och, 'tisnae what I want, but your words are wise. Mayhap by morn the rain will cease. Traveling through mud has been difficult on the horses."

At dawn, a feeling of urgency snaked through him. He turned to his friends as they saddled their mounts. "Make haste. I sense something is wrong." An image of Catherine lying wounded on the ground filtered through his mind. Jumping on his horse, he spurred it to a fast pace. He'd not had such a feeling since the day his mother died.

Had his fool wife endangered herself? Duncan couldn't shake the overwhelming feeling of dread. The heavy weight felt like someone sitting on his chest.

Although Duncan thought it took too long, they finally arrived in London, the place he considered a detestable town. He wasted no time finding her family home.

Every instinct warned something terrible would happen.

\* \* \*

Catherine sat on her bed and sighed. She felt restless, but didn't understand why. Being home hadn't given her the peace she searched for and the very walls where she sought solace seemed to close in on her, a feeling that had always frightened her.

Her lady's maid watched closely. "What causes you to fret, m'lady?"

"Father. He has done naught but rail at me." Not understanding her feelings, Catherine shook her head. "Mother and Trevor query repeatedly about what went wrong. Father calls my return a disgrace."

Now she belonged nowhere.

*Nay, if honest, I would admit I left my heart in the Highlands. How could I fall in love with people and a place so fast? Was I destined to be there?*

With a pang of longing for what she'd left behind, Catherine decided on impulse, "Let us walk outside. Mayhap to the far gardens." She rose and walked to her wardrobe to fetch a mantle. Opening the door, she tucked a stray curl behind her ear before heading into the afternoon's warm breeze. Memories swept over her like a wave caressing the shore. *Duncan always tucked that curl behind my ear.*

Catherine thought her heart would break.

\* \* \*

"Still pretentious," Duncan grumbled, looking at the well-groomed grounds of Catherine's family home. Guards at the gate were hesitant to let him enter the compound, but once he reminded them Catherine was his wife, they grudgingly conceded.

He pounded loudly on the entry door and requested an audience with his wife. When the doorkeeper looked down his nose and announced, "Lady Gillingham is not at home," Duncan wanted to plant his fist in the man's pompous face.

"Lady MacThomas." *By the saints, why did I say that?*

He insisted he didn't want the woman for his wife, yet grew offended when the servant used her maiden name. Scots women kept theirs. Since taking the husband's surname was an English way, he should abhor it. But something in him wanted to brand Catherine in every manner possible. How could one woman so twist his emotions?

"I shallnae leave until I see her," Duncan told the staid doorkeep.

Hearing the commotion, Catherine's brother, Trevor Gillingham, emerged to greet them less than pleasantly. He turned to his manservant. "That is all, Markham. You may leave."

With a frown at the Highlanders, the elderly doorkeep bowed and left the foyer.

"I am surprised to see you, MacThomas," Trevor said, an edge to his voice. "My sister tells me you left. What could you possibly want here now?" Duncan saw the impervious glare in Gillingham's eyes.

"I shall tell that to my wife."

"Your wife?" Gillingham's eyebrow rose. "I did not think you remembered you had one."

Anger filled Duncan, but he stood unspeaking lest he say something he might regret.

"If you came to argue with her, I suggest you leave." Aggravation edged Duncan's brother-in-law's voice. "My sister is not here, MacThomas. I shall tell her you called."

Duncan strode into the parlor, sat in a delicate chair with determination. "I shall await." He stretched out his legs and propped his boots atop a highly glossed table. When he tilted the chair back so it rested on two spindly legs, he had to hide his smile when his brother by marriage watched, mouth agape.

Gillingham angrily announced, "She seemed upset, so she walks in the gardens."

"Alone?" Duncan rose, glaring at his brother-in-law. "Are all English so lackwit? She was upset and you let the daft woman go outside alone in this bloody town?"

"Not that it is any of your concern, but she is not alone. She is with her lady's maid. And she is not *in town*, she is on the Gillingham estate."

"As I said...lackwit. What protection can a maid offer?" Duncan fumed.

Trevor strode to the door and opened it. "My sister's assessment of you appears correct, MacThomas. You are an arrogant arse."

Duncan suppressed an overwhelming urge to plant his fist in the young man's almost too pretty face!

Gillingham shot a scathing glance at Duncan. "Follow me, my lord ruffian. I shall escort you to look for Catherine. Then she may inform you she wishes naught further to do with you." He motioned two of his men-at-arms to join him. "John, Geoffrey, accompany us." Glaring at Duncan's heavily armed men, Gillingham arched a brow. "They look prepared to fight."

Duncan turned to his men. They had on naught but what they always wore when traveling—swords, targes, sgian dubhs, and dirks. What did the Englishman think they should wear when traveling in hostile country?

"We know how to protect our women folk," Duncan grumbled as they walked briskly across the manicured grounds. He cast a baleful glare at Trevor. "The woman is beautiful. Know you not the trouble she can get into? Guards should be protecting her. Cares your father so little, proper escort isnae provided?" Duncan groaned. Had he just admitted he thought his wife beautiful?

Trevor shot him a bitter smile. "I know my sister's beauty well—inner and outer. Know how easily she is hurt. She walks on Father's grounds. No Englishman would dare harm her."

Duncan bit back a retort, instead complained, "Can

we not walk faster? I didnae come here to leisurely stroll. I wish to reach Catherine. I dunnae want her alone." The disconcerting feelings grew, despite Trevor's feeble attempts at assurance.

Trevor glared at Duncan. Once more Duncan wanted to punch the condescending look from his face.

"From what my sister told me, you should have no say in the matter. You left her with no intention of returning. You relinquished all rights to say what she does, where she goes. If you wish naught to do with her, leave her in peace. Lest you forget, my sister was the innocent in our fathers' deal."

"*She* was the innocent?" Embarrassment warmed Duncan's neck. "I dinnae want the wedding. I was forced to come to this bloody town."

"So you chose to embarrass *her*?" Trevor mocked. "Only a callow man uses a woman in such regard. I saw no sword pressed to your spine forcing you to the altar."

"Nae one calls me callow and lives. If you werenae my wife's brother, I would toss my gauntlet."

Duncan gritted his teeth. He'd come to fetch Catherine back to Scotland, not trade insults with her arrogant brother. Yet why insist she return? This would be the perfect excuse to end his marriage. The very one he repeatedly insisted he didn't want.

But he did want her. Had wanted her from the moment he turned to gaze at her in the chapel.

Duncan saw Grant watching him. His best friend would know his nerves were stretched as tight as the strings on a *clàrsach*, a harp.

Duncan wondered why he thought of the calming

instrument now. He could think of nothing peaceful about this bloody town. He thought it rough, dirty, and dangerous. *Nae place for my wife to be.* Trevor was right. She'd been an innocent and he should have stayed to protect her. She needed—a husband. The one thing he couldn't seem to give her. Could he? Was there some way to still make this marriage work—after everything he'd done wrong?

# Chapter Eleven

Duncan stared into his wife's astonished eyes. He almost forgot how much she affected his senses. What a lie. He'd forgotten nothing. Her beauty haunted him every night. Her soft gold kirtle billowed in the breeze. She looked lovely—and safe. His worry had been for naught.

"Be you lost, wife?" Duncan raised an eyebrow. "Surely you dunnae think this my home."

"I certainly do not," Catherine answered frostily. "'Tis *my* home."

"Och, you err, my lady wife." He tried to keep anger from his voice. "Once we wed, Cray Hall became your home. My people treated you well?"

"Indeed they did. 'Tis more than I can say about their master."

Duncan felt the blow as if she'd slapped him. Her words stung with unexpected impact. He wanted to be...he didn't know what he wanted. That was a lie, too. He wanted her to love him, to need him more than anything.

"Naetheless," he said stubbornly, "I come to fetch you home."

Catherine balked. "I shall return nowhere with you. Since you hate all things English, especial me, there is no reason for you to remain."

She stunned Duncan by turning and walking off.

Duncan glared at her back. "You belong to me," he growled.

She spun around, her voice remaining surprisingly steady. "I *belong* to no one, Duncan MacThomas. Least of all an absent husband."

Although he'd admired her spirit during the time they spent together, he now found himself irritated with such fortitude. His stubborn wife dared to direct it against him.

Duncan's jaw tightened, trying to contain his frustration. He never expected such strength from her and was unprepared to handle it.

Trevor moved between them. "Shall we retire home to discuss this? Give tempers a chance to cool?" He cast a prodding glare at Duncan.

"Aye, we shall return," Duncan agreed, loath to agree with the man on anything.

"I have not yet finished my walk. I shall follow later."

"You willnae remain here alone." Duncan took a determined step toward her only to have Trevor place a restraining hand to his chest. Glancing down at it, Duncan growled, "If you value your hand, Gillingham, remove it." The man didn't flinch. Duncan gave him credit for that, but toe-to-toe he stared right back.

Gillingham waited three breaths to remove his hand, his way of indicating he removed it because he so chose, not because of Duncan's threat. Reluctantly, Duncan found a wee dram of admiration for his wife's irritating brother.

"My lord father said my wife was fully trained in the way of being a proper lady wife. How did she wind up with such a flaw to gainsay her lord husband?"

The corner of Trevor's mouth jerked twice as he fought a smile. He glanced to his sister, but not before Duncan saw a flash of growing respect in the eyes so like his stubborn wife's.

"Our mother tried to correct that, but I fear she found it a losing battle. My sister is quite stubborn."

Catherine huffed. She glared at her brother before shifting her gaze to her husband. "Do not speak as if I'm not here. I am here and here is where I shall stay. Now leave so I can enjoy the garden's beauty."

Duncan moved forward and wagged a finger in her face. "Your mam may have failed, but I shall correct that failing in the future."

Catherine's cheeks burned bright, her chest rising and falling with her fury. "As you told my brother, if you value your finger, Lord MacThomas, remove it from my face, or I shall...shall...bite it off."

Trevor tossed his head back and laughed. "Though it pains me, Cat, MacThomas is right in this. You should come home."

Catherine smiled at Trevor. "I shall return shortly— *when I am ready*." Then she turned to Duncan. "I will not, however, return to Scotland with you. I shall never go anywhere with you again. Should you wish a drink before your journey north, feel free to have one. However, I shall not be upset if you have departed before I return. I never wish to see you again." Her voice held a note of finality. She spun on her heels and marched away.

Watching his young wife calmly defy him stunned Duncan to the core. Why, of all the women in the world had his father selected this willful woman to be his wife? More to the point, why did what she thought of him matter? Duncan felt the flush of irritation creep up his neck. Every muscle in his body hardened, ready for battle. Only he'd never warred with a woman before.

Ill-equipped for such a battle, he opened his mouth to shout at her, but snapped it shut, unsure how to proceed.

Gillingham laid a hand to Duncan's shoulder. "'Tis best to leave Cat alone given her present mood. She shall stew over this, but will come home directly. She cannot hold tight to anger long. Her heart is too kind."

Trevor's words didn't appease Duncan. He shot one last glance over his shoulder at his obstinate wife. She stood proud and tall. She'd turned, her eyes shooting daggers in his direction.

He didn't have a good feeling about this. He wanted to return and throw her over his shoulder. He'd left her before and shouldn't have. Dare he leave now? That niggling sense of unease coursed through him anew. With grave misgivings, he followed his brother by marriage.

\* \* \*

Catherine slumped onto a fallen tree. Cut for cord wood, the woodman must have left it to dry. She felt confused. Seeing her husband again brought back everything she felt after their wedding. Why hadn't he stayed away?

Then she could hate him.

Indignation rose to her cheeks. She swung her foot back and forth, catching her toe on a rock. She yelped. Angry she'd let her husband upset her, she bent and hurled the rock against a nearby tree.

Rowena jumped at the sound.

"Rowena, forgive me. I should not have taken my frustration out on that silly rock. We might as well return home. I am too upset to appreciate the garden's peacefulness."

\* \* \*

A burly man appeared from nowhere and stepped from behind the tall boxwood hedge, the entrance to the maze. Trying to get over her upset at seeing Duncan, she hadn't seen him round the thick bushes. While she didn't know each of her father's servants by name, she knew instinctively this man didn't belong at Brentwood. It took her several breaths to understand why, but then it registered—he wore a plaide.

Uncertainty rippled up Catherine's spine. She suddenly wished she'd not remained so stubborn and had gone with the men. She darted a glance to see if they lingered nearby. Catherine's brows furrowed, but she remained polite. Mayhap she overreacted to this stranger.

"If you seek my brother, he is just down the path. Shall I call him for you?" She pointed down a pathway. "Come, I shall show you."

The man's muscular body blocked her. A sinister look appeared in his eyes and his lip curled in a snarl.

"Another lying female. Your brother and husband returned to that fancy palace you live in."

Shocked by his unexpected behavior, Catherine backed up a step. "If you will excuse me, I tarried too long. I must return." She tried to remain aloof, but the man caged her between himself and the maze. Catherine hated the maze, wished Father would raze it. As a child she'd wandered into it and become lost in the labyrinth of corridors. Trev had fetched her, nearly at dark. He'd found her in a corner, huddled and crying. Since that day, she'd refused to set foot in the darkened boxwood lanes.

There was a feral quality to the man's eyes, beady like an animal intent on its prey. She turned to call out, but remembered she'd sent everyone away. They were probably already at the house and wouldn't hear her.

Turning to Rowena, she urged, "Fetch Duncan." It didn't dawn on her she'd instinctively wanted her husband's help instead of her brother's.

Without warning, the man grabbed her. "I cannae believe you are finally outside alone." He half dragged, half carried her deep into the maze beside the tree-lined footpath.

"Who are you? Let me go!" She fought, dragging her feet and trying to gain purchase on the grass path, but his size and strength exceeded hers.

He laughed as he grabbed her around the waist, her back against his side. He picked her up and continued toward the middle of the high boxwood hedges—turn after endless turn.

Panic seized Catherine. All the fear she'd felt as a

child entwined with the terror of this frightening man. She put up her best defense, hitting and scratching him, yet he dragged her deeper into the endless walls of shrubbery. He moved through the maze as if he knew where he was going. Fear spiked through her as she heard a horse snort on the other side of the maze.

Catherine fought with every ounce of strength she possessed, her arms and legs flailing. If his intent was to rape her, she wouldn't make it easy for him. Twisting, she reached up and scratched his face, drawing blood, her reward being his yelp of pain. She bit down on his arm, hard. Repulsed, her stomach wanted to heave, but she willed herself to fight the instinct.

Catherine vividly remembered Trevor's instruction on what to do if ever in a dangerous situation. But she couldn't kick him from this position. She clamped down harder, tasting blood. He cried out and released her. With a rounding blow he backhanded her, sending her to the ground in a heap. Her mind reeled as lights flashed before her eyes. She fought hard to keep from passing out, knowing all would be lost if she didn't hang on.

Surely Rowena would have raised the alarm by now. Duncan and Trevor would arrive soon. She must struggle until they did.

He grabbed her by the hair and yanked her to her knees. "Settle down. I dunnae want you dead." His words broke through her haze of pain. "I but use you as a means to get to MacThomas. 'Tis pleasureable to hurt someone who means so much to him."

Confusion flashed through her mind, her voice shaking with fear. "What mean you?"

"I plan to kill your husband." He said it as calmly as if stating he liked his cider hot.

She cried out and tried to loosen his hand from her long hair, feeling as if he were pulling it from its roots. Almost to her feet, she was slammed back to the ground, pain shooting through her body. She continued to fight, her fists slamming hard into the man's groin.

"You bloody witch." He doubled over in pain, clutching himself.

As she crawled into the boxwood hedge, trying to drag herself up, he lashed out with his booted foot and caught her in the stomach. Catherine's body screamed in a thousand red-hot agonies. Blackness sucked at her, but she knew she fought for her life, her babe's life.

"I waited a long time for this day." He delivered his words with spittle trickling down his mouth. "You made it easy for me, wandering around your property with only that silly twit of a lady's maid. Now your husband will pay."

"Have mercy!" Catherine begged. "I am with child."

The wild look in his eyes revealed it had been a mistake to say that. A new calm possessed him as he smiled. A smile that told Catherine to expect neither pity nor mercy. Once again he kicked out, slamming into her stomach.

She raised a hand to stop him, but her efforts were like a feather batting at a whipping post. She tried to curl into a ball, but her strength failed. *My baby!* She released a scream of fury, of pain, of terror, fearing she might never stop.

\* \* \*

Duncan heard screams before they reached the house. He turned, seeing the young woman who'd been with Catherine running toward them, her skirt bunched above her ankles, yelling frantically. He couldn't make out what she screamed. He looked for Catherine, saw her nowhere. Fear ran through him. He'd been right. Catherine was in trouble. She needed him.

Once she caught up with them, Rowena doubled over, breathless. Her light brown hair was disheveled from running and her green eyes were wild with fright, tears streaming down her face.

Impatient, Duncan wanted to shake her, but watched as Trevor caught and held her while he calmed her enough for her to tell them what was wrong. Trevor asked patiently, "Rowena, where is Cat? Why is she not with you?"

Trevor's eyes scanned the area, as Duncan's already had.

The young woman breathed heavily. She shifted her eyes between Trevor and himself. "Catherine...hurt. I ra...ran to fetch you so...help. Hurry."

Duncan's blood froze. Frantic, he was halfway down the pathway before the other men turned to follow. His speed increased when he approached the spot where he left Catherine. His eyes searched the garden, the paths all leading to the maze. He saw her nowhere.

Duncan shouted at his friends, "Scour the grounds."

He couldn't breathe. *Where is she*?

They needed to spread out or they wouldn't find her. Why would she have come this far?

The yawning mouth of the maze beckoned to him.

He stood as if staring into the pit of Hell. He had only one experience before with a maze. At Castle Kerr. When he was a small, sickly child. The laird had beaten him, carried him into the maze and left him. He'd whipped him, the lash slicing into his back over and over, shredding his soft shirt. When the blood dried, the material stuck to the wounds. He had little doubt they'd fester. He'd already been sick that day. The auld laird was angered because he'd knocked over a pitcher of wine. Through the pain and agony, he'd lost track of how many times the braided leather cut into his back. The auld man dumped him in the very center of the overgrown maze and laughed. "If you find your way out, you can live. If not, I shall fetch my dogs to find you on the morrow." Duncan knew he didn't mean to find him, but to kill him. The night was cold, even snowing. He'd wandered down avenue after avenue, finding dead ends and having to turn back. He'd finally dropped in exhaustion, knowing he'd last no more than a few hours.

Grant's father had found him. Near death. He'd carried him to Drummond Castle and taken him in as a brother for Grant. Laird Drummond saved his life.

The scream broke him from the grip of that ancient nightmare.

He hadn't been in a maze since. Sweat popped out on his forehead and Trevor grabbed his arm. "This way."

Duncan dragged his feet until the second long scream ripped through the air. He was a battle-honed warrior, but entering the maze was a nightmare. But he had to do it.

For Catherine.

\* \* \*

"Damnation," the attacker fumed when he heard the shouts of men combing the maze. Shouts told him most didn't know the way to the center as he did. He'd taken plenty of time to study Brentwood, learned all its secrets. He stumbled onto the trick of the maze. Keep your right hand on the shrubbery and never let go until you get to the middle. When you wanted to return to the house, take the first left and keep your hand on the boxwood. But he knew there was a hidden door at the far side, the way he planned to take the chit out. He hadn't counted on the bloody witch fighting him. His arm throbbed where she'd near sank her sharp teeth to the bone.

He aimed another vicious kick at her belly, but she moved, so she took the blow to the hipbone. "You and your husband elude capture this day, but I shall be back. Remember that, woman. I will be back. You'll never know when I shall return."

The shouts neared.

\* \* \*

Duncan was close to losing his mind. What the bloody hell was happening to his gentle wife? He could hear her, tried to follow the sound, but kept running into dead ends.

"This way," Trevor hissed.

Duncan whirled around. "But the sound is there." He slashed at the ancient boxwood, trying to get through the thick mass.

"You waste time. Stay with me. We will move away from the sound before we circle back. The sounds come from the center. Come."

Not waiting for Duncan, Trevor vanished around another turn.

"Hell and feathers," Duncan grumbled. He took the turn Gillingham had, but the man was gone. He glanced over his shoulder in the direction of Catherine's screams. Now silent, he feared they might be too late.

After two turns, he still hadn't spotted Catherine's brother. "Gillingham!"

"Over here."

The call was deceptive. Duncan tried to follow the voice, but it seemed to shift. The wind was picking up and carried the words away.

Grant came up behind him and patted his shoulder. Grant was the only one outside of Laird Drummond that knew the terror a maze held for Duncan. "Hold fast, my brother."

Another call came. Duncan looked at Grant. His friend listened and shrugged. Alex came up behind them. Duncan flicked his eyes toward Grant. "Alex, take that path. Grant, the one on the right. I shall take this one. Shout if you find my wife or her brother."

Alex moved off at Duncan's order. Grant squeezed Duncan's shoulder. "I stay with you." He didn't say it, but his grey eyes clearly showed he feared Duncan near to cracking from the combination of memories flooding back from his childhood and worry over what they'd find when they reached Catherine.

"My wife..." Duncan sobbed, breath coming hard to his lungs.

"You waste time. This way." Grant urged him along.

Catherine's body ached. Her head spun and she

feared she'd pass out from the sharp, stabbing pains. She'd never felt such horrible cramps before, couldn't move. Groaning in pain and terror, shooting pains ricocheted through her body, no longer localized in her stomach.

"Duncan..." she whispered. She gasped when she tried to move, pain so intense she collapsed into a sea of darkness.

"Here!" Gillingham cried.

"This way." Grant yanked on Duncan's sleeve as they moved around another end and faced yet one more dead end. "*Merde!*" Grant muttered.

Then they heard rustling. Trevor was on the other side of the tall hedge. "This way."

They tried to follow his voice, but faced a second dead end.

"Here, MacThomas!" Then they saw. The boxwood was sculpted so the shadows hid the final turn to the center of the maze. They could have walked past it a dozen times and never spotted it.

Duncan's heart dropped as he spotted her. "Catherine!" Dear God, was she dead?

She wasn't moving and her leg was bent at an odd angle. His eyes searched her carefully, but didn't see her chest moving. She wasn't breathing. Nay! Blessed God in Heaven, he'd lost her. Carrying his anger with his father too far, he'd driven away one of the most important people in his life — and now she was dead.

He dropped to his knees and tenderly cradled her head while his men surrounded him helplessly. They turned to look at each other, but could do nothing.

His wife's maid knelt on the ground sobbing.

# **Chapter Twelve**

Catherine's lashes fluttered when Duncan knelt beside her and placed his fingertips to the side of her neck and felt the light beating of her pulse. Until that instance, he was unsure if she'd drawn a breath. He bent and brushed his lips over her forehead and heard her soft moan. The fear of losing her had crippled him, made him forget his warrior training.

Panic flooded him at that realization, how she had the power to destroy his life. That couldn't happen. He couldn't let his guard down for an instant. But saying the words and seeing them to action were two different things.

Trevor knelt on Catherine's other side. "Cat? 'Tis Trev. Waken."

Refusing to release her hand, Duncan noticed even now that silly tendril flopped over her forehead. He wanted to touch it. Touch her forever. Make sure she was all right. Her eyeballs moved behind her lids. Finally, they opened.

"Catherine, can you hear me?"

When she turned her head, she grimaced with pain.

"'Tis all right, lass," he said softly, his mouth lightly caressing her ear. "You shall be fine. I shall see you safely home." Looking at Catherine's brother, he knew the worry in the man's eyes matched his. "Help lift her into my arms."

Even with their care, every movement jarred her body and she screamed. Her eyes glazed over as she looked up at him. He feared every step would feel like a sword thrusting through her body.

Trevor kept pace beside him, gripping Catherine's hand.

Duncan shifted her in his arms. Her head rolled slightly as a cry lodged in her throat before she fell limp.

Duncan and Trevor's eyes locked. In unspoken agreement, they speeded up their pace.

\* \* \*

Shoving past hovering servants, Duncan charged into the house and up to the room Trevor indicated. In three strides Duncan was beside the postered bed. He laid Catherine on the embroidered coverlet. Still she didn't waken.

He sat, speaking to her, though he barely heard his words. His eyes took in everything. Catherine's long, wavy hair spread over the pillow. Her face, pale from the pain, looked as white as the bed pillows. The stark contrast of her dark auburn hair against her alabaster skin frightened him. He'd never seen a woman this pale before. Nay, that wasn't true. His mother looked like that the day his father took him away from Castle Glenshee.

Her face and body were battered and her lips were cracked and swollen. Blood oozed from the corner of her mouth.

Catherine's mother rushed in, the keys at her waist jingling as she wrung her hands in the skirt of her dark brown kirtle. Lady Gillingham shot a look of pure hatred. "Out of my way." Her eyes turned to blood staining the pale yellow kirtle. "Blessed God, my daughter may lose her babe."

*Nay*! His mind screamed. Terror raced through Duncan's veins. "I shallnae leave her."

He stared at Catherine's battered face, bruises already discoloring it and her arms before his eyes. He remembered the horror of seeing her lying on the ground. Blessed God in Heaven, what had that monster done?

Duncan barely took note of a female servant who bobbed as she entered the room, showing in an elderly man. A physician, Duncan assumed. The man motioned toward the hearth. "Kindle a fire. Gather clean rags to catch the bleeding. Cover the young woman from the waist down. Lady Gillingham and Rowena may stay. The rest of you leave."

Duncan didn't move.

The man pointedly cleared his throat, extended his hand to Duncan. "I am Thibideau Martin, the Gillingham family physician."

Duncan rose and shook the man's hand.

"You are the young lady's husband?"

"I am, and I have nae intention of leaving." Duncan's eyes didn't leave the man's wrinkled face. "She is with child."

"I feared such." His gaze went to Catherine, but he directed his words to Duncan. "Rather you a midwife be fetched?"

"We dunnae have time to wait for someone else to

arrive." Duncan choked out the words.

Sitting on bedside, the man drew a cone shaped implement from his bag. Lifting the blanket and her skirts, he placed it on Catherine's stomach and bent his ear to listen. His face revealed nothing. He reached under the blanket and pressed his hand on Catherine's belly, causing her to moan in pain.

Duncan squeezed Catherine's hand tighter. He knew the physician had to touch her, but he didn't have to like it.

Completing his examination, the physician stood and once again listened to Catherine's belly. Suddenly she screamed, her body arching off the bed. The doctor straightened, appearing uncomfortable. His eyes swept from Lady Gillingham to Duncan. "There is naught I can do to save the child. Whoever beat her did too much damage. Her body tries to expel it. The pains will continue until she delivers."

Duncan closed his eyes. What sort of animal would attack his innocent wife? The real question he couldn't wrap his mind around, however, was *why* someone would do so. She'd never hurt anyone. He rubbed his forehead with his sleeve. Since the servant lit the fire, the room felt stifling.

Catherine shifted in bed. She cried out as pains assaulted her body and her brow beaded with sweat. Duncan reached for a cloth, wetted and gently pressed it to her brow.

The night seemed to go on forever, the room darkening with long shadows. The fire was rebuilt, and rebuilt again. The physician firmly pushed on

Catherine's belly one last time. "'Tis over."

Duncan's eyes widened in horror at the blood. Merciful Saint Columba, did his wife bleed to death?

He saw the man furtively wrap something in a cloth and turn to hand it to the servant.

"My bairn, what was it?"

"Do not torture yourself."

Duncan reached out his hand to stay the man's arm. Gently he folded back the cloth and looked down at the too tiny face of his daughter. He refused to break down in front of strangers. *How could this happen? How will I break the news to Catherine?*

Catherine's mother sat in the far corner of the room, sobbing hysterically. Rowena opened the chamber door, letting in a faint ray of light. Trevor and Elizabeth rushed in.

The young girl hurried to her sister.

"Cat?" Elizabeth looked to her brother, then leaned down to touch her forehead to Catherine's. "Trevor said someone hurt you." Tears ran down her cheeks.

Duncan hadn't paid much attention to the young girl before, but he saw the resemblance. Elizabeth was a younger version of Catherine. Some day she'd be a beauty. Only now her face was blotchy and eyes were red from crying. He'd heard her wailing in the hallway. Trevor probably held her as closely as Duncan held Catherine when he carried her home.

Although Duncan thought the man irksome, he grudgingly admitted Gillingham loved his sisters.

The physician finished packing his small bag, then ran a hand through his already mussed hair. He approached Duncan and cleared his throat. "I am sorry, MacThomas. I wish I could have done more."

Duncan wished he'd done more as well. He'd failed Catherine yet again.

\* \* \*

Catherine's body screamed with pain when she moved. Her mother approached when she moaned. Catherine turned and saw Duncan sleeping soundly in a chair beside the bed.

"Mother," Catherine slurred. Her mouth felt as dry as if a cloth was stuffed in it. "Water."

Her mother filled a pewter cup and held it to Catherine's lips. After taking a few sips, Catherine had voice enough to query, "Why is Duncan here?"

Her mother glared at the man in question. "You have slept for two days. He refused to leave, no matter how often I insisted he do so. He is more obstinate than your father."

"But why—?"

Lady Gillingham handed her the cup. "Do not ask so many questions. Drink this and rest. You took a horrible beating."

Images coursed through Catherine. Eyes wide with fright, she looked up. "Why did that man beat me?" Tears pooled in her eyes. "I could not get away."

At the sound of her sobs, Duncan stirred.

In one fluid movement he rose and reached for her hand. Confused, Catherine jerked it away. Why was he being kind? She remembered their argument. Why was he still here? She raised her hand to her head, the movement causing pain to shoot through her, her stomach cramping.

Her hands flew to cradle her stomach. "The baby. Something is wrong."

Her mother glanced at Duncan. She bent to kiss the top of Catherine's head and patted her hand. Lady Gillingham whispered in her daughter's ear, "I love you, Dearling." She backed out the chamber door, tears glistening in her eyes.

Catherine watched her mother leave, knowing unpleasantness had always been something her mother avoided. With every fiber of her being, she sensed now was one such time.

Cramps tore through her again. Duncan's eyes were filled with empathy. Catherine's met his. "My baby?" Her hand instinctively fell once again to her belly, an unspoken plea in her eyes.

He sat on the bed, wrapped her in his arms and gently drew her closer. "The bairn is gone, lass."

"Nay!" Catherine choked on her torment. She didn't want to believe, but knew he bespoke the truth. She tried to push away, but he held tight and cradled her in his arms as cries of torment washed over her.

"You lie," she sobbed pitifully. "You want to hurt me again."

Duncan said nothing.

"P...please tell me 'tis not true," she pleaded.

The pain in Duncan's eyes was her answer.

She leaned against his chest and sobbed. He held her and rocked her as if a child, murmuring soft words of encouragement in Gaelic.

It was a long time before Catherine stopped crying.

The anguish more than she could bear, her grief plummeted into despair.

\* \* \*

For days Catherine didn't speak. Her eyes vacant, she refused to eat, but accepted fluids when they held the cup to her lips.

Her family coddled her, but nothing snapped Catherine out of her desolation. Even her brother's presence evoked no response.

Duncan grew desperate.

One morn Elizabeth exited Catherine's room, tears streaming down her face. She ran into Trevor's arms. "Cat will not speak with me, Trev. Is she dying?"

Duncan felt as if someone twisted a dirk in his heart. He stood aside and listened as Trevor consoled his young sister.

"Shh, Beth. Our Cat shall be just fine."

Duncan wished he believed Gillingham's words.

\* \* \*

His unease growing, Duncan reached the end of his patience. He told her family, "I am taking Catherine home."

Ready to break his fast in his Hall, Catherine's father laughed in condescension. "You abandoned her in your home."

"And you gave up the right to comment when you *sold* her to me for promises of wealth from your bloody king. I hope it was worth it. You should have protected her — regardless of financial gain."

Gillingham flung his goblet against the table. "How dare you speak to me thusly? I should throw you out. I no longer blame Catherine for feeling as she does."

"I blame *you*," Duncan hissed. "I intend to care for her far better than you did." He turned on his heel and left the drawing room.

Gillingham yelled, "Get out of my house."

"Happily." Duncan passed Lady Gillingham as he left the room. "Prepare your daughter, madame. I take her home." He headed to the stables and told his men, "'Tis time we take Catherine home. In Catherine's present condition, it shall take me awhile to fetch her back to Scotland. She suffered enough and I must take this journey slowly."

"We leave?" Angus queried, his eyes widening in surprise.

Duncan nodded. "Aye, shortly."

Alasdair's brows furrowed. "Is Lady Catherine strong enough to travel?"

"I believe so," Duncan said, raising a shoulder.

Turning to look at Catherine's family home, Grant nodded. "If you dunnae have needs of us, we shall depart. Tory probably paces the floor and wears a path in the rushes by now."

Before he left, Duncan carried Catherine downstairs and headed outside to the gardens. Veering left, he walked to the tiny plot of freshly dug earth.

"This is where our wee daughter Kaitlyn rests, lass," he told her, trying to keep his voice steady. "I saw her, you know. The physician showed her to me after…after…" He had to clear his throat to keep from breaking down. He couldn't do that. He must be strong for Catherine. "She was so tiny. Like a butterfly that flew to Heaven. Your mam suggested placing her near this beautiful fir tree rather than in the family vault beneath the house. The branches shall always provide shade for her. Is it not lovely?"

She said nothing, but tears rolled down her cheeks unchecked.

Duncan blamed himself. If only he'd insisted she leave the garden and return to the house. He should have carried her kicking and screaming over his shoulder. He'd felt a shard of fear when he left her, had paid no heed to that inner voice—God's warning.

In hindsight, Duncan knew he should have done a lot of things differently. "I gave her a name. God needed to know what to call her in Heaven." Duncan knew he rambled, but if he stopped talking he'd ball like a babe. He never thought anything could hurt this much.

Finally, he stood and lifted Catherine effortlessly into his arms. He headed for the litter. Her family waited—except her father. "Goodbye, Dearling," her mother told Catherine, wiping tears from her eyes.

Duncan placed Catherine on her feet and encircled her with his arms.

Trevor spoke to Catherine, but kept his eyes on Duncan. "Fare-well, Cat. If you need me, get in touch with me. Just like I said when we talked at your wedding."

Elizabeth could barely speak. She was crying too hard. She walked to Catherine and placed her arms around her waist. "Oh, Cat. I do love you. Please get well and come back and visit."

Duncan helped Catherine into the litter and tucked a

blanket around her legs for warmth. London always seemed damp to him.

It was time to go home.

He insisted they spend days enroute at various inns and halls, not wanting to discomfort Catherine. The farther they got from town, the harder it was to find places to stay.

Catherine stared vacantly into space and slumped against the side of the litter, saying naught.

\* \* \*

Weighed down with feelings of guilt, Duncan worried over how pale and shaken Catherine appeared. He watched her carefully for signs of pain. Her red-rimmed eyes revealed she succumbed to tears whenever he left their sparsely furnished, rented rooms. Neither had she regained the fire nor spirit he so liked.

How could he have been so insensitive to leave this beautiful woman alone? Duncan berated himself for neglecting her. While in London he'd taken a long, hard look at himself and seen things he didn't like.

Catherine's brother had been right. There'd been no excuse for his actions. Duncan vowed to spend the rest of his life making it up to her—if she let him.

Upon leaving London, he'd begun using the name her family called her. "'Tis time to break our fast, Cat," he cajoled, placing his hand beneath her chin and tilting her face up to meet his. "Will you not join me?"

Duncan thought it a miracle when her eyes rose to his and didn't waver. She seemed agitated and distraught, but took his hand when he extended it. She stood and followed him unsteadily to the door, her body weak from hunger.

Duncan wrapped his arm around her waist and escorted her downstairs to an empty table in the large open room.

They were soon joined by Angus, who smiled at the sight of Catherine.

Angus informed them, "Alasdair and Ian went outside to prepare the horses and litter."

Catherine reached across the table to pick up a wooden bowl and spoon the goodwife delivered. Her hands shook as she raised the spoon to her lips. Having nothing but fluids the past days, she was weak. Duncan took the spoon. After tasting the warm, creamy porridge himself, he smiled and offered some to Catherine. "'Tis good. Eat more."

She took the spoon from him and raised it to her mouth, but was so frail she dropped it. Frowning at Duncan when he picked it up and held it for her, she grudgingly ate a few spoonfuls.

Hope soared within him. He would care for her the rest of his life if that's what it took to fetch his beautiful, spirited wife back. He glanced at Angus and saw relief on the old man's weathered face and knew the look mirrored his own.

Surely Catherine just needed time.

# Chapter Thirteen

By the time she'd been home several days, solitude became Catherine's greatest wish. She realized soon enough it wouldn't be granted.

Why didn't Duncan leave? She thought he'd depart as soon as they arrived in Scotland. Hadn't he made it painfully clear he wanted nothing to do with her?

Now he expected to sleep in the same bed. He got into bed and wrapped his arms around her, just as he'd done on the journey home. As days passed, Catherine tried to ignore him, but his arms felt so good, so safe.

Then the bloody man's attentions increased. He leaned over the bedside table and blew out the single candle. Catherine felt the bed dip as he slid his big body beside hers. He moved close and wrapped his arms around her, planting her firmly against his side.

She tensed, but Duncan refused to release his hold. Instead, his lips brushed the back of her neck. They felt as light as a butterfly's wings.

Catherine turned to him, emotions she'd held in check exploding. She pummeled his chest with her hands. Tears choked her and filled her eyes, a low guttural moan escaping her lips. "As soon as you have your way with me you shall leave. Get out of this bed," she sobbed. "I want you nowhere near me."

His body tensed. She saw his look of shock. Anger soared within her to where she didn't care. The bloody man married her and left her. "Save us both the trouble and leave."

It was the first time she'd spoken since she lost the babe. The babe she wanted with all her heart.

His face remained impassive, but he held her with an iron grip. "I'm going nowhere, Catherine."

"You lie."

"I mean it, *Mo Chridhe*," he soothed.

Stray wisps of hair layered on her cheek. He brushed them aside, his touch gentle and undemanding. "I shouldnae have left. 'Tis difficult for a man to admit his error. I hope you can forgive me."

"Never," she cried, her voice ragged. Her lower lip quivered and tears pooled in her eyes. "And do not call me, Sweetheart. You'll not stay. You made it painfully clear you want naught to do with me."

Struggling in his embrace, Catherine turned her face away, hoping to hide her tears. She'd never let him know how much he'd hurt her. A part of her still needing his closeness, she buried her head in his chest and mumbled, "I do not want you either."

\* \* \*

Duncan rose early, having slept little. She didn't want him. He wouldn't accept that. *Couldn't accept that.*

He told Siobhán. "Help my lady wife dress. She shall join us below stairs."

He nearly held his breath waiting for Catherine. All eyes upon her, she forced a smile to her lips. In that instant Duncan knew she'd be fine.

She spent the day inspecting the Hall, then time with Cook planning upcoming meals. After the nooning dinner she headed to the garden. Duncan stood in the doorway and watched her lower herself to the ground. Smoothing her light green overtunic over her legs, she leaned against the fir tree. Its branches formed a wispy canopy and shaded her from the sun. She'd lost weight, looked tired, drawn.

He watched until her breathing evened out. She'd fallen asleep, appeared at peace. Would that he could bring that serenity to her.

After supper, the family bard regaled them. He'd come from Castle Glenshee after hearing of Catherine's condition. He wove tales of a handsome Scottish laird and his exquisite English bride. Duncan was pleased she smiled, usually when the bard made some outlandish claim about her. The eve drew late and Duncan rose from his chair, taking Catherine by the hand. He led her to their bedchamber, closed the door and drew her into his arms.

She turned away. "I want naught to do with you. Go find another woman."

Duncan persisted. "I want nae other. We are home now, Catherine."

"This is your home," she replied stiffly. "Not mine."

Duncan smiled. Och, she was obstinate. He turned her around and reached to loosen the front of her gown, but she jerked away. Not wanting to upset her, Duncan released her. He walked to his wardrobe, placing his plaide on the shelf. She needed more time—and he had the rest of his life to give her as much as she needed.

He turned and caught sight of her body in the chemise, rendered near transparent by the candle's light. The perfection of her curves made his body buck in need. He sighed deeply. As much time as she needed...even if it saw him a madman in the process.

Days passed and still Catherine's grieving didn't ebb. Duncan felt helpless, no idea how to help. He stayed close in case she needed him, leaving only to make the short trip to Castle Glenshee.

A sennight later Duncan received a summons from his father. He reread the missive and wondered why MacThomaidh requested Catherine's presence.

She demurred, but Duncan insisted.

As they journeyed toward the castle, Duncan knew it was past time to broach the probable reason for her requested presence. He cleared his throat. "Catherine, there are some things I havenae told you. When The MacThomaidh ordered me to wed you, 'twasnae the first time he ordered me to marry. To ward off his wishes then, I married another."

Catherine's eyes widened in surprise.

"You were wed?"

Duncan nodded. This would be an uncomfortable discussion. "Aye. Once she realized I had nae intention of living at the castle, she grew distant. She wanted the castle's luxury, not my home." Duncan shifted in his seat.

"Did you leave her, too?"

Had he loved his first wife? At least he'd wanted to marry the other woman. That knowledge hurt more than it should. After all, she cared nothing for him.

"Nay, she left me." Duncan cleared his throat,

looking uncomfortable. "After she bore our bairn."

*A child*? Pain slashed through her. Her hand flew to her stomach. He had a child, while hers lay buried in a cold, distant hill in London. Why hadn't he told her this before? She turned away, anger anew racing through her. He not only had a wife before, he had a child. Did it live at the castle? Did he expect to fetch the child home with them? She clenched her teeth and looked out the litter. She wanted nothing to do with another woman's child.

Her anger evaporated, Catherine slumped against the curtains. How could she think something so cruel? It wasn't the child's fault. Shame washed over her, pulling her deeper into depression.

She shook herself from her reverie, unable to stop a single tear, when he continued, "As soon as she delivered my beautiful daughter, she left. Wanted naught to do with either of us."

"Where is she now?"

"She died a year after she left, birthing another man's child."

"And your daughter?"

"I fought in many wars, most recently for Scotland's freedom. MacThomaidh took her to the castle. He thought his granddaughter should be raised there rather than by servants of an absent father." His jaw tightened at the memory.

He visited her as often as possible, just refused to do so when his father was home.

Duncan saw emotions warring on Catherine's expressive face. "What are you thinking?"

She turned. Curse it, her eyes held the same vacant

look she had after they lost their bairn.

Catherine remained silent for a long time before she blurted, "The same thing should have happened to me."

"Same thing...?" Duncan frowned. "I dunnae know what you mean."

"Like your wife. I should have died instead of our babe." She stared at him, but he doubted she saw him. Her eyes were sad and empty and she seemed lost in thought. Duncan thought he'd heard her wrong and was about to ask her to repeat her words when she whispered, "I wanted to, you know. For weeks after I lost her I wanted to die. It was my fault—"

"Nay," Duncan protested, aghast at her words. He reached across the vehicle to shake her. "Merciful saints, woman, your thoughts twist inwardly, fester your mind."

"I wanted to stay with my babe, but you took me away. Took me from the only thing I had left."

Stunned, Duncan moved to sit beside her and placed his arm around her.

"Our bairn is dead, lass."

She raised her eyes to look at him, tears streaming down her cheeks. "But I wanted her. I needed her. She was the only thing I had from our marriage. I wanted—"

"I wanted her, too, Sweetling. From the moment Angus told me, I wanted her."

"You did *not*. You didn't want her, didn't want me. She was all I had and I lost her."

Duncan caressed her cheek with his hand. "*We* lost her. We share the loss."

She stared, unspeaking.

131

"Dunnae ever think such a thing again. Life is the most precious thing we have."

She stammered, "But you'd not be saddled with me if—"

Upset, Duncan interrupted her. "I am *not* saddled with you, Catherine *MacThomas*. You are here because I wish you to be."

Tenderly he tipped her face to meet his. He cupped her cheeks between his hands, staring into her eyes. "How can I make you believe?" Och, he'd been a fool to leave. Could he ever undo the pain he'd caused?

Though he tried to gentle his voice, he ordered, "I mean it Catherine. Dunnae ever think such a thing again. Do you hear me?"

"It was my fault. I should not have stayed with Rowena. I should have gone to the house with you. I lost our babe—"

"We both should have done things differently," he said, sadness in his voice. "You think the demons of Hell dunnae torment me with *what ifs*?"

Catherine turned away.

Duncan refused to let the issue drop. His hands gripped her upper arms, turned her around to face him. He pleaded. "It wasnae your fault." His right hand caressed her cheek, his eyes holding hers until she nodded. He brushed away a tear from her cheek with the pad of his thumb. Her lips trembling, she looked like a bairn lost in the woods. He wrapped his arms around her, wanting never to let go.

\* \* \*

At the castle, The MacThomaidh met them in its

massive bailey. A tall, elderly man, he moved slowly, almost painfully.

He extended his gnarled hand toward the entry door. "Enter."

As Duncan guided her into the Great Hall, his arm encircling Catherine's waist, he noted MacThomaidh's eyes narrowed, scrutinizing his wife.

Duncan seated Cat in the most comfortable chair in the Great Hall, misgivings rising at his father's watchful gaze. He stood behind Catherine's chair, his hand caressing her shoulder.

"Why did you fetch this woman with you?" MacThomaidh growled.

Catherine blinked shock. Nervously she glanced up at Duncan.

"My lady wife goes where I do." This was hardly what he'd expected when he received the summons.

The auld man snorted in disgust. "I bid her here afore I learned of her flaws. She cannae even carry a wee bairn, they say."

Catherine inhaled sharply, a soft moan escaping her throat. She rose from the chair and swayed. Fearing she'd swoon, Duncan placed a protective arm around her. "Shut your gub, auld man."

MacThomaidh glowered. "You should have known I'd hear she lost my grandchild. If she had stayed where a wife belongs, the child would have been safely born at Cray Hall."

Duncan felt Catherine's body shake convulsively over his father's bitter words. "I am leaving," she told him.

Duncan's eyes narrowed, the battle-honed warrior surfacing. Holding his bride close, he informed his father, "My wife and I are leaving." He guided her toward the door. "Until you apologize, I shall never—"

His father's next words stopped him cold. "Dunnae you wish to see Meghan? Does the wee lassie mean so little to you?"

Duncan's head snapped up as if he'd received a physical blow. How *dare* his father insinuate such a thing?

He stalked to his father. Using his sheer bulk to intimidate the frailer man, he stared at him with a warrior's hardness. "Were you not an auld man, I would toss a gauntlet into your face, *amadan*. No man bears insult to my lady wife and lives to breathe another day."

"You call me fool?" MacThomaidh glowered, trying to meet the force of Duncan's stare, but blinked, both men knowing the line had been crossed and one step more would see Duncan's words made truth. "You dinnae answer me about Meggie."

"Of course I wish to see her," Duncan bit out.

"Then sit," the old Chief ordered. "I shall have a servant fetch her. If you leave, I shall tell her you dinnae wish to see her." Although the old man took a step back, his father's narrowed eyes warned it wasn't an idle threat.

Swearing under his breath, Duncan straightened to his full height. He looked to Catherine and beseeched, "Please understand. I must see my daughter."

He knew it cost her, but she pressed her lips together and stared at him long and hard before nodding. She sat in the cushioned chair, her back ramrod straight.

"Are you certain you can do this?" His father's cruelty lashed at her mind's wounds. After what she confessed earlier, how could he put her through something so traumatic?

Her jaw set, Catherine's eyes swung between him and his father. She nodded.

A small girl with dark brown hair and bright blue eyes—eyes so like her father—skipped into the room. Those eyes widened, adoration filling them. "Da!"

Duncan knelt on one knee expecting the wee lass to fly into his arms as she always did. Instead, her eyes shifted to the woman sitting stiff as a statue.

His daughter glanced questioningly at the woman holding her hand. "Ammie Tam?"

The rest of her question remained unasked, but his sister smiled and nodded, then released the young girl's hand.

Meghan flew into his arms, smothering his face with wet kisses. As he squeezed her, he glanced over his daughter's head at Catherine to ensure she was all right. Pain lanced through him at Catherine's sad expression. She sat so rigid. He saw the force she expelled not to shatter into a thousand pieces. Though it wasn't intentional, he'd hurt this beautiful, frail woman yet again.

Och, a multitude of sins stained his soul.

Catherine watched the tender scene, thinking the child a miniature version of her father. Tears for her own lost child sprang to her eyes. Would her daughter have looked as much like her father? She pressed a hand to her mouth and swallowed hard to rein in emotions threatening to swamp her.

The young woman who'd escorted the girl approached and extended her hand. "Since no one appears of the inclination to introduce us, let me be bold enough to do it myself. My name is Tamara Gray. I am Duncan's sister, Meghan's aunt. She cannae say auntie yet, so she calls me Ammie Tam."

Unlike her brother's dark brown hair, Tamara's was fiery red. "Actually," Tamara commented, "I was at your wedding. Considering the unfortunate circumstances, I doubt you remember anyone you saw."

Catherine tried to speak normally. "I regret I do not recall."

Tamara smiled in understanding. "I am sorry 'twasnae a happier occasion." She turned and glared at her father. "Unfortunately, as you probably noticed, men in this family work at being pig-headed."

That statement earned a glare from both men, which Tamara conveniently ignored. Pulling a chair closer, she sat beside Catherine. Her eyes were the color of jade, a lovely green.

Catherine watched Duncan cradle the young girl on his lap. He murmured soft Gaelic words into her ear and her returning smile lit up the room.

MacThomaidh interrupted the cozy reunion. "'Tis time you moved into the castle. I admit my mistake forcing you to wed." He ignored Duncan's glare and looked disapprovingly at Catherine. "I give approval for you to set her aside."

Tamara gasped and Catherine flinched as if she'd

been struck.

"You give your approval for me to break God's holy vows?" Duncan queried incredulously.

Catherine sat frozen in the chair.

Clearly struggling to contain his temper, Duncan lost the effort. "Auld man, you go too far." He turned to his sister. "Tamara, show Catherine the gardens. I must have words with *Athair*. Seems I am about to teach an auld dog new tricks."

Tamara extended her arm to Catherine as Duncan helped her rise. "Please join me." She turned to her brother. "Duncan, dinnae be too —"

"Outside, Tamara. Now," Duncan ordered firmly.

Tamara took Meghan's hand and guided her sister by marriage to the door.

Catherine was more than happy to leave, wishing she could continue to somewhere where there was no pain nor a small child looking at her with her husband's blue eyes.

# Chapter Fourteen

Tamara and Catherine strolled the garden footpaths. "'Tis always the same. They argue. Duncan is furious and I cannae blame him. Please let me apologize for Father's behavior. I cannae imagine what made him speak so cruelly."

A few paces ahead, Meghan tripped and fell. Unhesitating, Catherine reached down and helped Tamara right the child.

The little girl smiled bashfully at Catherine.

When they reached a shade tree, Catherine and Tamara sat, letting Meghan wander about picking wildflowers. She smiled at laverocks as they sang their merry songs. One bird flitted from branch to branch, enchanting her to giggle. Catherine watched the child, thinking the sound delightful...and yet a knife to her soul.

Meghan padded up. Biting the inside of her cheek and rocking on her heels, she addressed her question to her aunt. "Is she my new mam?"

Catherine gasped, her hand flying to her chest.

Tamara smiled and lifted the youngster into her lap. "Aye, Meghan, she is."

Catherine's eyes flew to Tamara's. "Actually, I am not—"

"Of course you are, my dear. You wed my brother."

"Aye, but we are not really..." Catherine searched for the correct words.

"Wed?" Tamara asked innocently. "You are. I was there, remember?"

"I meant..." Again, Catherine floundered. How could she tell this lovely woman Duncan didn't consider her his wife? It was humiliating. Instead, she changed the subject. "Live you here?"

"Nay," came Tamara's lilting response. "I was ordered here the same as you and Duncan. I arrived but yestermorn."

"Then who cares for the child?"

Tamara helped her niece to stand. "Go play, Sweetling." She turned back to Catherine. "Unfortunately, 'tis only Da and his servants. I hoped when Duncan wed he would fetch Meghan home. She needs her father." She waved at the small child as she played among the flowers.

"Where do you live?"

"Near Melrose. My late husband's estate is there. One I constantly must fight the English king to keep. He tries to wed me to Englishmen. I am tired of fighting, so I shall probably have to leave soon." She didn't turn away quickly enough and Catherine saw tears gathering. After a moment Tamara supplied, "My husband dinnae survive the battle at Stirling Bridge."

"I am sorry."

Tamara acknowledged Catherine's regrets with a small nod. She looked away, clearly remembering one of the saddest times of her life. "We thought we'd won our independence. We were fools." Valiantly trying to fight back tears, her hand covered her trembling lips. "I thank God Duncan returned unharmed, but I wish they'd never gone. 'Tis selfish, but I miss my husband. I shall never love anyone again."

Hearing Duncan was at Stirling sent a chill down Catherine's spine. Why? He meant nothing to her.

"Has Duncan told you naught of our family?"

Catherine shook her head.

"He dinnae have a happy childhood and tries to block it from his mind. Sadly, the memory haunts him. Running off to fight is his way of battling demons."

"What happened?"

"Damage inflicted by Father's neglect is etched in Duncan's mind," Tamara unhappily responded. "As a child he sent Duncan to foster with Clan Kerr. I feel certain Father dunnae know the cruelty Duncan experienced at their hands. If he did, I believe he would have fetched him back." Her hand flew to her mouth. "Och, but I say too much. Duncan would be angered if he knew I discussed his past. He thinks no one knows what happened to him. He is a proud man."

"But—"

Hearing a yelp, they turned. Meghan had fallen into bracken. An involuntary sound of distress escaped the young girl's lips.

Tamara rose and rushed to her. "You gave me a fright, Sweetling."

"Ammie Tam, I cannae get it out of my fingerpit," Meghan wailed.

Catherine thought she'd heard the child wrong, but

Tamara laughed at Catherine's perplexed expression. "Meghan learns body parts," she said, pulling the offending sticker from Meghan's fingers. "The men taught her oxter. I though armpit sounded better. Now she thinks everything has pits."

Eyes wide, Meghan bobbed her head, curls bouncing. She spread her fingers out before Catherine. "Want to see my toepits, too? I can take off my brogues and show you." Catherine tried to keep from laughing. She made the mistake of peering at Tamara's joyful countenance.

Tamara returned to sit under the tree. "As to what we spoke about, the battle between my father and brother goes back many a year. Unfortunately, now it affects my niece. Da loves her, but I hoped..." Tamara shrugged, seemingly unable to voice her hopes for her niece.

"Why does she not live with Duncan?"

"He traveled too much, off fighting one cause or another. Always valid reasons, but Meghan misses him." She turned her attention to Meghan as she approached with a handful of flowers.

She gave some to her doting aunt, then turned to Catherine and proffered the other batch. She scrunched her mouth and bit the inside of her cheek. "Will you put these on Da's table?" Her tiny voice quavered and her lower lip trembled as she awaited Catherine's answer.

"Indeed, I shall," Catherine assured with a smile. "Your father shall think they are lovely."

"Do you?" Meghan asked, eyes wide. "Dey are for you, too."

Surprised, Catherine answered, "They are beautiful. Thank you." She wrapped her arms around the small girl and hugged her.

"You welcome."

Looking into the face beaming up at her, Catherine lost herself in the doe-eyed grin. In that instant the innocent, tiny lamb captured her heart.

"Did Duncan tell you aught of our clan?"

Catherine rolled her eyes and shook her head.

"That surprises me. Although he and Da dunnae get along, Duncan is proud of his heritage. We descend from Clan Chattan Mackintoshes. Our people lived in Badenoch afore moving to Glen Shee." Tamara saw that meant nothing to Catherine. "Badenoch is on the other side of the Grampians, but enough about us. Tell me of your family."

Catherine shot Tamara a surprised look. "You do not really wish to hear about—"

"But I do," assured Tamara. "You are family now and I wish to know everything about you."

Pleased, Catherine answered, "I have an older brother, Trevor, and a younger sister, Elizabeth. She is at a difficult age, four and ten, so I left my lady's maid to care for her. Not that your brother would have let me bring anyone with me."

Tamara's eyes shone with laughter. "I am certain a lady's maid is the last thing Duncan thought of that day." Catherine thought her new sister lovely.

"Duncan was boorishly rude that day. I never saw him behave like that or leave a place as fast as he left your family home. I apologize for his behavior. He really is a gentle man."

Unbidden, images flashed through Catherine's mind—of him tenderly making love to her, holding her after their babe died, spoon feeding her porridge. She tried to push them from her mind.

They rose and returned to the Great Hall. As soon as they walked into the Hall both men fell silent.

Catherine wasn't surprised when MacThomaidh frowned at her, but he took her aback when he ordered, "Leave the room, Meghan."

The child's wide eyes shifted to her father, confusion flickering in them. "But Da is still…"

Before Meghan turned to leave, Duncan said, "Come, Catherine. We leave."

The old Chief's face grew tauter. He turned to Catherine and growled, "Dunnae bother returning to my home, woman. Hopefully, my son will set you aside shortly."

"Faugh, auld man. Did you hear naught I said?" Duncan stormed, taking a step toward his father. "I told you never to speak to my wife like that again."

Ignoring Duncan and swiveling to Meghan, MacThomaidh shouted, "I told you to leave."

Leaving Duncan's side like a bolt of lightning, Catherine approached Meghan, shooting MacThomaidh a quelling glare. "She is here because she waits for me to accompany her to her bedchamber."

Meghan turned to face Catherine.

"And why might that be?" MacThomaidh growled.

"Because she returns with us. I would never leave a child here. You are the rudest person I ever had the misfortune to meet," Catherine stated in disgust.

Duncan looked surprised. "Catherine, what mean you?"

Standing behind Meghan, Catherine turned the child to face the winding staircase before ignoring her husband and again addressing her words to MacThomaidh. "I know not if you are rude to everyone you invite to your home or just me, but I shall not allow this child to remain here another day. Meghan is Duncan's daughter and leaves with us as soon as I pack her belongings."

The old laird's face hardened and Catherine thought it best to leave the room and gather Meghan's belongings. Together they climbed the stone staircase, Meghan leading the way to her chamber.

MacThomaidh's bellow stopped her before she reached the landing. "My granddaughter goes nowhere."

Catherine wrapped her arms around Meghan to quell her shaking. "I take her home where she belongs—with her father. You are welcome to visit anytime you can keep your temper under control. If not, do not darken our door. You shall not be welcome."

She turned and climbed the remaining steps, leaving her husband and his father with mouths agape.

Tamara followed and entered her niece's chamber. Belowstairs men's shouts echoed throughout the castle.

Catherine folded clothes while Meghan rushed around placing items on the bed.

"Meghan, this pile is too unwieldy. I shall select several outfits while you concentrate on three items you wish to bring." Catherine smiled encouragingly and reminded her, "We only have a small conveyance with us, dear. We shall have everything else brought later."

"Oh," Meghan frowned. "I gotfor."

At Catherine's frown of puzzlement, Tamara corrected. "You *forgot*, Sweetling."

Meghan bobbed her head. "Aye."

"You're really taking Meghan?" Tamara queried in astonishment.

"She belongs with her father. Please do not try to talk me out of it."

"I have nae intention of talking you out of it. You are brave to confront Father, though. Not many people are courageous enough to do so. He can be quite—"

"Obnoxious?" Catherine hastened to add.

"Aye, that would fit." Tamara burst into hearty laughter. "Although intimidating was the word that first came to mind. I have never seen him so rude. I am pleased you are in our family, Catherine Gillingham. You are fearless."

"Fearless?" Wide eyed, Catherine shook her head. "Nay, in truth, I am terrified. I know not if I made the correct decision, but I must stick with it."

Tamara chuckled as she left the room.

Descending the staircase, Catherine headed to Duncan. A dark frown on his face, his arms were folded tightly across his chest.

Catherine bent to Meghan. "Tell your aunt farewell, dear."

Tamara knelt to give her niece a hug. Meghan then turned to her grandfather. Rushing to his side, she wrapped her arms around his knees. "Good-bye, Grandda. Miss you."

"And I shall miss you, my wee one."

Was that a sheen of tears in the old man's eyes? Surely her eyes deceived her. The man had no feelings. Boldly Catherine approached him and guided Meghan back to her waiting father.

As Tamara helped MacThomaidh rise, his eyes moved between Duncan and Catherine. They narrowed on his son. "You cannae rid yourself of her soon enough. I dinnae admit mistakes easily, but I made an error when I ordered you to wed this evil-tempered, vicious-tongued viper. Remove her from my home. Now!"

Duncan lifted Meghan into his arms. He shifted her to one side and put his other arm protectively around Catherine. He struggled to balance Meghan's belongings at the same time. Turning to his sister, he pressed a kiss upon her brow. "Come visit whenever you wish— provided you come alone."

# Chapter Fifteen

MacThomaidh shakily climbed the stairs to his bedchamber. Shoulders stooping, he stood at his solar's tiny arrow slit and watched the litter disappear down the well-traveled path.

His long-time man-servant and friend stood in the doorway. "You were hateful to that wee lass."

"I havenae lost my sense. I know what I did," MacThomaidh answered enigmatically.

Tamara stormed into his chamber. "*Athair*, how could you be so cruel to that gentle woman?"

When the litter vanished from sight, MacThomaidh walked to his massive four-poster bed and sank down heavily on the dark green coverlet, its side curtains pulled back and tied to the bedposts. A ragged sigh escaped his lips. "'Tis sad when one's own daughter cannae trust you to do what is right. Dinnae you see the way the lad jumped to her defense when I spoke ill of her? The lass has stolen his heart." Ruefully he admitted, "If he thinks I dunnae wish him with her, he is obstinate enough to keep her close."

His daughter and friend stared, mouths agape.

"That young woman is perfect. Mayhap she shall reach him where I cannae." The deeply etched lines of MacThomaidh's forehead merged together. "Sins of the father...I failed him in his youth. I must do this for him now. If she cannae teach him forgiveness and love, he shall go through life embittered and alone."

Tamara came, leaned to her father and kissed his cheek.

Grinning sheepishly, he glanced up to her green eyes. "You really believed I dinnae like the lass?"

She nodded.

"Good. Mayhap I convinced my stubborn son as well." MacThomaidh chuckled, but quickly sobered, rubbing his gnarled hand over the back of his neck. "I regret she lost her bairn and pray she shall have more. I would love more grandchildren afore I die."

His eyes softened as a flash of pain crossed Tamara's face. He knew how much she'd desired her own child. Unfortunately, her husband died before one had been conceived. He prayed some man would save his daughter from a life of loneliness. So much to do to see his children's lives set right...*so little time.*

\* \* \*

A sennight later Meghan ran up to Duncan, her face awash with excitement. Tugging on his larger hand, she entreated, "Come wif me and Mam to the garden, Da."

A strangled gasp escaped Catherine. Shadows of pain and regret crossed her face. He knew it wasn't easy having Meggie always underfoot. Sadness engulfed him, knowing time hadn't lessened her pain. Was it too soon after the death of her own child for Catherine to accept his daughter's loving endearment? Would she rebuff Meghan?

Pain stabbed through him. How could he comfort

one over the other?

Expectancy hung in the air like a raised sword poised to fall.

Conflicting thoughts clearly warred within her. Did emotions of their lost babe flood back? If so, she revealed none of them to Meghan.

She cast him a wan smile. "Aye, my lord husband, join us in the garden. 'Tis lovely outside this day."

Duncan knew he'd forever berate himself for hurting her. He approached and drew her close, her eyes sparkling with unshed tears. She was so endearing.

His mouth met hers for a brief kiss, then brushed her ear with his lips. "Thank you."

\* \* \*

Duncan and Angus planned to collect and deliver rents at Castle Glenshee on the next quarter day. Though he dreaded her reaction, Duncan told Cat, "Lammas heralds autumn and everyone looks forward to the beginning of the harvest. We must return to the castle."

"Never shall I set foot there again."

"I dunnae wish to, *Mo Chridhe*, but our clan celebrates Lammas. 'Twouldnae be fair to deny my men and their families the chance to celebrate. They willnae go without me."

At Catherine's continued frown, he took her hand and toyed with her fingers. "'Tis a day of fun, with games and contests of skill."

Meghan bobbed her head up and down "And a feast."

Duncan smiled at his daughter's enthusiasm. "Aye, from the first fruits of our summer harvest, *a leannan*."

149

He'd never called her that before.

"Sit a moment, my heart," he clarified, riffling his daughter's hair. "The sun-god Lugh ordered a feast to honor to his foster mother. We honor her life—and death—every year."

Catherine unhappily agreed to go.

Two days later they headed to the castle. "Look," she gasped in delight, seeing the castle grounds. "The booths look like a faire." Seeing the activity, she knew it wouldn't be difficult to avoid The MacThomaidh.

As the day progressed, Meghan ran to her side, grabbed Catherine's hand and led her into the crowd of laughing people. "March with us, Mam." She held Catherine's hand and giggled with delight.

Catherine saw Duncan amidst men paying their rents. As the Chief's son it was his duty to assist. Catherine watched, unable to avert her eyes. Realizing she stared, she turned away and laughed. *He's so handsome.*

Gloaming turned to evening and Duncan fetched her and Meghan. "Let us join our clansmen. They lit a bonfire over by yon hill." He wrapped his arms around them and headed to the hill.

Duncan ran his fingertips up and down her arm. She tried to ignore the shivers it sent up her spine. "As protection against storms and lightening, our homes will have fires in the hearths through the end of winter." He reached for her hand, running his thumb lightly over it, then leaned close to her ear and whispered, "But I am all the protection you need. I shall keep you safe."

\* \* \*

Riding home, Catherine leaned against his side for warmth while Meghan curled in her lap and slept. At times like this Catherine felt at peace, forgot Duncan didn't want her.

When he placed his arm around her, she looked up at him. "I heard of Lugh since London is named after him, but Father never held such a celebration. I am glad we went."

"As am I." He smoothed his daughter's hair from her face. "Meggie had fun."

Catherine nodded.

Reaching his hand under her mantle, Duncan brushed Catherine's breast. Her eyes rounded in panic, but he ignored her and kept talking. "You know, Lugh was ever practical. During one victory he spared a defeated enemy's life in exchange for advice on plowing, sowing, and reaping." He smiled in the dark. He had a different version of plowing and sowing in mind this eve.

Catherine's breaths grew ragged under his ministrations. She glanced down at Meggie, the tiny lass fast asleep. The growing love she felt for the small girl shone in her eyes. But Duncan saw something else, too. Desire. Shifting position, he knew all too well about desire.

"She had a busy day." He pressed a kiss to Catherine's cheek. Turning her face with his finger, he gently kissed her lips. Searching for an entrance, his tongue soon claimed her mouth.

Obviously flustered, Catherine moved away, seeking words as a shield against the passion that rose within her. "Does this celebration mark the end of work in the fields?"

Duncan laughed softly, causing Meghan to stir. So she meant to keep him talking. He leaned over and lifted Meggie from Catherine's lap, moving her to the opposite end of the litter. Resituating himself, he drew Catherine closer, trailed his finger lazily over her shoulder. "Bringing in our harvest actually begins our hardest work. We cut the grain, then begin the winnowing process."

"What is that?"

"Separating chaff from the wheat. 'Tis a back breaking process, but we must bring grain in afore winter storms set in. 'Tis usually a race against time, since we can rarely predict our weather."

This time Catherine laughed. She'd discovered Highland weather completely unpredictable.

Duncan trailed his finger from her shoulder to lightly circle her breast.

"Duncan, please," she protested.

"Please what, wife? Please touch you?" His strokes grew firmer. Her chest rose and fell in choppy breaths. She might try to deny it, but she was aroused. He unfastened the laces on her bodice and slipped his hand inside to cup her bare breast. He drew circles on it with his thumb until the peak hardened. "Aye, I wish to please you, wife."

He lifted her into his lap and trailed kisses down the side of her neck. He lowered his lips to hers, nipping her lower lip.

Arriving home, Duncan quickly exited and reached inside for Meghan. The small child slept soundly.

Turning, he handed her to the nearest servant. "See my daughter is put abed."

Duncan reached for Catherine, ensuring her mantle covered her gown. Without a word, he lifted her into his arms and headed inside.

"Put me down," she protested. "I can walk."

"Nay wife, I shallnae let you leave my arms this night."

Entering his chamber, Duncan kicked the door closed with his booted foot. He placed Catherine down gently. "Dinnae turn me away again, Sweetling." He'd been patient, not demanded his rights since they'd been home. It had been too soon after she miscarried. From her reactions in the litter, she was ready now, and he wanted her with an ache that bordered on pain.

Unfastening her mantle, he loosened the laces he'd not already unfastened. Pushing material aside, he soon had her breasts bared. He couldn't breathe. Merciful saints, he'd waited so long.

Removing his clothes with shaky hands, Duncan placed one knee on the bed. He bent to suckle a breast while his hands gently removed the remainder of her clothing.

Through the haze of his mind, he heard Catherine saying, "Duncan, we should not—"

"Aye we should...we most definitely should."

He covered her mouth with his to silence her. He kissed her forehead, her neck, her collarbone, working his way once again to her breasts. He heard someone groan, realized the sound came from him. He was so hard he thought he'd burst.

Nay, he'd not rush. He'd waited too long. Tonight he'd claim her, make her his all over again. His mind tried to convince himself to slow down while his body reveled in everything about her. When she arched against him, Duncan was lost. No better than an untrained lad, he opened Catherine's thighs with his knee. Sheathed inside her, her satiny insides were smooth, hot — and welcoming.

Duncan knew he wouldn't last long. Moving his hand between them, he caressed her womanhood while slowly moving in and out. When Catherine tensed and shuddered her release, Duncan joined immediately, feeling the waves of pleasure roll through his blood.

He lay atop her until she moved. Gathering his energy, he rolled to the side, taking her with him. He kissed her again and his manhood, nestled against her leg, stirred. *Aye, it has been a long time.*

He drew back, examined Catherine's face. Her eyes pooled with tears.

"Please do not do this, Duncan. I do not wish to be hurt again."

He knew she didn't mean physical pain. She still thought he meant to leave.

He rolled atop her and whispered against her mouth, "We both made mistakes. Hurt each other. I shall never hurt you again, *Mo Chridhe.*"

He kissed her tenderly, his tongue claiming her mouth and mimicking what he meant to do with other parts of his body. His erection pressed into her belly. Kneading her breasts with his hands, his mouth followed. He suckled each in turn, driving Catherine wild with desire. When his mouth lowered, Catherine ceased protests.

She surrendered, and Duncan claimed.

\* \* \*

With autumn coming, life was hectic. Catherine stayed busy doing everything except work in the fields.

"You go every day," she argued. "I can do anything you can—"

"I am certain you can, my pigheaded wife," Duncan laughed, "but I am not willing to let you do so." Och, this woman could still be as prickly as a Scottish thistle.

"I am not pigheaded," she shouted to his retreating back.

Duncan chuckled.

Catherine grumbled, but stayed inside the hall, helping to pack apples in straw in barrels. They'd be carried to storage pits below the ground's frost line. The rest of the harvest they cut into thin slices. They'd be set aside to dry or be turned into cider. Special treats in deepest winter.

Delivering another cartload of picked apples, Duncan paused to watch her working, drinking in the sight of her beauty.

Angus approached. "She tries to ignore her feelings for you."

Duncan wondered. Memories of their lovemaking the night before made him instantly hard. When he wrapped his arms around her at night and made love to her, Catherine seemed happy, satisfied. With the light of day she kept her distance. She was a conundrum he had yet to unriddle.

Although not much help, Meggie stayed close to Catherine's heels. Duncan was pleased Catherine allowed her to do so.

Delivering a cartload of supplies, he stopped in the kitchen.

Catherine turned to Meggie. "Sweetheart, hand me that moistened cloth."

Meghan got the cloth off the counter. She handed it to her and scrunched up her face. "Why say you Sweetheart? Da calls me Sweetling."

"Aye, he does," Catherine agreed. "Both are terms of endearment."

"Oh," Meggie said, scrunching her face again. "What is 'dearment'?"

Wiping her hands on the cloth, Catherine drew up a stool and sat. Duncan imagined her aching back and tired legs were grateful for the respite. She held out her arms to Meggie. "Come, Sweetling."

Meggie skipped over to her and raised her arms to be picked up.

Cat lifted Meggie and placed her on her lap. "An endearment is a word to tell someone you love them."

"Sweetheart means you *love* me?" Meggie's eyes grew wide.

"Aye, it does."

"Then you are *my* sweetheart," she said proudly. She bobbed her head, curls bouncing. "And Da loves you, too, 'cause he calls you Sweetling."

Catherine hugged Meggie tightly. She looked up and saw the man she was so uncertain about standing in the doorway. A fleeting streak of sorrow twisted her heart.

That wasn't true. One of the servants, Esme made certain Catherine heard whispers about Duncan visiting other women. Obviously she was no more important than other clanswomen. Why would the woman say it if it wasn't true? She handed Meggie an apple slice. "Cook says the kitchen moggie has wee kittens. Go see if you can find them."

As Meghan dashed from the room, Duncan approached. He made no comment about the child saying he loved her. Instead, he asked, "Where did you hear the word sweetheart?"

"From your Scottish abbey." She rose from the chair and went back to packing apples.

Duncan stepped behind her, let her feel his warmth. Finally he slid his arms around her waist and brought her back against him. "There is a Sweetheart Abbey in Dumfries." Nuzzling her hair, he breathed in the fresh lavender scent. "How heard you of it?"

"King Edward bragged about being there," she told him, her stiffness saying she was aware he'd not like her answer.

Taking her hand, he led her to the table and sat on the bench. "What did Longshanks say about our abbey?"

"Duncan, please, I do not wish to upset you."

"Tell me," he ordered, pulling her onto his lap.

Catherine exhaled loudly. Why had she thought he might back down? He was the most determined man she knew. "Edward said he stayed there after he sacked some castle and invaded a town called Galloway."

"Caerlaverock Castle."

"While there, the Archbishop of Canterbury sent him

a papal missive." He stared at her, but said nothing. "Edward took his time meeting the Archbishop, but when he did, the Archbishop ordered him to cease oppression of the Scots. Edward returned to England, but bragged about being there."

Duncan rubbed his hand up and down her back. She could tell he tried not to lose his temper. "Would you like to hear the abbey's true history?"

Catherine bit her lip and nodded.

"After Balliol's da died, John's mam was grief stricken. She refused to let them bury him and had his heart cut out and preserved." At Catherine's shock, he added, "Lady Devorgilla placed it inside a tiny silver and ivory casket and carried it everywhere. She called it 'her sweet, silent companion'."

Catherine wondered what it would feel like to have someone love her that much. She doubted she'd ever know.

"When she passed to Heaven, monks buried it with her. They thought it fitting she be buried there since she founded the abbey and dedicated it to his memory. Because of the love she showed her husband, the Cistercian monks called the abbey *Dulce Cor*, Latin for Sweetheart, beloved."

Duncan bent his head and placed soft kisses on her neck. "Now *Sweetheart*, 'tis time I get back to work. Crops willnae wait."

He rose and patted his hand against her bottom before striding out of the room. As he stepped into the sunshine, a smile of satisfaction crossed his face.

# Chapter Sixteen

Catherine tilted her head in thought. "Back home this is the beginning of Advent. We used the forty days before Christmas as a time of reflection."

Duncan cocked a brow and teased. "On the sins of the English? Och, lass, 'twould take far more than forty days."

Catherine swatted his arm and walked away. Duncan's rich, hearty laughter followed.

She walked around Castle Glenshee's grounds, the scent of meat pies wafting through the air. Unable to resist, she delighted in the beef and pidgeon pastie a pudgy woman with a flour coated apron and warm smile offered.

She ate while Duncan joined in games of skill. Unwilling to let him know she rooted for him, she refrained from outward display. He might misunderstand and think she cared. She could never let that happen when everyone knew he didn't want her.

She rejoiced when he won in the running match, but was chilled to the marrow when a red-haired bear of a man threw him to the ground while wrestling. She'd stifled a scream. Thinking him injured, she jumped to her feet to run to him, but caught herself. *Whatever was I thinking? He'd not want me out there.* She sighed in relief when he stood and charged the man head first. A roar of laughter sounded when his opponent fell to the ground.

Catherine couldn't help herself. She delighted in watching his muscles bunch together while tossing the caber. "He is magnificent," she sighed. *Clearly the handsomest man on the field. And the strongest.* She blushed when she caught herself thinking of being wrapped in those taut arms and the delightful things those hands did to her body. *How can fingers so strong in everything they do be feather soft when they caress my skin?* And when they found their way to her most sensitive spot, oh, the magic those fingers wove.

Catherine glanced to see if anyone noticed her besotted longing for a husband that didn't want her.

\* \* \*

Evening fell and stars emerged as Duncan searched for Catherine. "Come, lady wife. The *Seanchaidh*—storyteller—begins."

He unwound his plaide from his shoulder. He sat and patted the spot beside him. "Join me whilst we listen to tales he weaves. And here comes Alana bringing our Meggie. She looks exhausted."

"She should. She spent the day running around with the older children."

He situated Catherine in front of him while Meggie lay beside them on part of the plaide, quickly falling asleep. While people talked around them, he brushed his lips against Catherine's ear.

She leaned back and relaxed in his arms. He caressed her arms with his fingertips, sending ripples of pleasure through her. Ah yes, those fingertips. Hadn't she thought of them earlier? She shivered in delight.

Duncan felt the shiver, because he asked, "Are you cold?"

Catherine shook her head. She didn't dare tell him what she'd been thinking. He'd think her a wanton.

As though reading her mind, he lifted her and turned her in his arms. Facing him, her legs straddled his hips. The man had a strange smile on his face. "You would not dare!"

"I dare," he growled, placing his hands on her bottom and pulling her closer. Kissing her at the same time, his tongue mimicked his intentions. She felt his erection, rock hard against her body.

Catherine panicked. "Duncan not here."

He laughed and brought her bottom toward him again, grinding suggestively against her. In the next breath, he moved her aside and stood. He bent to pick up Meggie and grabbed Catherine by the hand, pulling her toward their litter.

When she finally caught his eye to see what was wrong, the bold man actually winked.

"Aye, wife, you have the right of it. We cannae stay here. You yell much too loudly when you find your woman's pleasure. You would surely embarrass me."

A blush heating her cheeks, Catherine gasped at his crude statement.

He roared with laughter as he placed his arms around her waist and lifted her into the conveyance. Meggie slept on the other side of the litter. It lurched forward as horses moved. Drawing Catherine into his arms, he removed her bodice. It hung to her waist as he buried his head in her breasts.

"Duncan, what are you....?"

Catherine said no more when he raised her kirtle and slipped his finger inside her. He groaned. He wanted her now. If Meghan wasn't with them, he'd take Catherine right in the litter. She made him lose every shred of control.

When Catherine wrapped her hand around him and caressed him, he thought he'd perish on the spot. As the horses slowed, Duncan wrapped his plaide around her, covering everything he'd revealed to his hungry eyes. He stepped to the ground and lifted her in his arms. He wanted her so much he had trouble breathing.

Looking around, he saw Angus had already arrived. Praise the saints. "Angus, please make sure Meggie gets tucked into bed."

Curse the auld man for smiling. It spoke volumes. The crusty old man knew exactly where Duncan was going — and why. These rides home were going to be the death of him. He'd never wanted a woman so badly in his entire life. Never felt such need with other women.

\* \* \*

Duncan wasn't surprised when Catherine elaborately acknowledged Christmastide. As his friend, Tory, had, Catherine brought many English beliefs with her. Chuckling, he thought his people in for a shock. Although they had their Yule celebrations, Christ's natal day had been a solemn day of prayer, then back to work. Their major festivities started days later and spilled over into the new year and Twelfth Night. Their biggest celebration was Hogmanay, the departure of the auld year and arrival of the new one.

"What does Hogmanay mean?"

Duncan shrugged. "I believe 'tis Gaelic for new morning, *oge maidne*. Others believe the name comes from the French *Homme est né*, Man is born."

Catherine whispered, "Jesus."

Duncan nodded.

"Tell me how you celebrated before."

"It matters not, *Mo Chridhe*. We shall celebrate both holidays from now on."

Catherine pressed, "I'll not have your people resenting me for changing everything. You already wish I was not here."

Duncan pretended he hadn't heard her last comment. Would he ever convince her of his need for her? "Mam insisted we attend kirk on the eve of Christmas and Christmas Day. Mam used the chapel at Castle Glenshee regularly. We dinnae have a live in priest, but one traveled there often. The day after Christmas, Mam recognized the Feast of Saint Stephen."

"The day of charity? When the church opens its alms boxes?"

"Aye, Mam gave wee gifts to everyone who served us. Grant's family, where I fostered, did so as well. His wife follows it now." Looking upset, Duncan paced the room. "Truth be told, the past several years I spent Christmastide with Tory and Grant, not wishing to be at Glen Shee."

"You missed Christmas with Meggie?" Catherine asked, aghast.

"Aye," Duncan agreed sadly. "'Twas my one regret."

He moved behind her and wrapped his arms around her. "I have decided to take you both to Crieff for a wee visit. 'Twill be difficult traveling, but there is something I wish you to see."

"What?"

"You shall see when we get there," Duncan teased.

\* \* \*

He'd sent Grant a missive, so he envisioned Tory decorating Drummond Castle. Christmastide was her favorite time of year.

Grant and Tory rushed into the bailey to greet them. Tory stood in her fur-trimmed mantle and hood, Grant in his plaide. Grant had his arms wrapped around her waist, his hand resting protectively on her belly.

Light flurries fell as Duncan helped his wife and daughter from the conveyance. After exchanging greetings with their hosts, they rushed inside Drummond's Great Hall to escape the bone-chilling cold.

Catherine gasped. She stopped in her tracks, her eyes sweeping toward a massive tree. 'Twas beautiful.

Speechless, Catherine looked at the elaborate decorations while Meggie jumped up and down. The room had evergreens with nuts and tiny bits of bright cloth scattered throughout branches. Candles were placed in the ferns. It reminded her of a faerytale.

"Mam, look," Meghan shouted, tugging on her hand. "Look at the tree." Eyes wide with awe, she turned to Duncan. "Da, look."

"I see it, Sweetling." He smiled at his daughter, then his eyes sought Catherine.

Hers darted around the room, but returned to the

festive tree. Red ribbons had been tied into bows around the branches. At the very top sat a silver coated star.

Catherine was speechless.

Duncan wrapped his arms around her. "This is what I wished to show you, *Mo Chridhe*." When she turned her head to look at him, he smiled. "'Tis a *tannenbaum*, a Christmas tree."

Breathless, Catherine whispered, "'Tis beautiful."

"The tradition came from Germany," Tory interjected, walking toward her guests, "although ancient pagans attached fruit and candles to evergreen branches in honor of Woden. To them, trees symbolized eternal life. I asked Grant if we could have one the first Christmas after he brought me here." She jabbed her husband with her elbow.

Catherine watched as her hostess swung her eyes back to her handsome husband. "He thought me daft to suggest a tree *inside* his Great Hall."

Catherine turned to Duncan. "Might we have a smaller one?"

Duncan's chest rumbled with laughter. "'Twould have to be smaller. Our home isnae as large. Aye, you may have a tree." His eyes twinkled.

Watching her youngest children run outside, Tory placed her arms around two young girls, drawing them close. "This young lady is our foster daughter, Annie." She turned to face the other child. "And this beautiful young woman is my sister, Ashleigh. She visits from England. They will show Meghan to their room."

Tory escorted Duncan and Catherine to their room. "I am certain you'd like to relax. Join us belowstairs after you have refreshed yourselves." She quietly closed the door behind her.

Catherine sank onto the bed. "I have never seen anyplace decorated like this. It..." She stammered for words. Looking around the bedchamber, she saw ferns and candles on small tables.

The next several days were spent in a whirlwind of activities. Catherine and Tory rarely separated and Meggie delighted in playing with the Drummond children. During frequent snowball fights, shouts abounded, punctuated by squeals of laughter.

Adults often joined the children. On one such trek, Catherine fell backward into the snow. Duncan rushed to her side, thinking her hurt. Instead, she moved her arms up and down and swung her legs outward in an arc. Finally she reached for him and he pulled her up.

"What in Heaven's name are you doing?"

She laughed and pointed at the ground. Everyone saw an angel—a snow angel. Soon children flopped backwards in the snow, giggles abounding. Catherine pulled Duncan forward, but he resisted. "Come husband. Be a child." Her eyes searched his face. It suddenly looked pained. "With the war ever continuing, you fret too much. For a short time, forget your worries." She let go of his hand and ran to a clear spot and extended her hand to him, her eyes beseeching. Duncan seemed to fight some internal battle, but joined her. She held his hand then turned him around. "On the count of three, fall backwards." He nodded.

"One. Two. Three!" Catherine watched her husband raise his eyes to Heaven before falling backward with her. A smile lit her face as she moved her arms and legs and she scrambled to her feet to pull him up. He yanked her into his arms to kiss her.

"Duncan," she squealed, "you will ruin the angel."

A tender smile crossed his face. "Nay, my love, naught will ever ruin my angel. She is perfect." He brushed the back of his hand lightly over her cheek before kissing her again, then let her pull him up.

Grant rushed to an outbuilding. He returned with several targes awaiting repair and bid everyone, "Follow me." Shrieks of laughter echoed as he sat on a targe and careened down the hill. By the time he walked back to the top, his older children were already sliding down the hill.

Catherine bent to grab one and sat on it. She went nowhere. Duncan laughed and leaned forward to push her. Plummeting downward, she screamed all the way down. She reached the bottom, picked it up and marched back up the hill. "Race with me, husband. I shall beat you."

Duncan laughed. "Aye, you would if I must push you first."

Catherine scrunched up her face and glared. He motioned Meggie to sit between his legs. With one hand around Meggie's waist and the other holding the targe, he waited for Catherine to situate herself. Ashleigh and Annie positioned themselves behind them and pushed. Meghan clutched her father's legs and screamed, "Aaaaaaah" at the top of her lungs. Catherine screamed just as loudly as she inched past them. Drummonds cheered, urging them onward. Catherine slid to the bottom a hairsbreadth before Duncan. She jumped up in excitement and reached down to lift Meggie high into the air, swinging the child around.

Grant watched their antics, a pleased smile on his face.

Meggie squealed, "Again, again."

Catherine swung to look at Duncan. Did his eyes shine with love? Aye, for Meggie. The two walked arm and arm up the hill. This time Duncan positioned Meggie between Catherine's legs and they raced Annie and Ashleigh. Giggles of delight echoed off surrounding mountains.

With snow antics behind them, Tory rushed everyone inside to change into dry clothes, not willing to risk anyone getting sick.

Too soon, the visit ended. Meggie scrambled into the litter, slid the curtain aside and watched her parents bid farewell to the Drummonds.

* * *

Safely back at Cray Hall, Duncan busied himself with catching up on current news while Catherine and Meghan settled into daily routines. Soon Catherine wished to decorate, so she headed outside to collect ferns and nuts.

Meggie delighted in helping and followed Catherine while she placed ferns around the outside doorframe. Catherine patiently lifted and held her while the child placed decorations where she wanted them.

Hearing footsteps crunching the snow behind them, Catherine turned to see a wide smile crossing her husband's face.

"Need help?" He reached around and held Meggie while she decorated the door to her—and Catherine's—satisfaction.

Meggie beamed at her father. "Look what I did, Da."

"I see, Sweetling." Squeezing her tightly, he gave her what his men called a bear hug.

Meggie's laughter peeled with delight and she squeezed back.

\* \* \*

Later that eve, Duncan sat before the hearth. Catherine walked past him and he pulled her into his lap. He wanted her near. He nuzzled her neck while his father's bard entertained with rousing tales. When Catherine wiggled in his lap, situating herself, Duncan immediately responded.

She froze, pretending she hadn't noticed.

Duncan leaned forward, whispered in her ear. "Too late, Sweetling. You woke him, now you must entertain him."

Shocked, Catherine swatted his arm. "Shh!"

Duncan rose in one fluid motion, Catherine still in his arms. He bade his men goodeve and headed to his bedchamber. They'd grown used to seeing him whisk his wife away. He was randy as a stag after a doe in heat.

# Chapter Seventeen

Duncan slammed the door shut with his foot and strode to their bed. Holding his arms out with Catherine still in them, he dropped her in the bed's center. He unfastened the ties on the bed's drapes, plunging them in darkness. Removing their clothes, he dropped them outside the drapes in a pile on the floor. They'd straighten everything in the morn.

He stretched his body beside her. Caressing her shoulders, his fingertips skimmed lightly over her arms. Soon he nibbled her earlobe, bringing the expected shudder. He shifted and claimed her mouth.

He'd wanted her all day, watched as she went about decorating. Every time she bent to place decorations, he'd wanted to walk behind her and plant his hands on her bottom. Wisely, he'd kept his distance, knowing if he went near he'd drag her upstairs. Why did she so affect him? He'd never desired another woman as he did Catherine. The power never lessened.

Lowering his head, he laved her nipple with his tongue, causing the tender bud to harden. He moved his mouth to her other breast, teasing both until she moaned.

Only then did he dedicate his attentions lower. When he entered her, Duncan feared he'd spill his seed immediately. He stayed his movements, had to slow down, not wanting this to end. His lips reclaimed hers. When her hips rose to meet his, Duncan fought to measure his pace. Plunging himself into her, he was surprised when she met him thrust-for-thrust. Their shattering climax left them both gasping for breath.

Duncan flexed his body over hers and whispered, "*A-rithist.*"

"And that means?"

"Again."

"A beautiful word. Oh, aye, *a-rithist.*"

\* \* \*

In the morn he headed outside to gather the much-awaited tree, taking Alex with him to carry it. Catherine's eyes lit up when he settled it in a corner while the children ran about the Hall, a flurry of energy. Calling them to her, she set them to decorating. She'd taken Tory's idea of the tree, yet made the decorations her own. She had the blacksmith make rings similar to what he forged for chain mail, only thinner, and looped them into a long strand. Entreating the children to help, they wound it around the tree. Next came a garland she'd created from sprigs of holly and bows fashioned from scraps of rags and yarn. Duncan smiled when she could no longer reach the upper branches. Walking to her, he did what she'd done with Meggie the day before—lifted and held her while she finished decorating. She giggled like a child, the sound musical, as she placed the star their blacksmith made atop the tree.

Everyone stood back and stared at the beauty and magic Catherine conjured for them. To the delight of each child, she rewarded them with several hazelnuts for helping.

Duncan decided traditions dear to Catherine would be continued. She told him, "Mother allowed the servant's children to reenact the birth of Jesus, when the Magi brought Him gifts." He watched as she coached his clansmen's children. He'd agreed when she asked, "May they perform it tChristmas eve?" He marveled at how she'd made the season come alive, bringing the message of Christ's birth as she coached them. Parents delighted their children were involved in festivities.

On a bright and sunny afternoon a sennight later, Duncan went outside to cut the Yule log. After bringing it in, he told Catherine, "It cannae be lit until Christmas-eve." He planted a kiss on her cheek as he walked to the hearth. "I think you shall like the ceremony."

"I am sure I shall, but the days pass too quickly to my liking."

It was time for Cook to serve supper, but everyone was reluctant to leave the tree. From behind, Duncan wrapped his arms around her and rocked her slightly. He kissed her temple. "Thank you for making this Christmastide special for our clanspeople. You bring much joy to us all." He nibbled her earlobe. "Especial me."

As they were seated for the meal, Duncan glanced at tables laden with Yule food, the pungent aroma wafting throughout the large room. Men placed roasted pigs on tables that groaned under weight of the food. "I dunnae think anyone shall go away hungry."

Catherine tried recipes she'd gotten from Tory. She couldn't wait to taste Black Pudding, but after doing so whispered to Duncan, "*Blech.*"

Duncan chuckled. "You dunnae wish to know what is in it."

When everyone said they couldn't eat one more bite, Cook entered with a holiday cake made with honey, raisins and nuts. Catherine chuckled when the men found 'a wee more room' to top off their meal.

Duncan rose and dashed up the staircase. He returned, unwrapping a small wooden knot. "Remains of last year's Yule log. We use it to light this year's fire to bring good fortune."

Men nodded affirmation as he went to the hearth and placed holly beneath the log to kindle the fire. He ensured everyone had gathered, then sprinkled the tree trunk with oil, salt, and mulled wine. He'd set the necessary items beside the hearth earlier in the day.

He drew Catherine to hearthside. "Join me." Their hands together, they put the tinder to the Yule remnant, setting it ablaze and in turn to light the new log. Reaching for a goblet of wine, he turned to his clansmen and raised it in toast. "*Slàinte, sonas agus beartas.*"

A cheer went up around the room at his wish of health, wealth and happiness.

Duncan picked up a sprig of holly and handed it to Catherine. "Toss this into the fire."

"Why?"

Duncan's smile faded. "To burn up the past year's troubles — we had enough of those. Let us put them behind us."

Catherine eyed him warily. Surely he didn't believe troubles vanished by throwing holly into the fire? She looked around and saw all eyes on her. All as hopeful as Duncan's.

Catherine couldn't spoil the day for them. With a smile she threw the holly into the fire. Others moved forward to do the same.

Deep in her heart Catherine knew it would take more than a bit of holly to make all well with the world. It wouldn't end the feud with England, and wouldn't bring her baby back.

*It wouldn't make Duncan love her.*

Pushing aside the painful thoughts, she cocked a brow. "Are there other superstitions that accompany this eve? You seem to have one for every occasion."

Angus chuckled. "You have the right of it there, lass."

"Aye, 'tis bad luck for the fire to go out."

Catherine's eyes danced. "Why?"

"Because the Sidhe are about on the longest night of the year and only raging fires keep them from coming down the chimney and paying a visit." Duncan looked like he tried to keep a straight face.

"Well we certainly wouldn't want anything coming down our chimney," Catherine teased, her mood lifting, "and I am quite certain you already arranged to have someone tend the fire."

Duncan grinned, revealing he had.

"Let us sit and watch all bad things burn away." She tried to hide a smile. Failing, she patted the spot beside her, indicating Duncan should sit. "I for one am tired and could use an excuse to rest."

Men sat before the hearth drinking whisky. Duncan

sat beside Catherine, one arm draped casually across her shoulders, Meggie seated on his lap.

"The Hall is lovely for *Oidche Choinnle,* our Night of Candles to light the way for the holy family. Thank you, wife."

Duncan ascended the stairs with her later, his mood mellow.

Closing the door firmly behind them, he drew her into his arms. "I am glad you shared the day with me, lass. 'Tis the first Christmas I spent with Meggie in many a year." He bent to feather a kiss across her lips, then whispered, "I thank you for that." His hand flexed in a squeeze on her shoulder.

Tired from the day's activities, they were soon abed. Duncan's arms encircled her and drew her close. She snuggled against him, her bottom against his hips. He fell sound asleep. Catherine lay abed and thought, *If only life could always be this simple. Our upcoming ceremony is about ridding ourselves of past year's problems. Would that it could be. Mayhap if I believe enough, this coming year will be free of problems.*

*If only…*

\* \* \*

Christmas morn dawned bright and sunny—with bitter temperatures. Duncan smiled upon waking, his first Christmas with Catherine in his arms. "*Nollaig Chridheil.*" He placed kisses lightly on her forehead and cheek.

"Happy Christmas to you, too," she murmured sleepily.

She looked beautiful as she lay beside him, her right

leg intimately flung over his. He caressed her lips. *I could kiss those lips for hours and not tire of them.* He'd never felt so at peace. "I know you would have liked to attend the castle service, but I refuse to set foot there and have this blessed day ruined."

He rose and dressed before traipsing outside to gather yew boughs to decorate the small room Catherine set aside for a chapel. His gift to her. Tiny, it barely accommodated twenty people, but his clansmen would wander in and out all day.

He opened the door and the fragrance of evergreens wafted out. He lit a candle, held it aloft to survey the room and stared in amazement. 'Twas already decorated. Tables lined the walls and were bedecked with candles and evergreens. He noticed a white cloth on the small altar and walked forward to examine it. Had Catherine embroidered it? Thinking back, he'd seen her ply her needle late into the night. Swirls of vines and flowers covered the cloth, a detailed crèche on each end. The intricate stitches were flawless. The perfect gift to pass to Meggie when she wed.

He walked around and lit every candle, then went to fetch Meggie and his beautiful wife.

Catherine had an overwhelming urge to hold Meggie on her lap during the observance. The thought of God's son being born brought special meaning to the birth of all children. Sorrow overwhelmed her, knowing she'd never cradle a babe of her own.

She realized Duncan watched her. Her cheeks flushed with embarrassment when he gazed lovingly into her face. Surely she just imagined it, just mists from her wistful dreams.

After the holy service Duncan led her to the trestle table in the Hall. Once seated, servants delivered the special courses. Duncan suspected Cook had taken great pains to ensure Catherine's first Christmas day dinner would be everything she expected.

The main course was roasted goose surrounded with rows of tiny beetroots. Also served were bannock cakes of oatmeal, a traditional Christmas treat.

Catherine had never had one before—never wanted one again. Inwardly she doubted she'd finish it. Was it her imagination or did it grow larger as she chewed?

Afterward, Duncan and Catherine presented Meggie with a new rag doll. Wanting it to be perfect, Catherine spent sennights making it. She'd sewn by candlelight in their chamber so there'd be no chance of the child seeing it. Her perfect stitches fashioned the face after Meghan's.

The child's eyes grew wide with delight and she rushed to hug both parents.

While she ran around and showed everyone her dollie, Catherine smiled shyly and handed Duncan a white linen shirt she'd made.

Startled, he'd not expected a gift from her.

He sat Catherine down before the hearth's warmth, walked behind her and drew something from his white fur sporran. He placed a delicate chain around her neck. When he extended his hand, he held a bracelet with three red rubies.

"Duncan!" She touched her necklace, her eyes holding a question.

"Aye," he confirmed. "It matches the necklace. The

three stones are for you, me, and Meggie. Our smith crafted it for you."

Catherine swallowed and stared at the beautiful red gems. "I cannot possibly —"

"Ah, but you must. 'Tis a gift." Before she could voice dissent, he added, "From me *and* Meggie."

Meggie chose that moment to reappear, smiling at sight of the necklace. "Do you like it, Mam? 'Tis from me and Da."

He knew Catherine well enough to know she'd never hurt Meggie's feelings by not accepting it. He'd thought that theory through before deciding what to gift her with.

When it grew dark, Duncan headed to the door to remove Catherine and Meghan's mantles from nearby pegs. He wrapped the pair of them and pulled the hoods over their heads. He held out the hand warmers Catherine and Meghan received that morn.

Meggie's eyes gleamed. "Da, I look like Mam." Duncan nodded, acknowledging her delight. He'd watched her emulating Catherine over several moons, giving him the idea of gifting them with the same item. Meggie's happiness told him he'd been right.

\* \* \*

Tamara arrived early the following morn, having spent Christmas day with her father.

She shook the snow off her burgundy mantle and stomped it off her soft brown leather boots before giving Catherine a cursory hug and heading to the hearth.

Tamara held her hands in front of the flames and turned to face her brother. "I hoped you wouldnae have lit a fire."

Duncan frowned at his sister. "You wish us to freeze? 'Tis cold, woman. Of course Angus lit our fire."

Duncan walked to Tamara and placed his hands on her shoulders. He scanned her face, not liking the agitation he saw. "What has you upset?"

"The ashes."

Duncan stiffened and they locked eyes. "Ashes?"

"Aye, I had trouble sleeping, so I was up early. I saw a footstep."

"'Tis naught but an old wives tale," Duncan said, his voice unconvincing.

Catherine watched in wide-eyed amazement. "What are you talking about?"

Duncan turned, moved Tamara with him. He looked over his sister's head. "There is an ancient custom that has to do with Christmas ashes." He said no more, but laid his head atop Tamara's. He felt her body shaking, bravely trying to stay her tears.

"And?" Catherine prodded.

Without a word, Tamara burst into tears.

Duncan closed his eyes and held her closer. He opened them when he felt a hand pressed lightly to his arm.

"Duncan, what is wrong?"

He sighed and looked into his wife's worried eyes. "Auld folks check the ashes the morn after Christmas. If a footprint appears, they believe it foretells events that shall happen during the upcoming year. A print facing the door foretells of death."

"The footprint faced the door. It must forewarn of

Da's death. He hasnae been well."

\* \* \*

Soon it was Night of Candles for Hogmanay, to light the way for First Footers. Duncan followed Cat as she put finishing touches to the trestle table trying to explain the tradition to Catherine.

"Rubbish. I cannot understand how you can believe dark hair indicates good luck."

"Most Scots have dark or red hair," Angus interrupted. "Norse invaders usually had light hair and fair complexions. Their vicious raids brought cruelty and hard times to our lands, so we tend to look upon such people warily."

To change the subject, Duncan drew Catherine to her feet and led her to the chair before the roaring hearth. Seating her gently, he presented her with a brooch.

"Duncan! 'Tis beautiful."

Leaning forward, he took it from her fingers and fastened it on the swath of MacThomas plaide flung over her shoulder. He took her face gently in his hands and kissed her.

"I have naught for you," she fretted.

A smile spread across his face. "You are all the gift I need."

A flush crept up her cheeks.

As midnight approached, Cat's anticipation grew. She found the festive atmosphere intoxicating.

When a knock sounded at the door, she jumped. They'd not been jesting. They'd really expected a visitor.

She followed behind Duncan to see who was there. When he drew the door open, Catherine couldn't stand the suspense. She poked her head around his large shoulder and saw Alex, accompanied by Duncan's cousin, Euan.

She stood on tip-toe to look over Duncan's shoulder. "Does he count? He lives on your land."

Duncan laughed. "Anyone who dunnae live in the house is a visitor, lass."

Alex brought all three Hogmanay offerings, or *handsels*. He carried a basket of food, drink and fuel for the fire. Duncan boomed, "Come everyone. Let us eat. Thank you for the gifts, Alasdair." He poured Alex a goblet of wine.

Catherine's brows drew together. "Why do you always call him Alasdair?"

"'Tis his name. Why else would I call him that? You'd rather I called him Geoffrey?"

She glared and placed her hand on her hip. "Duncan MacThomas, do not make fun of me. His name is Alexander."

"Actually," Duncan said, rocking back on his heels and thoroughly enjoying himself, "his mam named him Alasdair. 'Tis Gaelic for Alexander. We all have Gaelic names."

"You just make fun of me," she grumbled. She walked away, then quickly turned back. "What would your name be?"

"Donnchadh," came Duncan's smug reply.

Of a sudden, she smiled. She'd outsmarted him. "Catherine?"

Duncan thought a moment before a smile of satisfaction spread across his face. "*Mo Chride.*"

Exasperated, she stomped her foot. "Sweetheart is *not* Gaelic for Catherine."

"Och, in your case it is." He strode over and drew her into his arms. He bent and kissed her thoroughly, heedless of everyone present. Breaking the kiss, he took her hand and led her to the head table.

Afterwards, Alex headed to the hearth and threw the coal he'd brought with him onto the fire. Looking across the room, he told his friends, "A good New Year to one and all and many may you see."

Duncan held Catherine close. He couldn't think of a better way to usher in the new year than to spend it sheathed in his wife's body. Bidding his clansmen good eve, he led Catherine upstairs. The look in his eyes told her exactly what he had in mind.

*1305*

# Chapter Eighteen

Exhausted from lack of sleep, Catherine yawned and opened her eyes wide in an effort to stay awake. As they sat at the trestle tables that spanned the hall, Duncan smiled, clearly pleased with himself. He'd let her sleep not at all and she'd delighted in his attentions. She blushed thinking of it. In their bedchamber she could forget he didn't want her.

While they broke their fast, Duncan explained the day's tradition, the Creaming of the Well. "Unwed maidens race to the well in hopes of being the first to draw the water. If they succeed and get their *true love* to drink it afore day's end, they shall be wed within the year. 'Tis a ceremony I made certain to avoid."

Catherine listened to his story with mixed emotions. She thought it a sweet tradition—a woman filled with expectation trying to win a man she loves. Hoping he'd love her back. Laughter caught in her throat. Pain lanced her heart. She'd believed in love...once. That seemed so long ago—certainly before the king ordered someone to wed her who wanted nothing to do with her.

Exhaustion fogging her mind, she spoke from the heart. "I'm glad I need not participate. No one would drink water I drew."

At the shocked expression on Duncan's face, she realized what she'd said. Would he think her chasing after a compliment? Or would he pity her, seeing the truth of her words? She rose, rushing into the kitchen before Duncan responded.

She stood just beyond the door, wiping away tears and feeling like a silly fool. *Why can I not stay my tears? I am no better than children when they skin their knees. At least they have an excuse. I am just...weak.*

Why did hearing the simple tradition make her fall apart? Because she wanted to believe again. Wanted to have hope.

Needing to escape Cook's watchful eyes, she ran outside, only to find herself knee deep in snow. *I cannot even escape successfully. No wonder Duncan does not want me.* Thoughts continued to swirl. *Chin up*, she told herself sternly. *Trevor would be mortified if he witnessed such conduct. What did he tell me the day I wed? 'You can do anything if you put your mind to it.'*

Catherine dropped to the snow and let her tears fall. So much for getting hold of herself! Her husband didn't want her, she couldn't control her emotions and she'd landed in a family that believed true love came from drinking water! As if it was that simple. Duncan wouldn't love her no matter what. Bound to her by God's law, he tolerated her presence in his bed, naught else.

Her feet were wet—and she was freezing. She'd run outside without boots or even a mantle over her green kirtle.

The door opened and Duncan appeared. He took one look at her sitting in the snow crying and shook his head. Walking toward her, he squatted in front of her, his hand gently brushing her hair from her tear stained face. His eyes searched hers for a long moment, but held an unreadable expression. She gulped and sniffled, trying to stay her tears, not wanting to be a complete ninny. He caressed the side of her face, then gently kissed her forehead, his eyes holding a trace of a smile. He rose and picked her up in his arms like a child. His tenderness summoned more tears as she twined her arms around his neck and buried her face against his neck, feeling safe in his arms.

Saying nothing, Duncan carried her into the warmth of his Hall.

\* \* \*

The new year started with bitter snow storms. Shivering, everyone rushed inside as soon as they finished chores. Duncan, silly man that he was, thought it bracing. Catherine rarely ventured outside. Cooped inside the house for days, she spent hours plying her needle on a new kirtle for Meggie with other women before the hearth. She even tried her hand at spinning wool, a task she had neither knack nor patience for. Her strands went from too fat to too thin. Siobhán's nimble fingers pulled and worked the wool from the bundle while her foot kept a steady rhythm on the peddle, allowing her to spin the finest strands of wool Catherine had ever seen.

She went back to her sewing and spent the rest of the

evening listening to the *seanchaidh* tell his tales.

A sennight after the storms began, Duncan delighted her with an unexpected offer. "Would you like to learn how to play Chess? I could teach you."

Pleased he offered, Catherine nodded. Duncan was a patient teacher and she thought herself an apt student. They played most evenings, enjoying the comfort of the other's company.

Concentrating on the game, she was surprised when he brushed the back of his knuckles over her cheek.

She swallowed hard. "Are you trying to distract me, my lord husband?"

Duncan smiled, his eyes alight with mischief. "Distracting you is one of my many joys."

Catherine glanced around the hall to see if anyone heard. Why would he say such a thing? Like the women, Duncan's men also gathered in the Hall. Some sat on the floor, others on benches around tables, but none seemed to be paying attention to Duncan and her. She dipped her chin and pretended absorption in the game.

Rubbing his chin, Duncan watched Catherine surveying the Hall. It was obvious his statement shocked her. There had to be some way to tear down the protective barrier she'd built around herself and he was determined to try every one of them.

His men filled their time sharpening knives and whittling small animals to amuse the children, but he knew they felt restless, wishing to be outside. He did. Watching the men ply their knives, he thought of the apples they'd placed in barrels filled with straw after the harvest. Below the frost line in the ground, they'd be as fresh as ever. Smiling in satisfaction, he called to Alex. When the young man came, Duncan whispered orders to retrieve the precious apples.

When Alex returned a short time later with two youths carrying baskets laden with apples, Duncan rose to meet them.

"Thank you, Alasdair." He called to the youngsters. "Come quickly." Passing each child an apple, he said, "Take one to every person inside the Hall." They scampered off in all directions delivering apples. They returned to fetch more from the baskets and raced back to hand them out, squealing with delight.

Several young men gathered near the hearth and the ladies at their sewing. Catherine watched as they used their knives with painstaking care to keep the skin intact. Some swore when peelings broke. Laughing at her puzzled expression, Duncan leaned forward to explain, "They try to peel it so the whole skin comes off at once, not breaking."

"Why?"

"If they toss it over their shoulder and glance around quickly, they shall see their true love."

Catherine looked dubious.

"Care to try it? Or are you coward?"

With the gauntlet thrown, Catherine had every intention of peeling the apple and keeping the skin intact. Not because of his silly tale, but to prove she could do it. Reaching into her belt for the jeweled knife he'd given her, she wondered why Duncan challenged her. Concentrating on the apple, she took her time and peeled it perfectly. A smile crossed her face. She'd done it!

She looked at the peel in her hand and wondered what to do with it. Oh, why not? Allowing herself no time to think further, she tossed the peel behind her. Surprised to hear a sudden burst of giggling children, she turned to look over her shoulder. Duncan stood there with the peel between finger and thumb. His smile turned into a wide grin as he passed it to one of the children.

Catherine's smile faded. Why would he tell her that story? He had to know she'd rise to the challenge. And he deliberately placed himself behind her, to be the one to catch it. Why? Upset, she started to shake. She wanted to believe in happily ever after. She had when she'd been a child, but now she knew better. But then why…? Was this Duncan's way of telling her something or did he just delight in torturing her?

"Oooh, you are maddening!" Catherine stared into Duncan's eyes. His never wavered. Suddenly she *wanted* to believe he cared.

So her husband wanted to play games. Well, she could do that. She'd turn the tables on him—only play it better. Rising from her chair, she decided to kiss him and bedamn the consequences. For once she'd be brave enough to take the risk. She walked toward him. She touched his face with her hand, her fingers trembling.

Catherine pressed her body to his, then brushed his lips with hers. She whispered, "Now would be a really good time to take me to our bedchamber."

"I dunnae need a second invitation." Wrapping his arm around her waist, he guided her toward the stairway.

Meghan came out of her bedchamber and appeared at the head of the staircase. She held her rag doll in her hand, but dropped it. Collapsing to the stone floor, her small body was as limp as the dollie.

Catherine screamed and ran to the staircase and knelt beside her, Duncan at her heels. She placed her hand on the young girl's forehead.

"She burns with fever."

Duncan scooped the tiny girl into his arms and rushed to her room. Catherine stripped off the child's clothes while instructing, "Moisten cloths. We must cool her down. Duncan, go outside to gather snow. Once it melts, I can use it to sponge her down."

Despite their efforts, by evening Meghan was delirious. Duncan paced his daughter's room and despaired, "I feel inadequate. Give me a sword and an enemy. A sick daughter I cannae control."

A thought struck him. Surely his father hadn't felt the same when he'd been sick. Could that possibly be why...? Nay!

Hours turned into days and half the Hall's occupants fell to the spreading illness. With so many clansmen brought low by fever and stomach pains, Catherine set up a communal sick room belowstairs, trying to contain the illness. Concerned for his people, Duncan tore himself away from his daughter's bedside vigil to help her set up more pallets.

Shortly after returning to Meggie's room, Angus knocked on the door. "I must speak with Duncan."

The two men stepped into the hallway and spoke in hushed tones. When Duncan returned, he crossed to the arrow slits. Catherine followed. "Duncan?"

"Sad news. Elderly people from the village succumbed to the fever and three of Father's villeins died." He rubbed his hand up her arm and looked as if he'd say something.

When Catherine saw his bloodshot eyes, she ordered, "To bed with you, husband."

Duncan grumbled, "Nay, I am fine." Even as he said the words, he doubled over in pain, holding fast to his stomach. "Och, it feels like someone tosses a caber into my belly."

"Oh, aye. Fine as a newborn lamb," she huffed, fighting the edge of panic. "Off with you, before you collapse like our Meggie."

Duncan smiled despite the pains. Was that a burr he heard in his lovely wife's words? But what warmed his heart even more was her calling Meggie *theirs*. "Nay, my shrew wife, I cannae leave our daughter. She needs me."

His beautiful wife exhaled her frustration. "Then there is only one thing to do." Turning, she called out, "Angus, Alex, help me move Meggie into our chamber. I shall tend stubborn father and daughter together." She wrapped her arms around her husband to help him upstairs and Duncan thought some of the warmth running through his fevered body might actually be pleasure. If she wished him well, she must no longer wish to be rid of him.

Perhaps he made progress.

Days and nights ran together as Catherine numbly ran up and down the stairs tending people, pushing herself far beyond endurance. Exhausted, Catherine sat, half leaning on the bed as she bathed Duncan with ice water, fearful she'd get chilblains from the icy liquid used to try and break the fever.

"May I have a drink?" Meghan croaked.

"Meggie!" Catherine cried with delight, feeling the child's head, now cool to the touch. "Praise the saints. You are better."

She fetched Meggie some water, relieved color returned to the child's pale cheeks. Returning to her husband, she placed the back of her hand to his forehead, lingering to stroke his cheek. "What I would not give to feel you cool as well." Instead, his body ravaged with fever.

Deep into the night, Catherine sat beside him and moistened his brow while others slept. Her heart broke when he hallucinated.

"I love you," he said, then moaned again in pain.

Catherine thought her heart would break. 'Twas only his fevered state that made him mumble words she wanted to believe with all her heart. To do so would be folly. If only he meant those words. She'd not let herself believe them, even knowing she loved him. *Especially knowing she loved him.*

These past weeks he seemed happy. Oh, why hadn't he given their marriage a chance when first they met? She knew the answer only too well. He hated everything English. No matter how much she wanted the words to be true, a man didn't fight a foe and suddenly forget the woman he married is of their blood.

He sobbed like a child. "Da, dunnae leave me here. Come back."

Catherine soothed his brow, but he continued to weep.

"Da, I am sorry I have been sick. Take me home."

He tossed and turned, unable to rest.

"*Athair*, please dunnae leave me!"

Catherine lay beside him and wrapped her arms around his heated body. *How can I stop his torment?* She closed her eyes to plead with God.

Quieted by Catherine's ministrations, Duncan calmed, only to begin thrashing about again. "Laird MacGhillechearr, please dunnae beat me. Nay! I promise I shall ne'er drop the saddle again. I but felt weak from my illness. I willnae…Nay!"

This must be what Tamara intimated when they'd met at Castle Glenshee. Her strong, brave husband vividly remembered being abandoned and abused. No wonder he hated his father. Could she chase away shadows of his past? As she lay beside him, holding him to her body to still his shivers, she determined to try.

"Shh, Duncan. Naught can harm you now. Rest."

For hours she held him, whispering soothing words into his ear and placing moist cloths on his brow. She wept relief when Duncan, too, grew better. Being such a strong man, always pushing himself in the lists, he fought the illness off faster than most.

She mentioned nothing of his fever dreams. He'd be shamed if he thought he'd revealed something he perceived as weakness. Her husband was too proud to let that happen. Nevertheless, she'd set her mind to ridding him of ghosts of his past and she had every intention of seeing that through, no matter how long or hard the task proved.

Catherine concentrated her efforts on the room downstairs as people continued to fall ill. To her relief, a similar amount recovered. God blessed them and they'd lost no one in the Hall, although too many people had died in the village and at the castle.

What seemed like endless days later, Angus entered the sick room to see if any were well enough to partake broth Cook prepared. Catherine reached for the cup, but it dropped from her grasp. She sat with a small thud as if her legs wouldn't hold her.

"My Lady!" he gasped. "The fever is upon you." Angus spun on his heel, calling from the hallway, "Duncan! Lady Catherine is ill."

Duncan rushed into the room. He paused at the doorway, his eyes taking in his sick wife. Moving to her, he knelt on one knee. Running his hand over her cheek, he nearly flinched from how hot she felt. "How long have you been ill?"

Her eyes glazed, she tried to answer, but couldn't speak.

Sweeping her into his arms, a chilling fear filled his heart, as cold as Catherine's fever was hot.

He headed upstairs to place her on the very bed where she'd tended him. Fighting tears, he asked, "Angus, have snow brought and melted. I feared this might happen. She pushed herself too hard caring for the rest of us."

Now it was his turn to care for her.

She tossed and turned for days.

No matter what herbs people gave Duncan to try,

her fever didn't break. Reaching the point of desperation, he mumbled, "Damnation, woman if you even think to die, I vow I shall kill you myself." He couldn't lose her. He knew she didn't believe him when he told her he cared, but he did. That thought scared him to death.

The following days found clansmen mourning as they buried loved ones. Duncan came inside from helping them, then headed upstairs to his bedchamber and sat on the edge of the bed.

Would his beautiful young wife die? Nay, he'd not let her. "Fight, Catherine," he pleaded in a broken voice. He simply couldn't lose this stubborn woman. He needed her far more than he'd thought possible—far more than he cared to admit.

"Please fight. I need you to stay with me."

# Chapter Nineteen

When Catherine finally opened her eyes, Duncan felt as if an anvil had been lifted from his chest. The footprint in the ashes had been correct, but it hadn't taken his precious Catherine or Meghan. He'd been given a second chance with them both.

He spent Catherine's recovery regaling her about the Auld Ways, reveling in her reaction to his lore. When well enough to begin rebuilding her strength, he took her hand and drew her toward the outside doorway. "People believe a cloud in the shape of a bull shall cross the sky this morn, the direction it travels foretells our clan's fortune."

Catherine laughed. "Recently people were on their knees thanking God for allowing them to survive the malaise, now they scry the sky to see what direction a *cloud* travels? I misdoubt I shall ever understand."

Duncan smiled, pleased she felt well enough to jest, the sound of her laughter music to his ears. "Mayhap, woman, but outside with you now so we may see these ancient auguries." He patted her on her bottom as he moved her gently outside.

"See *what*?"

"Divinings," he clarified.

In the bailey, elderly men craned their necks to peer

at the heavens. Catherine turned to Duncan. "What do they think they see?"

Duncan drew her close, pressed her back to his chest. "See that cloud? It travels east, so we shall have a verra good year."

Catherine was in front of him so he couldn't see her face, but he knew exactly what she'd do — roll her eyes, pull her mouth to the right side and sigh. Och, his bonnie wife was so predictable, so precious.

He took her hand. "Let us walk. You need to rebuild your strength. Candlemas is our Festival of Lights, so I hope you feel well enough to go with me later to our torchlight processional around our fields."

"Why?" Puzzlement crossed her face.

"Why do I want you with me?"

"Why have a procession?"

"To purify the ground for spring planting."

"Everything is covered with snow."

"We bless the fields for later. I keep forgetting you were reared in a large town. It seems you have been here forever." He pressed his lips to the back of her neck. "You belong at Cray Hall."

Hope flared in her eyes, but died just as quickly. She jerked her head away to hide her longing.

*But he'd seen.*

He pretended he hadn't. "February second is St. Brìghde's feast day, the Celtic goddess of fire and hearth. Heard you of her?" The quirk of her brow told him she thought it a daft subject. "The list she's known for is lengthy, but the main thing is blessings she gives women set to marry. Women bear her name on their wedding day."

Catherine cocked her head in question.

"They are called brides."

A bewildered expression crossed her face. "Is that true, Duncan MacThomas, or do you spin tales?"

"'Tis true — and speaking of brides..." His expression sobered as he stared into her beautiful face. "I am late telling you this, but you were a beautiful bride on our wedding day."

Before Catherine could utter a word, he drew her into his arms. He kissed her in hopes of making her knees go wobbly, kissed her in hopes of reaching her heart.

Catherine knew he didn't want to be married to his English wife, yet he continually chose to be close to her. Would she ever know his true feelings? When he held her and deepened his kiss, she didn't care if she understood or not. She wanted to feel his strength.

Duncan brushed the lock of hair from her brow, a gesture he'd made a hundred times, but she pressed back against him, needing that physical bond. Why should a simple kiss overwhelm her, make her feel so much? He made her want — need — him so much, the force was bedeviling.

Duncan reined back, breathing heavily. He grabbed Catherine's hand and pulled her behind him. "If we see the sun this day, winter is over, but if it stays hidden behind clouds, more winter comes."

How could he do that? 'Twas most disconcerting. He continued with his lore as if naught passed between them. Only his labored breaths — and the very visible evidence beneath his kilt — belied the fact he'd been as affected as she.

Well, if the blasted man could do it, she could be just as nonchalant. "This is how you decide spring is upon us?"

"Tis an honorable way to foretell the weather." Catherine shivered and he wrapped his arm around her shoulder. "Let us be away to the Hall. I dunnae want you chilled. Whilst you were fevered, you hallucinated about being in the maze. I dunnae wish that to happen again." He hesitated. "I hate mazes. Something bad happened to me in one once, too. I almost..." He stopped, unable to continue.

Catherine looked at him expectantly. "What happened?"

He shook his head. "I dunnae wish to talk about it." He urged her toward their home, forestalling her questions.

* * *

Nearing the end of March, Duncan received a summons to Castle Glenshee. There was nothing to do but go. With foreboding, he told the courier, "I shall be there on the morrow."

He found himself impatient with these continual interferences. Why did his father desire contact with him now? What did he expect after having ignored him all those years? Did he think Duncan would forget?

The next morn Alexander and he entered Glenshee's Great Hall unannounced. He wanted the interview over with quickly and had no intention of staying. Now that Meggie was home where she belonged, there was no reason to tarry in the abode that held so many painful memories, so many regrets.

MacThomaidh entered the Hall. He walked slowly, seeming to age every time Duncan saw him.

"Good," the old man announced without preamble. "You came."

"I had a choice?" Duncan grumbled.

"One always has choices in life, son," MacThomaidh responded sadly. He turned away and sat at the nearest table. "Longshanks' forces are headed to Stirling. A messenger arrived with the news yestermorn. I would go myself, but we both know that would be folly. I am too auld. It pains me to admit that. I am a proud man."

Duncan's eyes closed as he accepted the inevitable, knowing his father's request—demand—before he voiced it.

"You must lead our clansmen."

Just when Duncan wanted to remain home, needed to be home, Edward again challenged Scotland. How many summers must they endure his coming?

"You swore fealty to Longshanks, ordered me to a wed a woman he chose, yet now you demand I fight him?"

"Figured you would ask that." MacThomaidh's lips quirked in a half smile, but quickly sobered. "Stirling must not fall. The castle's location is too important to Scotland. Situated as it is between the Highlands and Lowlands, whoever holds Stirling holds the country. We must hold it."

As much as it irked him, he had to admit his father was right. Stirling must not fall.

Duty would play havoc with the relationship he so

tentatively forged with his beautiful wife. On the ride home, he pondered how to break the tides to her. At times she seemed to accept their life, others she stubbornly clung to his foolish actions at their wedding. He'd never considered how deeply those actions would hurt her.

Catherine sat, finishing a new shift for Meghan. The instant she saw his face, she jumped up from her chair, the raiment forgotten at her feet.

"Duncan, what is wrong? You have the pallor of a ghost."

"Naught is wrong." He headed to the ale barrel.

Catherine followed. "Do not naysay me."

Taking a drink, Duncan put his tankard down. As she placed a hand on his upper arm, he admitted, "I have been summoned to fight."

Catherine barely caught her breath. "Fight?"

"Longshanks plans to lay siege to Stirling. We cannae let it fall to the English. Positioned as it is, if it falls, all of Scotland falls."

"Why must you fight?" She backed out of his arms and walked to the hearth, wrung her hands. "Please do not go."

He walked to where she stood by the fire. She tried to turn away, hide tears streaming down her face. He stopped her by putting his finger beneath her chin.

"Dinnae turn away, Cat. Tell me what is wrong."

"I cannot. You would think me silly."

Duncan drew her to him. He wrapped his arms around her, rubbing his right hand down her back, waiting for her to tell him what bothered her.

Looking into his eyes, Catherine blurted, "I had a dream."

When she didn't elaborate, Duncan urged. "And?"

She threw herself back into his arms and sobbed, "A foreshadowing of the future. I didn't tell you because I knew you would laugh."

He nuzzled his nose in her hair. "I am not laughing."

"A castle falls. Some strange monster, almost as tall as the castle throws boulders at it. I have never seen the likes of it before. Men scream in pain, trying to crawl to safety, trying to flee the stones crashing down around them. Blood...oh, so much blood. Everywhere." Eyes wide, she met his stare.

She shouldn't care what he did, shouldn't care if he left, but neither did she want him injured. She tried to tell herself she only worried for Meggie.

She knew it a lie.

"Dunnae worry. We shall be fine. We fought at Stirling before and won."

"It matters naught. Edward still comes."

Duncan frowned. "I dunnae like you hearing about—"

"War?" Catherine interrupted. "Death and war are reality, Duncan MacThomas. If you will not stay for me...you must stay for Meggie."

"Faugh, woman, dunnae put words in my mouth. I *must* leave. I have to fight for my country."

Catherine jerked away. She swiped the back of her fingers against her cheek to wipe away tears.

"I must pack some things. Come with me?"

"So you can bed me?" Catherine shot at him. "Nay!

If am not a good enough reason for you to stay, I'll not share your bed again. I want..." She paced the floor, stopped and glared, both angry and hurt. "'Tis clear what I want matters not."

Duncan knew not how to make it right. He was duty bound to fight for his country. 'Tis what men did—had to do.

"My heart." Moving a lock of hair from her face he tried to explain. "I dunnae leave because I want to."

"Do not call me my heart. Do not touch me!" Catherine angrily slapped at Duncan's hand before it could caress her cheek. "You think by bedding me or calling me some endearment you make everything okay. Well, not this time."

"Cat..."

"I will hear no more." She hiccupped, trying to stay her sobs. "I have this horrible feeling. Something shall go terribly wrong. I fear you will not come back this time, Duncan MacThomas. I know it. I told you what I saw in my dream. I saw a castle fall. Men lay all over—on the ground, the boulevard. Blood was everywhere."

"Catherine, that is nonsense. Stirling Castle is unassailable. It sits atop a mountain of rock."

"Stirling Castle be damned! You fight and chase Edward away. He just comes again next spring." Turning on him, Catherine beat her fists against his chest. "Your daughter needs you." She sobbed, "We need you."

"I will be back, my heart," Duncan promised quietly.

"Nay!" Sobbing, her plea had fallen on deaf ears. She pulled away and ran up the stairs.

Did she truly care about him? Would she care if he

was gone? Merciful saints, how he wanted that to be true. Following her, he entered their chamber. He drew a cloth over the arrow loop, darkening the room, then turned and lit a candle, its pale flame casting dancing shadows against the far wall. He wanted it dark, just not so dark he couldn't see her at all. A smile playing across his lips, Duncan determined this would be a night she remembered.

He watched her shaking her head. Going to her, he trailed his fingertips lightly along her tear streaked cheek. He eased her to the edge of the bed.

Sitting on the bed, he reached out, drawing her to him, but left her standing. Leaning back on his elbows, he watched the play of emotions on her face. How could this one wee woman so twist his heart? She didn't believe he wanted her and he'd done naught but try to show her how much he cared, how much he wanted her. Catherine was his, and he'd never let her go.

"I go to fight, Catherine. We won Stirling before. I hope we shall do the same this time."

Hesitating mere seconds to consider his answer, the barest hint of a smile crossed her face. She looked like she'd come to a decision.

Not taking her eyes from his, she unlaced her bodice. Inch by inch the material parted. A smile played over her mouth when his eyes widened as her breasts almost spilled out. Pausing, she licked her lips before sliding one side of the bodice back, exposing one breast.

She knew he was leaving the next day and she'd told him she felt something horrible would happen. She might not admit it to him, but she wanted this as much as he did. Duncan knew it to his soul.

Duncan's body jerked with crippling desire.

"Wife, are you trying to torment my weak and feeble body?" A smile spread on his face, feeling wolfish even to himself.

"Weak, feeble? I do not believe you are either of those, lord husband. The contradiction stands proud and tall beneath your kilt."

Leaning her head to the side, Catherine lifted her breast, the nipple showing her arousal. "As to whether I torment you, aye, husband, I am. Is it working?" She hesitated a moment before continuing, her lovely eyelashes fluttering, revealing her nervousness.

She removed her bodice from the other breast and Duncan nearly swallowed his tongue. He croaked, "Marginally."

Catherine crooked her eyebrow, placed her hands beneath her breasts, pushing them to prominence. She moved her thumb over one of the taut crests. "Marginally? This does not affect you?" She tilted her head. "That is a shame, because it makes me feel all strange inside when you touch me, stroke me, caress me." She stuttered.

Duncan smiled. His beautiful little temptress was trying to seduce him, but was nervous. Catherine turned sideways and wiggled her bottom so her gown slid the remaining distance to the floor. Her long hair hid only part of her from his view.

"Come here, Catherine," he growled hungrily.

She ignored him, bent to pick up her kirtle. His eyes shot to the dark triangle at the junction of her thighs. He had no doubt she could hear his ragged breathing.

As she came to the bed, the golden light of the candle behind her outlined her body. Duncan had meant to make this night memorable for her, but his wife had changed that. The image of her body, the curves, how the shadows caressed it, would be burned in his mind the entire time he had to be away. Oh aye, she'd done that apurpose.

He brought her down beside him on the bed and moved them both towards its center. Not taking his gaze from her eyes, he leaned on one arm and moved his free hand lightly over her body. He said nothing. Moving his hand from one breast to the other, he teased the tips until they hardened. She'd tormented him, now it was time for him to take the reins and drive his little wife mad with desire. He wanted to see her writhing with need, begging him to take her.

Catherine tried to turn so she could touch him as well, but Duncan stayed her movements.

"Nay, lady wife, you had your fun, now lie still and let me show you 'tisnae wise to torment your lord husband."

Moving closer, Duncan pressed his already firm manhood against her hip, a promise of things to come. When she squirmed beneath his ministrations, he kissed her. Her tongue mated with his. Duncan moaned. Or had the sound come from his Cat? His hand kneaded her breast, teasing the nipple while he claimed her mouth. Soon he moved his hand to her other breast and his lips teased the taut peak his hand just left. Her gasp sounded as needful as his had been moments earlier.

When her hand moved down to wrap around him, Duncan gave up all thoughts of prolonging this seduction. He would just have to love her again later. Moving over her, he opened her thighs with his knee. Positioning himself at her woman's opening, he nudged himself against her, but didn't enter.

"Duncan? Please…"

At her plea, he drove himself in, relishing the feel of her, the way her hips lifted to meet his. Oh aye, she was wet and ready. Duncan wanted to go slow, wanted to take every ounce of pleasure, but her body clenched around him, edging him on. Too soon his seed thundered through him and into her. Catherine screamed, following him over the edge of pleasure until they both collapsed. With barely any strength left, Duncan wrapped her into his arms and draped the woolen plaide over them. Wrapped in the comfort of each other's arms, they drowsed. Duncan stirred, Catherine's hair draped over his chest. She looked so peaceful lying beside him.

Peaceful? The little temptress had nearly milked him dry. He'd drifted off to sleep earlier, only to find his *innocent* wife lazily running her tongue down his stomach. And she hadn't stopped there! He'd quickly turned the tables on her. Starting at her lashes, he'd kissed his way to her nose, her mouth, her chin…continuing on, causing her to cry out time after time. He moved back up and entered her. His movements had been slow and sure and he took his time before bringing her again and again to her woman's release. Only when she cried out her pleasure one more time did he spill his seed into her. This time she slept.

Drawing the curtain on his bed aside, Duncan saw it was still dark. Time enough to love her one more time. He rolled over to whisper in her ear. "Cat? Wake up, my heart."

\* \* \*

The next morn Catherine came down the stairs, her eyes red. She walked out into the courtyard to see him readying his horse. Her lower lip quivered and her eyes pleaded for help.

Duncan glanced up, knowing he looked almost as bad as she. They'd slept little the night before, wanting to make each moment count. He had to leave, but knew he strained the frail bond they'd begun to forge.

He walked over to her and drew her into his arms. He'd already left his daughter crying in the Hall. He'd tried to explain what was happening while they broke their fast. She understood no better than Catherine.

"Catherine, dunnae do this. Please stop crying. I must leave, lass. My country needs me."

Catherine threw her arms around his neck. She mumbled something, but Duncan couldn't be certain what she'd said. Surely she hadn't really said, "I need you, too."

He was about to ask her to repeat it, when Angus called out, "Son, we had best leave. 'Twillnae get easier with time."

Duncan pulled Catherine close and squeezed her tightly. Dear God, he didn't want to leave. He started to pull away, but Catherine held fast, her body shaking with tears.

"Nay! Please do not leave. I…Meggie needs you."

"I must go. You know that."

"You aren't just using the battle as an excuse to leave again?"

He tilted her head up and lowered his mouth to hers, brushing his lips lightly over hers. "You know better than that. I leave because I must." He repeated what he'd said the day before. "I shall return."

Setting her away, he strode to his horse and mounted, praying his words would be true.

Riding off, Duncan brushed his hand against his face to clear his eyes. He was having trouble seeing. Blast, a man didn't cry. He had to help save Stirling Castle.

Was he ruining the fragile thread that had just begun to bloom between them? He glanced over his shoulder and drew in a breath. He shouldn't have looked back. Catherine had run to the edge of the wall. She grasped its edge, her body heaving with sobs, but she stood tall and proud—his warrior woman. His every instinct was to turn and go back, to hold her in his arms the rest of the day, make love to her all night. But he couldn't do either. If he went back now, he'd never leave.

And his country needed him. Curse Edward Longshanks for interfering again.

# Chapter Twenty

Duncan's forces arrived at Stirling, joining men from all over Scotland. In good cheer, men roasted a boar. Duncan stood with Grant, recalling the battle they'd fought here side by side in 1297, history revisited. Could they win again?

As anticipated, Edward wasn't long in coming. The brilliant scarlet standards with golden leopard had been visible a league away. Duncan and Grant stood on the battlements looking down at sheer chaos. For a sennight they'd watched tents being erected and the valley filled with wagons and horses, heavy horse of war, hobelars, siege engines and carts carrying huge boulders.

When the Scots refused to surrender, the mighty engines began pounding away at the ancient fortress.

Duncan rubbed his neck in exhaustion. "By the saints, I tire."

Grant nodded. "Aye, I havenae slept since they arrived. How can anyone sleep with those bloody siege engines pounding away every day? The whole castle reverberates with constant slamming—twelve bloody monsters at last count."

There was little to do but endure. They slept in shifts, deep in the caves under Sterling Castle. Only a small respite from the endless pounding.

Still, few found peace as each day their situation worsened.

* * *

Catherine sat beneath the huge copper beech tree. She was tired, having not slept well the past few nights. Strange images had interrupted her sleep and she'd been afraid to drift off again. She'd sit and rest awhile before going back inside the Hall.

A strange lightness enveloped her. She felt herself drifting. *She saw the ground below, clouds above. What was happening? Where was she? Suddenly she saw Duncan. Was he home? Nay, he climbed to the allure of a castle she'd never seen, and there was Ian.*

*"Duncan, Ian, what are you doing here? Where are we?"*

*They didn't hear. Instead, Ian surveyed his long time friend and frowned. "Have you eaten this day? You look like hell."*

*"As do you," Duncan quipped. Pausing, he seemed to be thinking.*

*Catherine worried. Had he eaten? He looked so tired.*

*"The last meal I actually remember was the roasted boar we had before the English arrived. When we still foolishly thought this battle would be over in nae time."*

*Catherine eased closer. She needed to make certain he ate. Silly man. It was just like him to think of everyone else before himself. "Duncan, come with me. Let us find the kitchen. You must eat." They didn't appear to hear her.*

*"Damnation," Ian swore, drawing Catherine's attention to the crenellations. He watched as Longshanks approached on his daily ride to survey the walls, making certain to stay out of reach of any arrows. "The man is in his sixties, yet rides here*

*daily to harass us."*

*Slender, almost bony in appearance, the king's height was accentuated by his long legs. Edward's snowy mane of white hair blew behind him in the breeze. He wore his scarlet surcoat over his armour, three golden leopards upon his chest.*

*Someone catapulted a large stone down toward the king, causing his horse to throw him. He rose and brushed the dirt from his clothes before remounting his steed. Angus grumbled, "What will it take to kill him? Again the bloody devil walks away unscathed, rubbing our noses in the fact he has us trapped."*

*Catherine watched the arrogant king and wondered how she ever thought him in the right.  He didn't really want Scotland. Certainly didn't need it. He just wanted the feel of them under his thumb, wanted to grind them into the earth until they begged his mercy. Didn't he understand these Scots wouldn't do that?*

*Grant stepped behind Duncan. Peering over the ledge, he groused, "Look at the bloody devil. 'Tis his daily tweaking of our noses. Well, I for one have had enough." Reaching behind him, he grabbed an arrow from his quiver and nocked it. He raised his bow arm, drew back the string until his thumb was against his jawbone and his index finger almost touched the corner of his mouth, just as his father taught him.*

*Catherine saw what he meant to do. "Nay!" she screamed, placing her hand on Duncan's arm. "Duncan, stop him! Know you not Edward will only make things harder for you?" Why didn't he pay attention? Why didn't they listen to her?*

*Taking a breath, Grant aimed and released the arrow, aiming for Longshanks. He let out a shout when it went through Edward's surcoat and lodged into his saddle. "Fires of hell, I missed."*

*Furious, Longshanks reined his horse back, releasing a string of expletives as he grabbed his leg. He looked up toward the battlements and shook his fist. "You shall pay for this you bloody heathens. You shall rot in hell before I let you escape. You just sealed your doom! I shall see you gutted and hanged."*

*Grant turned to Duncan, his face somber. "Och, it felt so good to do it, but I fear I've cast our fate. Longshanks will raise the dragon standard now, see us all fodder for ravens."*

*Duncan sighed. "You think we werenae before?"*

*Catherine sobbed, "I tried to warn you. Tried to stop you. Why would you not hear?"*

*The men turned to walk away. "Duncan!" she shouted. "Do not leave me here. Why won't you…?" Dear God nay! They don't see me. They cannot hear me. They…I…what is happening?*

Catherine screamed, the sound waking her in the garden. She was safe at home. If she was here, how had she seen Duncan?

Weapon drawn, Alex squatted beside her.

"Alex!" she sobbed. "I saw Duncan…"

"'Twas just a dream, my lady," Alex soothed, helping her rise. "I am sure our men fare well."

\* \* \*

Over several moons Duncan survived while Scotland's great castle was bombarded by siege engines of war. The English stripped lead from nearby kirk roofs, melting it down to round balls. They flung them from the trebuchet along with large boulders. Oftentimes, pots that were lit and flung at the castle exploded on impact.

He and fellow Scots valiantly fought back, but grew

weaker every day from lack of food and sleep. He only hoped he'd be blessed enough to return in one piece. He'd promised Catherine, after all.

*All I want is to be back with Catherine and Meggie*, he thought, fogged by exhaustion. *Bloody hell, at this point I'd even be willing to see Father again.* They'd wasted so much time arguing and hating each other — to what end? He could die any day now, and hating his father didn't seem to matter so much anymore. It hadn't changed anything, had nearly cost him Catherine's love.

Longshanks returned daily, taunting, always staying just out of reach. Grant stood on the boulevard and watched the pageantry. "I told you we were dead. His banneret flies the *dragon standard*, Edward's way of saying he gives us no quarter. He flew the same dread pennant before he sacked Berwick and before he let loose his dogs of war, putting nearly all to death — including Father."

Heartsick with worry, Catherine stood on the walkway atop Cray Hall, staring at the horizon. She blinked as the stinging wind brought tears to her eyes. *Duncan, where are you? Why haven't you returned? You promised.*

*A strange feeling overtook her. Lightheaded, once again she saw Duncan and Grant as clearly as if she were with them.*

*Grant bemoaned, "We lose ground every day. Bloody hell." He pointed to a barrel of oil. "They try to breach the curtain. Someone help me heat that."*

*"Aye," Duncan agreed, "and where is the molten lead others worked on earlier? Pour that down the machicolations."*

*Screams resounded as Englishmen were burned by the*

heated lead. Catherine leaned to peer through the crenellations, aghast at the carnage she saw below.

Bolstered by sounds of agony, Scots ran outside to fight the English garrison.

"Nay," Catherine shouted. "Do not go outside the wall." They paid her no heed. Why could no one hear her?

A shiver of dread coursed down her spine and her hand flew to her mouth. Nay, her mind screamed. Duncan was in trouble. Shouts from the battlement warned him to return. He needed her. She felt it, felt him. Tears streaming down her face, she reached her hand out and cried, "Duncan!"

Duncan paused, dizzy from exhaustion. He looked out over the horizon. Blinking disbelief, he saw Catherine in the distance. If he died here, would she ever forgive him? Ever believe he loved her true? She stretched out her hand to him and relief poured through him. Duncan reached for her...just a few more steps and he'd be with her. "Dunnae cry, *Mo Cridhe*." Two more steps. "I told you I would return." One more step. Mayhap if he leaned forward...

Grant grabbed him, looked at Duncan in shock. "Man, are you daft? You nearly fell through the crenellation."

Duncan stared at Grant in shock, looked around at his surroundings. He still stood on Stirling Castle's boulevard of the battlement. The bloody English were below hammering away at the castle. *But he'd seen Catherine.* She'd been real. He turned to Grant and placed his hand on his friend's arm. "I saw Catherine. I vow, she reached toward me. She called to me." He slammed his hand into the wall. "Bloody hell. Have I begun hallucinating?"

Grant rested his hand on Duncan's shoulder. "You think I dunnae dream of Tory? She is with me every breath I take."

Shaken, Duncan turned from his friend, walked down the steps and into the castle. He had to get some rest if he was to return home. Had Grant not been with him, he'd have fallen to his death. He smiled ruefully. At least the bloody English would have been deprived the joy of killing him. He headed into the castle caves, exhausted, hungry, yearning for home. He wondered how long this battle would continue. With little food, they couldn't hold out much longer.

* * *

Duncan leaned against the castle wall. "Why are we doing this when the Comyns and Bruce have sold out? We've been here nigh unto four full moons. I want to see my lady wife. The rest of Scotland goes home to their families."

Later Grant sat beside Duncan and whispered, "The food has run out."

Duncan snapped, "Dunnae you think my stomach rubbing against my backbone already knows that?" As Grant's eyes widened in surprise, Duncan caught himself. "Sorry, my friend. I dinnae mean to shout. I worry I shall die on this bloody rock and never see Cat again, never have the chance to tell her I am sorry for being such a bloody fool, never get to tell her...I love her more than life."

"I fear the same."

"And for what?" A sob caught in Duncan's throat, at

the end of his tether. They'd nearly run out of water. He was so thirsty his voice cracked and came out a hoarse croak. "Why are we still here?"

When their commander made his rounds, Duncan stopped Oliphant and demanded, "William, why are we here instead of home with our loved ones? Every noble in Scotland has gone unto Edward's peace. We started with seven score men and have only sixty left. We have no food, little water. We shall die, whether from starvation or from enemy arrow. All we have accomplished is to give the Comyns time to broker a better deal with Longshanks for Scottish nobles. Only Wallace still holds out. 'Tis time to end it, my friend. Whether we admit it or not, we have lost." Murmurs of agreement spread throughout the battlements.

The time had come for surrender. The following morn Oliphant sent word to Edward. "We surrender if granted our lives." Duncan joined men gathered at the wall to wait for word. The end was near. *Dear God, nae matter what happens, please let Catherine know I love her.*

When word came, a wave of horror swept through the tattered warriors. Edward refused, wanting an unconditional surrender. Duncan groaned, "I am not shocked with Longshanks' ruthlessness. The sack of Berwick lives forever in my mind. This is nae different."

Oliphant sank to the ground. "Longshanks asked me at the beginning to surrender. I refused. This is his way of paying me back." He turned to those gathered. Most barely had enough strength to sit and lean against the castle wall. "I am sorry. I thought we would win. My error in judgment cost us dearly. We are nae match for whatever Edward plans to throw at us on the morrow."

The next morn Edward unleashed his final horror.

Catherine tossed and turned, alone in her large bed, afraid to fall asleep for fear she'd again *see* what was happening at Stirling. Every time she drifted off, she saw Duncan and the war. She'd finally quit telling Duncan's men for fear they'd think her daft. Mayhap she was. Who in their right mind watched her husband fight a battle daily? Saw him wounded, hungry, tired, and could do naught about it. Strained to the point of exhaustion, Catherine surrendered to sleep.

*The English garrison brought forward the Warwolf while Edward laughed and raised his arm. "Defend yourselves as best you can." He lowered his arm to begin the onslaught, a vicious act of carnage.*

*Sweat running down her face, Catherine screamed. This was the monster she'd warned Duncan about! She had to save him.*

*Standing on the ramparts, Duncan and his fellow warriors stared in shock at the fifty foot beast that stood before them with its huge counterweight and mighty beam.*

*They banded together to fight – or die.*

*"Nay, my heart, do not think that." Catherine willed her thoughts to Duncan. "Come back to me. Come back…"*

*Boulder after boulder pummeled the castle. Screams of pain were heard as chunks of wall broke off and slammed into them. To a man, the Scots, battered and wounded, battled on and on.*

*Catherine saw Angus fall to the ground, blood streaming down his leg. A boulder crashed through the wall where Duncan and Grant stood.*

Catherine screamed! Shot up in bed, the linens twisted around her. *Duncan! Dear God, please protect Duncan. Bring him home safely.*

\* \* \*

Duncan held his breath as Oliphant again offered their surrender to Edward, the bloodthirsty man finally accepting. Despite previous threats, he didn't kill remaining survivors. Obviously thinking the thirty men too weak to fight further, he proved lenient. Even more to Duncan's surprise, the only person Longshanks ordered seized, made prisoner, and taken to the Tower of London was Oliphant.

Untrusting of Edward's peace, Duncan and others seized the opportunity and slipped into the dark of night. Starving, exhausted, and injured, bone chilling rain poured down on them as they struggled to climb hills that would lead them away from Longshanks and home to their loved ones. Warm tears filled his eyes, mixing with the icy rain as he looked to the heavens, wondering if they'd escape. *Is this one of Edward's cruel jests that we fight our way to the top only to find the English soldiery waiting there?* The night nearly spent, he staggered to the safety of nearby trees, remembering to stay in the shadows.

Hearing his name whispered, he saw Grant several yards away, limping, but making his way toward him. Ready to drop where they stood, the two men couldn't help but rush to each other. They gripped hands in a handshake and clapped each other on the back, squeezing each other tightly. Both laughing and crying.

They'd survived. Acknowledged God spared them.

One by one they located other survivors.

Duncan heard sounds of the English searching for them. "Hide in that nearby cave." He and Grant dragged branches in front of the entrance, requiring every ounce of their failing strength. Safely hidden, they silently prayed for God's cloak of protection.

The next day they found Angus near a burn trying to fetch a drink of water. Duncan and Grant treated his injuries. "Och, not only did the bone break when part of the castle wall catapulted into his thigh," Duncan groaned, "a jagged edge gashed through the skin." He turned to Ian and Grant. "Hold him whilst I reset the bone." He mumbled, "Forgive me," then slammed his fist into Angus' chin. Two days later, it was a sad parting when Grant and Ian broke off to head east toward Drummond Castle. "Good bye, my friend," Duncan said before he and Angus proceeded north toward Cray Hall.

Though limping and in excruciating pain, the elderly man tried to keep pace with Duncan. He'd refused to let Duncan carry him on a litter of twigs tied with vines. To elude recapture, they traveled only by moon's light. Duncan's legs nearly gave out when he finally sighted Cray Hall's stronghold. He was home. Suddenly, people streamed out the gate, crying their greetings. His eyes hungrily looked for Catherine. He was glad when Alex relieved him of Angus' weight. Others helped them inside the stone walls.

Everyone rushed up, patting him on the back and hugging him, dozens asking questions all at once. Still, he sought Catherine. He'd seen her beautiful face many times. It was her vision that kept him going.

"Duncan! Thank the Blessed Lord, you're alive." Tears of joy streamed down her face as she rushed headlong into his arms. She kissed his face and wrapped her arms around his chest, squeezing hard.

When he winced in pain, she stepped back, taking in his appearance, seeing the chest she just hugged was hardly that of the man who'd left in April.

Then her soft eyes shifted to notice men gingerly helping Angus to a chair.

"You have been gone so long." Catherine glanced around the Hall, question lighting her face  when she realized only Angus was there of the men that left with him. She took Duncan's arm and helped him to a chair. Holding the chair's arms, he settled into it heavily.

"Duncan? Are the injured outside?" The question turned to fear as she glanced toward the main door. "My dream. 'Twas right was it not?"

"Nae one else survived," he admitted sadly, leaning heavily against the table. "We lost Stirling."

Behind him, women wailed.

Too tired to move, he turned to Alex. "Praise the saints most of you remained to guard our land." He tried to catch his breath, but it hurt to breathe. "We must send word to Castle Glenshee. MacThomaidh must be told our men perished."

"Grant?"

He knew she was terrified to hear the answer. "Injured. He and Ian survived. Everyone else perished. Once again, Clans MacThomas and Drummond sacrificed their life and breath to Scotland's cause. I dunnae know why God spared us."

220

Tears streamed down Catherine's face. The stress more than she could handle, she looked ready to pass out.

Duncan caught Alex's eye and nodded toward her. He was so weary he couldn't move. *Dear God, I know I dunnae talk to You as often as I should. Thank You for bringing me back to my Cat.*

Alex rushed to her and quickly lowered his lady to a chair.

She roused herself from her anguish. "Worry not about me. We must care for Duncan and Angus."

She faced Duncan, but directed her words to Alex. "Take my husband to our chamber. I shall tend him there." She turned toward Angus. "Take Angus to—"

"See to Duncan, kind lady. Angus shall be well cared for," Dohmnall assured her.

Duncan leaned heavily on Alex and Colin. Fearing his wounds had festered, the image of Andrew de Moray sprang to mind. Would he die now as Andrew had, cut down in the prime of his life? If he did, would Catherine leave and remarry? The thought of her in another's arms was not a thought he liked.

Duncan's throat worked to swallow the pain. Had he fought his way home, just to lose it all?

# Chapter Twenty-One

Alex pressed, "M'lady, we havenae the luxury of time. His wounds poison."

Catherine hesitated less than a breath to make a decision. "I shall open the wounds."

The two men eyed her warily. "*You* shall lance the festering?" Alex queried.

Catherine nodded, grimness molding her mouth. "How difficult can it be?"

"But—"

"My lady wife shall tend my wounds," Duncan asserted, cutting off further discourse. "I trust her to do so. The healer tends Angus."

Her eyes never left Duncan's, thanking him for his trust. "I shall do whatever it takes to see you well."

Duncan nodded.

Later, Catherine thought, *I should have called the healer. 'Twas folly to believe it a simple matter.* She'd almost gagged over his injuries. Alex and Euan held him down. She dug down and endured, fearing she might pass out.

The healer cackled when she inspected Catherine's work. "You did well, lass, though you look a might peaked. Sight of rotting wounds more than you bargained for, eh?" She perused his naked form. "Och, your husband is a braw and bonnie lad. Small wonder you wish him hale and hearty."

Catherine blushed and Duncan scolded weakly, "Leave be, Maddie. My lady wife has been through an ordeal this day." He held Catherine's hand and linked fingers.

Maddie walked to the hearth. Drawing worts from the cloth bag hung from string twined at her waist, she spread them onto a cloth, folded it, then saturated it with hot water. "I use woad to staunch the bleeding." She crossed to Duncan, slapped the hot poultice onto his leg.

"Fires of Hell, Maddie. What means of torture be this?"

Catherine gasped and bent to remove it.

Maddie shoved her hand aside. "Leave be. You want him healed or rotting?"

"Healed," Catherine answered, aghast, "but that hurts him. 'Tis hot."

"Of course 'tis hot. 'Twould do nae good otherwise." She quirked a brow at Duncan, but voiced her comments to Catherine. "Are you saying our braw laird cannae take a wee bit of pain?"

Outraged, Catherine exclaimed, "Wee bit of pain? He survived a horrible battle. He—"

Duncan raised his fingers to her lips to stay her torrent of words. "Dinnae fash, *Mo Chride*."

His eyes locked with Catherine's. "She knows exactly what I have been through. Her son was with me at Stirling." He nodded at Maddie. "Continue your torture, auld woman."

* * *

The man was driving her daft.

"I want to go down the stairs, woman. I am fine."

"Fine? You have broken bones, festered wounds, and have barely eaten in a sennight. You are *not* fine," she bullied, rather than letting him see her upset.

He gave her his sexiest smile. "Aye, but you care for me so skillfully I dare naught but get well."

"You are right," she argued. "'Tis for me to say whether you get out of that bed or not. And I say not!"

The door opened and Catherine rushed to shoo his men. "Out, the lot of you. Duncan rests."

"We must see him," Dohmnall said.

"I give up." She threw up her hands in resignation. "By all means, come. See that he lives still—through sheer stubbornness."

"Lady Catherine," Siobhán said, entering the room and crossing to the table to refill the ewer and basin, "you must rest. You weary yourself."

"I shall rest when he fares well," Catherine challenged. "Until then, I go nowhere."

Duncan groused. "My lady wife is too stubborn to listen to reason. 'Tis a flaw I havenae yet corrected."

Siobhán teased, "Aye, 'tis one of the reasons you love her."

To ease the embarrassment of her friend's words, Catherine busied herself with changing the foul-smelling poultices.

Duncan's eyes followed her every move, though he conversed with his men on clan business.

Alex winked at his laird and told those gathered, "We should leave. Duncan is in fine hands."

Duncan caressed her arm when she brought him

water to drink. Every time she got near, he touched her, skimmed his fingers over her cheek, her hand, the end of her braid as it hung over one shoulder.

Finally, his eyes drifted closed.

She wanted to touch him, but feared she'd hurt him. Instead, each night she waited until he slept, then skimmed her hands over his arms, his chest, his cheek. She told herself she only did it to ensure he was fine, had no fever. What a lie!

"My wounds itch, wife. Means they heal. 'Tis time you rest. Come lie beside me." He opened his eyes and patted the bed. "Or want you I should pretend to sleep so you can stroke me?"

"You…oh…" Shocked that he was awake, she stepped back.

Catching her off guard, Duncan pulled her down so she sank to the bed. He drew her close and brushed his lips over hers, soft as a feather. He wrapped his arms around her, held her close, then whispered, "Sleep, stubborn lass."

Despite her body reacting from being against him, she felt her eyes drift shut, safe in his strong arms.

\* \* \*

At sennight's end, Tamara arrived. Sobbing, she flung herself into her brother's arms as he sat in bed.

"No need for tears, wee sister. I fare well," he assured with a grunt. "Or was until you reopened my wounds."

She drew back, looking horrified, but Duncan smiled. "I tease. I could be below stairs, only my vixen wife willnae let me go down. She holds me prisoner."

Tamara eyes were full of womanly wisdom. "Because she loves you."

Catherine's mouth dropped open, aghast.

Duncan's gaze settled on Tamara, doubt showing in his eyes. Catherine's love was something he could only hope for.

Tamara interrupted the uneasy silence. "Da is concerned for your welfare."

"While I misdoubt that, tell our sire I fare fine." Immediately, he remembered the feelings he'd had when he thought he'd die. Had their quarrel gone on long enough?

After Tamara's departure, Duncan returned to seducing his wife. It was difficult to charm Catherine when he barely had enough strength to sit, but he determined to try. It was important to reestablish the closeness they'd achieved before he left for Stirling. He grabbed her wrist to pull her down beside him.

"Duncan! What are—?"

He silenced her with a kiss.

"Duncan, you are injured." She tried to pull away. He wrapped his arms around her and held her fast. "We cannot—"

His tongue mated with hers, stilling her protests. When he hiked her skirt up and caressed her, Catherine forgot to argue.

With a throaty sigh she asked, "Are you sure...?"

Duncan groaned in frustration, drew back to meet her eyes. "I thought of you day and night, Cat. 'Tis the only thing that kept me alive." He pressed his hand to the side of her face, touching her gently before running his fingertips down her cheek and neck.

"Duncan MacThomas, you have no idea how I fretted. I dreamt over and over of a horrible battle and feared you'd not return."

"My men told me. I needed you at Stirling, *Mo Cridhe*. I need you now. Make love to me."

Her lashes fluttered, revealing her nervousness. Did she fear she'd hurt his wounds? He didn't care. He'd waited so long.

Removing her clothes, he tossed them on the floor. Gently he kissed her face, her neck. He reverently cupped both breasts, her nipples tightening in response. He lowered his mouth, drawing one then the other into his mouth. With a restless moan, she pressed closer. He ran his fingertips down her arms, over her ribs, up again to her breasts. Lowering his mouth to one breast, he cupped the other with his hand.

"Now, my heart. Show you want me, yearn for me." He shifted, placing her atop him. He was still too weak to maintain the lead for long, wanted to draw this out as long as possible. When she groaned her desire, her need, he lifted her hips and drew her down onto his shaft. Slow, sure movements brought a smile to her face. She quickly picked up the pace, delighting him as she began to tantalize him. She ran her finger lightly over his lips, tracing the outline before levering herself forward to kiss him. She feathered her hands over his chest, teasing the soft whorls of hair. Nearing her woman's pleasure, she rose up and arched back, her eyes closed. Duncan's agonizing moan of release followed hers, unable to hold back.

After their labored breaths evened out, Catherine trailed her fingers lightly over his bandages.

"Looking for signs my wounds reopened?"

"I see no blood. All right, my lord husband. You are well enough to leave our room."

"Care to put it to the test again—just to be sure?"

\* \* \*

Duncan yanked on the girth of his saddle and then secured his pack to it. "I am loath to leave."

"Then I shall ride to Crieff with you."

"Nay, my heart. Stay with Meggie. I travel faster with just my men and will be back on the morrow."

"Stay home—or send a messenger."

"Cat, I shallnae rest easily until I know how Grant and Ian fare. It took Angus and me longer to heal than I liked. Grant would tell a messenger anything to save me worry. I must see them to know naught dreadful happened."

She tried not to pout. "All right. I shall prepare a room for Tamara. According to the missive last week, she should be here soon."

Now she and Meghan stood in the doorway and waved goodbye as he and his men rode away.

Meghan and she watched the men ride out of the bailey. It hurt. This was the first time he'd been away since his return. It brought back too many memories of his leaving for Stirling, the dreams, his return.

The following day she felt restless. Nagging fears haunted her, so she sought a diversion. She'd already prepared the room for Tamara's visit. Everyone else was busy carding wool. Suddenly, Catherine brightened and rushed downstairs.

"Cook, Marjory just had a babe. I'd like to take bread and cheese to help until she feels stronger. Meggie enjoys playing with Nettie. I shall take her with me. Would you prepare a basket?"

Cook frowned. "'Tis a grand idea, m'lady, but you shouldnae go out. My auld hip is aching this day. Means a storm brews."

Catherine sniggered. *Now they foretell storms with their silly omens. Hip joints foretelling rain, indeed.*

"I shan't be gone long. Only a quick stroll to Marjory and Liam's croft. After Meggie and Nettie play, we shall come right back."

"Be sure you take a guard with you," the auld woman barked.

Catherine laughed. She could just imagine her mother if their cook had dared to give orders. Here everyone was one big family. "Of course. How could I go anywhere without an ever present watchdog?"

\* \* \*

Catherine lost herself in the wonder of the small babe, couldn't take her eyes from him. "He is perfect. Look at his wee fingers and toes. Oh, I wish..." She stopped, not allowing herself to finish. Merciful God in Heaven, she wanted a child so badly—Duncan's child, but feared it would never happen. The physician said it wouldn't. She rose and stared out the door so Marjory couldn't see her tears. *I wonder what my daughter would look like now. Would she have Duncan's beautiful blue eyes or would they be brown like mine?* Would she look like Meggie, or be a smaller version of herself?

A thunder clap snapped her out of her reverie. Clutching the tiny babe to her chest, Catherine glanced up to see clouds darkening. She'd been engrossed and hadn't noticed storm clouds approaching. She turned to Marjory. "I must leave. I've tarried too long." Reluctant to return the infant, Catherine nuzzled her face in the soft wisps of hair on his head.

She raised her eyes to the young mother, unable to hide the longing. "Care for him well. He is a blessing from God." Her heart hurt thinking about the babe she'd never have.

She dashed out the door and collected Meggie, her eyes searching for her guard, Tanner. Surely, he was aware of the approaching storm and knew the need to return home quickly. She called to him several times, the rising wind carrying her voice away. She glanced nervously to the sky. It had that strange yellow cast it does when hail comes with the storm.

"Meggie, we cannot wait for the lad. We may have to run home to keep from getting wet. Come, we must hurry."

Catherine glanced about the croft, uneasy to where Tanner had gone. Duncan wouldn't be pleased the lad was lax in guarding her.

They got only a short distance before the first light patter of rain fell. Catherine raised her face to the droplets. "I cannot wait to hear what Cook says about this. Her hip was right after all."

Nearly halfway there, the rain fell harder. She glanced in the direction of the croft. It was just as far to go back and it was to the Hall, so she pressed on, the disquiet over Tanner's absence growing.

The landscape grew darker, the oddly colored clouds lending eeriness to the path through the woods. Catherine fervently wished she was already home. She quickened her pace.

Meggie twirled in circles, her arms spread wide. Catherine reached down to grip her small, trusting hand.

Catherine snapped around to look behind her, a shiver of fear snaking down her spine. What gave her this feeling of foreboding? She'd had this same sensation before. When? Realization slammed into her — she'd had it as she approached the maze on her father's estate.

In the distance, a rider approached, the horse riding hard. The destrier's hooves cut deep into the soft sod, sending clumps flying in its wake.

Coming toward them. Closer, closer.

# Chapter Twenty-Two

Duncan was relieved to reach the safety of Cray Hall just as the storm broke. His eyes searched the courtyard, seeking Catherine. Why hadn't she met him at the door? The hairs on the back of his neck rose. Something was wrong. He had the same feeling he had when he fetched her in London. Catherine was in danger.

He could feel it.

He rushed into the house, glad to be out of the rain. He missed Catherine and wished he'd taken her with him. She'd have delighted in visiting Tory.

Shaking his head, he wondered when his fae wife had become so important.

"Where are Catherine and Meggie?"

Busy setting up tables in the Hall, women shrugged. "We were busy carding wool and dinnae notice our lady left. Tanner's gone, so she took the lad with her. Dinnae fash, m'lord."

Blast it, that answer wasn't acceptable!

Something was wrong. He felt it clear to his toes.

\* \* \*

The sound of pounding hooves drew closer. The rider looked familiar. Suddenly she remembered. London! The man who'd beaten her in the maze! Why did he wear the MacThomas plaide? What was he doing on Duncan's land?

The slashing hooves made Catherine want to run, but she held her ground. Holding Meggie protectively to her side, Catherine faced him. "Are you mad? How dare you come here?"

Behind her, Meggie tugged on her skirt and whimpered. "I afeard, Mam."

In London he'd said he wanted Duncan to pay. For what? A chill rolled through her as she recalled his threat. "*I shall be back. Remember that, woman. You'll never know when I shall return.*"

"Run, Meggie. Fetch your da," Catherine whispered to the child. If he beat a helpless woman, kicked at her stomach when she begged she was with child, she shuddered to think of this brute getting his ham-fisted hands on Meggie. She had to distract him, give Meggie time to escape.

Meghan stood rooted to the ground, frozen in place by fear.

Catherine watched the child face her fears. She had to get the three-year-old moving. She pushed the child from her. "Please, Meggie, run. Follow the path back to Cray Hall."

Meghan's eyes grew wide.

"The path with pretty flowers we took to Marjory's home. Remember."

Biting her lip, Meghan nodded.

"Go that same way. Do not stop to gather any flowers. Run straight to your da."

Meghan kept her eyes on Catherine.

"Can you do that? Tell your da—or Angus—about

this man as soon as you arrive home. Do not wander about the Hall or go to your room." She kissed Meghan on the cheek. "I shall lead this man away, so do not be frightened when I leave. I shall see you again as soon as your da comes to find me."

She pushed Meggie toward the pathway.

Not hesitating to see if Meggie obeyed, Catherine rose and ran in the opposite direction, determined to draw the madman away from Meggie.

Erwin spurred his horse after her. Like a game of hound and hare—Catherine as the hare.

"Leave me alone," she shouted as she ran from tree to tree.

The man snorted. "I waited too long to catch you alone."

"I have a guard." Her hair lifting in the wind, her eyes darted back toward Meghan. Pride and hope swelled in Catherine's chest seeing her turn towards home, her little legs running. *Please God, protect my little one. Do not let anything happen to her.*

She had to keep this ogre distracted.

"Mean you that stripling lad? He made nae sound when I sliced his gullet—from ear to ear. Duncan must not value you much if that is all the protection he gives you."

Chest heaving from exertion and fear, Catherine suppressed feelings of rage boiling to the surface. This man caused her to lose her child! She had to keep her wits to save herself until help came.

He spurred his horse, herding her, ever closing the distance between them.

Catherine stepped back and tripped on a gnarled tree root. She tumbled backward, her head striking a small stone. Rolling to her side, her heart leapt as she closed her fist on the rock.

"What do you want?" Her buttock hurt and her head pounded. She was dizzy, but she couldn't give in to it or she'd be at the mercy of a man who had none. Her breathing labored, she glared at the horseman. With all the strength her rage afforded, she flung the rock at her tormentor's head.

"Silly wench. You want I should hold the horse still whilst you try again?"

Catherine seethed. He mocked her ability to defend herself. She grabbed for the nearest thing, a long stick, determined to let him see he'd derided the wrong woman. It wasn't long enough to reach his head, so she jabbed it into his leg, stunning him a moment. Pressing her advantage, she swung again, but he caught the stick and jerked it from her hand. Breaking it in two, he tossed the halves away.

"Now you've done it, lass. You will pay with that pretty flesh on your back."

Swinging the horse around, he leaned from the saddle and grabbed her hair. Yanking hard, he nearly jerked her off her feet, bringing her dangerously close to the horse's prancing hooves. Catherine screamed and kicked. This man *wouldn't* hurt her again—ever. Planting her feet and pulling hard, she freed her hand, then swung her fist into his shin—hard. She wasn't sure what she hurt the most—her fist or his leg—but his grunt of pain was music to her ears. Before he had time to react, she sunk her fingernails into his shin and raked a trail in his flesh.

With barely suppressed rage, the man shot his foot out of the stirrup and kicked her in the ribs, sending her to the ground. She saw the horse advancing on her, not giving her a chance to rise. She frantically crawled backward, but kept slipping in the mud. Not able to see where she was going—just the monstrous hooves coming nearer, nearer—her shoulder slammed into a tree. Pain flashed brilliant in her mind, pushing her toward blacking out.

He jumped from the saddle. Grabbing her arm he jerked her to her feet. But not before she grabbed another rock. Catherine gripped it and rounded her swing, striking him in the head, connecting with a satisfying thud. He cursed and held his head, his hand falling away from her.

In that instant of freedom, Catherine lifted her kirtle and ran. Too late she realized the gentle roll of ground led to a sharp descent. She tried to pull up, right her balance, precariously teetering at the edge. She flapped her arms frantically, searching for something, anything, to grab. He was upon her. In a last ditch effort to keep from going over the edge, even her terror didn't prevent her from latching onto her tormentor. The fabric of his plaide slipped through her fingers as she felt nothing beneath her.

"Ahhhhhhh!" she screamed, careening over the side. She plummeted down the incline, the fall finally broken by several scrub pines, snapping them in two. She landed in a heap against a boulder at the base of the ravine.

Bruised, battered and unable to move, she saw the evil man picking his way down the hillside. *Merciful God, nay!* He closed the distance between them before a distant noise stilled his steps. "Again someone rescues you?" His jaw flexed with rage as he flailed his fists at her. "Beware woman. When you least expect it, I will be there. Your luck cannae hold." She heard his curses all the way up the hill, then the sound of his horse's hoofbeats fading to distant thunder.

Catherine lifted her head, trying to see where she'd landed. The pain proved unbearable, a groan escaping her lips. She spit damp leaves from her mouth, her arms too painful to reach up and remove them.

Fearing she'd pass out and not be found, despair overwhelmed her.

Catherine worried. Had Meggie arrived home safely yet? A tear fell as she thought of him having to tell Tanner's mother of his death. Forever her fault. She'd lost her babe because she'd been too stubborn to return with Duncan. And this day she just had to get away from the Hall, merely to relieve her restless feelings. Now a young man lie dead, and Meggie…

She noticed blood on the rocks—*her blood*—but it only distantly mattered.

"Duncan, hurry. I wish to see your face…to tell you …I love you." Her whispered words were drowned by the falling rain. Pain sliced through her with every breath. Her vision swam. She fought the welcoming darkness. "Please, let me see him…one last time."

\* \* \*

Rain grew heavy as Duncan raced to his horse. Cook

informed him Catherine fetched a basket to the family with the newborn. Saddling his mount, he rode through the gate at breakneck speed. Reining up, his blood chilled when he heard Meggie's piercing, "Da!"

She ran toward him — alone!

He was a man used to riding into battle, used to fighting with his men beside him, facing life and death situations. Yet never had he been as frightened as when he'd heard Meggie's shout and saw Catherine nowhere with her.

He couldn't lose Catherine. God spared his life at Stirling to return him to her. He refused to lose her now.

\* \* \*

Strong arms gently encircled Catherine. Pain wracked her body with each movement. She opened her eyes, unable to see anything but shadows.

Through a blur of senses, she heard, "Hang on, lassie. You shall be fine. Dinnae give up now. Hang on until the lad comes." The man's arms were strong, yet held her gently. The voice sounded familiar.

Catherine moved her lips, but only a moan emerged.

"Dinnae fash, lassie. I have you." A roughened hand pushed tangled hair off her face. "Can you hear me? You shall be fine. Hang on now. The lad needs you. You must be strong for Duncan. He cannae live without you." The man continued to talk in a low, calm voice.

Catherine blinked uncomprehendingly. *Duncan not live without her? Nonsense.* Mayhap she hallucinated. If only Duncan did love her.

The pain in her heart, combined with the pain in her body, threatened to drag her under, but the persistent man kept her awake by nudging her and repeating gentle assurances.

Shouts and the sound of approaching horses rent the stillness of the area. Pain lanced through her as she tensed. *Does the rider return?* She shook in terror. The gentle voice soothed, "'Tis all right, lassie. The lad comes. He shall care for you, so you dunnae need me." He lowered her to the ground.

She tried to tell him not to leave, but slipped into the eddying blackness.

When she awoke, firm arms encircled her and Duncan's voice penetrated the haze of her mind. He knelt beside her, cradled her—sounded frantic. "Cat? Cat, wake up. Please my heart, wake up."

*Duncan, I'm awake. Why do you keep repeating yourself?*

Drops of rain fell on her face. Nay, these droplets were warm

She fluttered her eyelids, trying to awaken. "Och, thank the blessed Lord."

Catherine couldn't focus. Duncan. Handsome Duncan. His face held such strength. She needed that now—all the strength he could give her.

"*Mo Chridhe*, what happened?"

Pains shot down her leg and up her back, making movement impossible. A scream trapped in her throat, her answer fading to an anguished sob.

The horse! The rider headed for Meggie. Had the child gotten away?

"Meg…gie."

"She's fine. Dunnae fash." His voice cracked.

Duncan lifted her into his strong arms. She felt so

safe, yet screamed from the pain of being moved. When she looked up, his eyes held tenderness.

He placed a kiss atop her head. "I am sorry, Sweetling, but I cannae fetch you home without hurting you."

Catherine bit her lip, trying to stifle cries of pain. This man was her haven of safety. If only she could stay in his arms forever. Duncan would never let that horrible man get to her again.

"Yell if you must," he said with gruff reassurance. "I know it hurts."

Catherine felt like someone stabbed a burning poker into her back and legs. She passed out.

To awake in her own bed.

Duncan sat, a worried expression on his face. "I sent for a healer. You've been unconscious for hours." His voice was hoarse, ragged.

Maddie the healer. Through the haze of blackness, Catherine remembered the words. "Use these herbals to ease the pain, but there is naught else I can do. I fear your lady willnae walk for a long time...mayhap never."

After Duncan saw she was awake, he questioned her about what happened. Her speech slurred and her eyes appeared wild. "I do not 'member his face...blue and g...geen MacThomas plaid. I...seen him before. I r...ran." She raised her hand to massage her sore head.

Duncan listened intently, holding her other hand and stroking it gently.

"After I fell, someone came...stayed with me, held me..."

Duncan's brows knitted together. "I held you."

She tried to lift her head, but it hurt too much. She softly moaned. "Before that... someone else."

Duncan patted her hand. "We shall talk later. Rest now. You are safe."

Safe. Safe and Duncan. Aye, she could rest now.

# Chapter Twenty-Three

A sennight. She'd been in bed only a sennight, yet it felt like a full moon's passing. Catherine knew every crack in the wall, the placement of every object.

A small knee pushed against her leg, sending a shaft of pain through her. She cried out, unable to suppress the pain.

Duncan's hands stilled on her ankle.

Meghan froze, no longer squirming on the bed. "I sorry," she pouted, her bottom lip puffing out. Tears threatened to drip from her beautiful blue eyes.

Catherine breathed deeply and reached over to soothe the small child. "'Tis all right, Sweetheart. 'Twas just a wee bounce." She took Meggie's small, chubby hand and cradled it.

"Duncan," Catherine grumbled, returning her attention to her husband. "I cannot stay abed forever. I hate being separated from everyone."

"You cannae walk about on your leg until 'tis properly healed." After the accident, Maddie fashioned a splint hoping the crushed bones would heal. The yellowing bruises from her fall still mottled her creamy skin. "I cannae move you yet. Dinnae argue."

"You need not mollycoddle me."

\* \* \*

A fortnight after Cat's accident, Duncan sat at his desk in the counting room beside the Hall trying to concentrate on balancing his accounts, but his mind drifted back to her pleas to leave the room. His spunky Cat was too restless to stay abed much longer.

Her scream made his heart stop. He dashed up the steps two at a time, dropping to his knee beside her as she lay on the floor. Taking her in his arms, he offered soothing words. "'Tis all right, *a leannan.*" Picking her up, he placed her atop the bed. Her face deathly pale, Catherine's chest rose and fell with sobs. They tore at his heart.

"When I tri...tried to walk, my right leg felt leaden. The pain was horrible."

Duncan's heart broke as wrenching despair flashed across her features.

He knew the leg would take a long time to heal. "You must begin exercises to rebuild muscles in your back and leg." He leaned over and positioned pillows around her. He sat beside her, gently kneading and massaging the muscles not covered by the splint. The smallest movement sent shocks of pain though her. "I know it hurts, but you must exercise or you shallnae regain your strength."

Her jaw clenched and moisture covered her face. He was proud of her for uttering no protest and following his instruction without complaint. She grimaced, but stoically bit back her moans.

He smiled and moved his hands down to her foot, again massaging the tightened muscles. Smoothing his thumbs along the slim arch, he slowly moved the foot back and forth.

"I shall roll you onto your stomach now." He massaged her back and legs.

With her face buried against the pillow, she brushed away tears at each kneading motion, hoping he wouldn't notice. She knew Duncan meant well, but merciful heavens how it hurt. She jerked when he exerted too much pressure. "Duncan, stop!"

He circled her with his arms. His fingers stroked her back and he kissed away her tears.

Exhausted, she rested against his broad chest.

\* \* \*

Resting after a strenuous workout, Catherine rolled over on the bed and saw an unfamiliar woman steal into the chamber. Catherine didn't recognize the woman. As she drew closer, recognition dawned. Tanner's mother! She looked as if she'd aged two score years. The woman, when she'd seen her at Tanner's funeral, was still handsome for her age. This woman was wasted by grief. Tears welled in Catherine's eyes.

"You dinnae know me..." the woman whispered hoarsely, her eyes mad with pain.

"You are Tanner's mother."

"Was...are nae more. My precious son lies cold in the grave because of you. My braw young lad, only six and ten summers, had his throat cut because you, Lady High and Mighty, couldnae stay in your laird's house like a good wife shoudst. His death is your fault. Who will die next protecting you? You bring naught but death and doom."

Her hand flying to her chest, Catherine screamed.

Duncan and Angus rushed up the steps and slammed open the door. They charged into the room, saw a mad woman leaning close to the bed, screaming at Catherine.

Duncan subdued her. Motioning to Angus, they ushered the woman out of the solar. Belowstairs, Duncan motioned Alex forward. "Help Angus take Martha to her home. She is distraught and needs someone looking after her."

He rushed back up to console Catherine.

Refusing to tell Duncan what the woman said, she sat on the bed shaking, crying uncontrollably until she thought she might shatter into a thousand pieces, the distraught face of Tanner's mother burned into her mind.

* * *

Catherine spent the next moon doing exercises, swallowing fears she wasn't getting better. Thoughts of Tanner's mother were never far from her mind.

She was frustrated she couldn't remember more about the man who'd forced her over the hill. One thing stuck in her mind. The man had paid no heed to Meggie when she ran home. *He told me he uses me to get back at Duncan. Still, Meggie could have been hurt while in the woods alone. I'd never forgive myself. And Duncan. The man thinks me the weak link in Duncan's armour. What if he's injured protecting me? Hadn't Tanner died a needless death because he guarded me?* Visions of Tanner's mother flashed through her mind. She remembered the woman's tortured words, "Who will die next protecting you?" *I cannot allow another to be injured because of me.*

Duncan's arms were firmly around her, holding her up while she tried to take a step. Every time she stepped on it, pains shot up her leg and back, causing it to buckle. After all these sennights, she still couldn't walk.

For the first time Catherine considered she might never walk again. *I cannot do that to Duncan. Knowing how he was mistreated as a child because of health problems, he'd never turn away someone in need. He'd keep me here and care for me. But can I ask him to do that? Watching me would be a constant reminder of all he went through in his youth. Protecting me could cost him his life. Tanner died because of me. How can I stay and continue putting Duncan and Meggie at risk?*

She slumped deeper under the bedcovers before making a decision and calling Siobhán. "Fetch a piece of parchment." She sat, quill in hand, and pondered all that happened, recalled Martha's words. Wondering what details she should give him, she wrote a note to her brother.

\* \* \*

Yet again, Duncan tried to help her walk. Weak with exhaustion, her legs trembled. "Let me try it on my own."

"Nay, I shallnae allow you to fall."

"I do not wish to have you mollycoddle me every minute."

"I am not mollycoddling you. I but wish to help."

Trevor appeared in the doorway, headed to Catherine's side. "I got here as quickly as I could. What happened, Cat?" He ran his hand gently over her arm.

She threw her arms around his neck in greeting. "Trevor!"

"What right have you to barge in here without a by your leave?" The man was Cat's brother, but that didn't mean he liked her being in Gillingham's arms.

Trevor snapped back, "Catherine's, actually. She wrote and told me to come fetch her."

Duncan's jaw set. "By all the saints, fetch her where you please. When she is ready to travel. Not before." He stormed from the room, his expression black.

\* \* \*

Over the next days, Trevor watched his sister closely, wondered if Duncan would let her go. Mayhap he wouldn't want a wife who could never walk again. Somehow he had trouble believing this of the man. Would he convince Catherine her injuries didn't matter?

Trevor found it difficult to watch Catherine do Duncan's bidding. He thought Duncan right in thinking Cat needed to gain her strength back, but thought the pigheaded Scot handled her too harshly. Why would he work so hard to see her walk again if he wanted to be rid of her? Questions troubled his mind.

Or had Cat been right from the beginning? Was her husband a monster?

One afternoon he stood beside the hearth in contemplation. Duncan's entrance drew him from his reflections. Fed up with the man's behavior, he snapped, "How dare you be so heartless? Cat cannot withstand the discomfort you put her through."

Duncan ignored his brother by marriage and grabbed a tankard of ale. "They help. I willnae stop."

"They do no good," Trevor spat. "She walks no better than when first I arrived." His eyes narrowed as he watched his brother-in-law. "I plan to take Cat back to London on the morrow."

Duncan closed the distance between them. "Over my dead body."

"Easily arranged," Trevor snarled. "Tell me where and when and I shall happily handle that minor detail." He threw his goblet against the massive hearth.

"I willnae fight you, Gillingham. I couldnae do that to Cat. She loves you too much."

"You think you'd win?"

"I said I willnae fight you. Cat is in enough pain without discovering her husband and brother at each other's throats whilst she lies helplessly abed."

"You cannot stop me from —" Trevor began.

"I bloody well can —"

"Stop it." Tamara Gray strode into the room eyeing both men with disgust. "You both act like spoiled bairns. Think of that beautiful woman lying abed up those stairs."

"I am," Duncan and Trevor said in one voice. Their heads snapped to the other, glaring.

"*Amadan*," Duncan growled lowly.

"I assume that is some form of insult." Trevor sneered.

"It means fool," Duncan chuckled.

"There's a fool present all right, but 'tis not me," Trevor retorted.

"Enough! Both of you."

Trevor turned to look at the woman who had the audacity to yell at him. He stared, awestruck by the beauty of the woman in high dudgeon before him. Her bright red hair and flashing green eyes made her the picture of a warrior woman ready to protect her loved ones. A warrior he'd love to tame. One whose image haunted him since he'd first seen her in London.

Trevor pushed his attraction aside and gathered enough wits to defend himself. "I think only of Cat." He jerked his thumb toward Duncan. "Your brother tortures her. I have seen her cry."

"Go home then and you willnae have to see." Duncan slammed the tankard down on the trestle table.

Speaking words he loathed, Trevor said, "'Tis clear she shan't walk again. I shall take Catherine home where she can find peace."

Duncan's mouth opened, but Tamara stayed his words with a raised hand. She spoke to Trevor. "*This* is her home." Trevor started to argue, but she shot him a silencing look. "Your sister is married, Lord Gillingham, whether you approve or not. She is my brother's wife. 'Tis time you realize your sister is an adult and leave her to live the life your father chose."

Trevor was shocked by the sensibility of her words. She was not only beautiful, but intelligent. He met and held her eyes. "I never approved of Father's actions."

Tamara stepped closer and placed her hand gently on his forearm. "Naetheless, my lord, she is wed. Please let my brother and your sister live their own lives."

His eyes shot daggers at Duncan. "He hurts her."

"Nay," she said calmingly, "he doesnae."

Trevor's jaw flexed in frustration, but anger no longer edged his voice. "How can you say that? Have you not heard her screams?"

"I have," she said gently while motioning Duncan to leave. "I love Cat, too." She steered him toward the fire.

"Dunnae you realize what it does to Duncan every time she cries out? Instead of being angry with my brother, watch *his* face at her cries. 'Tis a dirk to his heart."

"He cares not—"

"Och, there you are wrong. My brother loves Cat verra much."

"He abandoned her."

"Aye, he did." She tried to be patient. "Now he wishes he could take back his words and actions."

Trevor shot her a look of incredulity.

"Have you never made a mistake, Lord Gillingham?" When he didn't answer, she said, "There are circumstances you dunnae understand, but Duncan loves your bonnie sister."

Trevor looked ready to protest, but she raised her finger and laid it gently against his lips to stop him. His eyes locked on her and an odd expression crossed his face. Tamara froze. The way he was staring at her! Merciful saints, what had she just done? It wasn't proper to touch him. She snatched her hand back. Embarrassed, a flush crept up her neck as she dared to look into his eyes.

They burned into hers. It had been a long time since she'd seen a look like that. Not since her husband carried her to their bed. A shiver of excitement snaked down her spine. She moved away, his body too close. Radiating heat. Making her forget her words.

She drew a shaky breath and tried to blot out images flashing through her mind. Wanton images of moving closer and placing her hand on his chest. She gulped. "If my brother could, he'd change places with your sister in the beat of his heart. He'd take her pain upon himself."

Trevor watched her, unable to tear his eyes from her face.

"Your husband is a fortunate man, Lady Gray." Shifting uncomfortably in his seat, he couldn't believe the erotic thought he'd just had when she'd raised her finger. He wanted to wrap his lips around it, suck it into his mouth. His lips burned where she'd touched them. He'd frightened her, had seen it in her eyes. Never in his life had he wanted another man's wife.

*He did now.*

Tamara's eyes clouded with regret. "My husband is dead, killed seven years past during one of Scotland's battles. 'Tis why I wish to see my brother's marriage salvaged." She turned away, but wasn't quick enough to hide her anguish. "I wish one of us to be happy."

Pleased to hear she wasn't wed, he couldn't take his eyes from her face. He shifted again, hoping she didn't notice his discomfort—or his erection.

\* \* \*

Trying to gentle his thoughts, Duncan entered their room, saw Catherine leaned against the bolstering pillows on the bed. He went over and sat beside her, picked up her hand and held it between his own.

Catherine's eyes shot to his as he gently rubbed his thumb over her palm.

"Your brother plans to take you back to London." Duncan raised her hand to his lips. "I naysayed him."

"But—"

"Why did you write him?" After all he'd done to help her, she'd written to her brother behind his back.

Asked him to come fetch her. He'd been such a fool. At the first sign of trouble, she wanted to leave. "I thought Cray Hall was your home."

"I place everyone in danger being here."

"Nonsense."

"The man who attacked me came after me to get to you. He told me that in London. What if he'd chased after Meggie because she was with me?"

Duncan's brows furrowed.

"I love her too much to put her in danger. To put everyone in danger. Who knows what such a madman has planned? 'Tis best if I leave. Then you'll not have to protect me—or get hurt trying." She tugged away her hand and straightened in bed. "I know how inconvenient it must be having me here. Accept Trevor's offer."

Duncan's eyes turned as hard as steel. "You are home! You're my lady wife and shallnae leave. 'Tis my duty to protect you and a madman's threats willnae stop me from doing so." His jaw clenched, daring her to contradict.

"I am not afraid of returning to London. I—"

"I know," Duncan shouted in exasperation, jumping up from the bed to leave the room. "You are afraid of naught—except needing me."

## Chapter Twenty-Four

Duncan stood in the chamber doorway, pleased his brother by marriage was gone. Thanks to Tamara's intervention, Trevor returned home alone. Meghan was curled at Cat's side listening to her weave tales of faeries. Catherine spent the last sennight drawing a *book* for Meghan with whimsical creatures. Each time they perused the tiny drawings she created a new story. Duncan delighted in seeing the look of joy on his daughter's face as they *read* the book together, a single candle nearby.

Catherine wore a wildflower in her hair, obviously a gift from his ever-thoughtful daughter. Though she'd been all smiles with Meghan, she grimaced at his approach. "Can we not forego this? I do not feel like—"

"You are the one who told your brother you wish to leave," he shot at her, more upset than he cared to admit over her writing Trevor to fetch her. "You shallnae contrary me about our sessions."

"Do not tell me what I cannot do," she said in aggravation. "Tell me what I can."

Duncan smiled, having won this round. "Och, that is easy. You shall do your exercises."

Catherine glowered. "That is not what I meant and you know it."

Eyes wide at the exchange between her parents, Meghan scampered from the room.

To Duncan's surprise, Catherine put extra energy into her efforts. Her muscles had to be screaming, the pain unbearable, but she refused to cry in front of him.

Proud of her efforts, Duncan praised, "You did well. Keep it up."

"I knew you wanted me to leave. Is that why you're pushing me so hard?"

Duncan laughed. "Again you twist my words. How do you do that? Only hear the part you wish to hear."

"Leave me be."

Ignoring her protests, he laid her on the bed and skimmed his hands over her body, smoothing, teasing. He pressed gently with his thumbs, massaging her entire body.

Catherine moaned with pleasure.

Above her, he smiled, leaned down and placed tender kisses along her neckline. Catherine squirmed beneath his ministrations, his motions soon turning to caresses.

Duncan turned her so she lay on her back. He looked deeply into her eyes, didn't need to voice his desire.

"Duncan, I cannot. I cannot move my leg."

"Dunnae worry." She sounded so vulnerable, like one of the soft, mewling newborn kittens Meghan showed him near the hearth. So in need of protection and tender care. "I shallnae hurt you."

"But—"

"Hush, Sweeting. If it starts to hurt, tell me and I shall stop."

Untying the ribbons of her gown, his soft caresses and tender kisses silenced her.

Lying in bed later, a smug smile spread over his face as he held her in his arms. Between the exertions of her exercises and his very thorough loving, she'd fallen asleep. Though probably not the best way to show her, it was the only way he knew right now to demonstrate how much he wanted her. He had so much he wanted to say, but his bloody tongue twisted in knots and the words didn't come out right.

\* \* \*

For a fortnight Duncan maintained the same schedule. He carried her down to break her fast, then in late morn carried her upstairs to rest before doing her leg exercises.

Approaching their open chamber door, he heard Catherine telling Meghan about her youth. He leaned against the doorframe and listened.

"My brother always grew frustrated when I did not let him get his way."

"Laird Trevor got angry wif you?" Meghan questioned in awe.

"Not angry. He thought he was right about everything. But I didn't back down."

*Och, so my bonnie wife was a force to be reckoned with as a child, too. That doesnae surprise me.*

Too soon her story ended.

Catherine rolled her eyes when he entered the room.

Meghan reached up to hug her father, leaned over to kiss Catherine on the cheek, then scrambled off the bed and left the room.

"What?" Duncan queried with a laugh. "Nae argument?"

"'Twould be futile."

She pushed herself to her limits, he saw, determined to show him she could do anything he said. She did so well, Duncan added new stretching motions. He straightened her leg and tried to raise it in the air, then pressed it gently toward her chest.

She bit her lip, finally shouted, "Duncan! Try you to fold me in two?"

Though he tried to keep his voice light, his tone grew serious as he lowered her leg to the bed. "What I try to do is take your pain away. I feel helpless and inept."

* * *

Duncan sat at his desk but could think of naught but his bonnie wife. He loved the way Catherine regaled the clan youngsters with imaginative tales. Only this morn, they'd gathered around her on the bed. When Duncan bundled her in blankets and placed her in a chair before the hearth, they sat on the floor at her feet. Their carpenter made a wooden box so she could stretch her leg in front of her and Duncan covered it with soft animal fur so it wouldn't chafe her skin. The sight of her surrounded by children reminded him of Grant's wife.

Perhaps Tory could help. He sent a missive to his friends, explaining the situation and asking them to visit. He looked forward to seeing them and thought a visit from Tory just the medicine Catherine needed.

He realized what he felt for the gentle woman in his life far outweighed whatever feelings he'd ever had for his best friend's wife. He grunted in surprise. He'd fallen in love with his own wife.

Taken aback by his feelings, he headed upstairs, approached the bed and sat. He watched Catherine, but said nothing. Instead he kneaded muscles, caressed the instep of her foot with his thumb. She made him feel awkward. He could never tell her the depth of his feelings. She'd laugh in his face.

# Chapter Twenty-Five

Duncan watched Alexander approach and sit opposite him, knew from the young man's expression he had a burr under his saddle. "Are you not being too forceful with the lass? We hear her cries down the stairs."

His friend's voice resonated concern, yet Duncan couldn't stop disappointment from roiling in him. "Forceful? I try to make her walk again."

"Can you not accept her as she is?" Alex challenged. "The rest of us dunnae care if she walks again."

Duncan frowned over the rim of the tankard. He set it down untouched and shook his head chidingly. "I thought everyone understood me better. I dunnae care if she ever takes a step. I would gladly carry her about every day for the rest of her life."

"Then why...?"

"For *her*. She has been through too much. First her da gave her away for promises of wealth from his king, then she lost our bairn, now this."

Duncan leaned back in his chair, conveniently leaving out how he'd left her. He tried hard to forget the worst mistake of his life. "I cannae let this defeat her. She had such resolve right after her accident, determined to walk again. But now...mayhap because it takes longer to heal, doubts set in. *I* think nae less of her because she cannae walk, but *she* does. Of late she doesnae want my help. She pushes me away. Tries to do everything on her own."

"Think you 'tis because she still cannae walk?"

"Nay, something festers in her mind. I wish I knew what. Mayhap she thinks she is less of a woman."

"But she's—"

"Beautiful—inside and out." Duncan's shoulders slumped. "What can I do, Alasdair? She is perfect, but I dunnae think she'll believe that, especial until she walks on her own. Somehow that must happen."

Shoulders still slumped, he rose and slowly climbed the staircase to his chamber.

\* \* \*

The following sennight, Catherine grimaced as she slid her leg forward, trying to walk. She started to fall, but Duncan caught her with steady arms. Frustrated with the pain and lack of improvement, Catherine lashed out, "Is this how you plan to spend the rest of your life? Caring for a cripple? Even Father's money cannot compensate for that."

*Merciful heavens*, she thought as soon as the words were out. *I did not mean to say that. Duncan knows only too well how it feels to have someone care for him that doesn't want to. And from what I've heard of his treatment at the hands of Clan Kerr's laird, he'd never hurt someone he thought weaker than himself.*

Duncan's face turned to stone. "You seem determined to leave. Fine. As long as you walk out the door on your own two legs."

Catherine's mouth dropped open, abruptly shut.

With the gauntlet thrown, she renewed her efforts. After Tanner's mother's visit, she'd written to Trevor, thinking only of Duncan and Meghan's safety. She didn't want to leave, but couldn't bear the thought of another innocent dying because of her. Who knew what the vile man that attacked her would do next—or when he'd strike again?

"I accept that challenge, Duncan MacThomas."

* * *

Duncan heard a commotion outside. Peeking through the arrow loop, he saw his friends had arrived.

Tory's face bloomed with radiance, motherhood on her again, and Grant strutted as if delighted at the prospect as he helped her from the litter.

Duncan crossed the courtyard to greet them. "Thank you for coming so quickly."

Tory knelt in the dirt and drew Meghan to her, hugging her tightly. "I cannot believe how you've grown since last I saw you."

Meghan's cheeks dimpled. She raised her hands and put up four fingers. "I am this many summers now."

Happiness shown on his friends' faces. Duncan remembered when they first met, were incredibly stubborn, and their happiness had been a long time coming. Mayhap there was hope for he and Cat yet.

Duncan led everyone into the keep. "Sit while I fetch Catherine." Carrying her into the Hall, he asked, "Sweetling, you remember Grant and Tory Drummond?"

Catherine gave him an incredulous look as he lowered her to a chair beside Tory. "Have you taken leave of your senses, husband? I injured my back and leg, not my mind."

Duncan and Grant reminisced for hours, so Tory took advantage of her time with Catherine and continued the sessions Duncan had begun. She leaned forward and braced pillows against Catherine's lower back, trying to make her comfortable. Catherine raised her leg and held it with her hands under her thigh.

"That was good, Cat," Tory encouraged. "Now let us have a go at this instead." She stretched out on the bed, raised her leg and rotated her ankle, demonstrating exactly what she wanted Catherine to try. She laughed when her expanding belly got in the way. "I fear I am clumsy these days." She turned on the bed and raised herself on her elbow. "Whether you ever walk again is not what matters to Duncan. He only wants you safe and happy." Tory shot Catherine a look that told her she'd best not argue.

Downstairs, Tory rubbed her lower back and teased Duncan. "I took the liberty of making a few *wee* changes in your regimen. You work with an injured young woman, Duncan MacThomas, not your rowdy men-at-arms. You need adapt to Catherine's lesser pain level. Do not force her muscles. Be gentler. If you do not exert quite so much pressure, she shall probably heal faster."

She took him back upstairs and showed him exactly what changes needed to be made. Before entering the room she added, "Congratulate Catherine more. Make her feel she truly accomplishes something. Have her sit in a tub of warm water every day. Add this salt I fetched with me." Tory handed him a leather pouch. "It comes from Epsom and has healing qualities. 'Twill soothe her sore muscles, reduce swelling. When she is abed, elevate her injured leg. You do not wish the area to swell like it has. You told me you did so at the beginning, but you must continue. Swelling slows healing."

Grant joined them. "I shall send you one of the chairs our carpenter made for Tory. With its curved rungs, it moves back and forth. Its motion should soothe you."

Tory could tell Catherine doubted she'd ever see it.

Catherine and Duncan reminded Tory of Grant and herself at the beginning of their relationship. They too locked horns like the great red deer of the forest, but fell in love while doing so. She believed Duncan had done the same. She just couldn't ascertain Catherine's feelings. Wanting nothing to disrupt their growing friendship, she approached the subject cautiously, but finally asked, "How feel you about Duncan?"

Catherine repeated what she told everyone. "He does not want me."

Observing Catherine closely, Tory decided the young woman had fallen in love with her husband, but feared admitting it because she believed he didn't want her. Yet there was more. Tory just didn't know what. Catherine watched Duncan with longing, yet pushed him away when he tried to help.

Two stubborn people.

\* \* \*

After Tory and Grant left, Duncan used the new motions Tory'd shown him. Gradually Catherine could move her leg on her own. He was thrilled at her progress.

Over the past sennight he'd held her close and helped her move across the room. Still supported, but walking.

Now they stood beside the bed and he felt foolish. He was scared to release her to let her try and walk.

"Let go, Duncan. I can do it myself." Her eyes shimmered with tears. He knew not if they were tears of excitement or fear.

He moved away and she stood unmoving. Finally she slid her leg forward. It didn't buckle! Eyes wide, hers flew to his. She took a few tentative steps and stopped. Her shoulders heaved with sobs.

He could stand it no longer and rushed to her side, wrapped her in his arms and held her close. He was perilously close to tears himself. She'd done it! His stubborn wife had prevailed. Each day she'd grow stronger.

Not wanting to wear her out, he lifted her in his arms and carried her back to bed.

Eyes wet with tears, Catherine beamed up at him. "I did it, Duncan. I walked."

\* \* \*

Clan business required Duncan to be away a fortnight. He worried how Catherine would take his absence. Hated to leave when she finally made progress walking. Tory's treatments had helped.

Now he carried a flower, feeling a fool for doing something so sentimental. Seeing Catherine resting before the hearth in his Hall, he walked behind her, brushed her ear with the flower before kissing her cheek. "I missed you."

Catherine reached up to take the flower, pressed it to her face. She closed her eyes as if in pain. Duncan tensed when a tear trickled down her cheek.

"I am glad you are home, m'lord." She opened her eyes. "I have been waiting for you. We must talk. The time has come for me to leave. I can walk out the gate on my own—with the help of the walking stick you made me. You said when I could do that, you wanted me to leave."

He feared this might arise. Now he knew.

He'd looked forward to coming home. Planned to make love to her all night. Wrap her in his arms, sheath himself in her body. He hadn't even had a chance to kiss her.

Angry over his welcome home and how she'd twisted his words, he pursed his lips. "I shallnae stop you. If you're determined to leave me, get out of my house." For this he'd rushed home? Faugh, he'd known all along she'd leave. Known from the beginning. She was no different than Helen or his father. How foolish of him to believe.

"I shall, after I pack my things...and tell Meggie good-bye."

"If we...she...means so little to you that you can so easily leave, then you must say naught." His steely gaze locked on her face. Deeply pained that she wanted to leave him—them, Duncan chose the only way he knew to hurt her back. His voice hard, cold, he flung his next words cruelly. "'Tis so wonderful you lost our bairn there. Run back so you never have to worry about bearing my child again."

All color drained from Catherine's face. Duncan wished he could rip his tongue out. Blessed St. Andrew, how could he have voiced the one thing he'd known would hurt her the most?

Her gait labored, she turned and fled the room. Straight to the stables.

Duncan's impulse was to go after her, pull her into his arms and tell her he was sorry. Pride stopped him. She was leaving him.

He heard shouts. Going to the door, he opened it to assess the commotion.

Catherine rode out the gate. Bloody hell, his stubborn wife rode out unaccompanied. Racing like the Bansidhe howled at her back.

He'd driven her away with his heartless words. Why hadn't he just demanded she not leave?

He couldn't let her depart. Not like this — *not ever*.

Knowing he needed her more than life itself, Duncan raced outside to mount his steed. His response anticipated, a horse was already being saddled.

He raced after her, pushing his horse to full gallop. "Please, God, dunnae let her injure herself," he cried aloud.

He finally saw her, pushed to overtake her, knowing the fool woman wouldn't stop. Drawing abreast, he shouted to her.

She barely spared him a glance, concentrated on riding.

She was going too fast.

Duncan feared the horse would stumble. She might lose her grip on the reins or saddle. Bracing his knees to maintain his balance, he reached over to grab her reins. She jerked them away. Not wanting to startle the horse, Duncan took only the space of a heartbeat to make a decision. Bending to loop his arm around her waist, he pulled hard, jerking her from her horse.

Catherine shrieked.

Trying to situate her on the horse with his left arm, he yanked on the reins with his right. She flailed, trying to escape him.

"Let me go!"

He brought the horse to a stop and dismounted, bringing her with him.

She pummeled her hands against his chest. He didn't stop her. He'd hurt her, deserved it.

Her knee buckled and she dropped to the ground, sobbing. "How dare you...how could you...how...?"

"Shhh, my heart, I am sorry. I didnae mean—"

"You did!" Her shoulders shook with uncontrolled sobs.

Duncan drew her into his arms, held her while she sobbed. "You leave me. Why?"

"Does it matter? You never wanted me in the first place, just the coin my father paid you to take me."

"Dunnae dredge up the past that is better left buried."

"Like our child lies buried—" She choked back a sob, putting her fist to her mouth to keep the pain from escaping.

"That has naught to do with you leaving now and you know it!" He grabbed her shoulder and shook her. "By all that is holy, you owe me that much. Tell me."

"I leave to protect you."

"What? You think to leave...to protect me? What sort of corked-brain notion is that? Did you fracture your skull as well as your leg?"

"Tanner's mother—" she began only to have him cut her off.

"Is a woman filled with black grief. It rots her soul, twists her mind inwardly."

"With cause! Her child is dead, as is mine, by the hand of same man. I cannot risk being near another person....having them....I do not want you to..." Her tear filled eyes lifted to his. "Do you not see...Tanner is dead because of me! Because he protected me. If you protect me...you will...I am naught but a bringer of death and sorrow. Mayhap I...."

"Tanner lies dead, as does our babe, because of a madman. You had naught to do with it. Can you not see?"

"Duncan, I fear your death. Dreams haunt me nightly. I see you and this man, swords drawn, there is blood." She glanced down to her hands as if see them stained with it. "Mayhap if I go away I can stop this."

"Cat, 'tis only a dream, not augery."

"I saw Stirling. I was there. Do not naysay me now. This, too, shall come to pass."

"You said the man wants to kill me. You were the instrument to lure me into his trap. Well, I know naught about him. He could be stranger or friend. He could come up to me and stick a sgian dubh in my heart and I wouldnae suspect him until too late. You leave me to that? Would you not protect me more by keeping watch over me, saving me from the hand of an assassin who I might think is kin?"

"I..."

"How are you protecting me by leaving if 'tis *me* he wants to kill in the first place? If you leave, you abandon me to this madman. Only you know what he looks like. Is that how little you care about me?" He met and held her eyes.

"Do you?" he queried, running his fingers lightly up her arm.

"Do I what?" she sniffled.

"Want to stay. To hold on to what we have? Or want you to throw it all away?"

She gazed into his eyes a long time before heaving a loud sigh. "I would much rather be miserable with you than without you."

Duncan shook his head. "'Twas that a compliment? If so, we both must work on what we say!"

# Chapter Twenty-Six

Within two moons of Catherine walking, Duncan and Catherine were summoned to Castle Glenshee. *'I hold a supper for John Comyn and his betrothed, Isabel MacDuff in honor of their upcoming nuptuals. I want you both present,'* MacThomaid said in his message.

Catherine sat in Duncan's lap by the hearth. "Why hold this supper while his health deteriorates?"

He cradled his cheek against her hair, breathed in the scent of her. Reluctant to speak of his father, he finally answered, "He often entertains earls loyal to the Crown. Feel blessed we usually dunnae have to attend. The thought of being in the same room with Comyn makes my stomach turn. He saw naught wrong with Longshanks' murder of Wallace."

Grudgingly, they headed to Duncan's childhood home.

Meghan rushed to her grandfather and wrapped her arms around his knees as soon as she saw him. "Grandda," she exclaimed in unabashed delight.

Laughing, he lifted her and swung her around, then crushed her to his massive chest. "Och, lassie, 'tis good to see you. I miss your bonnie smile."

"I miss you, too, Grandda."

Catherine and Duncan's eyes locked, surprised at the

tender interplay between the two.

Tamara, also summoned to assist with the supper, just smiled knowingly.

Under the scrutiny of Duncan's probing blue eyes, Tamara led him to the side of the room. "Are you alright? I heard many had hurt feelings when your wife voiced her desire to leave. You included."

She smiled when he gave her a look indicating he cared not one way or the other.

His eyes returning to his wife and daughter, Duncan murmured dryly, "I felt naught when she wished to leave. I..."

"Och, Duncan," she sighed and wrapped her arms around him. "You may fool your friends, but you cannae fool me. I know you well. You love that bonnie lass. Just remember, she isnae Helen. The only reason Cat may ever think to leave is because deep down she still thinks you dunnae want her. Although misguided, there is a difference."

"She had other daft reasons. Thought I couldnae protect her. Nay, the fool woman thought to protect *me*." He turned away, saying no more.

They turned when Meghan shrieked. She'd fallen and skinned her knee.

When Catherine took Meghan into the Great Hall to tend her wounds, The MacThomaidh held the child. He rubbed his calloused hands lightly up and down her back and crooned to her to keep her from crying.

"'Tis all right, lassie," he soothed. "You shall be fine once your mam fixes your wounds. She will make you good as new. Be strong now. Be brave for Grandda."

Catherine returned with necessary herbs. The old man's words seemed out of character, but she paid little attention. MacThomaidh set the child down so Catherine could tend her. She dipped a soft cloth in water and cleansed Meghan's palms and knee. Applying a bread poultice, she sprinkled it with a small amount of grated Solomon's Seal root, wrapped strips of torn cloth around the tiny knee to keep the poultice in place.

After giving Meg a kiss on the cheek, Catherine rose and headed to the other side of the room. The MacThomaidh reached out and drew Meghan near. "Come here, lassie." He picked her up and placed her on his bony lap. "I am proud of you. You were a brave girl for Grandda."

The words had scarcely left his mouth when Catherine remembered what he'd said when she entered the room with her herbs. Her hand flew to her mouth. "'Twas you," she said in disbelief. "You held me the day I fell down the hill."

"Nonsense, woman. You dinnae know what you speak of. I was on my own lands, nowhere near—"

"You were," she insisted, interrupting him. "I know not how or why, but you comforted me, kept me awake until help came." Her eyes searched his in non-understanding.

Of a sudden, memories flooded back, her heart flying into her throat. Her hand on her chest, she turned to Duncan. Worry lines etched his brow. "I remember."

Duncan walked toward her. "You remember what?"

As Catherine tried to remember, the tragic events unfolded. "Everything. The man that charged me and

Meggie wore the MacThomas plaid." She rushed on excitedly. "He dragged me into the maze on Father's property." Breathing deeply, she sank into the closest chair and rubbed her hands over her forehead. "How could I have forgotten? Hitting my head must have done more damage than I thought," she murmured, excitement filling her eyes. She squeezed her eyes shut as she tried to recall that horrible day.

"I remember one thing." She smiled weakly. "The angrier he got, his speech changed. Like yours does when you're angry with me."

Duncan glowered at her choice of words.

Catherine continued as if his expression hadn't changed. "He jeered 'twas good to hurt someone you cared about, said 'twas time he paid you back. *You*, Duncan. 'Tis not just some stranger with an unknown blood oath. This man knows you." Her voice reached a fervent pitch.

"Did he lay hands on you?" Duncan stormed.

Catherine's gaze moved to his, her brows dipped to a frown. "He beat me."

"I dinnae mean that. I mean did he..."

When he couldn't finish, Catherine realized his intent. "Nay, husband, he did not touch me that way."

Seemingly mollified, Duncan grumbled and turned to the hearth, then faced his father. "Is it true?"

MacThomaidh stared in confusion. "Is what true?"

"You comforted my wife?"

MacThomaidh didn't answer for a long time, finally nodded. "I received a missive about Robert. I thought to bring word myself. When I heard the lass' screams, I but did what anyone would do."

Duncan studied his sire, a questioning look on his face.

* * *

A fortnight after Trevor was notified Catherine remembered everthing, he arrived at Cray Hall. He motioned his hand toward the heavy oak door. "I brought Catherine a small gift. Mayhap you could help me bring it inside?"

Duncan eyed Trevor warily. "And what *small gift* might you bring my wife that takes two grown men to haul inside?"

"A settle I had made in London," Trevor answered jovially. "I thought you could place it before the hearth in your chamber or main Hall. Cat probably still must rest quite a bit."

Carrying the heavy furniture inside, Duncan and Trevor discussed the direction of Robert Carrick's true loyalties.

"Thus far, Edward thinks Bruce again supports the English," Trevor said, "but I wonder. Bruce knows he'd have to fight not only Edward, but half of Scotland were he to claim the crown."

Duncan swore under his breath. "Will Longshanks never leave us alone?"

After arranging the settle in the main Hall, Duncan called into the kitchen for his wife. Seeing her brother, she rushed to his waiting arms. Her leg tired just before she reached him and she fell, but his strong arms safely caught her. He crushed her to his chest in a bone-crunching embrace.

Trevor looked at Duncan over her head, concern in his eyes. His brother-in-law smiled and mouthed the words, "She is fine."

When Trevor finally released her, Catherine saw the settle. Her eyes flew between Duncan and her brother.

"'Tis but a small gift." He smiled at his sister lovingly. "Made especial for you. You left so quickly, you did not get a wedding gift from me. I brought several trunks with me. They are in a cart that has not yet arrived." He turned to Duncan. "Once I reached your property, I fear I left them behind. I was too anxious to see Cat."

Meghan rushed into the Hall. "Mam, Mam, a cart comes. We have comp'ny." She started to pull Catherine toward the door when she saw Trevor standing beside her father. "Oh." She drew her tiny brows together. "Our comp'ny is here."

Raising her face to Trevor's, she asked, "How did you get here?"

"On my horse, little lady," Trevor teased. He knelt before her. "I hope you do not mind me visiting your mother. I brought her some lovely presents." He smiled and teased. "I believe I may have a gift or two for you as well."

"Truly?" Delighted at the prospect, a smile flashed across her face. She raced outside to meet the approaching cart and crashed into her aunt, who'd just crossed the threshold.

"Meghan, dear, do slow down," warned Tamara. She rose from straightening her côte-hardie when she looked up to see her brother already had a guest.

"Oh, do excuse me," she murmured in embarrassment. "I shouldnae have arrived unannounced." She flushed when she realized all eyes were upon her.

Duncan noted especially the eyes of the tall man beside him. Cat's brother flashed a perfect set of white teeth. Duncan felt like putting his fist through them. To his amazement, he saw his sister was flustered. He frowned, not sure how he felt.

"You know you are welcome. You just surprised us since Cat's brother arrived moments before. I am surprised you dinnae cross paths." Duncan's brows dipped in suspicion. "They dinnae cross, did they?"

Duncan's eyes swerved to Trevor. He'd seen the look of embarrassment passing between his visitors. Suspicions deepened. "Trevor Gillingham, I believe you remember my sister, Lady Tamara Gray."

Trevor approached, bent over, and pressed his lips to Tamara's outstretched hand. "Charmed, Lady Gray." The corner of his mouth twitched with a suppressed smile. "It appears I arrived at an opportune time."

Catherine broke the tension. "I am sure you are both thirsty. Could I have Cook fix you a repast?"

Trevor turned to Duncan, his eyes alight with pleasure. "I would like some of your whisky. I have acquired a taste for it since my sister wed you."

"I dunnae think that is the only thing in Scotland you like." A silent understanding passed between them.

While the men proceeded to the trestle table, Catherine escorted Tamara upstairs. Cat noticed Tamara's backward glance to the two men tipping goblets to their lips, noted the blush tinge Duncan's sister's cheeks when Trevor raised the cup to her.

While the women hung Tamara's garments in the oaken wardrobe, Meghan entertained herself by having her kitten chase a string.

Catherine could tell Tamara lingered. Drawing chairs before the hearth, she queried, "What is wrong, Tamara? Has aught happened?"

Meghan climbed into Catherine's lap.

"I havenae been in Melrose." Tamara's hand flew to her chest. "I remained at Castle Glenshee with Father."

Catherine stared at Tamara expectantly. No one had told Duncan this.

"He is dying."

Catherine gasped. She'd known he hadn't been well, but hadn't imagined how ill.

"The only thing keeping him alive is feeling he cannae leave this earth while Duncan still hates him."

Catherine's eyes widened.

"He acknowledges his error and regrets the time they lost. He has admitted that to everyone except the person who matters most."

Her eyes beseeched Catherine. "I need your help, Cat. Duncan must return to Castle Glenshee. He and Father must talk." She sighed heavily. "I know you are not fond of Da and Duncan certainly holds nae love for him, but..." She stopped, uncertain how to continue. Her eyes closed in anguish before looking to Catherine again. "But, he is my father as well—and I love him. What Da did to Duncan was wrong, but he was a loving father to me—in his own way. He just has difficulty showing it sometimes."

Her face paled. Catherine set Meghan aside and rushed to the small table. Lifting the porcelain pitcher, she poured water into the basin. Wringing out the excess from a soft cloth, she brought it to Tamara to hold on her face.

"What do you wish me to do? You know how stubborn Duncan is. We will be there for Lord Comyn's and Lady MacDuff's supper, but I misdoubt they shall talk then."

# Chapter Twenty-Seven

Finally, the object of Duncan's turbulent thoughts walked through the door. He'd spent too much time waiting for Catherine to return home. Why had he agreed to let her help prepare for the upcoming supper?

He didn't understand why this woman meant so much to him. He only knew he wanted to be with her, wanted her as close as two bodies could be.

He approached Catherine, a smile on his face.

His father probably worked her endlessly. Yet he knew enough about his stubborn wife to know she'd not leave until she'd completed the task. Usually tireless, her shoulders drooped. His eyes moved to her face, an answering smile curving her lips.

He drew her into his arms and kissed her tenderly. Cupped his hand against her cheek.

She leaned her head against his hand and peered into his face, her eyes holding a multitude of questions.

"I missed you."

"I was but at your father's."

"Exactly." His smile faded. "You spend too much time there. I shall be glad when this fête is finished." He reached for her hand and pulled her toward the staircase. "Come."

"Duncan, what are you…?"

She had dirt on her nose and cheek and looked like she'd been cleaning all day. She'd never looked more beautiful. "I am taking you to bed."

"I am not that tired."

"I dunnae intend you to sleep." He enjoyed the astonished look on her face.

"But Duncan—"

"Dinnae 'but Duncan' me. You have been gone too much and I want you close. I intend to make love to you all night." His eyes glinted with passion as he lifted her into his arms and strode to their bedchamber.

Laughing, Catherine protested. "But..." She stopped the instant he pushed open the door. A steamy tub sat in the middle of the room, candles set all around. He'd kept it refreshed with warm water, had put a lot of thought and effort into this.

"How wonderful!" She pressed a kiss to his forehead.

Duncan delighted in her response. When he set her on the floor, she stood on her toes and kissed him. She untied the laces on one shoulder, letting the material fall. She cupped his cheek with her hand as he'd just done to her, then untied the other laces. Her shift fell to the floor.

His eyes feasting on her, Duncan extended his hands to lift her into the tub. She moved into his arms, wrapped hers around his neck.

Duncan lowered her into the tub immediately. If he didn't, the water would turn cold again. With her body this close, he wanted to love her now. He bit back a groan.

Stretching her arms above her head, she relaxed in

the tub while Duncan washed her, taking every opportunity to caress her body with his fingertips. She leaned her head against his chest as his lips trailed in a gentle caress against her shoulder. He reached around her and lightly trailed his fingertips along the inside of her thigh.

Duncan leaned across the tub and claimed her mouth.

Catherine sighed with pleasure. Placing her hand against his chest, she pushed him away, rose, and stepped from the tub.

He sat back on his heels and watched, spellbound.

Smiling, she inched her way back to their bed, water dripping across the floor. Cocking her head to one side, she lowered herself to their massive bed. Her eyes beckoned and it was all the invitation Duncan needed. They'd worry about wet linens later.

Control deserted him and his clothes were stripped off while striding to the bed. Placing one knee on each side of her, he leaned down and crushed his mouth to hers. Soon he had her moaning and writhing beneath him. Pushing down his own desire, he slowed his motions. He'd not rush this joining. The tip of his tongue laved her earlobe, nipped at it with his teeth. She again moaned, caused his manhood to harden even more. Duncan pulsed with need. They loved each other the rest of the night.

\* \* \*

Quail, roasted pig, and fish with herbs and spices graced heavily laden tables. Servers barely had time to rest before another course was provided.

Catherine was surprised when The Black Comyn and Lady MacDuff brought uninvited guests. Duncan leaned close and whispered, "You should have expected as much from a conceited earl." Comyn had several friends with him and Isabel brought her cousin, Morag.

Being Bruce's cousin as well, the young woman was the recipient of many glares from the Comyns. After Duncan told her the reason behind them, Catherine thought Morag handled the situation with grace and diplomacy, thought her a very brave young woman.

When the men rose from the Great Table, the women drifted out to the garden. The full moon and bright stars illuminated the pathways. Chatting amiably, Catherine discovered Isabel was knowledgeable of the situation between the two countries. She found her open and forthright and liked her immediately.

Morag was beautiful and younger than her cousin. Catherine thought she might be close to her own age.

While Catherine admired Isabel, she was drawn to Morag. The young woman's honesty and thoughtful nature emanated from her every action. Throughout the evening, she'd put her own comfort aside ensuring Isabel had everything she desired.

Catherine looked about often to find male eyes fastened on Morag's every move. The slender woman had long red hair and green eyes that clearly captivated many MacThomas clansmen.

"You and Lord Comyn seem ill-matched, Lady Isabel. Is the betrothal one to your liking or was it planned for you?" Catherine thought back to the events leading up to her own marriage. If only the king hadn't interfered.

"What a question, my dear. I shall become Countess when the nuptials are complete. Why would I not desire such a union?"

Although Isabel kept her voice light, Catherine wondered if she'd heard an under current of tension. Were things not as happy as they seemed?

Gusts of wind wrapped skirts around their legs and whipped hair into their eyes. A chill moved inland, so they headed back to the castle's warmth. Catherine escorted the two women to their room, seeing every amenity had been provided. After ensuring Isabel was comfortable and settled for the evening, Catherine and Morag brought needlework downstairs and talked until the men retired for the evening.

By the time the entourage left the following morn, the two women had formed a true friendship. Catherine regretted Morag didn't live closer, but had every intention of convincing her to join them at Christmastide.

"I couldnae possibly come then," Morag initially argued.

"Why not?" Catherine shot back stubbornly. "We had such fun these past days."

"I am quite certain Isabel will need me to do something for her." She sighed. "She always does."

"Will you live with Lady Isabel after she and The Comyn wed?"

"Nay. She shall be a Countess and Comyn servants will do her bidding. She shallnae need me."

Catherine nodded in satisfaction. "Good. Then you being away a few sennights should not matter, either. If she complains, remind her she shall be so busy with Christmastide she'll not have time to focus on wedding plans. After Hogmanay you shall be refreshed and can plan her wedding with renewed vigor."

Laughing, Morag's eyes widened. "I cannae believe you came up with such logic."

Duncan entered the room, laughed as well. "You mean illogic, but you might as well give in. My lady wife willnae give up until she wears you down. Last eve she mentioned she desires you to visit." He turned his smile to Catherine, placed his arm around her and drew her close. "'Tisnae often she tells me she wants something, so when she does, I like to grant her wish. I would consider it an honor if you joined us during Christmastide."

Morag looked from Catherine to Duncan. "I appreciate your kindness and would love to visit again sometime, but—"

"It would also be my pleasure to send my men to escort you. Your coming here shall cause no hardship on your home."

"You would have a wonderful time, Morag." Unable to resist, Catherine teased, "And from what I saw last eve, you would make many of our clansmen very happy."

Morag blushed. To Catherine's delight, she finally nodded. "Aye, I would be pleased to spend the season with you."

After seeing their guests off, Catherine looked up at Duncan and walked back into the house chuckling. "Did you notice how quickly she changed her mind when I mentioned the men would be happy?"

Duncan wrapped an arm around her waist, caressed her arm with his other hand. "Aye, our Alasdair seemed fair smitten."

\* \* \*

As promised, Duncan sent an escort to fetch Morag to Cray Hall. Catherine acted as much a child as Meggie while she awaited her friend's arrival. She bustled about and checked Morag's bedchamber at least ten times to make certain it was just as she wanted. Finally cornering her, Duncan grabbed her and dragged her to the chair near the hearth. He pulled her onto his lap, framing her face with his hands.

"Relax. Morag visits *you*, not to see if she finds a speck of dust on our bed frame or hearth."

"I want everything perfect. I want—"

"You want a friend," he said in understanding.

She nodded. "I never had a friend before."

"Am I not your friend?" he inquired quietly.

"Sometimes." She swallowed the tear clogging her throat and changed the subject. "A courier came earlier. What news did he bring? You did not fetch me."

Duncan chuckled. "I thought you were too busy running around to take notice."

"And you evade the issue," she teased. "I know not why you bother. I never let you get away with it."

She was so endearing, and so bloody bossy! Yet she had a right to know. "Robert paves the way to claim Scotland's throne. I think he would have made the move before now, but 'tis rumored when Wallace was seized he carried secret papers from the French to Robert promising aid should he stand against England's king.

'Tis why William returned to Scotland after all these years. They trusted nae one else to carry such a missive. Robert has lain low since August, waiting to see if this is true, see if Longshanks demands his arrest. I misdoubt he would suffer the same fate as Wallace. I should worry, based on past actions, but he has proved to be a natural leader. He is older now. Ready, I think."

"Soon he will try to be king?"

"I believe so," he said, looking into her tired eyes. "But 'tisnae something we need worry about now. We shall only concentrate on Christmastide."

Catherine leaned into him and cradled her head in the hollow of his neck. Although activity abounded around them, Duncan chuckled when her breathing evened. She'd gone non-stop for so long, she slept the instant she relaxed.

A shout sounded outside.

Awake in an instant, Catherine bounded for the door. "My friend has arrived."

Only Duncan staying her arm with his hand made her stop. Reaching toward a peg on the wall, he retrieved her mantle and wrapped it around her, pulling the hood over her head. As they stepped outside, snowflakes lightly swirled through the air creating a wonderland.

When the curtains to the litter parted, Duncan reached up to help Morag alight. Her eyes were wide with excitement.

Arm in arm, the two women headed inside the keep.

"After you rest, I shall show you the tree Duncan brought in for us. If you feel up to it, we can decorate on the morrow."

"Must we wait? I would love to start now. I have never seen a tree the likes of what you described when last I was here."

Hours later the room was bathed by candles aglow on the tree.

*1306*

# Chapter Twenty-Eight

Surprised to have Grant call him aside immediately after arriving with Tory, Duncan glared. "What news?"

"Tisnae good. I wish our visit to Black Comyn's wedding could start on a better note." Grant stared into the fire. "The Bruce has finally been forced to take a stand, one that will plunge Scotland into war. In January, Comyn and Robert were at Longshanks' court in England. Comyn and Robert signed a pact."

"Red Comyn and Bruce agreed on something?"

"Aye, on this they did. Bruce told Comyn he'd either give all his lands in Scotland in exchange for Comyn's support for the kingship or Comyn could give Bruce all the Comyn lands and Robert would support him as king."

Duncan almost howled at the madness. "A mooncalf's bargain. The two would rather stick their dirks in the other's heart."

"They nearly did," Grant bit out, running a hand over his face. "Instead of keeping the pact, Comyn ran to Longshanks with the news."

"Someone should kill the traitor."

"Someone did."

"Comyn dead? How? When?" Duncan closed his

eyes as the impact hit him.

"Save your questions, friend, and let me tell you the whole mess at once."

Duncan nodded, almost holding his breath.

"Comyn headed to Edward to lick his boots. He turned over papers showing Carrick and the Bishops Wishart and Lamberton backed Wallace and Bruce— behind the scenes. When Wallace was seized last year he carried similar papers from the French court. Edward plays games with his brother-in-law, the French king. He cannae confront him with evidence because it might push the French into openly supporting Bruce. Comyn's evidence nearly sealed Robert's death warrant. Had he not held such a high place in Edward's esteem, Edward loving him more than he does his own son—"

"Small wonder," Duncan scoffed.

"Edward summoned Bruce to court. Suspecting naught, he arrived with Elizabeth, but quickly discovered Edward in a poisonous mood. Later that night, Bruce heard a knock at the door. Fearing the worst, he opened it expecting guards to seize him and throw him in the Tower. Instead, a servant of the Earl of Glouchester presented Robert with twelve pence, a pair of spurs and the message, 'My lord sent these in return for what he got from you yestereve.' Robert understood clearly. The money and spurs meant to flee before it was too late. He did, barely escaping Edward's grasp."

"Frankly, I am surprised Longshanks didnae toss him into the Tower immediately."

"Edward thought to toy with him. Plus there was the problem of Elizabeth. I dunnae think Edward expected

Robert to bring her with him. De Burgh being Edward's closest friend, it might cause problems if de Burgh's daughter Elizabeth was implicated in her husband's *lese majesty.*

They escaped, made it back to Galloway. Robert waited until Comyn returned and sent word he wanted to meet. Thinking the meeting a trap, Comyn demanded it be on Holy Land—Greyfreirs Church in Dumfries."

"What happened?"

"Both accused the other of being traitors, which led to a fight between them. As you say, they'd rather bury their dirks in each other's heart, which they clearly tried to do. Comyn is dead. That is all anyone knows. Some scream Bruce did it. He says he only defended himself and dinnae mean to kill Comyn. Naetheless, Comyn is dead. Bruce ran to Wishart who confessed him, shrived him and gave him dispensation and absolution. The Comyns are howling mad. Bruce had two choices—flee Scotland and take sanctuary at his sister's court, the Queen of Norway, or stand and fight for the crown. He chose to fight, already taking castles left and right. Word is out he'll soon be crowned at Scone's Abbey."

"That puts us in the thick of it. There is nae way to back out of attending Buchan's wedding, yet the instant we do, Robert will see us as siding with Clan Comyn."

Grant sighed. "We are damned if we do, and damned if we dunnae show."

\* \* \*

Though Duncan had no desire to do so, there was no choice but to attend Isabel and The Black Comyn's wedding. He wore his blue and green MacThomas

*Feileadh Bhreacain*, full plaide, along with the white linen shirt Catherine made him for Christmas.

Eyeing the sky warily, he thought it might soon rain. At least they were having an early spring.

When he entered his bedchamber to check on Catherine's progress, he stopped in the doorway, unable to move. Her beauty astounded him.

Her côte-hardie's emerald green satin bodice snuggly caressed her curves. The velvet skirt fell in soft folds from beneath the underside of her breasts to the top of her shoes. Beaded lace edged the bottom of her long-flowing sleeves and rested atop the seam below her breasts. The scooped neckline exposed no more than Catherine thought proper for a kirk wedding.

Siobhán had woven tiny seed pearls throughout Catherine's curls, her hair piled atop her head with loose tendrils framing her face.

The maid began to fasten the jewelry when Duncan stopped her. "Thank you, Siobhán. I shall assist my lovely lady with her jewels." He left the room and returned with a necklace and earbobs—gold set with emeralds.

"These belonged to my mam." He brushed her cheek with his fingertips. "She sent them to me at Drummond Castle years ago with a note to give them to my wife." He took in every creamy inch of Catherine's exposed neckline. "I believe they go well with your raiments." He fastened them, stood back to admire her. She took his breath away.

He'd watched the play of emotions as they flitted across her face. She'd gone from questioning, to wonder, to doubt, to hope.

Catherine gazed into his rugged face, blushed under his intense scrutiny. She glanced into the looking glass. "Duncan, I could not possibly accept these. They are too beautiful."

"As are you."

Catherine lowered her eyes.

"As Grant and Tory once told me after a debacle they had over a gift, one dunnae refuse a gift given in love."

Running his hand over her cheek, across the line of her chin and down her neck, he leaned forward and kissed her. Held her tightly against him. When he released her, she stood breathless before him.

A gift given in love? Catherine looked into Duncan eyes. How could he say such a thing? Oh she wanted him to, but it'd never happen. She shouldn't read anything into his actions. But she wanted to. By the saints, she really wanted to. Catherine found her vision slightly blurred with tears of hope.

\* \* \*

Pleased that Morag greeted them prior to the ceremony, Duncan thought the young woman bloomed in her sapphire blue côte-hardie. She invited Catherine and him to stand with her even though Isabel had many family members present.

Catherine laughed as Duncan's companions made no secret of trying to edge their way beside Morag. To no one's surprise, Alex won.

Tamara and The MacThomaidh arrived just before the ceremony began. She'd voiced concern he might be too ill to travel, though she was pleased with spring's early arrival. Hopefully, he wouldn't catch cold outside during the ceremony. They slipped in beside Catherine and Duncan, and Cat did a double-take when her brother followed behind them, possessively holding Tamara's arm.

She arched her eyebrows, but they ignored her and focused their attention on the beginning ceremony.

Catherine thought it a faerytale wedding. She tried not to think of her own ceremony, which had been such a farce compared to this solemn day. *Nay, I shall not think of that now.* Her throat painfully tightened.

Within the space of a few heartbeats, Isabel MacDuff became the Countess of Buchan and Fife.

As soon as everyone adjourned to the Great Hall after the couple moved inside the chapel to have their union blessed, Catherine pinned Tamara and her brother with a glare. "Is there aught I should know?"

Trevor grinned like a schoolboy and Tamara tried to look innocent. She failed miserably.

\* \* \*

Isabel was a beautiful bride, but glancing sideways at Catherine, Duncan thought she outshined the new Countess. If only he'd paid attention to her at their own wedding. Regrettable actions often came back to haunt a person—often for a lifetime. Watching the blessed ceremony that just ended, he knew he'd forever ruined that day for his own bride.

Duncan never doubted Comyn's wedding would be elaborate. He expected no less from the earl. His own people could have eaten for several moons on the courses offered during the wedding banquet.

When the entertainment began, tables were dismantled or moved aside so people could join in the festivities. The bride and groom led the first dance, an eightsome reel, and soon everyone joined them. Looking around the Hall as he twirled Catherine around the floor, Duncan saw Trevor dancing with Tamara and Alex dancing with Morag.

Contrary to Duncan's earlier fears, they had a lovely evening. Occasionally he could tell Cat's leg bothered her, but she refused to discuss it except to say, "There are not many occasions when I get to dance with you, my lord husband, and I shall let nothing cut short this evening."

The ground was soaked from torrential rains, so guests spent the night encamped in every available chamber. Catherine and Duncan retired to their appointed room. He watched her as she removed pearls from her hair. Since Duncan already helped her out of her côte-hardie, she sat clad in her chemise.

When she raised her hand to brush her hair, he strode to her side and took the brush from her.

"You are mine, Cat," Duncan said with a feral growl. "Never forget that."

Catherine turned on the small seat to look up at him. Her eyes sparkled with happiness, but she stayed his hand with hers. "Duncan, what bothers you? You have been upset ever since Lord Dinraven asked me to dance. Did he say aught to upset you?"

"He said naught of import," Duncan interrupted, carefully avoiding her eyes.

"Then what has you troubled?"

Duncan didn't like having such possessive feelings, didn't want to care. He glared at Catherine. "He wants you."

"I beg your pardon?"

"Dinraven wants you in his bed," Duncan clarified. His eyes turned dark. He reached down and pulled Catherine to her feet. "I willnae have it, Cat. I willnae be made a cuckold again."

"He said that? He told you—?"

"Of course not," he shot back. "He dinnae have to. I saw the way he looked at you."

"Duncan, I would never—"

"Would you not? If a handsome, wealthy man such as Dinraven asked you to his bed, you wouldnae willingly agree?"

Catherine's eyes held a disturbing combination of anger and hurt. "That is exactly what I am telling you, Duncan MacThomas. I would never dishonor my vows—and that you have such low regard for me is intolerable."

Her face set, she grabbed a robe and started for the door. "I knew you did not want me, but I thought you respected me. I thought…"

She got to the door and opened it when Duncan reached her and slammed it shut. He grabbed her arms and swung her around.

Catherine opened her mouth to rail at him at the very moment he pinned her between his hard body and the heavy wooden door.

A strangled cry of rage threatened to erupt from her throat. It faded at the feral look in his eyes.

Scant heartbeats passed before he crushed her mouth with his own.

Catherine placed her hands flat against his chest and pushed.

He didn't budge, but pressed her harder again the door.

His breathing increased and Catherine felt his manhood harden.

Keeping her pinned to the wall, he released her mouth, moved his head back and looked deeply into her eyes.

"Cat?"

Catherine saw the pain in his eyes. She raised a finger to his lips to silence him. "I shall never bed another, Duncan. I believe you know that about me. It matters not who he is — a great Chieftain like Dinraven or even the king of Scotland. I made my vows before God the day we wed and it goes against the tenants of my faith to dishonor them." She rubbed the backs of her fingers against his cheek. "I heard what your first wife did, but I am not Helen."

Duncan lowered his mouth to hers, breathing easier. The kiss didn't have the urgency it had only moments before. Now he savored her. Lifting her legs around his waist, he carried her to the bed.

Placing her on it gently, he lowered himself atop her and kissed her tenderly.

The bed in the great mansion was comfortable, but Catherine and Duncan got little sleep. His eyes smoky with desire, he was too busy showing her how much she meant to him.

Safely wrapped in Duncan's arms, she thought he whispered, "I am sorry I ruined your wedding. It should have been as beautiful as the one we witnessed this night."

Her lashes softly fluttering against his chest, Catherine smiled.

* * *

Catherine stood next to Duncan observing the ceremony, clutching his arm, fearing how this event might shape their lives. She glanced to Tory standing beside Grant, the same expression of fear in her eyes. They were two Englishwomen with Scottish husbands who might have to defend their land. Catherine thought of Trevor likely forced to ride at Edward's side. She lived in dread her husband and brother might face each other across a battlefield.

Wearing robes borrowed from the Archbishop of Glasgow, Robert rode to the Abbey of Scone where he was crowned with formality and solemnity. Bishop Wishart—a long-time, silent organizer of Scotland's rebellion—hid the trappings to crown the new Scottish king. Now he placed the gold circlet upon Robert's head, while the great banner of the kings of Scotland—the lion with scarlet lilies—was unfurled behind The Bruce.

Noticeably absent was the young Earl of Fife. Held in Edward's *safekeeping*, the lad was unable to perform his hereditary office of crowning the King of the Scots. Grant whispered, "'Tis doubtful he would have done so even if not in Longshanks' clutches. He is close kinsman of Red Comyn and his sister Isabel is wed to Black Comyn. Talk about sticking your hand in a hornet's nest."

Duncan nodded. "The lad likely feels relief the choice was taken from him."

Nearly seven months to the day after the death of William Wallce, Bruce was king. The first king not crowned on *Lia Fail*, the Stone of Destiny. The first not to receive the crown from the hands of the Earl of Fife.

"God save the King!" someone shouted.

Grant said softly, "God save us all."

Catherine and Tory echoed his thoughts. "Amen."

\* \* \*

Duncan helped Catherine from the litter, then moved up the steps to join Grant and Tory already there. They'd come this bright Spring morn, a morn full of hope and promise, to pay homage to Robert Bruce, Earl of Carrick, Lord of Annandale, King of the Scots. Catherine heard Duncan's and Grant's whispers long into the night, discussing what Edward's first move would be when learning of Robert's coronation. Though she couldn't decipher most words, their expressions revealed their worry. Both feared vengeance like that directed at William Wallace would be unleashed across the land. Edward thought sending William's severed limbs to the four corners of Scotland would see an end to the rebellion. Instead, he'd martyred Wallace. Now Bruce picked up Scotland's banner for freedom, but the two friends feared he'd first plunge the country into civil war. By swearing their oaths to The Bruce, they'd be bane to Clan Comyn, so they'd face an enemy from the South as well as ones at their backs.

"Robert waits, eager to get his government in place,"

Grant said solemnly.

A clatter of hooves rang out as a small band of men galloped toward them. Catherine gasped. "'Tis Isabel."

Sure enough, hair flying like a warrior's pennon, barefoot and riding astride, Lady Isabel, Countess of Buchan, led a cadre of men, some wearing Buchan colors, some of Fife.

She leapt from the horse's back and ran up to them. "Am I late? Since my brother cannae crown our king as is his office, I came to see Bruce crowned properly. I stole my husband's best horses and rode with haste. I brought men willing to fight for Robert."

Catherine stared at the young woman, her eyes aglow, hardly recognizable as the lass who married the elder Comyn. The fire of rebellion burned in her soul and 'twas obvious she saw Bruce as a hero.

Duncan shook his head. "They crowned him yestereve."

The Countess frowned, then her face brightened. "Then we shall just have to do it again. Nae man can be King of the Scots until the Earl of Clan Fife places the crown upon his brow. I shall perform the office in my brother's stead, then nae one dare claim Bruce is not our king."

"Oh, aye," Duncan grumbled, "so Edward can be twice as angered."

On Palm Sunday, two days later, Catherine, Duncan, Tory and Grant witnessed the second crowning of Bruce, as the Countess of Buchan placed the gold circlet upon Robert's handsome brow.

# Chapter Twenty-Nine

"He is a monster!" Tears streamed down Catherine's face when news reached Cray Hall about the capture of Bruce women.

The courier reported, "Edward moved swiftly in two spearheads, leading one himself, his son, the Prince of Wales the other. Bruce's forces were too thin to man the borders, having only five score landed knights. Bruce left his queen and her ladies in the care of his younger brother Nigel, while he raised an army of nearly five thousand men. Upon hearing the approach of Edward's host under the Earl of Pembroke, Bruce moved to Perth."

When the courier departed to share his news with the rest of the country, Duncan and his men rehashed the horrible events. Duncan knew his stubborn wife wouldn't cease her interrogation until she heard all the sordid facts. "After fierce fighting, Bruce, Jamie Douglas and Neil Campbell barely escaped into the night after Pembroke struck. Later Sir Simon Fraser and Sir Christopher Seton were captured at their castles." Duncan walked to the fireplace and stared into the cold hearth. "Edward had Fraser and Seton executed in the manner of Wallace. It seems nobles are no longer exempt from the poison that rots Edward's soul. Bruce sent word to Nigel to fetch the women, knowing he had to bring them into his protection." He swore. "I hoped to let them stay here, but 'twasnae safe after Edward heralded throughout the land proclaiming the Bruce women and any with them were to be treated as outlaws. He granted leave to any and all to rape or murder them and they'd be rewarded. I couldnae put you all in such danger."

"How can one man be so...vile?" Catherine couldn't find the words to explain her horror.

"Elizabeth, the Countess Buchan, Bruce's daughter Marjorie, and his two sisters were captured." Duncan closed his eyes against the horrible images. There was so much more he knew, but had to spare his wife from hearing. Her heart was too tender.

"Nigel Bruce was put to death after being dragged through Berwick's streets, hanged and beheaded."

Catherine choked back a sob. "Oh, Duncan, he was such a beautiful lad, so full of life. The ladies adored him."

"I guess killing Nigel, Fraser and Seton spent Edward's spleen. He spared the women from being put to death, though 'twasnae for mercy. Edward has ordained wooden and metal cages be built jutting from the battlements of Castles Berwick, Roxburgh and Kinrose and the women be imprisoned there. One is being built at the Tower of London for Marjorie." Duncan fought the wave of nausea trying to overwhelm him.

"Duncan, she is but two and ten! A child! 'Tis inhuman." Catherine wanted to scream her outrage, but knew it would do no good. "And Morag? Was she with Isabel?"

"Aye." He nodded sadly. "She was put in a cage at Kinrose."

"Duncan, please, we must do something. We cannot leave these poor women to this fate. Morag is as dear to me as my sister."

Duncan paused while pacing the Hall. "Sweetling, dunnae you think people have already tried to free them? 'Tis impossible. You heard what the courier said. The cages are heavily guarded. Longshanks uses them as bait for Bruce, *wants* him to come for them."

Devastated they could do nothing, her voice shook with emotion. "Let me return to England. I shall beg the king for her freedom."

"As long as there is breath in my body, you shall do nae such thing."

"But surely he would listen to me. I did as he asked when we wed."

Duncan walked toward her, drawing her into the safety of his arms. "Ah, wife, Edward listens to nae one. I am sorry about Morag. I wish you could have convinced her to come back with us, but I shallnae let you bring attention to yourself. In Edward's twisted mind, he might throw you in a cage, too. 'Tis a pity Morag is Bruce's cousin, elsewise Longshanks might have been lenient when he caught her with the Countess."

Catherine leaned against him and sobbed.

\* \* \*

A sennight later the Drummond family arrived. Although Grant used delivery of the chair he'd promised Catherine as an excuse, Duncan knew he wished to talk about the sad turn in recent events.

Duncan eyed the women while raising the metal quaich to his lips. "Catherine is upset about the women being captured—Morag in particular."

Grant watched the women head upstairs.

"She bonded with the lass."

"Aye. Morag visited during Christmastide. Can you believe my daft wife actually wished to request an audience with Edward to beg his lenience?"

Grant quirked a brow.

"She thought he would grant her an obligement since she did his bidding and wed me." He rolled his eyes. "Daft logic. As if the English king would be lenient to any Scot. I'll let her nowhere near that blackguard."

"Not to mention all the handsome men at court who would undoubtedly try to talk your lovely wife to their beds," Grant teased—quickly realizing it hadn't been the wisest thing to say.

Duncan threw his goblet at the hearth, his eyes revealing his pain and uncertainty. "If anyone touches her I shall kill them."

He didn't realize the depth of feeling his words revealed.

"Catherine considers the lass a friend. And from what I have seen, Catherine doesnae think she has many friends."

"Batherskite. Everyone loves her." Duncan's brows furrowed at the suggestion it might be otherwise.

"You know that, but does she? Everyone, originally, was your friend. She may think they only like her because of you."

"Look at how she and Tory get on."

"Aye, like sisters," Grant agreed, rubbing his chin. "And whose friend was Tory before Catherine came here?"

Duncan opened his mouth to answer, shut it without uttering a sound. Instead he tipped his drink to his lips and drank.

"But Morag likes her for herself."

"'Tis why we all like her," Duncan argued. His tone indicated he realized he was losing the battle. "Afore I came back, my people fell in love with her, were ready to form an insurrection had I not returned on my own."

Grant chuckled. "And well they should have, you great lout. They were smarter than you."

\* \* \*

Catherine joined arms with Tory.

Just before reaching the bottom landing, Catherine stopped on the steps. She turned to Tory, glanced toward her husband. "They plan to free the women from those hellacious cages."

"They plan to *try*," Tory agreed sadly.

"'Twill be dangerous." Catherine made no attempt to hide her fear.

"Aye. Men have been killed trying. Edward has no intention of freeing them, uses them as bait to trap Bruce." She stopped before they neared their husbands. "Will you try to stop him?"

"Stop Duncan from doing what he feels strongly about? What he feels is right for his country? He'd never listen. Part of me wants them to try. I even offered to try and free them myself."

"You what?" Tory asked, aghast.

"I suggested I return to England to speak to the king." Seeing the shocked look on Tory's face, Catherine affirmed. "Duncan refused—or should I say that is a polite version of what happened." After a moment's thought, she continued, "I tried to stop him from leaving once before, Tory. I did not succeed. 'Tis who he is. 'Tis one of the many things I… admire about him."

"What you mean is, 'tis one of the many things you *love* about him."

Cat's eyes swung to Tory at the bold words. Biting her lip, she nodded. "Aye, 'tis one of the things I love about him. How did you know?"

"That you love him?"

Catherine nodded.

"Everyone knows. Except for Duncan. You are just afraid to tell him." Catherine started to protest, but Tory held up her hand. "Do not argue with me. You would waste your time and mine. I did not say you had to tell him—although I am certain my dearest friend would love to hear the words. But you should admit it to yourself. Your husband is much closer to winning your heart than you ever thought possible, Lady MacThomas."

Throwing her arms around Catherine, Tory hugged her. "Oh Cat, if you only knew how much you remind me of myself when I met Grant."

Catherine's eyebrows furrowed at her words.

"Never fear. When the time comes, you shall admit your love for him. You shall see." Tory turned toward the outer door, but felt the threat of an approaching storm. She knew not if it was a storm of harsh weather or of impending violence.

"For now, we must concentrate on what will happen to the women Edward holds hostage. And pray for our husbands' safe return."

# Chapter Thirty

They rode and rode hard, threaded their way through the mountains, keeping to the mists. The Highland way. Use the fog as a shield against English troops unfamiliar with the lay of the land. The men were exhausted, their mounts pressed hard, but they had to keep to the circular path back to Drummond land. What good would rescuing Morag do if the English followed them?

Duncan glanced over at Alex, holding Morag before him, wrapped her in his plaide to keep the mist from making her worse. He worried about the lass. She'd lapsed in and out of consciousness. Sometimes she slept. Alex must weary from holding her, but he stubbornly refused to let anyone spell him. Grant had offered and Alex looked like he might take a dirk to their friend.

Duncan's mind conjured an image of Catherine. Likely Tory and she were wearing holes on the soles of their *ghillies*, pacing, frantic with worry. He could understand Alex's need to hold Morag. Had it been Cat in one of those cages, he would have been out of his mind. Cat would be relieved their efforts secured Morag's release.

They'd studied information gathered on the cages holding Isabel, Bruce's sister Mary, and Morag. They could do nothing for Elizabeth, Robert's Queen. She'd been taken to England. Informants swore she was treated well, not out of respect for her being a queen, but simply because she was de Burgh's daughter. Longshanks couldn't afford to turn his long-time friend and ally from his side by horrific treatment of his beautiful daughter. No word had come back yet if Edward made good the promise to cage Bruce's child at the Tower of London as he did the other women. Some heard she'd been sent to a convent.

There was no getting to Isabel at Berwick. She signed her fate with Longshanks when she placed that crown upon Bruce's brow. She, above all others, he held most securely in his fist. Roxburgh Castle proved impossible to breach, so they could do nothing to aid Mary.

However, Morag was merely a Bruce cousin, not quite so important in Longshanks' mind. 'Twas why he chose the wee fortress on the hillside as the site to hold her. The castle was in an area that was supportive of Bruce. While the English garrisoned the fort, it was with a much smaller force. Scots living in and around the castle were furious at Morag's treatment, so were willing to aid Duncan and Grant's men.

Morag was seized by a coughing fit. It pained Duncan to watch. He only hoped they'd not been too late to save her. "How fares she?"

Alex's hand trembled on the rein. "We must get her someplace warm—soon."

"Hang tight, lad. We are almost there."

They'd gotten into Kinrose Castle easily through the escape tunnel, using a map drawn by the former Gate

Keep.

Duncan feared Alex would go wild when he first saw Morag. Her eyes glazed, she hadn't recognized him, hadn't responded in any fashion. He'd had to step into the cage, risk being seen to get her to come inside the castle. As Alex spoke softly to her, Morag bestirred and tilted her head against the comfort of his fingers. Her eyes didn't move. Duncan saw tears streak his friend's face.

Suddenly, the English were everywhere. They had to fight. At Morag's scream, instinct and training ruled. Alex raised his sword to ward off the blow aimed at his head. He shoved Morag behind him to protect her. Swords swinging, he and Duncan jumped into action and fought as if they'd both been born Berserkers.

The sound of clashing swords and Morag's screams served as a beacon to other guards, summoning them into the passageway. The first two were felled by Duncan. Two more appeared. The guards brandished their swords and Alex suffered their slashes. Morag screamed behind him, but they dared spare no glance. Over and over he and Alex slashed and lunged, super human strength finally felling their opponents.

Alex grabbed Morag's hand and advanced mere steps when more guards charged. Grant, Ian and their men appeared, giving Duncan and Alex a shield so they could free Morag. They formed a phalanx and cut their way like a spearhead through the *Southron* soldiery.

They'd rescued her, but not without cost. They left dead on the bailey ground of Kinrose.

From there it had been a running game of hound and

hare. When the pandemonium calmed, Duncan motioned for Alex to lift Morag into his arms. Carrying her, he wended his way through town. Everywhere they turned, they neared English patrols.

Duncan warned to keep Morag silent. They couldn't risk having her moan. Alex placed his hand over her mouth.

When the enemy passed, they crept to the next building—and the next, and the next. They hid from the English *hobelars*, while escaping into the hills. At one point when they got too close, Grant and Ian split their forces and led the English away. Duncan held his breath until they met again.

Grant winked at him, saying the way was clear to make the final run to Drummond Castle. Tory would kill him if anything happened to her black-haired husband.

Catherine paced the Great Hall of Drummond Castle, unable to stay still. The dream had come again. The one of being in a place so dark daylight never seemed to penetrate, of Duncan and that man locked in a battle to the death. Even now, that might be taking place. She put a hand to her heart to still her mind. She wouldn't think upon that. The prospect terrified her.

"You miss him, don't you?" Tory asked.

Close to tears, Catherine nodded. "I desperately wanted Morag's release from that horrid nightmare, but not if it means losing Duncan or Grant. This wait seems eternal."

A page dashed in, out of breath from running with the news. "Men come."

"Can you tell if they are our men?" Tory asked.

"Nay, about two score ten, mounted and moving fast. Not English."

Women and children alike ran from the keep as the call when through the fortress 'twas Laird Grant returning. Emotions ran high as they waited for the men to ride under the portcullis, each woman seeking the face of her loved one. The warriors all had their plaides wrapped around them as a mantle, the color of their hair obscured under the makeshift hood of wool.

Frantically, Catherine searched their countenances, but failed to find either Duncan or Grant. Then the final four riders moved under the murder holes and into the bailey. Ian, Grant, Alex and Duncan sat upon their monstrous stallions. Alex held the huddled form of a woman before him.

They were safe!

Alex sat as if he couldn't move, as Grant and Duncan lifted Morag down. Ian took her from them, then they helped Alex from the horse's back.

Tory couldn't wait, but flew into Grant's arms, hugging him.

"Have mercy, lass, you squeeze the breath from me."

With a trembling hand, she wiped tears from her eyes. Trying to regain control of her emotions, her sad eyes looked up at him and asked the question everyone feared to voice. "How many did we lose?"

"Six."

Catherine stood rooted to the group, watching. Lightheaded. She feared if she moved she would faint. Everyone was covered with blood. Even Duncan!

He came to her, stood before her, his blue eyes

almost drinking in her image. Then he looked down at the blood. All the wounds were slight, just in places that bled like a stuck pig.

"Lass, there is naught I want more than to kiss you, but—" He made a face at the blood and dirt caking his plaide and shirt.

Catherine didn't hesitate. She flew into his arms. He held her tenderly, brushing his knuckles against her cheek to remove tears.

"Hush, lass, I am safe."

Embarrassed at her unbridled response, Catherine buried her face in his shirt.

He was alive. Nothing else mattered.

* * *

Tears streamed down Catherine's face as she helped Morag sit. She was as weak as a newborn babe. "Oh, Morag, they freed you." Catherine's eyes traveled the length of her friend taking in every bruise, cut, and stain.

"Blessed Holy Mother, what did the English do to you?" She had cuts and slashes everywhere and the torment she'd experienced from lack of food and exposure to the elements was obvious. How had she survived?

Morag turned to look at Catherine, but her eyes were glazed. When she tried to rise, her face turned deathly pale and she passed out.

"Duncan!" Catherine screamed.

Duncan helped Alex lay Morag on a straw pallet. Tory tore herself away from Grant to assess the damage.

Though wounded with cuts and slashes of his own, Alex held Morag's hand, stroking it with a feather touch while Tory treated her injuries.

Wrapping the final strip around Ian's chest, Catherine turned to Alex. "Let me tend your wounds while Tory cares for Morag. She is in good hands."

Raw emotion in his eyes, he adamantly refused. "Not until I know she will live. I feared she wouldnae survive the ride. I held her…feared if I let go she'd slip away." He looked at Morag's still figure resting on the pallet, his eyes revealing something inside him would die with Morag if she didn't pull through. "Without everyone's help, we would be dead."

"Alex," Catherine soothed, "you protected her as well as possible."

He shook his head, denying her encouraging words.

"You will do Morag no good if your wounds fester and you die."

His expression of exasperation looked like one she frequently received from her husband. Men were so thick headed.

Warwick rushed from room to room, delivering hot water and ensuring clean cloths were torn into binding strips. "Och, I am getting too old for this," he grumbled to no one in particular. He glanced around for Agnes. "I am glad you are here to help."

"You just like having me at your side."

Catherine smiled when Agnes approached Alex. The auld woman moved a cot beside Morag's. "Sit on that, young man, and remove your plaide—now."

He glared at Agnes. "I said I wouldnae—"

"I know what you said. Now I tell you what you shall do. If you wish to care for this young woman after we tend her, you will need your strength. Letting your wounds fester is daft. Now remove your plaide or I will do it for you."

From the other side of the room, Warwick shouted, "Best you do it, lad. You willnae win against my Agnes."

Once everyone had been treated, Tory stretched her sore muscles and told Cat, "I go in search of Grant. I know exactly where I shall find him—propped against the hearth in the Great Hall. Likely, Duncan is with him."

Grant and Duncan had been treated, and as they assured, the wounds were shallow. They now slept in the chairs where they sat before the fire, tankards of ale still clutched in their hands.

Tory crossed to Grant and gently placed a kiss to his cheek. He instantly jerked awake and blinked. "Are they alright?"

"In time. Some are worse than others."

Duncan awoke as well. "And the lass?"

Tory's eyes locked with Catherine. "Time will tell. She is very ill. I mourn our lost men, but you did a good deed in saving her. I believe, if left untreated another day, she would have died."

* * *

Duncan tugged on Catherine's arm so she'd sit before him. He held her as if he'd never let her go. Tears flowed down her face. She'd fought an emotional battle while Duncan had been gone—and lost.

The fear demonstrated what she'd not admitted. She loved him with her whole heart.

Unable to speak of her own feelings, Catherine told him, "Your sister hasn't said anything, but I think she has feelings for my brother. Will you find problem in that?"

"They are their own people. 'Tis their lot and right to walk their own path. I spoke to her. She vowed never to give her heart to another after losing her husband. Worse, she thinks your brother deserves better than a childless widow. Trevor will have a hard road to travel to win her. She may never admit her feelings."

Catherine's lashes swept down, shielding her inner pain. "Sometimes 'tis hard to speak of matters of the heart."

\* \* \*

Nearby, Warwick sat slouched over a table. "Och, I need to sleep, but am too tired to stand."

Agnes sat beside him and reached out to gently pat his hand. "Go to bed, auld man."

"I shall if you come with me."

She elbowed him in his side. "As if you could…"

"Nay, auld woman," he laughed. "For once I couldnae. This time I just want to sleep, but I would like to wake with you beside me."

Duncan chuckled at the banter between the aged couple, wondering what he and Catherine would do when they were old.

Agnes said nothing, but squeezed Warwick's rough, wrinkled hand. She rose and tried to help him to his feet. "Then come along and I shall tuck you into bed like a wee bairnie."

Warwick laughed and pushed himself to his feet by placing both hands palms down on the table. Finally standing, he grabbed Agnes' hand, reached up to touch her face with his. "Woman, you are beautiful—wrinkles and all." Duncan watched them walk together toward Angus' room.

Agnes grumbled all the way. "The impression we must be giving everyone."

Warwick chuckled, placed a hand to his chest. "Och, aye, two auld people heading to bed. I misdoubt there is a man here that doesnae believe we shall do aught but sleep." He released her hand and slapped his on her bottom. "Now quit grumbling, auld woman, and let us sleep."

\* \* \*

Stretched out on the bed, Duncan cradled Catherine in his arms. He'd loved her several times over the past hours. He should have been sated, but every time he woke and felt her body snuggled beside him, he craved her again. He'd come too close to not returning. The English had been everywhere. "I love you, *Mo Chride*," he murmured into her ear.

He felt her heart lurch, but she buried her face against the curve of his neck. "Shh, husband, sleep. You must rest." Her mind shouted at her to tell him she loved him too, but she bit her lip and stifled the thought.

# Chapter Thirty-One

Catherine grimaced when Tory brought a quaich and set it down before her while breaking her fast. Noticing the face she made, Duncan picked it up to smell it and promptly set it down, making a face.

"What foul smelling potion is this?"

"Something she must drink for awhile," Tory evaded answering. "Do not fret. Catherine looked a bit peaked and these herbs should help."

Catherine wrinkled her nose after sipping the liquid. "She's made me drink this every day since you departed for Kinrose." She grumbled and made a face at Tory. "It tastes as horrid as it smells."

"Fares she well?" Duncan's eyes slowly searched his wife's face, his hand rising to lightly caress it. "Should we—?"

"You need do naught. She just needs drink this each day." Tory rushed on, "I prepared enough herbs for you to take with you. Ensure Catherine takes this after you return home." She whirled on her heel and walked away.

\* \* \*

A fortnight later, Duncan stood in the doorway and watched as Alex and Morag rode into Cray Hall along with men he'd left to guard them at Drummond Castle. They arrived just before the sky lit with jagged lightning bolts. Alex dismounted and reached up to help Morag before aiding her towards the door.

Inside, Morag removed her mantle. "Alasdair, stop being so stubborn. I should return home."

"Dunnae be daft. That's the first place the king shall look. You can never return there. From now on you shall live with us."

"I cannae—"

"You must," Catherine said, hurrying across the hall. She wrapped her arms around Morag and drew her close. "Duncan and I insist you remain here."

Alex pressed, "'Twill be difficult enough to hide you until the king ceases searching. I dunnae wish to be worrying you shall try to leave."

Taking in the homecoming, Duncan interceded. "I dinnae misdoubt the king's cohorts search even now. 'Tisnae my wish to frighten you needlessly, lass, but treatment you'd receive would be far worse than anything you experienced during your imprisonment. Edward declared you an outlaw. He has set his dogs loose to do as they please should they get their hands on you."

Duncan turned to Alex. "I offer Morag sanctuary." Duncan smiled, trying to place Morag at ease. "We shall see her safe whilst she recovers."

Morag doubled over with a coughing spell, ending all arguments. "I am sorry to trouble you."

Alex put his arm around her, smiled at her tenderly. "You are nae trouble."

She shook her head apologetically when she straightened. "I shall be but a nuisance." She sat ashen faced as she looked about the room.

Moving forward, Catherine cast Alex a reassuring smile, then helped Morag to her room.

* * *

Although he'd rather be anywhere else, as Chief of Clan MacThomaidh, Duncan's father had the right to know they harbored a fugitive. If discovered, it would impact the entire clan, not just Duncan. The next day Duncan went to see him.

Her body wracked with fatigue and injuries, Morag had been abed when he left the Hall.

Catherine wished to accompany him to Castle Glenshee to stave off arguments between him and his father, but finally she agreed to remain with Morag.

Alasdair accompanied him. "I was the one to suggest she stay with us. If you receive punishment from our Chief, I share the blame."

To their surprise, Tamara met them at the door. She'd been crying. "Da's ill."

Duncan hesitated a heartbeat to let his sister's words sink in, then strode upstairs to his father's bedchamber. His step faltered at the sight that greeted him.

His burly father—the man he'd hated for so many years—appeared as weak as a newborn bairn. He lay abed, bolstered by pillows.

A hint of a smile crossed his lips. He raised a hand and motioned Duncan to sit beside the bed.

His breath shallow, it appeared he forced himself to speak. "Now I know I am dying. Either that or something brews. Which is it that brings you to my bedside after ignoring me these past years?"

The lump in Duncan's throat grew, but he finally spoke. "I am responsible for another life."

His father's eyes slid past him to the doorway. "Young Alasdair accompanies you. That means the new life is the gel you freed from Kinrose's cage."

Stunned, Duncan's mouth dropped open. "How did...?" He stopped mid-sentence. Did the king know as well?

"Did you really think to keep me in the dark? Och, you should know better than that." After recovering from a coughing fit, he continued, "I know everything you do, have for years. Just been too bullheaded to admit it."

Duncan stared at his father, but said nothing.

"I dinnae have much longer, son. 'Tis time we clear the air. I cannae go to my death without admitting the truth."

Duncan stood. He didn't want to hear this. Over the past moons Catherine insisted he needed to mend the rift with his father. It wasn't possible. Yet, there was something healing about being in this room. He couldn't explain it.

"Sit, lad. 'Tis much we need speak of and I tire."

Duncan remained standing.

"You dinnae have to listen to me as my son, but as Chief of Clan MacThomaidh I can command you listen. I would rather you sat as my son."

A coughing fit again sapped his energy. He removed a cloth from his mouth and Duncan noted specks of blood. He tensed. Did his father have it aright? Was he dying? After but a moment's hesitation, he did as bid without arguing. From the corner of his eye he noticed

Alex disappear from the doorway.

"Tamara has been here for days. She has been sad too long since the death of her husband. I feared she would never allow her heart to love again. Now I see a spark in her eyes. Mayhap she will yet wed and have a child of her own."

Duncan grimaced without thought.

"I am sorry. I dinnae mean to dredge up sadness. I am sorry for the loss of your child. You have Meghan, though, and she couldnae be more delightful. I have missed her. She was a ray of sunshine to my days."

Surprisingly, Duncan believed him.

Alex returned. "I fetched ale. I thought you both could use it." He took MacThomaidh's to him then handed the other quaich to Duncan before once again leaving the room.

Duncan turned back to face his father. Memories flooded over him. He'd been right to feel the anger he'd harbored over the years. So why suddenly feel defensive? He sensed his father meant to bring up a subject he didn't wish to discuss.

Within the space of several heartbeats, his father said, "We must talk. I dinnae have the luxury of time anymore to hope we can work this out slowly."

"There is naught to work out," Duncan said gruffly. His chest felt tight and it was difficult to breathe.

"Och, there is and well you know it."

Duncan rose and headed for the door.

"Dinnae walk out on me, Duncan MacThomaidh. When I meet my Maker I wish to go with a clear conscience."

Duncan turned and swore. "A clear…How *dare* you suggest such a thing? You *abandoned* me."

There. He'd said it. After all the years of holding it inside, he'd finally revealed his innermost feelings to his father.

MacThomaidh looked overcome by remorse. "Aye, I did."

Duncan stared at his father, never expecting that admission.

"I realized years ago I erred, but by then there was naught I could do. The damage had been done. You were grown and wanted little to do with me. I dinnae blame you."

"You expect me to forgive you now?" An angry flush rose to Duncan's cheeks. "You willnae die. You are too mean."

Duncan stood resolute. The auld man brought this upon himself. Duncan vowed years ago never to forgive him.

"I knew this wouldnae be easy. I hoped with time we might grow closer." Duncan raised a brow at the declaration. "You have softened some since wedding the lass." MacThomaidh tried to catch Duncan's eye, but Duncan refused to look at him.

"Duncan," MacThomaidh thundered. "We must talk."

"We have naught to talk about." Duncan's tone was hard.

Behind him, a melodic voice said, "Please Duncan, listen to Da. He means what he says. He told me his regrets years ago, but made me promise to hold my tongue. He wanted to work it out in his own way, his own time."

Duncan spun on her. "You talked about me?"

"Because we love you, you great lummox."

"*You* love me." He motioned to his father. "He—"

"Loves you as well," Tamara interrupted.

His senses reeled. How could Tamara do this? She knew what their father had done.

True, men fostered their sons out to other clans to learn the art of warfare—but they didn't forget about them. He vowed his sons would never… Duncan drew his thoughts up short. He'd never have sons, never have the one thing his father had squandered—a son's love.

From the massive bed, MacThomaidh watched his son. How could he have been so daft as to throw one of his children away? That's what he'd done. No matter what excuse he'd made at the time, he'd freely given away his own son. Surely there could be no greater fool on the face of the earth.

Aching emptiness overtook him. So many years lost, never to be returned. Why hadn't he listened to his wife? She'd not wanted Duncan to leave. She'd pleaded to let him stay.

He'd turned a deaf ear.

Now he'd give anything to have Duncan's forgiveness, but doubted Duncan would give it. Whether Duncan admitted it or not, he was much like himself. Having made up their minds, it wasn't easy to change.

MacThomaidh's temper flared. Curse it, he'd not give in this easily. He was clan Chieftain. He'd fought all his life.

"Duncan, sit."

Duncan's eyes narrowed. "Dunnae order me about."

"Sit," MacThomaidh ordered. "You will hear me out."

"I need do no such thing. You gave up that right—"

His father shook his head sadly. "Years ago. I know. You repeat that oft enough. Have you made nae mistakes in your lifetime you wish you could change?"

One sprang immediately to mind. He'd left Catherine.

He said nothing.

The old man smiled. "Och, I thought so. None of us are perfect—even though we act like we are."

"I never claimed to be perfect"

"Good, and as much as it pains me to admit in my auld age, neither am I."

MacThomaidh sat forward and looked into Duncan's eyes. "I made mistakes raising you, but there is naught I can do to change that. I only hope someday you can forgive me. Until you do, I believe you will always hold part of yourself away from your beautiful wife."

"My *beautiful wife*?" Duncan frowned suspiciously. "I thought you dunnae like Catherine."

"She is perfect—and you know she is."

Understanding hit Duncan like a pike. He let loose a stream of curses. "Again you manipulate my life?"

"You left her," MacThomaidh groused. "Were you not wrong to do so?"

"That is my concern, not yours."

"There you are wrong," his father shouted. "My newest daughter *is* my business. Especial when I see you making the same mistakes I did."

Duncan's eyes narrowed. "What are you blethering about?"

"You left her just as I left you. You disappointed me when you did that. I never thought to see you make the same mistake I had and couldnae let you continue to do so. What I did was wrong, but your actions were just as wrong. I knew if you thought I dinnae like her, you'd stay with her to spite me. Just like you left because I chose her. I hoped if you spent time with her, you'd realize she is perfect for you." He held up his hand when Duncan opened his mouth to interrupt. "And you did."

"That is why you comforted her when she fell over the ravine?" Despite himself, past events fell into place.

"Aye," MacThomaidh admitted, embarrassment flooding his face. "I couldnae let the wee lassie die. You hadnae admitted it, but I knew you needed her. As much as she needs you now, only she too is too proud to admit it. She still believes you dinnae love her."

Duncan wondered why his father's words made sense. Och, had Catherine turned him soft? He shouldn't listen to his father.

He fell silent and shook his head.

MacThomaidh pressed the issue. "Soon you shall be clan Chief and will be a verra good one. I have every confidence in your abilities." He blinked back tears. "I am proud of you, son. That admission comes many years too late, but I want you to hear it. I am verra proud of the man you grew to be. The fact I can claim no part in building your character causes me great pain."

Duncan's chest grew tight, expanded. The barrier

he'd spent years building around his heart came crashing down.

He rose and ran from the room.

Jumping onto his horse, he raced home.

\* \* \*

When he threw open the door and strode inside, Catherine took one look at his face and paled. "Your father?"

Duncan found it difficult to speak. "He lives."

She rushed to him and wrapped her arms around his massive body. "Then what is wrong? You look as if you saw a ghost—or had a vision."

Duncan rested his chin atop her hair. The light scent of roses wafted to his nose.

When he still didn't speak, Catherine drew back and looked into his face. She took his hand and led him to a chair by the hearth. "Sit. Tell me what happened."

Hearing Catherine order him to sit, just as his father had so recently done, moved him to tears. Like a child who'd fallen and injured his knee, Duncan wept. He felt a fool. Men didn't cry.

Catherine wrapped her arms around him and kissed the top of his head.

His men quietly exited the Hall, clearly unable to face the torment on their young laird's face.

Catherine placed her hand beneath Duncan's chin and turned him to face her. He looked haggard.

"You finally realize your father loves you? He does, you know. As you have been unable to forgive him, he's been unable to absolve himself for the way he treated you. However," she stopped and smiled, "I have it on good authority he loves you very much."

"What authority?" he challenged.

"Why your father, of course."

Duncan roared. "You spoke to Da about me?"

Catherine shrugged. "Mayhap a time or two."

"When did you plan to tell me?"

"I did not plan to mention it. 'Tis between you and your father. 'Twas not my place to meddle."

Duncan laughed. "You meddle into everything else in my life. Why should this be different?"

"Do not yell at me, Duncan MacThomas—and I do not meddle." She stopped to form her words. "I merely *help* situations along sometimes."

"Well there is naught to help. He wishes to ease his conscience before he meets his Maker. I have no intention of helping him."

"Duncan you must—"

"I need do naught. He abandoned me, left me with Clan Kerr."

"He but meant to foster you. He knows now being worried about your health was wrong."

"Worry about my health?" Duncan choked. "Is that what he told you? He cared naught about me, thought me an embarrassment. 'Tis the reason he left me."

"But—"

"But naught! Have you never wondered at the scars on my back?" A sob broke from his throat as he said the words.

"Of course. I wanted to ask about them many times, but feared you would be angered. I thought you would tell me when you were ready."

"Well, I am ready. These scars are a *gift* from Father."

"Duncan! Surely your father never beat you."

"He dinnae have to. He let someone else do it for him."

Catherine placed her arms around him. "I do not believe he would do that."

"He left me with Clan Kerr's chieftain. I dunnae know why the man hated me, but he did. When he wasnae starving me, he beat me. Remember I mentioned how I hated mazes? When I was but a small lad, and so sick, he beat me until I couldnae stand. Then he carried me to the center of Castle Kerr's maze and left me. I would have died had Laird Drummond not come upon me and taken me to Drummond Castle."

Sucking in his pain, he raised his face to the ceiling as if seeking answers. "How could Da let him do that, Cat? Why did he hate me? I tried to be the son he wanted. I couldnae help that I was sick."

Catherine drew him closer. Her head to his chest, she heard the racing of his heart. His pain that never healed was now her pain. She murmured words of encouragement.

He moved away and looked into her face. "I loved him, Cat, and he threw me away. He dinnae want me!" His voice caught. "What did I do wrong? Why couldn't he love me?"

# Chapter Thirty-Two

Catherine thought her heart would break. Her brave, strong husband once again sat before her like a little boy lost. She drew him close and kissed his forehead, his eyes, his nose, brushed her lips gently over his mouth.

Duncan clearly didn't realize it, but the war he'd waged with his father finally drew to a close. He'd just called him Da. Not my da, my father, or that auld man, but Da. In no way did she think his pain would fade any time soon, but the first steps toward healing had begun.

She just had to figure out how to get him back to speak with his father. She tried a different tact. "Was your father upset about Morag being here?"

Duncan drew back from her embrace, a hint of a smile etching his lips. "Changing the subject, are we?"

Catherine shrugged, but couldn't hide her smile. "Obvious, am I?"

"Aye."

She refused to give in. "Was he?"

"Nay. Actually, he already knew. He surprised me when he told me about her."

"How did Alex take the news?"

"He wants a wedding at Castle Glenshee. Although Da can be as contrary as a bear, Alasdair wishes to honor him by having the wedding at the castle while Da still lives. Alex finally wore Morag down and convinced her he loves her. Remember the conversation we heard a sennight past?"

Catherine laughed. "How could I forget?"

Duncan chuckled. "When he threatened to claim her as Scots are prone to do with unwilling wives, Morag glared at him and stomped her foot."

Looking into his eyes, Catherine stifled a laugh.

Duncan boasted, "I knew something brewed between them from the beginning. My beloved friend and the bonnie lass are destined for each other—as you and I are."

She thought it odd Duncan would make such a strange statement. "Morag told me she thought she'd never be strong enough or well enough to be worthy of him."

"He is as determined to help Morag as I was to help you after your injury. Can you plan it quickly?"

"When would it be? A moon's passing? A bit of a rush, but I could throw a lovely wedding by then."

"Within a sennight."

"Duncan MacThomas, are you daft? I cannot possibly put together a proper wedding that quickly. They could not cry the first bann by then."

Duncan patiently explained. "Castle Glenshee's priest agreed to perform the ceremony, granting dispensation for needs of haste because of Da's health. Can you arrange everything?"

"I cannot possibly..." she wailed.

"You can do anything you set your mind to. You are the most amazing woman I e'er met." He held her close and ran his hand over her back. "Alasdair wants a simple Highland ceremony — with a nice celebration afterward."

Catherine tilted her face up to his and he bent to kiss her.

"Duncan..." She stepped back. "You just told me I have less than a sennight to plan a wedding. I do not have time for *that* right now."

She turned and dashed for the kitchen.

Duncan frowned, mumbling, "There is something you would rather do than have me make love to you? 'Tisnae right, wife."

Catherine stopped with her hand on the door. "Nay, husband. I would rather be making love with you, but for once that will have to wait. I promise I shall make it up to you, though."

As she swept through the doorway, Duncan cocked a brow. He'd not meant her to hear his words, but he'd hold her to her promise. He headed outside to join his men on the training field, needing to work out his frustration.

* * *

Catherine was amazed at how quickly everyone brought the wedding together. Her stomach felt queasy as she bustled about. Probably from the frenzy of activity.

Before the light of dawn she rose and dressed. Everyone would arrive shortly and she wished to make changes to the upcoming meal. Suddenly lightheaded, she shook her head to clear it, thinking she'd risen too quickly.

She headed down to the castle's massive kitchen to

find MacThomaidh's cook preparing bread for the day's activities.

The heavyset, elderly man nodded in greeting.

Hearing her husband's voice in the Great Hall, Catherine dashed out of the kitchen. Barely through the door, dizziness assaulted her again, causing her to slump to the floor.

At her side in two long strides, Duncan cradled her in his arms and tried to rouse her.

Catherine opened her eyes and smiled at him. "I did not hear you arrive, husband. I am pleased you are here so early."

"Woman," Duncan barked in an effort to cover his worry. "Why did you just faint?"

Catherine tried to sit up. "Do not be silly, husband. I never faint." She stopped a moment. "Well, except for one other time. And then again when I fell down the ravine after that madman chased me."

"Och, you just like sitting on the ground?"

Looking around, Catherine realized she was, indeed, on the ground. She felt awkward, not knowing how to respond. "I know not what happened, Duncan. I felt lightheaded, but am fine now. Please let me up. I have much I must do."

Duncan helped her rise and guided her to the Great Table. "You will do naught until we break our fast."

Cook signaled servants to bring the food when everyone was seated at tables. Since the MacThomaidh didn't feel well enough to come downstairs, Duncan sat in the head chair with Catherine beside him.

Speaking with men seated nearby, Duncan kept a

watchful eye on Catherine. She was right. She wasn't prone to fainting spells. Although she mentioned there'd been one other time. He wondered when.

And why now?

A strange look suddenly crossed Catherine's face. She jumped up from the table and dashed outside.

Duncan swore and followed her. What was amiss? He found her beside the castle, doubled over in pain. The contents of her stomach lay scattered on the ground.

Smiling weakly, Catherine ran a hand over her face. "The day's events must have beset me more than I thought. I shall be fine, husband. Pray worry not. Once the day is over, I shall be fit as ever."

Duncan took her hand and led her back inside, hoping her words proved true.

\* \* \*

By mid-afternoon all the guests had arrived. Catherine was pleased Grant and Tory were able to come on such short notice. Having no time to prepare for a lengthy stay, they'd left the children behind. Catherine left Duncan to chat with them while she went upstairs to check on Morag.

When she opened the door, she found her friend sitting on the bed, staring ahead.

"Worried?"

Morag nodded, a sheen of tears in her eyes.

"Alex is a kind man, Morag. He shall care well for you."

"'Tis naught that which worries me."

Catherine wrapped her arms around Morag and squeezed. "You needn't worry. He is a rogue no more, my dear. He loves you too much to be unfaithful."

Morag smiled faintly, embarrassed. "What if I dunnae please him? What if I cannae bear a bairn after Edward's vile treatment?" The instant the words were out of her mouth, she stifled a gasp. "Oh Cat, I dinnae mean..."

"I know you did not. I try to accept I shall never bear Duncan's child. If he can forgive me that flaw, I must ask God for strength to see His wisdom."

Morag stood and hugged Catherine. "Come, friend, help me dress."

Catherine brushed away her tears. "Aye, a handsome man awaits you by the chapel."

\* \* \*

Catherine headed to Glenshee's chapel. Her husband stood talking with Grant and Tory. Raising up on her toes she placed a kiss on Duncan's cheek, then turned to hug her guests.

While so embraced, Tory whispered, "Duncan worries about you. He told me what happened this morn. Have you fainted before?"

Catherine shook her head. "Nay, this morn was the first time." She tilted her head as she thought. "Although my stomach has felt queasy nearly a sennight. 'Tis just because I bustle about preparing for the wedding."

Tory looked into Catherine's eyes. "Aye, probably so. Do you still take that herb I gave you each morn?"

Catherine made a sour face. "Aye, I have not forgotten. I am glad you love your husband so much, else I would wonder if you poisoned me so you could have Duncan."

"I am happy with my Highland rogue." Tory linked her arm though her husband's, a wide smile crossing her face.

When Morag walked to the chapel, Catherine smiled at the glint that lit Morag's eyes when she saw her future husband. Blushing, Alex rocked on the balls of his feet. How fortunate they had been to find each other.

Morag moved beside him and he grasped her hand, holding it between both of his.

The priest stepped forward to begin the ceremony. Catherine looked over those gathered and saw The MacThomaidh sitting on a chair near the others, too weak to stand. Instinct warned too soon the priest would be performing funeral rites for their clan Chief. It wouldn't be an easy time for her husband...her Highland rogue.

Catherine turned her attention back to the present. For now she'd concentrate on the task of life. Death would intercede soon enough.

"Friends..." Joining Morag's and Alex's right hands, the priest covered them with a small cloth Catherine embroidered for the occasion. He intoned God's blessings on their lives.

After they received the marriage blessing, the priest gave Alex the kiss of peace. With a lump in her throat, Catherine watched Alex lean forward and pass the kiss on to his new bride.

Catherine tried to keep tears from falling, although happy for the two lovers. She couldn't help but remember her own wedding day when Duncan turned his back to her and refused to give her the kiss of peace. She'd been embarrassed down to the tips of her toes, wondered what everyone thought. She'd seen the pity on their faces.

She bit her lip to keep from crying. Curse him for giving her such a sad memory.

Curse him for not loving her when she loved him more than life itself.

\* \* \*

Later in the Great Hall, Duncan and Grant seated The MacThomaidh in his large chair. Although clearly tired, he insisted on presiding over the festivities. Catherine knew that meant a lot to Alex. Knew it meant a lot to Duncan's father. There seemed to be a truce between father and son.

Everyone joined in festivities. Jugglers performed and people danced, ate, and sang their way through the eve.

Duncan stayed nearby. He lightly caressed her cheek with his hand, ran his fingertips over the curve of her mouth, pressed his cheek to her hair.

Catherine smiled as she watched Alex with Morag. Pleased with her friends' happiness, she couldn't keep tears from flowing down her cheeks. She loved the two people who'd just professed their love to each other.

Morag joined her new husband on what was now being used for dancing. Tables still heavily laden with food had been pushed to the side of the room, allowing people to feast throughout the night.

"Dance with me," Duncan whispered in her ear. When the musicians started to play, she gladly obliged.

Throughout the evening Duncan watched Cat. Occasionally she'd stared wistfully at the happy bride and groom. Now she sat cradled in his arms as she listened to the bard weave his magical tales. He handed her a cup of mead. "Alasdair told me earlier the ache and emptiness he felt his entire life are gone. He's finally found the other half of his heart."

Catherine felt a lump in her throat. She'd found the other half to her heart, too. If only she could tell him.

Nearing the midnight hour and many drinks later, Duncan rose from his chair and went to speak with the priest.

Catherine walked about the Hall, ensuring everyone had a wonderful time. The woman never rested.

He circled the room and spoke to several of his men, then headed for Catherine. "Come, wife, we have something we must do."

Catherine backed away. "Duncan, we cannot leave the celebration. Alex and Morag will be hurt."

"We are not leaving," he said dragging her behind him. This was something he should have done a long time ago.

While he led her behind him, Catherine looked back to see Grant and Alex helping The MacThomaidh to his feet.

What were these men up to? Was The MacThomaidh finally letting them take him to his bedchamber? He'd pushed himself past all measures of endurance.

Soon the priest rushed past them and headed toward the chapel. Duncan followed behind him, as did all the guests.

Catherine paled. Was something amiss? Why did everyone return to the chapel?

Duncan led her all the way to the chapel's door, then turned her to face him. He cupped her chin in his hand. Standing tall, his words resonated throughout the room. "Catherine Gillingham MacThomas, will you marry me?"

Catherine thought her knees would buckle. She was glad Duncan had one arm wrapped around her waist.

"Wh…what?"

"I brought you to our chapel to do it right this time. Will you marry me—again?"

Tears flowed down her cheeks. Duncan no longer held her chin, but she didn't turn away. Her eyes locked on his.

"Do you mean it?"

"I never meant anything more. I ruined your wedding day and would like to rectify that. Since my dearest friends are here, I should like them to witness this as well. The only person missing is Tamara."

Catherine was afraid to move. She feared herself dreaming and if she moved the spell would be broken.

Duncan tilted her chin and lightly kissed her mouth. "Please?" The words were a whisper against her lips.

She couldn't speak, but nodded. Surely she'd never been so happy.

At ceremony's end, Cat knew that for a falsehood.

Duncan said his wedding vows freely this time, smiling down at her all the while. She thought her heart would burst and take wing. This was the happiest moment of her life, and she felt wonder and amazement.

When jests grew too ribald, Duncan took his bride's hand and departed the Great Hall.

Aided by two friends, MacThomaidh crossed to

Catherine and placed a kiss on her cheek. She detected a hint of tears in the crusty old man's eyes.

# Chapter Thirty-Three

Catherine lay abed, basking in the afterglow of Duncan's lovemaking. He'd been so tender with her. She still couldn't believe he'd married her again—willingly. She thought she'd burst with happiness when they repeated their vows. Not only had she said hers happily this time, Duncan freely voiced his. He'd pressed the back of his hand against her cheek as he said, "I do." And instead of the kiss of peace, he kissed her until she thought her blood would boil—to the cheers of his clansmen.

His father had looked so ill during the day's festivities she feared his death was imminent. Somehow she had to get Duncan back to the castle to talk with him.

She turned in his arms, ran her fingertips lightly over his chest. "Why did you want a second wedding ceremony?"

"What?" He drew her closer.

"Do not pretend to be deaf. Why was it important to have our ceremony at Castle Glenshee?"

Duncan didn't answer. Instead buried his face in her hair.

Catherine edged back. "Do not try to ignore me. 'Tis important we discuss it."

"Father chose well for me. Except for his actions, I

339

wouldnae have you in my life. I...owed it to him to let him know that."

"We do owe your father. I know you do not want to return, but you must speak with him. You made a beginning the other day. You must return."

"I dunnae need to—"

"Stubborn man." She placed a finger to his lips to silence his argument. "Duncan, I know you're upset about your childhood. You have every right to be, but you know not everything."

"He left me. What else need I know?"

Catherine drew in a deep breath, then exhaled. She leaned down and wrapped her arms around him. "Your father did not want to leave you."

Duncan bolted upright. "Dinnae speak such nonsense. He couldnae wait to rid himself of me."

"I cannot tell you why he sent you from him. If you wish the answer, you will speak with him. I can tell you after he left you, he almost returned to take you home."

"Where did you get such a daft notion?"

"While preparing for the Countess' party at the castle, I came upon your father staring out the door near the garden. When he turned to look at me, he looked like his heart was breaking. He told me he remembered the day he left you."

"I believe none of it," Duncan said, switching position and holding her in his arms, "but I shall return to the castle. Just to silence you. But then, there are more pleasurable ways to silence you."

And he did.

\* \* \*

The next day he rode to Castle Glenshee and headed upstairs to see his father.

He knocked, entering without waiting. Inside the doorway, Duncan paused, nearly swaying as the breath felt knocked from him. He finally moved to sit at bedside, staring at his father. The man had always looked larger than life. Now he appeared a shadow of his former self.

Duncan swallowed hard, knowing his father would soon cross to Heaven. His beautiful wife was right. He needed to know the truth.

"What did I do wrong?"

Before a fit of coughing stopped him, MacThomaidh frowned. "When?"

"When I was little. Why did you hate me?" Although intending to reveal no emotion, Duncan's voice cracked.

"I never hated you."

"Then why did you send me away?" He raised his hand when MacThomaidh opened his mouth to answer. "I dunnae wish to hear fostering is normal. I know that. But other families keep in touch with their children. Why dinnae you visit me?"

"I…"

Duncan's lips thinned when his father didn't continue. "So, even you cannae think of an acceptable reason."

"I left you with a good chief. Knew he'd teach you everything you needed to know to grow into a fine man, mayhap become a knight."

Duncan choked. "That *good* chief hated me. Why? What did I do that made everybody hate me?"

"Duncan, what speak you of? Of course Kerr dinnae hate you. He promised he would train you well. He—"

"He trained me all right," Duncan said, his hands clenched in his lap to keep from trembling. "Trained me to hide from him whenever I made a mistake, because if he found me he'd beat me. Trained me to eat whatever I could when I got the chance, because I never knew when he'd punish me by taking away my food. Trained me to—"

"Cease!" MacThomaidh shouted. "What nonsense do you spout? Kerr would never treat anyone like that, let alone a child in his care."

"He did." Duncan rose and paced the room. "It dinnae matter what I did wrong. If I dinnae learn fast enough to please him or if I dropped something, anything, he'd punish me. Beat me."

"I dunnae believe you. He would never—"

Duncan tore off his plaide and pulled his shirt over his head. "Think you I gave *these* to myself?"

MacThomaidh gasped. "What happened?"

"I told you. Kerr beat me on a regular basis. Had Laird Drummond not arrived and taken me to Drummond Castle, I probably would have been dead within the moon's passing."

Duncan watched his father age before his eyes, slump even more in the bed.

"So that is what happened. I always wondered."

"Wondered what?"

"How you wound up at Drummond Castle and why Drummond forbade me to see you."

Duncan's brows furrowed.

"I received a missive from him informing me you lived with him. Said he planned to raise you as his own and threatened my life if ever I came to Drummond lands to see you. I wrote and told him that was nonsense, but he answered immediately. Said that would be his last correspondence with me. He called me every name imaginable and reiterated his men had been informed to kill me on sight."

A fit of coughing overtook him. Blood stained the cloth after he wiped his mouth.

"I realized then something happened, but never knew what. I convinced myself you were better off without me, probably wanted me nowhere around, so I stayed away."

"How convenient."

"I must explain why I sent you away."

"I know why. You dinnae want me. I was a mistake in your life and you wished to rid yourself of me." He fisted his hands in his plaide to keep them from trembling.

MacThomaidh swore. "Nay, son. You werenae a mistake. You were one of the few true blessings in my life. The day you were born was one of the proudest of my life."

Duncan could stand it no longer. Tears welling in his eyes, he broke. "Then why?" he choked out.

"Because I thought myself a failure." MacThomaidh mirrored his son's former movement and raised his hand to forestall him speaking.

"I am clan Chieftain, Duncan. Our people look up to me—as they will you one day. I helped them, worked beside them, provided for them. I did everything they needed, but I couldnae help my own son. Everytime you had difficulty breathing I feared you would die. I felt a failure. Nay, I *was* a failure. A failure as a man and father. I thought I needed to be invincible. Needed to do anything to prove I was a good chief. After all, our clansmen needed my support. How could I expect them to trust me when I couldnae do the most important thing in my life? Care for you—find someone to heal you."

MacThomaidh placed a hand to his chest. Breathing irregularly, he continued, "Pride reared its ugly head. I had to keep our people's respect. Our clan wouldnae prosper without that. I thought if I removed the one thing I was a failure at, I would keep their respect. And I did—I thought. In the long run everyone but me realized I'd done the wrong thing. Took the coward's way out. Did just the opposite of what I tried to do."

Duncan stopped pacing, again sat beside the bed. His tone incredulous, he said, "You couldnae heal me so you sent me to die somewhere conveniently out of sight."

MacThomaidh roared. "Merciful God in Heaven, son, I loved you more than life itself. I wanted you well, but no matter what we tried, naught helped. You coughed and had breathing problems. I feared you'd have a spell and stop breathing for good. I couldnae face that. Couldnae face what your death would do to your mam. Kerr's wife was a great healer. I hoped in time she might heal you."

Duncan stared, dumbfounded. "You loved me?"

"Of course. I loved you then. I love you now. I—"

Words barely came. "Why did...you not tell me?"

Duncan sobbed, now on his knees beside the bed.

"You wouldnae have believed."

"I...I..." Tears flowed down Duncan's cheeks unchecked. "All I ever wanted was your love. I needed..."

Rising, he faced his father. When the old man raised his arms to him, Duncan threw his large body upon the bed and let his father enfold him in his arms as though still a child. He wept for all the years they'd wasted.

\* \* \*

Two days later, The MacThomaidh passed through the gates of Heaven.

While Tamara and the MacThomas clanspeople mourned, Duncan tried to come to grips with his feelings. Though awkward admitting it, he felt an overwhelming sense of loss and sadness. He and his father could have had so many years together, could have built memories. Instead he had nothing but a feeling of emptiness, regret.

He and his father had made their peace, but years had been frittered away. Why hadn't they spoken before? If not for Catherine, they'd not have done so now. He never would have learned the truth. Now they'd have no more time together. He had no happy recollections to fall back on as did Tamara.

Moving to the castle proved difficult. He and Cat spent the past nights in an empty room. His people removed everything from his father's solar and cleaned the room, but he couldn't move in. The time would come when he could do so, but not yet.

Duncan looked up and saw Catherine was finally

back in the Great Hall. Smiling tiredly, she walked toward him, raising her hand to her brow to wipe away a sheen of perspiration. The lass had tired herself trying to comfort their people.

Only a few steps away, she slumped to the ground.

Duncan was beside her in a heartbeat, kneeling and patting her face with his hands. "Cat, wake up." His eyes shot to Tory who'd entered the Hall with Catherine. "What is wrong with her? This is the second time in a sennight she fainted."

Tory knelt beside Cat's just as her eyes fluttered opened. "Naught is wrong a bit of rest and a few moon's passings will not take care of."

Duncan frowned at the odd words and placed his arms around Catherine, helping her to sit.

"Dunnae blether in riddles, woman. What is wrong with her?"

Tory's eyes danced to her husband's. When his eyes widened in understanding, she turned back to Cat and Duncan. With a smile on her face and love radiating from her eyes, she reached out to hold their hands.

"You are going to be a father. Cat is with child."

Laird and Lady MacThomas sat speechless. Finally Cat and Duncan spoke simultaneously, "But that is impossible. The physician said…" and "But Cat cannae…"

"The physician said he did not *believe* you could bear a child again. I am pleased to tell you he was wrong." She smiled into the eyes of her startled friends and started to laugh. "I never thought to see you without a swift comeback, Catherine MacThomas. Are you really at a loss for words?"

Raising Catherine to her feet, Duncan looked into her eyes. No longer aware of anyone else in the room, he drew her close, lowered his mouth to hers and held her tightly. When he released her mouth, he twirled her around in circles.

Behind him, he heard Grant. "That maynae be the best thing to do to a woman who just fainted."

"Och, you are really irritating when you are right," he shot at his friend. Ignoring him, he swung Catherine around again, then hugged her to his chest and kissed her.

# Chapter Thirty-Four

Catherine remembered the moment they found out she carried a child. Duncan had thrown his head back and shouted, "I am going to have a son."

Tears of joy had spilled down her face. "Duncan, Tory said we are having a babe. She did not say 'twould be a son."

A broad smile split his face and he placed his hand gently on her stomach. "She doesnae have to tell me. 'Tis a son." He turned to look for Meghan. "Meggie, love, you are going to have a braw wee brother."

Now, a fortnight later, she sat busy with her sewing, placing perfect, delicate stitches on a collar she'd been working on for Meghan. The young girl stood beside her, watching her ply the needle in and out of the cloth, a frown on her face.

"What has upset you, Sweetling?"

Meghan bit her lip, but didn't speak.

Catherine placed her sewing in her lap, giving her full attention to the young girl. "Meggie, is something wrong?"

"Nay."

"Something upsets you. I see it on your face."

Reluctantly, Meghan nodded.

"Can you tell me what it is? I cannot help solve the

problem if I know not what it is." Catherine caressed Meghan's cheek.

"I want the bairnie to be a girl and not a boy," Meghan said so softly Catherine had to lean forward to hear her.

Catherine had been afraid of this. Duncan was so excited at the prospect of having a son that she feared Meggie might be jealous.

"Your da will not love you any less," Catherine assured her. "You shall always be the pride and joy of his life."

Meghan's eyes held a question.

"That is what bothers you, isn't it?"

Meggie shook her head.

"Then what has you upset?"

Meghan scrunched her face up, clearly searching for words. She finally blurted, "I want the bairnie to be a lassie and not a laddie so I can be a big sister and not a brother."

Catherine couldn't stop herself. She burst out laughing. 'Twas obvious the wee child didn't understand the difference between boys and girls. She rushed to assure her, "I promise your da shall make quite certain you are always a sister, whether it be a boy or a girl."

When Meghan looked appeased, Catherine went back to teaching her a few stitches, chuckling all the while.

She couldn't wait to tell Duncan.

\* \* \*

Nearing Catherine's woman's confinement, Duncan was in the midst of an argument with Angus. He shouted, "Why dinnae you tell me?"

Patiently Angus looked his Chief in the eyes. "You werenae here—and at the time stubbornly vowed not to care."

"You told me the woman cleaned my home. You couldnae tell me she fainted when she carried my child?" Glaring at his friend, he stormed into the keep. Mayhap he should chain her to their bed so she couldn't get in any trouble.

Catherine was distracted by Tory and Grant's arrival, children in tow. She looked at her guests, aghast. "Forgive him. He seems to be—"

"Upset," Tory finished. She carried her new son, Andrew, in her arms. She cast a glance at Catherine's belly. "Good, you haven't had the babe yet. I assume from the discussion we just witnessed you must have fainted again."

Catherine nodded.

"I've tried to visit for over a sennight now, but things kept requiring Grant's attention. I finally told him if he didn't leave immediately, the children and I would come ourselves."

Trying to regain his good mood, Duncan turned and slapped his old friend on the back when Catherine escorted everyone inside the Great Hall. "So, you still dunnae trust her out of your sight?" He remembered she'd been Grant's prisoner when first they met, his men constantly watching her. She'd hated that and rebelled. He knew she still felt closed in if followed too closely. Duncan knew his friend only did it now for her safety, just as he did with Catherine.

"Not for a moment," Grant agreed. "The woman gets into too much trouble."

Tory rolled her eyes.

Once everyone settled into their rooms, Catherine showed Tory around the castle.

"Isn't it amazing?"

Tory nodded just as tiny Andrew wailed. "'Tis time for him to suckle."

"Let me take you to your room so you can get comfortable," Catherine told her, leading her toward the staircase.

Settling herself into a comfortable chair, Tory unlaced her bodice and let Andrew root around until he latched onto her breast. His wails stopped and sucking sounds echoed throughout the room.

"He is a lusty eater," Catherine commented.

"Aye, like his father." Tory blushed, realizing the double meaning behind her words.

\* \* \*

Deciding the weather was too nice to stay inside several days later, Catherine and Tory walked outside the gate, Catherine waved up at the guard on the tower. She raised her basket so he'd know she was out gathering herbs.

Linking arms, the two women strolled along. The sun shone and a soft breeze whispered through the trees. Walking slowly, they chatted amiably, taking in the splendor of the sun-kissed mountains.

Busy pointing out local herbs, Catherine said, "There is a little patch of herbs on the other side of that copse of trees, but we have already come too far. Should we take a quick look or turn around?"

Tory assessed the area. "It should not take long to go there and head right back to the castle. I shall gather a few herbs to take home with me and then we can return. I do not think our guard will mind too much." She bent, but grabbed her back and stood.

"Are you with child again?"

"Nay, not yet. My back just hurts. Probably from wee Andrew kicking me all the time before he was born. What about you? Would you like more?"

"Oh, aye, but I do not believe that will happen. I thank you for the herbs you made me drink, although I never tasted anything so nasty."

Tory watched her expectantly. "Too horrible to take now you know what it was for?"

Catherine's eyes widened with hope. "You think it might help again? Oh, if I thought there was a chance I might bear Duncan another child, I would drink that horrid taste the rest of my life." Her eyes twinkled. "How long must I wait before I can try it again?"

"Naught in the herbs will harm a babe, but you should probably wait six moons."

A thought instantly struck her. "Will you use a milk mother?"

"Nay." Catherine looked aghast at the suggestion.

"Not many Chief's wives nurse their children. Grant told me most have milk mother's living in the castles. I didn't care. 'Twas the one thing I was adamant about. I almost died birthing Jamie, but as soon as I recovered, I nursed. I wanted him looking at my face and hearing my voice crooning to him, not another woman."

Cat smiled in understanding. "Duncan suggested we get one, but I waited too long to have a child to relinquish any of the joy."

Standing straighter, Catherine gasped and grabbed her back. A crippling pain shot through her.

# Chapter Thirty-Five

Catherine leaned against Tory as they walked upstairs and turned toward the master bedchamber.

"Why did you not tell me you were having back pains?" Tory frowned as she helped Catherine out of her outer tunic and into bed.

"Because you would not have gone with me and I needed to walk," Catherine answered. "I did not want my confinement to start so soon. I wish to wait as long as possible."

Tory moved pillows around Catherine, then sat on the edge of the bed. "What can I do to make you more comfortable?" She reached out to hold Catherine's hand.

"Nothing, I…" She stopped, unable to go on.

"Cat? Tell me."

Catherine's eyes met and held Tory's, imploring her to listen. "I do not wish to start my confinement yet. I spent so much time alone when I hurt my back and leg. I do not want to do that again. I…"

Tory squeezed her hand. "I shall stay with you. 'Twill be a long time yet since your pains just begin in earnest, but I will stay until you have your babe." Looking at her friend, she smiled. "'Tis alright to be frightened you know. You needn't hide it. For now, just rest."

"I did not tell Duncan my pains began. I feared he would panic."

Tory laughed. "Your husband fought in many a battle, came close to dying many times. You believe he would panic just because you have his bairn?"

Catherine shrugged, uncertain what to say.

Tory kept laughing. "Of course he will, silly girl. Grant falls apart every time I give birth! Duncan trains in the list with Grant now and will be busy for quite some time. Do not worry about him."

A sound from the far side of the room drew Catherine's attention. "Did you hear that?"

The scratching sound continued.

"Aye, I do." Tory got up and walked toward the wardrobe. "But I see naught."

Without warning, the wardrobe door banged open, knocking Tory to the floor.

A man stepped out, reached forward and grabbed Tory as she scrambled to her knees to stand. Jerking her up against him, he slid his dirk along her neck. He turned to Catherine and warned just as she opened her mouth, "Scream, Lady MacThomas, and your friend dies."

Shaking with fear, Catherine closed her mouth without making a sound.

The man drew Tory closer to the bed. She twisted and tried to scratch his face. "Let me go, Erwin MacComas. How did you get in here?"

Catherine gasped. "You know him?"

"Aye, he's Duncan's former clansman." She jabbed her elbow back, but he grabbed it and twisted, moving the dirk away from her neck.

Catherine sat bolt upright in bed. "This is the man that beat me in London. He made me lose my babe and made me fall over the hill!" She swung her legs over the side, trying to stand.

Erwin pushed her back down. "Stay there or I will gut your belly like I gut my fish."

Catherine looked toward the wardrobe. "How did you get in here? How—?"

He narrowed his eyes. "I grew up in this castle. I know everything about it."

Her eyes shifted to the wardrobe and back to Erwin. "Nay," she cried when he pushed Tory down to her knees.

He grabbed ropes used to tie back panels on the four-poster and pulled Tory's arms behind her back. He looped the rope around her wrists, fastened a cloth between her lips and tied it behind her head.

Kicking him with her foot, Catherine reached forward and twisted her fingers in his hair. She yanked—hard.

He flung his arm out and backhanded her across her face, the impact forcing her to fall backward on the bed. He used the split second she was incapacitated to grab her arm and pull her toward him.

"Let me go," Catherine yelled, growing angrier by the minute. "Why are you doing this? What do you want with me?"

"I dunnae want you," Erwin growled. "I want your husband to suffer afore I kill him. You are bait—a means to an end."

Catherine glared. "I lost my babe because I am the

means to an end? I stayed in bed for almost a year because I am *the means to an end*?"

Erwin shrugged. "What happened to you matters naught to me."

"What does matter?"

"Getting this castle. 'Tis mine."

"Castle Glenshee?"

"Of course. 'Tis mine by rights."

"You are daft," Catherine shot at him.

"What you think doesnae matter." He jerked her to her feet. "Now move, and remember, both of you, I shall have a knife to her fat belly the whole way. One slip and I will gut her." He jerked them both toward the wardrobe.

"What are you doing?" Catherine screamed. She locked eyes with Tory. How could they escape this madman?

"What does it look like?"

"Like you plan to walk into the wall!" Catherine tugged against her bonds. "Where do you take us? Let me go. Let Tory go."

"We use the escape passage, you stupid cow," Erwin grumbled. "It shall take us all the way to the cave I hid in whilst keeping watch on you."

"You spied on me?"

"Aye. I hoped you would come outside the gates without a guard, but Duncan always had someone with you." He turned to glare at Tory. "Earlier you came out with Lady Drummond. I have a score to settle with her as well, so I thought about kidnapping you then, but you were too well guarded. 'Twas then I realized I must make my move now."

"Duncan will know I am missing. He will follow me."

Erwin laughed. "Your husband dinnae grow up here. His father—my father—dinnae want him. He sent him away and never went to see him. Your Duncan knows naught of this passage."

"What do you mean *your father*?"

"My mam was a servant here. The laird thought her good enough to bed, but not to marry." He shoved Tory through the narrow entrance and pulled Catherine with him, the knife against her child. She tried to hold onto the wardrobe, but Erwin jerked her forward. Her undertunic caught on a wooden peg and tore. She grabbed one last time for the doorframe, where the wardrobe opened into a tunnel, catching her hand on a jagged piece of stone and cutting her palm.

Erwin slid the secret door into place and pulled the two women behind him by yanking on the rope.

Catherine froze, the dark stone walls seeming to close in on her. "Nay, I cannae see, I cannae breathe."

"You dunnae need to see. I know exactly where I go."

"But 'tis dark, 'tis suffocating. Let us out of here."

Erwin ignored her pleas, still moving forward.

As they moved away from the castle, Catherine felt a chill to the air and the stone beneath her feet vanished, replaced by something softer. Tears poured down her face as she fought her panic. If she could just see Tory, it would help. She tried to gain purchase on the ground. Erwin jerked her forward, causing her to fall. She cried out in pain.

Beside her, she heard a thump and Tory's groan. Had Erwin kicked her or had she run into something? In the next instant her question was answered when she heard a slapping sound and Tory cried out.

"Leave her alone," she shouted. She received naught but a laugh in return.

Catherine kept losing her balance, feared harm would come to the babe.

Tory kicked Erwin and mumbled. Kicked him again until he jerked the cloth from her mouth. "Do that again and I gut your friend."

Tory protested. "Untie my hands and I will help her walk. You can move faster that way."

Catherine opened her mouth to ask why she would help this madman, but Tory pinched her. She felt movement and Tory's hand was on her arm, urging her forward.

It seemed like the passage went on forever. *Dear God, please get us out of here. I…*

Pain lanced through her lower back again, bringing fresh tears, but she forced herself to keep moving. She shrieked when she crashed to her knees. An overwhelming pain hit her stomach. The baby!

"Please take us back. I am sure Duncan will give you whatever you want. He would —" She knew it was useless to plead, but couldn't stop herself, her fear of losing another child so great.

"Your husband has taken everything that should be mine."

Catherine couldn't see him, though she wasn't sure if it was a blessing or a torment. She too easily imagined his glowering face.

"The auld laird dinnae bother to claim me as his son. Why should he? Right after he married the worthless woman who took my mam's place, she bred with child. Mam told me this castle and clan should be mine." His voice rose in anger. "Why should Duncan be clan chief? He dinnae even grow up here."

How long had they been gone? Would Duncan miss her yet? Had he even come inside from training in the lists? Catherine sent out a silent plea. Would he sense it? Could he know she needed him?

"When Laird MacThomaidh set me to travel with Duncan, my hopes soared. I thought mayhap he'd finally acknowledge he was my da. But nae, he just wanted a companion, a protector for his weakling son." He jerked the rope so both women stumbled. "'Tis mine. Do you hear me? This castle is *mine*."

Soon he stopped. Catherine heard a creaking noise, like a rusty door being opened. Had they reached the end of the tunnel? Suddenly Erwin jerked on the ropes again, yanking them out behind him. Catherine heard a loud thump, then a click as the door's lock obviously shifted into place.

Moving her body from side to side to test her surroundings, she still felt walls around her. They were inside another dark tunnel, could see nothing. Nay, she had to get out of here!

Did Duncan know of the tunnel's existence? He'd not mentioned it. Terrified, she screamed. She felt the sharp edge of Erwin's dirk against her throat.

\* \* \*

At Castle Glenshee, Duncan grew concerned when his wife didn't come down before the evening meal. He sent a servant upstairs to see if she felt well. When the young woman returned and said, "No one is in your chamber, my lord," Duncan charged upstairs to see for himself.

*She wasn't there.*

Rushing through the castle, he found her nowhere. Duncan ran up the steps to the promenade above the castle. "Have you seen my lady wife?"

When the guard shook his head, panic formed a knot in Duncan's belly.

"Hellsfire!" He slapped his hand against the wall in frustration and shouted, "Get Grant. He needs know the women cannae be seen from here either."

He ran down the steps to the courtyard and headed back into the keep and up to his chamber. He'd heard from several people that Catherine had trouble walking into the courtyard. Why hadn't they sent for him then? Surely it meant the bairn would be born soon. If so, why wasn't she abed?

Grant joined him, followed on his heels, back to search the bedchamber. "No sign of them?"

Duncan shook his head.

"'Tisnae like Tory to wander off," Grant grumbled, worry apparent on his face.

Duncan walked to the bed. "Catherine was here. The covers are turned down." Suddenly he stopped, tilted his head as he stared at his bed. "The ropes."

Grant raised a brow. "What?"

"Ropes that tie the bed drapes back during the day.

Two are missing." He pointed to drapes hanging down instead of being tied back.

Grant's eyes narrowed. "Something smells foul about this. Tory would never leave on her own." He walked around the chamber, eyes searching everywhere. Suddenly they widened.

"Duncan. Here."

Duncan hurried to the wardrobe.

Grant pointed. "Look."

All color drained from Duncan's face—specks of blood dotted the floor.

He moved closer, picked a piece of cloth off the wardrobe. His eyes narrowed. "'Tis from the undertunic Siobhán selected for Catherine this morn."

# Chapter Thirty-Six

"Finally, I get you where I want you," Erwin said, pushing the women into a large opening.

A cave! The tunnel led into a cave. Rays of light seeped through branches covering the entrance. Catherine edged away while his attention was focused on Tory. She turned to run, trying to get to Duncan, but the man quickly caught her, slapping her face. "Dinnae try escaping again, Lady MacThomas. If you do, I shall stick my dirk in your friend's heart."

Catherine eyed Tory and knew she couldn't leave her friend. He dragged Catherine to a fallen log and fastened her to a tether. He ran his finger lightly up and down her jawline. She jerked away, his attention sending shivers up her spine. He pressed a dirk to her throat, toyed with it as if he meant to slice her jugular.

"Leave her be," Tory shouted at him, disgust clear in her tone. "You are insane. Let us go, Erwin. You know Duncan and Grant shall find you — they shall kill you."

Erwin waved dismissively. "They willnae find us. At least not until 'tis too late for the pair of you. And you, Mistress High and Mighty," he said, hard, steely eyes glaring at Tory, "willnae escape me this time. I waited a long time to bed you. My waiting has come to an end. When I am finished, your beloved husband shall have naught to do with you."

"Grant would never—" Tory protested before he cut her off.

"Dunnae fancy he cares that much about you. The Drummond is too proud to take back tarnished goods." The evil in his voice chilled Catherine's blood as he taunted Tory. "By the time I finish, you shall be *verra* tarnished and have my bairn in your belly."

He laughed, the most terrifying sound Catherine ever heard. This man truly was demented. How could they possibly escape?

"You vile, evil man!" Tory lunged at Erwin only to have him grab her and twist her arm behind her back.

Tory swung her free arm, trying to hit him, but he twisted it again, threatening to break her bones.

He glared at the woman he'd once desired. "I know you well enough, Lady Drummond. 'Tis why I dunnae tie you up. You shallnae abandon Lady MacThomas."

"You know naught you worthless excuse for a man." Tory narrowed her eyes and glowered.

"Should you try to escape, Lady MacThomas will be dead afore you reach the cave's entrance, but first I shall slice that bairn from her belly."

As if the matter was settled, he set about to make a fire, humming happily to himself.

Catherine stifled a moan and sat with a thud.

Tory lowered herself to the log beside Catherine. "What is wrong? Have your pains increased?"

Catherine's eyes met Tory's. She shook her head, trying to deny anything was wrong.

Tory smiled at Catherine. "Your husband is right,

Cat MacThomas. You are a horrid liar. Duncan once told me you did not lie well. He said he could always tell when something bothered you, because your face showed every emotion. He said 'twas one of the things he so loved about you."

"He does not love me," Catherine protested.

"Cat," Tory said in exasperation, "will you stop being so thick headed? Your husband adores you."

"He—"

"Has done everything possible to convince you of his feelings," Tory challenged, "but you refuse to believe anything he says. For once in your life, quit arguing. This is not the time or place to talk about it, but if you refuse to believe what he tells you now, why cling to fool words the man said when first you met?"

Catherine seemed about to answer when she doubled over in pain.

Tory's eyes widened. "You are having the babe! *Now*?"

When the pain ebbed and she was able to sit upright again, Catherine met her eyes and nodded.

"When did your pains start in earnest?"

"When I fell in that horrid tunnel. Before Erwin cut your bonds and you were able to help me. Oh, Tory, I hate small places. I know not how I survived the walk through that dark place."

"After all the time we have waited, you choose now to have Duncan's baby? Friend, you astound me."

"I do not believe I particularly have any say in this," Catherine said through gritted teeth. Her eyes swung to Erwin who was busy building a fire. "How do we keep *him* from knowing?"

Tory admitted. "Soon 'twill be too obvious. The man is evil, not stupid." She reached out and held Catherine's hand. "I do not wish to frighten you, but your pains shall get worse before the babe arrives."

Catherine gulped and nodded. "How know you him?"

"He's a former member of Clan MacThomas, once was one of Duncan's most trusted companions. One night he seemed to snap. Afterwards he blamed me. Something ridiculous about wanting to bed me and Duncan let Grant steal me away."

Erwin walked over to where they huddled together. Towering above them, his eyes glinting with malice, he informed them, "It amuses me to take something away from your husbands. I have waited long for this day."

"You think they will not find us?" Catherine taunted. "They are excellent trackers and will have men from the keep with them. Just because you do not possess such skills, does not mean they are failures like you."

Erwin backhanded her, the stinging force causing her to fall off the log.

Tory helped her up, trying to cover Catherine's grimace. She engaged Erwin in conversation, clearly trying to keep him from noticing Catherine was in labor. "Why did you come back to Scotland, Erwin? You had to know Grant and Duncan would come after you after what you and Grant's brother did to me. As I recall, you tied me up then, too. Is that the only way you can get a woman? What a pathetic excuse for a man."

Another sharp pain engulfing her, Catherine drew in

a sharp intake of breath.

"Pathetic? I dunnae think so, lady," came Erwin's harsh words. "I have exactly what I want now." He gave her a crooked, gap-toothed smile. "If you do as bidden, you willnae die. One of you I mean to bed, the other I shall kill her child—just as I did in London." His cold eyes regarded Catherine.

Hers widened at his brutal words. She shuddered and stifled a cry.

Tory gasped at the sickness in his admission. "You really beat an innocent woman? Made her lose her child?"

"I intend to rid her of this one, too," he boasted. "The world doesnae need another MacThomas from Duncan's line. The foul spawn would likely be sickly like his weak sire."

"You traveled with Duncan. What turned you against him? He did naught to you," Tory pointed out.

"Faugh," Erwin snarled. "He gave you to that nae good husband of yours. Had he fought for you that night instead of handing you over with nae argument, I would have made you mine as soon as he finished with you." He cursed. "But nae, he handed you over with nary a word. I vowed that night I would avenge myself."

Catherine couldn't stop the shivers that shook her body. Some was fear, but the cold was seeping bone deep. There was no way to stay warm in the chemise. Erwin squatted and added more twigs to the fire, but the pale light neither gave off heat nor dispelled the inky darkness of this crypt-like cave.

Another shudder racked her body. This one dread.

Her dream...Catherine bit her lip to hold back her scream. This was her dream. She looked at Erwin, knowing soon Duncan and he would be locked in a deadly duel to the death.

He turned his head back to Tory. "Nae one will find this cave. I watched the castle with this as my base. I used the tunnels to get into the kitchen at night to fetch food. I could live here forever without someone finding me."

"Do not use me as an excuse," Tory shouted. "There is more to your hatred than not bedding me."

"It matters not," he said, his mouth twisted in a sneer.

Turning his head, he narrowed his eyes at Catherine, lewdly appraising her body in the thin chemise. "Once I root out the bairn she carries, I shall plow her as well."

"Root out?" Catherine screamed in alarm. "Nay, you cannot hurt this babe. I shall not let you." She tried to stand up, but her bonds jerked her backward. No longer focusing on concealing her pains, she cried out as the next one engulfed her.

Erwin narrowed his eyes and stared. When she clutched her belly, he laughed, "Looks like I shall be spared the trouble of finding a stick to root it out. Let nature take its course, then I shall kill it. Mayhap throw it in the nearest loch to drown — or let it lie outside for hungry animals."

"You are despicable," Catherine shouted, her hands clenched in fists. "I vow on my life, you will *not* harm my babe. I will kill you first."

Erwin shifted position and Tory scurried to her feet to stand between Catherine and him.

"The hare squeaks." With another burst of laughter, Erwin left them alone and walked outside the cave.

Tory rushed to Catherine's side. "Shh," she consoled, rubbing her hands up and down Catherine's arms. "'Twill be all right. Just help me keep him talking. The longer he talks, brags, the more time it gives our men to find us. Our husbands shall be here soon."

"Oh Tory, I had a dream…of a crypt-like cave and endless darkness…blood…and men fighting with swords." Catherine gulped back her tears.

"Never fear, Cat," Tory assured. "We shall get out of here." She placed her hand on Catherine's belly and added, "All three of us. There is no way I shall let this man harm you or the babe you and Duncan waited so long for." She paused. "Grant did not tell me Erwin was responsible for you losing your babe. I misdoubt he knew."

Catherine shook her head, took several deep breaths. "I did not know who he was. I had no name to give Duncan." She looked to the cave entrance and back to Tory, "How will we escape?"

"I have no idea. With you so close to delivering, we are vulnerable." She smiled. "So, we will keep our wits about us, see he talks and give us time to let our husband's find us. Grant never lets me go far. You'll see."

"Please do not let him kill my baby, Tory," Catherine pleaded, her chest rising and falling with gulps of air. "If I could free myself of these bonds, we could rush him, mayhap knock him to the ground."

Tory shook her head. "Despite the enormous danger to yourself, you would charge him?"

Catherine nodded. "Of course, I must get back to Duncan. I fear him coming to the cave and fighting Erwin. I saw so much blood in my dream."

Tory put her arm around her. Catherine felt the warmth of her body. "Did you see Duncan die in the dream?"

"Nay, but I…"

"Then trust in Duncan, Cat. As I trust Grant."

\* \* \*

Duncan grew frantic as he desperately ran his fingers over every spot on the wall. "There has to be a catch here."

"You are certain you dunnae remember your mam or da mentioning an escape tunnel?" Grant asked.

"Nay, I spent little time in their chamber. Da dinnae like me in there." Raking his fingers through his hair in exasperation, he said, "I dinnae even know we had a tunnel system at Glenshee."

"But someone who lives here must."

They immediately called for Angus. Duncan also issued the order to, "Set the men to search outside the castle pale. See if they pick up a trail away from the castle."

Grant glared at the wooden wardrobe. "Nae need for a secret latch if we use an axe." His sharp eyes narrowed. "Look at this carving on the side. It looks like an arrow."

"Mayhap it points to the lever?" Duncan joined him, inspecting it. "Push it."

They pushed against the heavy piece. At first nothing, but then it moved away just enough for a body to squeeze through. Hope rose, until they faced a stone wall.

"Now what?" Duncan groused.

Grant glanced back at the wardrobe. "The arrow no longer points to the wall." His eyes looked to the fireplace just to the side. "It points here."

Grant ran his hand over the fireplace's mantle. Over the hearthside tools. Then he noticed the lions' heads on either side of the stone mantle.

Angus walked in and was quickly apprised of what they searched for.

"'Tis the lion's head on the left," he informed them.

Grant slowly jiggled the head until he was able to pull it a hand's length away from the wall. As he did, they heard a heavy grating sound and the wall behind the wardrobe moved just enough for Grant to get his hand through it.

Duncan instantly noticed the darkened stain on the wood frame.

They put their shoulders to it, but almost fell in as the hidden door moved easily.

"I'd say someone uses this rather frequently." Grant grabbed a torch off the hallway wall and followed Duncan into the tunnel.

Duncan was in absolute panic. The narrow corridors seemed to go on forever, the incline steep. More than once they were faced with one that branched off.

"Slow down, Duncan. Use your tracking skills. Tory might have left clues," Grant insisted.

"How many paths wind beneath the castle?" Duncan bemoaned.

"'Tis something we can discover once our ladies are

tucked up safely."

The hairs on the back of Duncan's neck prickled as it registered the tunnels were like an underground maze. His breath nearly caught, but he forced his mind to deal with it, and pushed on.

Catherine needed him.

*Where are they? Will they be safe when we find them?*

Terror drove him forward.

"Who took them? One of the neighboring Farquharsons? Mayhap hoping to claim blackmail over our longstanding feud? How would they know of the tunnel?" Words came from his mouth, though he little recalled speaking.

Concentrating on the path in front of him, he pushed his tired body onward. Everyone veered right when Alasdair found signs the women had turned in that direction.

Grant hushed him. "We need to listen for sounds. Here." From marks on the ground, one of the women had fallen and been dragged before standing and walking again.

Duncan glanced toward Grant, who looked just as angry as Duncan felt.

He growled his frustration.

How far ahead could the women be? Had they been taken while he trained in the lists, or had his wife's life become at stake while he lazed before the hearth in his Great Hall? If he'd checked on her sooner, this might not have happened.

Fear churned his belly.

Did whoever took them think himself too good to be

found?

How foolish.

A sea of rage spurred him on.

"Another corridor." Grant paused, waving the torch inside each trying to see if there were signs to see which way they came. "Listen…I hear voices."

Eyes fixed on Grant, he stood at the mouth of two tunnels trying to determine which way the voices came. They echoed, reverberated, distorting sounds to where he couldn't tell. "Should we separate? You take one and I take the other?"

"Hush, listen," Duncan cautioned, holding his finger to his lips.

Muted voices came and Grant jerked his head to the right. "This way."

A scream echoed along the stone.

Duncan pushed past Grant and the torch, racing in the direction the sound had emanated.

He recognized the scream.

Cat.

# Chapter Thirty-Seven

Approaching stealthily, they again heard a shrill scream. Louder this time. Locking eyes with Grant, Duncan mouthed the words, "What does this monster do to them?"

"Shut her up!" The angry shout came from up ahead, but they could see no opening. Only cave walls.

The women were being held captive only a few yards in front of them, but how could they get to them? Years of training asserted itself and the men transformed their strategy to battle behavior.

Duncan's chest tightened at the sound of another terrified scream.

"Shut her up, I said."

"You fool. I cannot do that. She cannot help it."

*Tory. That was Tory talking. That affirmed the person yelling was Cat.*

Duncan's heart slammed against his ribs.

Filled with blind rage, he started to charge forward, but Grant grabbed his arm.

A familiar voice said, "Stuff summat in her mouth. I dunnae wish to hear her screams. How much longer will it take?"

"You lackbrain." Tory voiced her loathing. "No one can answer that."

*Merciful Lord, is Cat dying? Is that what Tory cannae ascertain? Please protect her.* Duncan's heart felt like it would break in two. *I cannae lose Cat now. We have come too far and I am too close to reaching my goal – her heart.*

"Listen," Grant held his fingers to his lips, then jerked his head toward the tunnel on the right. "This way."

Duncan followed on his heels as they charged down the black tunnel, finally coming to a dead end.

"A latch is here someplace, and if 'tis the last thing I do, I shall find it," Duncan vowed, running his hands over the wall. "Hellsfire," he cursed, his anxiety rising. "Where is it?"

"Here." The sound of Grant working the lever was music to Duncan's ears.

"Help me push it so we dunnae make any noise."

They opened the door slowly, grimacing when it creaked.

Drawing their swords, they stormed through it, yelling the MacThomas and Drummond war cries at the top of their lungs.

The sound was deafening with the cave's echo.

Startled, the wretch who'd taken Cat spun around, kicking dirt onto the fire, dousing the feeble light, plunging the cave into darkness.

In the split second before the firelight went out, Duncan placed a face with the voice. Erwin. The man who'd caused Grant and Tory so much pain. His former right hand man.

He swung his sword at the spot where he'd last seen his former cohort, to no avail. Tory shrieked in pain.

"Stay back," Erwin warned through the darkness. "If you come closer, I shall kill your women."

Catherine let out a blood-curdling scream.

Duncan thought his heart would leap from his chest. "What happens? What are you doing to my wife?"

The torch Grant carried now cast eerie shadows on cave walls.

No one moved.

Erwin stood with his dirk pressed against Tory's throat. A look of madness upon his face. He turned his eyes to Grant, who'd just stepped through the entrance. The gleam in them was devoid of all humanity. This was a cornered animal that would kill to save himself. And would take pleasure in the killing.

Grant coldly eyed the man who had caused so much pain in his and Tory's lives. Duncan had seen that countenance upon his friend's face before in battle. A man focused, ready to kill.

Duncan's attention moved from Grant. Catherine. Where was she?

Another scream echoed through the cave. Were there others with Erwin? Who tortured Catherine? He saw no one.

Of a sudden Duncan gasped. All eyes followed the direction of his gaze. Catherine was bound to a fallen tree. There was no one around her, yet she continued to cry out. Had Erwin fatally wounded her? Was his beautiful wife dying?

Tory met their eyes and shouted, "The babe comes."

They stared at her in stunned disbelief.

Erwin yanked on her hair and ground out, "I told

you to shut up. One more word and—"

"And nothing," Grant said coolly, with a smile. "Harm one hair on my wife's head and I promise you willnae die quickly enough to suit you."

Erwin laughed, a look of triumph crossing his face. In his madness, he recognized in Grant's eyes he was already a dead man.

"You are in nae position to threaten me, *Laird Drummond*." Erwin spat Grant's name like an epithet. "Neither is my auld friend, Laird MacThomas." He swung his eyes to encompass Duncan. "As long as I have your wives, I do as I please." Erwin released Tory's hair and reached his free arm in front of her. His grin licentious as he watched Grant, he kneaded her left breast.

Grant smiled, then shifted his eyes to Duncan. With a quirk of the eyebrow he said, "Now."

Duncan and Grant lunged toward Erwin.

Erwin pushed Tory toward Catherine and grabbed for his sword, swinging it up to block Grant's, then Duncan's.

Erwin mocked, "Remember when we were like brothers? Brothers? You dinnae know that is what we are. My mam said it should all be mine. Said your father bedded with her, ignored her when he wedded with your mam."

Duncan drove back with the hilt of his sword, slamming the pommel into Erwin's nose, breaking it.

The weasel shouted in pain, blood streaming from his nose. "Blast you to Hell, Duncan MacThomas. You have no right to claim what should be mine. But for the side of a blanket, Clan MacThomas should be mine."

Despite his pain, Erwin continued to fight, a frightening opponent driven by madness. He used the sword with a chopping swing, the power of his beefy arms saw his blade clang against Duncan's, sending the blade flying from his grip. Erwin swung at Duncan, a blow that would have cleaved him in two, but Grant was there blocking the sword.

Grant smiled as he backed Erwin step by step away from the women. There was an unholy light in his eyes, a light that would make a sane man shudder, but Erwin was too far past rational thought. The two adversaries fought, their broadswords locking, then it became a test of sheer strength.

Duncan, his sword in hand again, shouted, "Stand back, Grant. This scum belongs to me."

With a snarl, Erwin swung at Duncan. "I always had your leavings, MacThomaidh's weakling son. This time I shallnae fail. You shall die. I shall claim what is mine."

Their swords clanged, echoing as they hammered at each other. Well matched, once they'd fought for the same cause. Now they fought to the death. Duncan watched Erwin summon every ounce of strength. A blow that rained down knocked Duncan's sword from his hands, the blade slicing into his upper arm.

Grant took up the fight as Duncan grabbed his dirk from its sheath with one hand and the sgian dubh from his boot with the other. Grant nearly lost his footing on the rocky cave floor, giving Erwin chance to swing his sword at Duncan.

Duncan jumped back, but not before the blade

ripped his shirt and sliced across his chest. Blood stained, Duncan was little aware. When Erwin raised the sword to crash it into Duncan's head, Duncan lashed out with his booted feet, catching him in the ribs, falling to the ground. Feinting to the side, he jumped to his feet, crashed his shoulder into Erwin's. They fell to the ground, grunting from impact. Duncan grappled with Erwin to wrench the sword from the crazed man's hands.

Erwin grabbed the small dagger from his waist and jabbed it into Duncan's side, but the pain of it could not stop the thrust of his dirk as it slipped easily between two of Erwin's ribs.

Eyes wide, Erwin howled in pain and bared his teeth. With effort he rolled away from Duncan and rose to his knees, but could rise no farther. Refusing to give up, he threw his dagger at Duncan's heart. With a quick movement of his arm, Duncan deflected the dagger, feeling the sharp pain as it entered. Erwin fell forward.

When he didn't move, Grant moved forward to grab his hair. He stared at Erwin's open mouth, the eyes devoid of life. "He is dead," Grant said, breathing heavily, "his poison gone with him." He let the man's head fall back to the ground and turned to stare at Duncan. "Methinks you need to spend more time in the lists training than in bed with your wife. He almost had you there. Dunnae ask me to stand by and watch you fight alone. I shall never do so again."

Observing no other enemy, Duncan rushed to Catherine.

His heart pumping wildly, he knelt beside her. He tried to lift her in his arms, but she was still shackled to the large log. When he moved her, she screamed in pain. He laid her back gently, his eyes searching her body for signs of injury. He saw bruises and cuts, but nothing that would cause the pain she seemed to experience.

Biting her lip to keep from yelling, Catherine reached for Duncan's hand and refused to let go. "Hold me," she begged. "Please do not let go."

"*Mo Chridhe*," he shouted with raw emotion. "What did that monster do to you?"

Duncan felt Tory lay a hand gently on his shoulder. "She is fine, Duncan. I swear. I told you, she is having the baby."

Duncan looked at his friend like she'd lost her mind. Had the stress proved too much? His wife would never give birth to their child while tethered to a log in the middle of a dark, dank cave!

He turned his gaze back to Catherine, hoping she'd tell him what was wrong. He found her eyes glazed with pain and her skin covered with a sheen of sweat.

Seeing Duncan no longer paid attention to her, Tory turned into Grant's embrace. Through his panic Duncan realized Tory and Grant stood wrapped in each other's arms. "You found us," Tory breathed.

"Aye, my love, we found you," Grant soothed, rubbing his hands up and down her back.

"She is having her babe, Grant. She is bruised, but fine. But she has been exposed to the chill of the cave too long. We must warm her."

Duncan's eyes shot between his friends and his beloved wife. He tried to speak, but barely croaked out the words, "She has our bairn? *Now*?"

"She cannot have it here. She will sicken. We must get her back to the castle afore it is too late," Tory told him.

Catherine nodded slowly. Keeping her eyes open seemed so difficult. She felt cold. She weakly rubbed a hand along Duncan's whiskered jaw and marveled, "You came for me. Tory told me you would, but I did not believe her." She grabbed for Duncan's arm and squeezed, her face contorting in pain as another contraction hit.

Duncan gently pushed the damp hair back from her face. "Why dinnae you believe Tory?"

"Because I have done so...many foolish things," Catherine mumbled, her head lolling to the side. Why did it take so much effort to speak?

"I always came for you, *Mo Gràdhaichte*. I always will."

"You called me...beloved...," Catherine smiled, her breathing ragged.

"Of course I did." Duncan wrestled with his emotions. He wanted to shake this woman and clutch her to his chest at the same time. "You are my life. Naught else matters."

"I never believed you truly loved me," she confessed, voice cracking.

Her admission stunned him. "And now?" He was afraid to breathe, afraid to hear her answer.

"Now I believe you love me...as I love you." She struggled to smile, her voice a mere whisper.

Duncan felt weak with relief. It had been a long time coming, but their arduous journey back to each other was now complete. But in the next breath, Catherine lapsed into unconsciousness.

Tory urged, "Hurry! We must get her back into the castle. She is too cold. She risks losing the babe unless we get her warm."

"What is wrong with my lady wife?" His eyes swung to Tory, pleaded as Grant helped him lift his wife. "Tory, tell me what is wrong!"

"Her breathing slows. Too slow."

"The bairn?"

"I know not."

# Chapter Thirty-Eight

"Tory, tell me she will be all right."

"I know not, Duncan. Her body is too cold. We must do something—fast." She grabbed Catherine's hand and rubbed it. "Cat, wake up. Please, Cat, do not die."

Color drained from Duncan's face. "My lady wife willnae die." He gently shook Catherine. "Do you hear me, wife? You *willnae* die!"

Catherine's body shook uncontrollably. She lapsed into chills. That scared Tory. Continuous chills was a sign Cat was too cold. When they came in waves, the body was giving up the fight to stay warm. Cat's breathing slowed, a sure sign her heart was slowing, and so would the babe's.

Duncan turned his face to meet Grant's. "We must get her back to the castle. I cannae think! Which would be faster? Through the woods or back through the tunnel?"

"The tunnels. It starts to rain. Getting her wet would only make her colder," Grant cautioned.

"Then the tunnel it is."

"We cannae be sure how we came," Grant said. "There are many trails."

Tory sobbed. "It helps; my right hand was on the wall the whole way down. My hands were tied behind my back, but I made him cut my bonds so I could help

Cat. I used one to hold her and dragged my right hand along the wall. I never took it off until the last turn, and then we turned left."

"That's my smart lass," Grant chuckled. "Ever resourceful."

Duncan nodded. "We use the tunnels." He placed a kiss on Catherine's head. "Did you hear, Sweetling? You will be fine."

She didn't move. Didn't open her eyes. Her breathing grew shallower as they rushed through the tunnels thanks to Tory's directions.

He buried Catherine's face in the hollow of his neck, murmured encouraging words in her ear. "I love you, *Mo Chridhe*. Dunnae forget that. Wake up now. Come on, Cat, please wake up."

Duncan felt her body tense several times as contractions wracked her body. But even they seemed weaker than before. Did the cold affect their bairn as well? *Please, God, dunnae let us lose this bairn, too. Grant me the chance to make up for all the wrongs I have done.*

The false doorway to their room stood open. Duncan breathed a prayer of relief. Everyone rushed through it and Duncan headed to their bed. He placed Catherine gently on it, smoothed her hair from her face. She was so cold.

Tory ordered, "Fetch blankets. Pile them atop her to warm her." She turned to look for her husband, "Grant, lock that wardrobe door. I know I saw Erwin die, but I wish to take no chances. Then, build up the fire. I care not how hot you make the room. Catherine must get warm."

Her husband moved to the wardrobe, ran his hand

along the inside and moved the door back into place. "There is a lock inside," he announced. It clicked loudly as he secured it.

Turning, Tory saw worry in everyone's eyes. "Move everyone! Find Siobhán, then have Cook boil water and heat a broth."

While Grant built up the fire, he turned to watch his wife. "Thank God Tory is a healer. Otherwise we would have to wait until someone else could be found."

Tory smiled at her husband. Duncan felt her hand on his arm. "Help me get Cat into dry clothes. Her chemise is wet from the cave's dampness."

Duncan rushed to the wardrobe and found a shift. Tory stripped Catherine's wet clothes off while Duncan brought the dry garment to her. He raised Catherine up so Tory could slip it over her head.

His eyes swung to her, took in her wet clothes. "What about you?"

"No time now. Once we get the heating stones around her, then I shall change."

Siobhán rushed into the room, her arms loaded with sheets of wool. Tears streamed down her face. "They heat the warming brick as we speak. What can I do?"

"Watch the fire. Keep adding peat." Tory pulled the blankets over Catherine with Siobhán's help.

Next, Tory bound Duncan's wounds. "This is temporary. I shall tend them fully later. Right now, get into bed with Cat. Warm her with your body."

He turned to look at the woman he loved. The stark contrast of her dark auburn hair against her alabaster skin frightened him. He'd never seen a woman this pale.

A memory flashed through his mind. Nay! She looked like this the day she lost their bairn in London. *Please God, dunnae let that happen again.*

He slid in beside her. Leaning against the headboard, he embraced Catherine in his arms and cradled her against his chest. He gently tapped her face with his hand, trying to revive her. "Cat, wake up. You must fight, lass. Fight for our love. You told me you love me, said so in the cave. I shall hold you to that."

As time passed and she didn't move, a tear trickled down his cheek. The contractions slowed. Her body no longer fought to bring their child into the world. She was still too cold. He was cold, too, fear spreading through him. If she lost their bairn, he'd lose her, too. He wouldn't survive that.

Angus rushed in with two lads, pails full of heated bricks. Grant, Siobhán, and Tory stacked them on both sides of Catherine. Siobhán kept tucking the blankets around her as though fearful of leaving.

Duncan looked up when Tory stroked his cheek. "The bricks shall warm her. Already I see a bead of sweat on your brow."

"I willnae let her go." He held her cradled like a babe in his arms, hoping to lend her his strength.

Grant rose after adding another brick of peat to the fire and walked to Tory. Drawing her into his arms and placing a kiss on her forehead, he told her, "We have done all we can for the nonce, now get you into dry clothes before you grow ill as well."

"My clothes dry on their own," she protested.

Duncan urged, "Make her leave, Grant. Dunnae take

nay for an answer. We dunnae need her falling ill."

Tory saw there was no standing against both of them. Nodding, she allowed Grant to lead her from the room. She paused at the doorway. "Siobhán, promise you'll fetch me if you need me?"

Grant departed, dragging Tory who kept tossing one instruction after another over her shoulder with him. She shouted down the stairs, "Angus, fetch Duncan some *ùsigue bethea*," before Grant closed the door to their chamber.

Duncan leaned his head against Catherine's. Her body bowed with another contraction, making him flinch in helplessness. He ran his hand along the top of her arm, murmuring words of encouragement. "I love you, lass. You are fine now. We are safe in our room."

Finally he could stand it no more. Catherine still hadn't opened her eyes.

"Please, *Mo Chridhe*. Fight for our bairn."

Catherine stirred, but didn't waken.

"Cat, please. I need you. I cannae be alone again, I was alone so long. I wasted years fighting with Da. I never would have reconciled with him if you hadnae forced me. I need you, need your common sense. I spent so many years thinking nae one loved me. Dunnae leave me now that I know you do."

He looked up as he realized Tory had returned. Tears streamed down her face. He glanced to see Siobhán crying as she headed toward the hearth. He didn't care. Didn't care if they thought him weak.

He needed Catherine.

"Please, lass. I need you to wake up. Need you to

forgive me for being daft enough to leave you in the beginning. I didnae want to, you know. I wanted to stay with you, but feared you'd leave me. I loved you from the moment I saw you—and I love you now. And now you shall leave me anyhow. Just when we find our way back to each other. Well, I willnae allow it. Hear you that, Catherine MacThomas? I order you to wake up." Tears streamed down his face just like they did Tory's. "I order you to…"

Catherine stirred, moaned, her eyelids fluttered open.

Duncan buried his face in her hair. "Thank you, God. Thank you for bringing my Cat back to me."

Every hour or so Duncan went outside to breathe fresh air. "How bear you this?" he asked Grant. "How stand you the uncertainty when Tory births her bairns? I am about to lose my sanity. There is naught I can do to help her through the pain. I feel useless."

Grant tried to reassure him, his face showing he searched for the right words. "I would tell you it gets easier with each child, but that would be lying. I worry about Tory every time she gives birth." Breathing deeply, he continued, "Dunnae madden yourself with worry. All you can do is pray. As Agnes once told me, 'she is in God's hands now—and that is the best place she can be.'"

Duncan knew that was true, but it didn't make waiting any easier. Walking back inside, he stared at his chamber door at another shout from Catherine.

Many hours after they found her and she'd regained consciousness, Catherine gave birth to a wee baby boy.

When he let out a lusty howl, one of the men

standing downstairs said, "He has the lungs of a wolf. He shall be strong and hale." No one had any doubts it was a male child.

Duncan sat behind Catherine on the bed, her body braced against his chest.

"'Tis a laddie," Tory told Duncan as she tore off her underskirt and wrapped the baby in it. He laid Catherine gently to the bed, rose and paced his room. Tory handed the babe to his father, her face wreathed in a wide grin, then pushed the damp hair off her face.

Tears rolled down Duncan's cheeks. He cared not who saw him. "I have a son. God blessed me with another healthy bairn." He offered up a silent, fervent prayer of thanks as he unwrapped the cloth and gently touched his son's tiny toes.

"I cannae wait to introduce him to his sister." His eyes swung back to Tory. Nervously he asked, "And Cat? Is she…?"

"She is weary from the exertion of childbirth, and the cold in the cave sapped her strength, but she fares fine," Tory assured him, smiling. "Take the babe to his mother so she can see him. She worked hard to bring this tiny miracle into the world."

Duncan stood with mouth agape, not truly believing the wonder he'd just witnessed. He gazed in awe at the most magnificent sight he'd ever seen—his son's tiny body wrapped in Catherine's loving arms. This tender moment had been missing when Meggie was born. Her mother couldn't wait to hand her over to the milk mother. That would never happen with his Cat.

He closed his eyes and thanked God for sending

Catherine into his life. Opening them again, he moved closer and sat beside his wife and son.

He quickly turned to Tory. "What is wrong?"

Tory frowned. "Naught is wrong. They are both fine."

"Then why does my wife cry?"

Tory laughed. "You dolt, ask her. She lies right beside you. But if I were to guess, they are tears of happiness."

"Happiness? That makes little sense." He placed his hand lightly on Catherine's arm.

"What is amiss, wife?"

Catherine hiccupped, trying to stop her sobs. "He is beautiful."

Duncan thought she'd lost her mind. "Aye, he is."

She reached up to draw him closer. "Duncan, I waited so long for this—and he is perfect."

Duncan played with his son's toes. "Aye, my heart, he is. As are you."

Eyes alight with amusement that something so tiny could turn a mighty warrior slackjawed, Catherine told him, "Since I am certain you wish to show him off to everyone, make certain he is swaddled like Tory had him and take your bonnie wee son downstairs."

"Aye," Tory agreed. "While I take care of your wife. I have things I must do to ensure Catherine heals properly. I want to keep her well covered to bring her body temperature back up. Her skin feels clammy and she shivers even though the room is hot. If I didn't already know Erwin was dead, I would kill him for putting Cat through that. After I take care of her, she shall be more than ready to see you both again."

Duncan's brows creased to a frown. "Will she be…? Is she…?" His gaze swung to Catherine's. He reached out to take her hand. "Tory, please tell me…?"

"Duncan MacThomas, your wife will be fine. 'Twill just take a little longer than normal. Now go, show off your son."

Duncan smiled as he rose and lifted his son into his arms. The wee laddie had surrendered to a peaceful slumber in his mother's arms.

Tory pushed him out the door, closing it firmly behind him.

As soon as Duncan walked downstairs, everyone rushed forward.

Grant smiled and rushed up the staircase. He called out, "Tory, are you well?"

"Aye." Her voice came on a sigh. "Tired, but fine." Then she laughed. "Although after everything Cat has been through, I am not the one to complain about being tired."

Grant heard rustling inside the room, then Tory poked her head outside. Grant immediately wrapped his arms around her and held her close.

She raised her eyes to his. "Cat is fine, but I must return inside. That monster put her life in danger. Sitting on the cave's damp ground was too cold for her. She shivers still."

"Will she fare well?" he asked, pulling her closer.

"She and the bonnie bairn are fine. God willing, she and our dear friend, Duncan, shall have many years of happiness ahead of them."

*Two Years Later*

# Epilogue

Catherine couldn't believe it was almost Christmastide again. Like her friend Tory, she had a decorated tree in the Great Hall every year. She loved having the tree with tiny ribbons and nuts around it. Candles were the perfect touch.

Now she just had to figure out how to keep her two youngest children from pulling all the decorations down. Wee Alasdair thought it his lot in life to remove nuts from the tree and eat them, and since she was just learning to walk, Bláithin giggled while using the lower branches to pull herself up.

More amazing, her children were already two and one. While they usually called him Alex, just like their friend, Alasdair was the apple of his father's eye. As her name denoted, Bláithin was his little flower.

Although she constantly ran after two tiny people, she and Duncan were pleased Tory's herbal decoction had once again worked.

Only Meghan left the tree alone. She was, after all, seven summers now, and to hear her tell it, "I am all grown up." She delighted in helping Catherine look after her small brother and sister.

Catherine smiled as she watched Meggie and Alex helping her carry fern branches inside to decorate the keep. Dropping the branches inside the castle door, she and Meggie took off their winter mantles and boots, shaking off the snow before they entered the Great Hall. Meghan had insisted, "I want a mantle just like Mam's," so Catherine happily sewed one for her. She left the boots to Duncan to obtain. While Meghan reached to hang their mantles on the wooden pegs, Catherine bent to remove Alex's outerwear.

Catherine already helped Meggie place ferns around the outside of the door. That had been Meggie's idea. Catherine agreed, thinking it a wonderful addition. "Your Da will be pleased, Meggie." Unless they were getting into mischief, which was all too often, Duncan enjoyed anything his children did.

Catherine wanted the castle to look perfect. Even though the weather made travel difficult this time of year, if her parents kept the promise they made several moons earlier, she expected their arrival the next day. Her mother wrote she had a surprise for her.

It would make Christmas day perfect. She'd start the day with her entire family around her while they attended mass in their chapel. She couldn't be more blessed on such a holy day.

Then, after they all enjoyed the Christmas feast she had planned, the celebration would begin. She'd arranged for jugglers and tumblers to perform, then hoped everyone would join together and end the evening in song.

Although they were making up for lost time now, Catherine was sorry for the time she wasted not believing Duncan truly loved her. She watched his every step as he entered the Great Hall and walked over to her. She smiled when he wrapped his arms around her and bent his head to kiss her. Ah, she loved this man.

He turned her to face the tree, circling his arms around her waist. "The tree is beautiful, *Mo Chridhe*." His breath fanned the nape of her neck as he brushed her hair aside and placed tiny kisses there. "But not as beautiful as you."

Catherine smiled a secret smile. Mayhap after everyone retired for the evening after Christmastide festivities were ended, Catherine would give him his last present.

She'd tell her Highland rogue he was going to be a father again.

What a wonderful way to start the new year—with the promise of a new life. A beautiful beginning to the rest of their life.

## *Author's Note*

The information I've used on Clan MacThomas, a clan my husband belongs to, has been moved up to the early 14th century to accommodate this story. Following is information from the Cockstane Journal on the clan from their official webpage:

Thomas, a Gaelic speaking Highlander, known as Tomaidh Mor (Great Tommy), was a descendant of the Clan Chattan MacKintoshes, his grandfather having been a son of William, 8th Chief of the Clan Chattan. Thomas lived in the 15th century, when the Clan Chattan confederation became large and unmanageable. He took his kinsmen and followers across the Grampians, from Badenoch to Glenshee, where they settled and flourished, being known as McComie (phonetic form of the Gaelic MacThomaidh), McColm and McComas (from MacThom and MacThomas). To Edinburgh's government they were known as MacThomas and are so described in the Roll of the Clans in the Acts of the Scottish Parliament of 1587 and 1595. MacThomas remains the official name of the Clan to this day.

The early chiefs of the Clan MacThomas were seated at the Thom, on the east bank of the Shee Water opposite the Spittal of Glenshee.

The incident with Edward punishing the women of Bruce's family is accurate, with the exception of Morag. The Countess and Bruce's sister, Mary, hung in cages from the respective castles for many years. Neither lived long after they were finally released, the ravages of their treatment and the weather taking a mighty toll. The women's movement is actually believed to be founded on her. It was the call to remember all the Countess sacrificed that led to rights women today are afforded.

# Meet the Author

*L*eanne Burroughs has been married for 36 years. She and her husband have two children and three grandchildren. She is currently a member of Romance Writers of America, President of Outreach International, Secretary of Hearts Through History RWA SIG, and Newsletter Editor of Outreach International. In addition, she is a member of Celtic Hearts RWA SIG, RWA Online, First Coast RWA, Central Florida RWA, Florida Writer's Association and Historical Novel Soceity. A life-long, avid reader, she particularly enjoys historical romances. While researching her husband's genealogy, she fell in love with Scotland.

That led to extensive research, several trips to Scotland, and her first novel, *HIGHLAND WISHES*, about the Scottish War for Independence. It was a winner in the Reader's and Bookseller's Best, 2004 Published Laurie's – Historical Division. She is working on several upcoming books—a sequel to *HER HIGHLAND ROGUE* with Trevor and Tamara; *KEEPER OF THE STARS*, a story about the aftermath of Scotland's Battle of Culloden; a Viking historical, *THE POWER AND THE PASSION;* and a Scottish time travel.

*She loves hearing from her readers. Please feel free*

*to contact her at* <u>*Leanne@Leanneburroughs.com*</u>

Printed in the United States
42164LVS00002B/1-75